ENCRYPTION OF THE HEART

AN EERDEN ROMANCE

STARFISH
INK

C.E. CLAYTON

ISBN-13: 978-1-952797-12-5
ISBN-10: 1-952797-12-8

Printed in the United States of America

www.ceclayton.com

• Cover Design by
https://jabdesignstudio.com

• Interior Design by Tyffany Hackett
www.tyffanyhackett.com

ALSO BY C.E. CLAYTON

The Monster of Selkirk Series

1. The Duality of Nature
2. The Heart of the Forest
3. The Machines of Theda
4. The Intrigues of Arcadia
5. The Spark of Divinity
6. The Wrath of Silence

Ellinor Series

1. Resistor
2. Deadlock
3. Symbiotech

Paradigm Flux

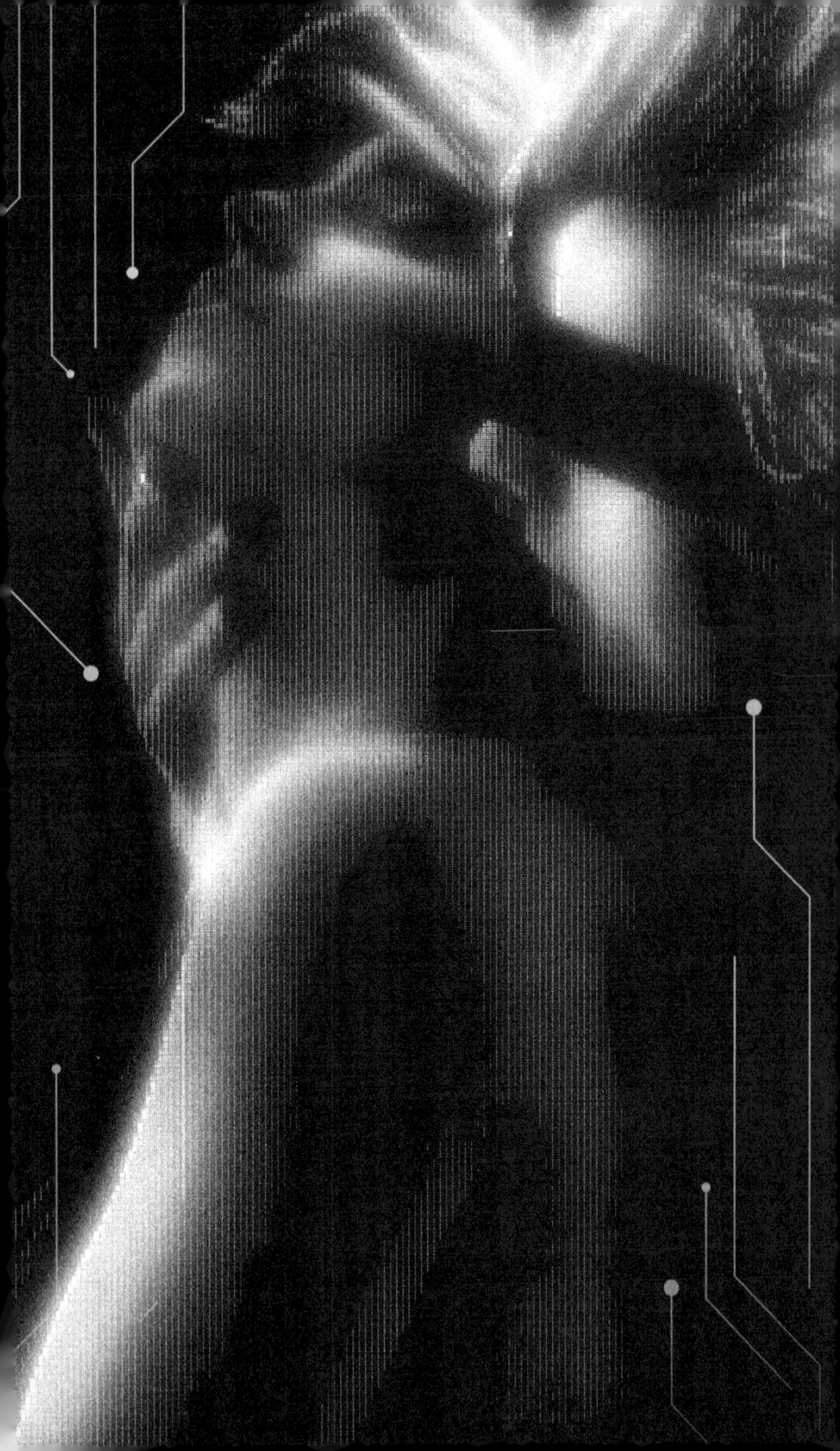

To everyone who promises they'll stop romancing Astarion, and then never does.
This one's for you, darling.

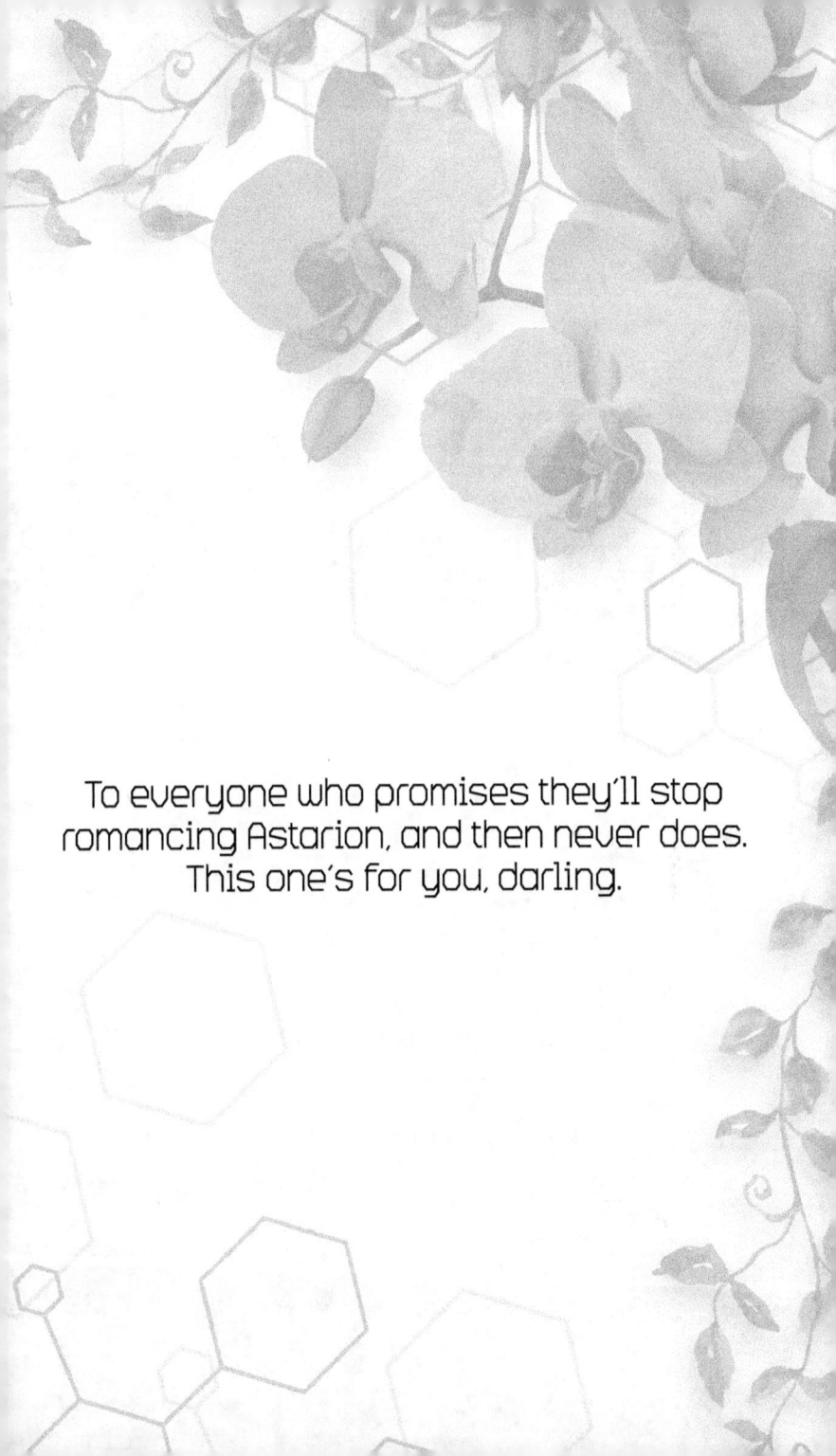

CHAPTER 1

The first day of any new job is stressful. More so when you have the added excitement of moving to a brand-new city on top of it. Which is exactly what Olline Tavos decided to do. And she *was* excited, stressed and nervous to where she thought she may throw up, of course, but mostly excited.

The hardest part of the relocation was moving all her plants to her new apartment. Well, it wasn't *the hardest* thing, but it was the thing she could control and therefore fixated on.

She had been so worried about the trauma of the move for her flowers that four hours before she was due at the Police and Securities Department in the Government Plaza, she was wide awake and tending to her ferns while still in her pajamas. But her plants didn't mind the faded turquoise shirt—it had been her mother's—or the boy-short underwear.

Olline hadn't unpacked most of her other belongings yet, just a few clothing essentials, and, of course, all her greenery. The new job and relocation had been so fast, there had been no time to unpack properly, even with her anxiety keeping her from sleeping.

Accepting the position almost immediately had definitely *not* been an impulse decision born from embarrassment and betrayal. Who would even think that?

Olline hummed as she gently brushed her hand over the fronds of her ferns. Squinting out her window—what a novelty!—she switched the ferns with her giant split leaf monstera, allowing the ferns to have the indirect light instead. Natural light, like from the large bay windows in her new apartment, was something Olline never had before. She misted the monstera leaves, marveling at the view she now had. She was high over the residential sector of the city, with a nearly unobstructed view of the businesses and government center downtown. The vista was mesmerizing. The aerial vehicles whizzed by below, the twinkling city lights reflected from the miles and miles of steel and glass making up the mega-sky towers surrounding her, with the occasional blip of light as a drone sped by.

She could spend a lifetime right in front of this window and never tire of the view.

Yes, moving to the other side of Audamar, out of her home city-state of Cyneburg to get a fresh start, was *precisely* the thing she needed. She would take no questions on that at this time, thank you very much!

Pleased with the ferns and monstera, Olline moved next to her collection of pothos and philodendron vines. Their big leaves of emerald and lime green, or jade and moss, were still curled, as if comforting themselves after the ordeal of transit. She moved the plants to have their vines frame the entryways into the wide living room with its tall, arched ceiling. But the vines didn't seem to have the strength or will to grow in the direction she wanted. With a sympathetic tut, Olline put her fingers into the soft soil. She touched the thrumming heat deep in her chest where her magic lived and let the ethereal tendrils of her power find all the roots—from the small fragile hairlike roots to the thicker branches—and spark health and vitality into the struggling plants. Warmth bloomed in her, and she sighed blithely. Savoring the contented connection she felt with her plants, she allowed her mind to wander.

Olline used her magic all the time for work, but she had always loved using her earth abilities to make things grow. It was frivolous, of course. There was no point to plants in the city-states if they weren't explicitly for food or oxygen production. But that was what Olline loved most about it.

She loved the bright green of a new leaf just before it unfurled, and watching it turn to jade as it matured. She loved encouraging exotic blooms to climb her walls to hide the grime and stains of the other people who had once called her apartment home. All the orchids and vines, the leafy ferns and gem-colored succulents she kept, would have died within hours outside of special hothouses. Unless you had water or earth magic—like Olline Tavos.

For the first time in a decade, Olline wasn't answering to anyone but herself. Free of a corporate culture that sneered at her for embracing her earth magic for more than advancing the metals in the hardware they worked with. Far away from crushes—*coworkers* that faked being interested in her only to steal her work, share it with their actual lover, and then get her fired for confronting them over it.

The big leaves of the vines shuddered. Olline opened her eyes and stepped back. Putting her hands on her hips, Olline smiled. The vines clung to the walls happily now, twisting up over the arched entryways. Leaves unfurled in delight. She admired her work for a moment longer before heading into her bedroom, where she kept her most prized blooms—her hybrid orchids.

Her bedroom was the smallest of the five rooms, but she liked the coziness of it. Especially with the two dozen orchids she had transported. Each was a special creation all her own. Some had two toned blooms of baby blue and soft pink. Others, a soft antique peach with lavender spots. A few of her orchids were a pearlescent, shimmering white, while others were a midnight blue with magenta veins. Olline crafted each orchid by hand, using her magic to coax permanent colors into the blooms impossible to achieve otherwise. She kept the furnishings of her room—from her many cozy blankets to her chair and desk—a soft heather grey; her orchids as bright as neon with the contrast.

She lightly stroked the stiff emerald leaves. Yet the normal joy she felt when her plants quivered in response to her touch had waned. Memories tickled in the back of her mind around why she and her orchids were here instead of back in Cyneburg.

Olline sighed, her shoulders drooping. She had shown her crush—*coworker* her plant-based hobby once, and he hadn't . . . reacted how she would have liked. She had showed him things she was most proud of, and then he shared it with the woman he was actually sleeping with, and they laughed at Olline behind her back. All while he had been telling Olline *she* was, instead, the special one.

With a shudder, she let the smooth leaf of the deep amethyst orchid she was tending to slip through her fingers. Obviously, the need to flee—*move* had been her fault. She'd been too naïve, had trusted the wrong person to be vulnerable around. She would just keep herself too busy with this new contract to do something silly, like try to make friends.

Workaholism would be her cure for loneliness. It was the perfect plan.

Taking a deep breath, she squared her shoulders and forced a bright smile. "It's the past, Olline," she reminded herself. "Cut away the dead leaves so new growth can come in and all that." With a nod, the words settled in her heart a bit more firmly, like roots gripping the soil to anchor her in place. "No one can take advantage of your trust when you work for yourself. No one can make fun of your passion if you're too busy with work to bring anyone home. Ever." With a happy sigh, she ran her nose over the silky petals of her orchid. "Besides, I can't be alone when I have you ladies, right?"

The stems of her orchids straightened slightly, the blooms moving up and down, nodding in agreement. With a grin, Olline meandered to the kitchen, where she kept all her miniature, gem-colored succulents and cacti. Olline didn't cook much, which afforded her ample room to put the plump little succulents in jars others would have used for food storage into almost every ounce of space. Leaving the counter island in the center of the kitchen free for her second most prized possession: her coffee maker.

Her holo-tablet was next to the vintage coffee maker where she had left it the night before. As she fussed with the settings to make certain her next cup of coffee was perfect, Olline couldn't resist reading over her offer letter and contract once more.

Her title wasn't fancy, which was a bit of a bummer, but oh well. She didn't have anyone but her dad and half-brothers to brag to anyway. An "independent contractor for data analysis and storage with the Police and Securities Department" was, categorically, a very unsexy title. At least she could make her own hardware without having to be monitored like most casters who created magitech. Another perk of working with the government rather than a private corporation, in Antal or Cyneburg.

Antal had opportunities that the corporatocracy of Cyneburg didn't, though. Antal had a more traditional governing system with Under Senators, Senators, and a Governor to oversee them. All elected by the people and not chosen by some rich board of directors to represent a business entity. They were chosen *by* people, *for* people.

Olline found that rather novel.

Or, in theory, that was how it was supposed to be. She had

read the comments the news feeds in Cyneburg had made regarding their trade partner. According to the snide comments made by the news feeds in Cyneburg, the governing body of Antal was supposedly set up to be a thinly disguised front for organized crime. But she wanted to give the system a chance, to see it in action for herself.

Plus, the government of Antal was offering a stupid amount of money for someone just like her.

As a humani caster, she was free to move to any city she liked without her magic suffering, cut off from its place of origin. While that restriction limited others—like seersha and seerani casters—Olline was as powerful anywhere she went. And with her expertise in metal and ore manipulation? They scooped her up for this position alarmingly fast.

It was impossible for her, even now, to stifle her excited grin as she looked at the starting salary, all for a six-month long trial contract with the potential of extension. Of course, there had been a lot of scary language in the agreement about what would happen should she be in breach of contract, or abscond with the signing bonus before delivering on the promised hardware and software. But Cyneburg took contracts so seriously that people had been killed for violating them. Thus, making "potential incarceration" seem relatively benign in comparison.

Once she was positive that the old coffee maker wouldn't fuck up her next cup of real coffee—Olline could always tell the difference between cultivated beans and those artificially grown thanks to her magic—she pushed away from the kitchen island.

Olline glanced over her shoulder at the digital clock. She still had hours before she needed to be anywhere, but she figured now was as good a time as any to get ready. It gave her plenty of time to perfect her new look.

That had been the second hardest thing about leaving Cyneburg. Saying goodbye to her father while trying to explain the reason for her "drastic" change in appearance.

Once upon a time, she had bought in completely to the corporate culture. Especially for her first job. Looking back, it hadn't really made sense. When you had seersha working in the same department, you couldn't really adhere to a standard "look" no matter what the shareholders wanted.

Seersha were such a visually bright and uniquely wonderful race of people that Olline often believed that humani were more likely to alter their appearances in comparison. Humani often tried to compete with the seersha, whose eyes and hair could be any color in the world. Some seersha had horns like her half-brothers, or long pointed ears, or both. Their skin tones were far more varied than a humani's. Olline wasn't self-conscious of her looks, but she often envied the seersha—and seerani, the product of seersha and humani parents. Like the flowering plants she cultivated, their uniqueness was a splash of color in a world dominated by steel and glass.

But with her father's reaction to her new style, Olline could have sworn she had shown up with horns instead of new piercings, a haircut, and a neck tattoo. She had needed the change after Achan, her not-quite ex. She had needed the control. And given she was her own boss now, she figured, well, why not? Why not do something just for her, just this once?

Oddly, her father hadn't cared as much about the thorny rose tattooed in crisp black and grey on the side of her neck. He'd merely frowned at the vertical iron bar pierced through her eyebrow, an addition to her already pierced ears. No, he cared the most about her hair.

"Why would you dye it, Olline? You have—had your mother's hair," Zachery Tavos had moaned. His voice still echoed in her mind, even as she styled her hair that early morning.

She reminded her father she technically still did. She had merely cut her long, smoky black hair to accommodate a tidy Mohawk with the rest tied in a bun at the base of her skull. If she chose, she could easily remove the deep, moss green highlights. Besides, there was so much more to her that was distinctly her mother's that she didn't think her hair altered things that much.

The freckles, the color of rich soil, across her nose and cheeks, were the same smattering that her mother had. Even their bronze-touched rosy skin tone was the same. The only thing Olline had that was her own, that didn't belong to anyone else, was her clear, unnaturally bright emerald eyes. The color signaled her caster ability as clearly as the tattoo on her neck. But her hair—hair identical to her mother's—was still there, just with, as she explained to her father, a twist.

Olline thought the changes made her look edgier, less innocent, braver even. Less like the woman who was only worth loving if she had something someone else could profit from.

Thanks Achan.

That part, she hadn't explained to her father. She didn't want his pity. Besides, it was done now, and Olline liked the change.

"New growth," she murmured, a reminder to herself as she carefully styled her Mohawk between the thin braids on the side of her head leading to the bun at the back. The braids showed off the green best, and that was, arguably, Olline's favorite thing about the style. That, and it suited the clothes she enjoyed wearing far better than the stuffy corporate black and grey she had worn daily for the past decade.

She wiggled into her favorite pair of tight, faded, low-slung jeans. Pulled on a pastel teal and pink crop top with cartoon palm-trees and an over-exaggerated sunset. Slipped into the oversized, slouchy white jacket that felt like a hug each time she put it on. Then, and only then, did Olline grab her bag, slide on her massive headphones, wave goodbye to the feathery purple passion plant by her front door, and head out—two hours before she was due in the office.

Whoopsie.

CHAPTER 2

The guard at the Police and Securities front desk stared at Olline with bleary, bloodshot eyes. The holo-tag on his faded uniform read "Brayden G". He didn't introduce himself though, and Olline thought it would be awkward if she greeted him by his first name. He barely gave her credentials—which she held out, not in the least embarrassed by the big grin on her badge photo—more than a cursory glance.

Rude.

He waved a security bot forward, its red laser scanning her from head to toe. The cylindrical robot beeped at her and flashed a green light before rolling back behind the front desk.

At least the bot said good morning. Or she thought it had. She was going to assume it did.

Olline smiled, her mouth opening to exchange the normal pleasantries you're supposed to go through on the first day of a new job. Brayden gave a heavy exhale through his round nose, stopping her mid inhale. "You're early. Your supervisor hasn't clocked in yet. I'll have to get an assistant drone to lead you down."

Olline blinked at him, her body tensing at the imposition she was already causing on day one. "Yes, I guess I am," she said with an uneasy giggle. "I didn't think I needed to check in with anyone when I got here." She shrugged, unsure what else to do.

Brayden frowned at her, then pointed down the long, shiny chrome corridor. "They have you stationed in sub-basement thirteen. Take the last elevator bay down this hall." He taped on his wrist-communicator for a moment, then added, "The assistant drone will meet you at the elevator."

Olline glanced down the empty hall, nodded to herself, and silently walked away. "Do me a favor," Brayden said, voice harsh. She glanced at him over her shoulder, the blood draining from her cheeks. "Touch nothing until your lead checks in with you," he warned. "You have a high security clearance, but you don't need to be *anywhere* but sub-basement thirteen. Your supervisor is going to explain it to you, so don't let me catch you wandering in the meantime. Clear?"

Olline swallowed the lump in her throat. She nodded vigorously, ignoring his grumbles about "fucking morning people" as she scurried away.

True to Brayden's word, an assistant drone hovered by the elevator waiting. It was an automated bot, not equipped with a voice box or holo-screen. Its sole function being to lead people to where they were meant to go and ensure they didn't break anything along the way. With how eerily quiet the building was, Olline kind of wished it was a droid. The robots weren't real AIs, but it didn't feel as awkward talking to a droid as it did a drone.

The bot trilled at her, then rotated toward the elevator, which it unlocked with a series of beeps. Following the little gun-metal grey drone, she touched the side of the elevator wall. The slight vibration of the hydraulics coming through the wall were the only sign the elevator was moving.

The doors opened silently, and the drone floated out first. Olline poked her head out into another empty hallway. The ceiling lights turned on as the drone flew down the room, illuminating the path she was to take.

The drone beeped at her, warning her to follow faster. She narrowed her eyes at the machine, letting a wisp of her power leak out and curl around its metal components. The bot didn't care. But it was a pleasant reminder to Olline that a little assistant drone couldn't boss her around. She scurried to where it waited for her in front of room two-hundred twenty-three, regardless. The only things she passed as she went were two security bots similar to the one at Brayden's desk. Though she knew there were dozens of tiny, cloaked surveillance drones in the ceiling to monitor everyone's comings and goings.

The drone, hovering by the door, put a spotlight on the scanner beneath the shiny gold "223". Once she waved her credentials over the door, it slid up, granting entrance. No sooner had she cleared the threshold when the door closed behind her with a soft *hiss*, the soft puff of air tickling the back of her neck. The assistant drone hadn't followed her.

Perhaps it waited outside for when her supervisor arrived, making sure she didn't wander off.

The room was filled with shadows, and the stacks of blinking servers loomed over her as she carefully tip-toed to the table in the center of the room. The servers were so jammed together that it would be easy to hide amongst the stacks. With the various lights blinking at inconsistent times, making the shadows move, it gave the impression that someone was lurking in the corner of her eye.

Taking a deep breath, Olline pushed away the paranoia and smiled into the shadowy room. This was *her* office. Just hers. She didn't have to share space with a dozen other programmers where half were sick at any given time. That kind of freedom was worth the creepy office.

Feeling lighter than she had when she first entered, she pulled out her various holo-tablets, laptops, and folding keyboards, then connected her devices to the first of many server stacks. Brayden may have warned her not to do anything until her supervisor appeared, but surely that didn't include setting up? Though she had never really understood why she needed a supervisor.

The job she was there to do, at least to start, wasn't difficult. Just tedious.

The Police and Securities Department wanted to upgrade their old servers, ones that kept ancient evidence and cold cases, into a secure proprietary system. Her task first was to move the original files into a safe temporary digital storage device. Once she had a firm grasp of how big the new server needed to be, she would build the magitech hardware from scratch. Olline would use her earth caster abilities to craft something far smaller and more secure than what the Department currently had.

Until Olline reached the hardware crafting phase, she would have to work hard to suppress the curiosity that arose when her mind wasn't occupied. She knew, despite her security clearance, that peeking at any of the evidence files would be a very unprofessional thing to do, even with no one currently snooping over her shoulder.

Once Olline powered on everything and set up her devices to her liking, she glanced at the time. She cringed. It was still a good hour ahead of when she was supposed to start. She considered familiarizing herself with the room, but the thought of casually strolling through the shadowy stacks sent a shiver down her spine.

Olline took a deep breath and sheepishly glanced around. "Well, no one's here to tell me not to start. Maybe they'll give me another bonus with the next contract if I finish early," she said, perhaps trying a bit too hard to convince herself it was all right to bend the rules.

As always, she became instantly engrossed in the work when dealing with raw code and data files, sending smoky whispers of her magic through the copper wires to coax the software to move and duplicate into new locations in ways normal coders couldn't do. It didn't take long before she completely hunched over, with the collar of her white jacket in her mouth, idly chewing. Her eyes glazed over, completely oblivious to the room at large as her ethereal magical fingers did the navigating for her.

Olline had only been working for a few minutes when something interesting caught her eye. She blinked, her gaze coming back into focus, trying to catch up with what her magic had seen before her eyes could make sense of it.

"Huh," she murmured, leaning forward until her nose nearly poked through the holo-projection in front of her. Her jacket collar, already saturated, fell from her open mouth. So far, all the evidence files had been available to her with her temporary administration account. But this file set was *encrypted.* Coded with at least seven layers of tangled encryption, its code was almost a living thing with its complexity.

Nothing else had this level of security around it. Stranger still, she was working in a pretty innocuous cold case area of the server to start with. More than just odd, it was *curious.*

Most earth casters had a level of empathy where they could sense others' emotions, the natural flow and pull of someone's feelings, and how it affected the world around them. Olline didn't have that. Not truly. Sometimes she could get a feeling from others, but after, well, *after,* she didn't trust those sensations anymore, especially when it came to men. What she had was a curiosity, a gut feeling, and while it did little for steering her away from shitty relationships, it often bubbled up when there was a technical challenge before her.

The feelings that tugged her down an inquisitive hole? *Those* she trusted.

Of course, she *knew* she shouldn't mess with the file. Olline was alone though, and was still, technically, not on the clock for another ten minutes. She didn't see the harm in making a door, in a sense, and having a teeny-tiny peek. Well, she did, but she ignored that and pretended this was *research.*

"Talent recognizes talent," she said cheerily at the projection. "I just want to see and appreciate what your creator did, little file."

Pulling up a prompt, she began writing a back door code that would tell this file that there was a system update to be installed. The temporary administrator account would allow her access into the file, despite the encryption.

Once the code was written for all viable systems housed within the folder, she took a deep breath, her finger hovering over the enter key. Olline gnawed on her lower lip for a moment, considering if her curiosity was worth the risk. A slow grin pulled her lips up.

She pushed the code. The system updated. Olline could now peek at the different layers of encryption this strange file held within.

"This doesn't make sense," she whispered, her eyes tracking the different lines, but unable to decipher exactly what it did, or what the different sub-folders were for. From what she could tell, they were external biomagitech chips of some kind which fed back to this server.

She couldn't tell what the chips were supposed to do, or how many were currently active. And why was the file on *this* server? They weren't attached to any cold case. They didn't belong here. But here they were, all the same.

"So, so weird," Olline mused.

Her finger hovered over the open command when the door to her office slid up and the assistant drone flew in. Hovering behind it was a larger drone with a holo-projection screen. Illuminated in the projection was a grumpy humani man. His bushy, blonde brows were pulled down over his small blue eyes. Thin, cracked lips were equally tugged down in a frown. Even with a soft filter on the projection, there was no hiding the dimpled scars on his tanned skin, nor his annoyance that Olline was already at work.

With quick, subtle movements, she closed the folder she had been snooping in. Olline licked her lips and glanced at the time as the man continued to glare at her from the projection. *Now* it was officially time to work.

"You're Olline Tavos?" His voice was gravelly and full of irritation.

"Y-yes, sir," she answered with a slight wince. Nervous sweat began collecting around her hairline. A tremor entered her hands she hoped he couldn't see. Did he know what she had done? Had the assistant drone tattled on her?

No, impossible, she reminded herself. *Those bots aren't sophisticated enough to spy on me or my magic.*

He grunted. "Karter Wayser," he barked in return. "I'm your supervisor. But clearly," he said, the projection drone hovered closer, moving around her to look at her holo-tablet. "You don't need me." His tone was flat, and she didn't know if he was pissed or relieved.

The drone zoomed in front of her again, moving down to

be eye level. "I'll make this quick. I may be the one signing off on your paycheck, but Under Senator Straub was the one to hire you." Olline opened her mouth to ask who that was. She didn't recognize the name from her offer letter, but Karter had already moved on. "He's the one who will decide if you get an extension. My job is to make sure you clock in and out, and you don't take any evidentiary files from the building. That you *only* move the digital cases from this room to your designated space and build the required hardware. If you try to go into other departments' files, I *will* know and there *will* be consequences. Understood?"

Bobbing her head in a nervous nod, she said, "Understood, Mr. Wayser." He frowned at her, and Olline moved her hands away from the holo-tablet at last, rubbing her clammy palms on her jeans.

"Call me Karter. No need to be formal with me. You're barely one of my employees."

The way he said it sent a chill down her spine. Like the distinction mattered, but she couldn't say why. Before she could ask though, the drone rotated and flew to the door. As Karter left, the speakers on the drone rotated to face her, and he said, "I won't be here until I absolutely have to be. If you show up early again, fine. Just clock in so the IT teams know you're here and in the system. You won't get overtime, though."

As if on cue, the door hissed open again and a short, bored looking humani woman waltzed in. The drone swiveled. "Good," Karter said. "Perfect timing, Camirin." The drone rotated back to Olline, who blinked in confusion as the woman, Camirin, tossed her dark brown ponytail behind her back and disappeared in the server stacks without a word. "Speaking of letting IT know you're here," Karter said. "Meet Camirin. She's your point of contact if you need anything for the servers, or if passwords give you any issue. Be sure to bother her, not me."

Olline whipped her head around to see what Camirin was doing, or talk to her more about the equipment. But Camirin apparently already finished what she came down to do. Her hazel eyes briefly glanced over Olline, before turning her attention back to Karter. "All good here," she said, tone just as uninterested and monotonous to match her demeanor.

"Excellent," Karter responded, moving his drone to address Camirin like Olline wasn't even there. "Now, if you need anything, who do you bother?" he said suddenly, barely glancing at Olline, the only sign that he was talking to her.

"Um, Camirin?"

Camirin gave a lazy wave, the only response to her correct answer. In unison, her supervisor and IT contact turned to leave. "Welcome to the team," Camirin said belatedly as the office door opened once more.

Before Olline could respond, the door slid down behind the drones and Camirin. Olline was alone once again.

Olline let out a slow breath, relieved that Karter didn't know she had already violated her work order. If nothing else, the fake update she pushed wouldn't affect the chips' ability to communicate with the server; no one would ever know she snooped around. The chips would sync with the new, dummy version and continue doing whatever it was they were told to do without a lapse.

"No one will know," she told herself again, flexing her fingers. *Unless there's outdated chips connected to the server . . .*

But with a shake of her head, she dispelled the thought. Who would have active biomagitech chips so old that they wouldn't reconnect with a simple server update?

The passing of time went unnoticed after her rocky start. Karter never came to check on her—in person or otherwise. Occasionally, she noted the sounds of movement beyond the room that served as her office. She wasn't alone on the floor anymore, but no one came in to introduce themselves or invite her to lunch. Olline's shoulders slumped, deflating slightly, and she decided if they didn't want to say hi to her, she would not make the effort either. At least for today.

It was only by happenstance that Olline looked up from her latest transfer to note that business hours ended over three hours ago. Her jaw dropped at the realization, and as if on cue, her stomach grumbled. "I'll bring more snacks tomorrow," she murmured.

She got up, stretched until her shoulders popped, and prepared to immerse herself in work in a similar capacity tomorrow. The Police and Securities Department should have given this contract to a team of engineers, not one person, even if that person was an earth caster. So, Olline was determined to prove they hadn't made a mistake. That she alone could, in fact, handle the workload.

Plus, she was good at it. Like really good.

She left her devices where they were, activating her three-factor authentication before shutting them down. Just because she had snooped in files questionable for her to look into, didn't mean she wanted others to do the same.

The long hours of the day slammed into her as soon as she exited the room. Her shoulders sagged, and her eyelids were too heavy to raise all the way. Olline was slow leaving the server room, waving her digital fob over the door to clock out for the night like Karter said. She was only vaguely aware that the hallway looked exactly as it did when she arrived. Completely void of other breathing life.

Or so she thought. She wasn't so tired to miss the shift in shadows from the corner of her eye.

She was, however, too sluggish to move out of the way.

CHAPTER 3

"Umpf!"

The air rushed out of Olline's lungs as the figure slammed her against the wall with their forearm pressed against her throat. Something sharp pricked her bare skin, just under her crop top. The scent of eucalyptus and lavender musk filled her nose.

Olline's mind spun. Panic threatened to make her scream, if it weren't for the arm against her throat. It kept her from moving so she could see who had her pinned.

All she could croak out was, "Badge!"

"Badge?" A smoky voice, like satin sheets rustling in the dark, whispered in her ear. "You want my badge? Darling," the figure said, a chuckle rumbling in their chest that rattled Olline's ribcage, "*I* don't need a badge."

"No," Olline sputtered. "Me. I have . . . a badge."

The figure—a decidedly very male figure—went still for a moment before abruptly taking a step back. Olline never got a good look at the sharp object he had pressed against her abdomen, but she wasn't looking for it all that hard once she could see her assailant in full.

He was *beautiful.*

Which she knew was the wrong thought to have immediately following the encounter, but she couldn't help it. A breathing work of art had just assaulted her, short-circuiting every synapse in her brain—an otherwise very smart and clever brain, but still. Her magic hadn't even stirred to warn her about this man's clearly evil intentions. Just more proof that her magic was completely ineffective in sensing threats and shitty behavior from men.

The entire ordeal had left her too surprised to reach for the natural metals in her piercings and use her magic against the stranger.

She eyed him warily, and rubbed her throat, trying not to get hung up on how tight the shirt and coat pulled against his lean muscles as he crossed his arms over his chest, returning her scrutiny with his own. Olline tried to ignore the perfect line of his nose and definitely did not notice the razor-sharp angle of his jaw. She certainly didn't make note of his cloud-like curls, or how the silvery tones of those curls perfectly matched the details in his clothes.

He was taller than her by *maybe* a hair or two at most. He was dressed in black, from his fitted pants to the tailored shirt, and the long coat with its silver detailing. Simple, but refined. It added to the deadly beauty of the man before her.

The pillow that was his lower lip was fuller than his top, accentuating the coyness of his slight smirk into something that sent a shiver down the base of her spine. It was then that Olline realized she still hadn't spoken. But neither had he, so maybe they were both assessing what the actual fuck was happening?

His eyes trailed over her, languid and penetrating, with just a hint of confusion. That had to be because he was realizing she was a nobody. Or, at least, not a threat.

And those eyes!

His eyes were such a rich mahogany that when the light caught them in full, they shone blood red. No humani, caster or otherwise, had red eyes. The man was clearly a seerani of some kind, like her half-brothers. This felt all the truer as she better observed the linen white quality of his skin and yet he somehow avoided looking sickly. He reminded Olline of a marble statue in twilight; which made no sense and yet fit him perfectly.

He rubbed his chin with his hand, eyes narrowing as he assessed her. She tracked the movement as subtly as she could. For safety, of course. His hands were large, but his fingers moved with grace. He had a painter's elegance to him that accentuated his devastating beauty, and made the dangerous quality he had unfairly alluring.

He just tried to stab you, stop it!

"Who the fuck are you?" Olline croaked, then winced. Hard to be intimidating now.

The flick of his gaze from her lips to her eyes, as she spoke, had her breath hitching in her chest. He tilted his head, hair shifting to expose long, elegantly pointed ears, as if he heard the hiccup of breath.

His gaze slid from her face to the door she had exited, before slowly gliding down her body again, resting on her hips—where her security badge dangled off a belt loop.

Oh, right. The badge.

She couldn't quite suppress her shiver as he leaned closer, his fingers brushing the badge to look at it better. "Adorable," he said, his voice husky in a way that made her feel like she was wearing far less than she actually was.

A tickle in her throat had her coughing again. *Focus, Olline, this guy could be a serial killer! Being stunning doesn't mean they aren't a murderer!*

She swatted his hand away. "Who the *fuck* are you?" she repeated, doing her best to look threatening. Olline called to her magic, pulling it beneath the surface of her skin, ready to fling it out and grip the natural ores in her earrings and brow piercing and . . . what? Eviscerate him?

Gross. But hadn't he been about to do that to me? She shook her head, clenching her fist around the magic; she would do what she must.

"Were you working here today? Alone?" he asked instead, jerking his narrow chin at the door next to her.

"Obviously." She rolled her eyes at him. "You saw me exit when you pinned me to a wall!"

"No need to shout, darling," he said, glancing around the hall. He hunched his shoulders forward slightly, taking a step closer, as if worried he was somewhere he didn't belong.

"Oh no? You tried to kill me! I'll scream if I have to. And

use my magic if that doesn't work," she said, widening her eyes, so he got a good look at the brilliant emerald color that confirmed her threat. "Now, who are you? And," she added, deciding that if she was going to make demands, she might as well go all the way, "stop calling me darling. It's patronizing."

He took a step back, sucking in a breath. He, unsuccessfully, tried to hide his confusion by looking at his nails, pretending to be bored by the question. Yet she caught how his eyes twitched from her eyes, to her badge, and back to the door again, like he was trying to figure something out. After a mere breath of a moment, he tilted his head again, appraising her once more. He clenched his jaw, the lines of his face hardening in determination.

"My apologies. You can never be too careful this time of night, no matter where you are." The expression he wore was cool and considering. His easy, casual smile was as disarming as before, but when he licked his lower lip, Olline's stomach gave a little flip. It really was unfair how gorgeous he was.

"The name is Casimir Everhart and, never fear, I'm not some scoundrel lurking about. Security is too tight for that, now isn't it?" Olline narrowed her eyes, and this time Casimir cleared his throat. "I work for Etzel Straub, in a manner of speaking."

Straub . . . that name sounded familiar. Hadn't Karter mentioned an Under Senator with that last name? It felt so long ago now she couldn't be sure. She continued to glare at him, her magic bubbling like magma in her veins.

He sighed, shifted his stance, exasperated, and rolled

those dark red eyes at her. "Under Senator Etzel Straub? He's rather famous in Antal, you know. Etzel is the only one who's held his seat for nearly two centuries. It's quite impressive." Casimir said as if reciting from a script.

Olline's eyes narrowed slightly. Casimir grinned and added quickly, "If we're actually exchanging pleasantries, this is the part where you'd offer your name, and some explanation why you're in the evidence archives so late when there's an entire city teeming with life waiting for you. It couldn't be," he said conspiratorial in a way that made it seem like they were old acquaintances, "that you're so green to Antal that you know nothing of the city and how it functions."

She noted that none of what he said was a question.

His gaze stayed fixed on her, giving her his full attention, waiting for confirmation. Desperate for it, even. Olline tried to hide the tremble in her legs when his eyes became half lidded, as if they were out enjoying said night life somewhere and not in the middle of a quiet hallway.

An empty hallway.

Olline cleared her throat again. "I *was* working. First day. I lost track of the time transferring files." His eyes fluttered, and there was a tick along his jaw when she mentioned "files". She quickly glanced at the door to make sure it was securely closed. "I'm Olline Tavos. Freelance data analyst and program engineer. Now that those *pleasantries* are out of the way, I should be going."

Casimir hesitated, his body going stone still. Just as quickly, his shoulders relaxed and his easy, coy smirk returned in force. "I knew it. Allow me to show you around the city. *Please,*" he said, his words rushed, holding the hint of desperation.

It was the "please" that had Olline tensing. It came out heavy, almost like a plea. An entreaty now hidden as he continued, his tone more casual, "It's the least I can do for, well, pinning you against a wall. At least without your consent."

Olline's throat went dry at his words. Was he honestly *flirting* with her? Now? After what he did? And was it honestly working on her?

Get over yourself, Olline. He's just apologizing for trying to kill you. Or something . . .

"Um, I'm good. Thanks. I'm just going to go home now." Sliding away from him, she forced herself to walk calmly back toward the elevators, keeping her magic close to the surface. A second later, she heard his steady footfalls behind her. "Stop following me," she snapped at him.

"Darling,"—she glared at him—"Olline. These are the only elevators that lead to the entrance. Please, I think we've already established that if I truly wanted to harm you, I could and would have. And you would use your pretty magic to deflect me, and things would get very messy. But *I* don't want to hurt you." His voice was steady, and Olline almost believed him.

Almost.

"It was an error on my part. You surprised me, is all. Still, I shouldn't have reacted the way I did. But I've already apologized, so I don't know what else you want me to do. Unless you let me take you out."

Again, there was that soft plea to his offer.

She narrowed her eyes at him, wishing the elevator would hurry. He chuckled, raising his palms in a placating gesture. "Out on the town. Or out to dinner. Your choice. I promise you, it's nothing nefarious." He paused, his smile softening. "Unless you want that."

"I'm good, really," Olline answered, scurrying into the elevator as soon as the doors opened so he wouldn't see her cheeks flaming. Casimir stalked in behind her, a predator out for a casual stroll. He shoved his into his pockets as he leaned against the mirrored wall.

The elevator doors closed, and they began moving. Olline did her best to stare straight ahead and not let her gaze slip to the man in the corner. But he didn't give her much choice. "You *are* new to Antal though, aren't you, Olline?"

"Yes, you already guessed that. So what?" she replied tersely.

"Just confirming an observation." Casimir said no more, and Olline glanced at him from the corner of her eye. He didn't seem to notice her looking at him. His expression remained thoughtful, his silvered brows pulled slightly together in thought, his eyes downcast in a way that seemed so natural that it looked like he was permanently sad.

Which made no sense. Olline would not humanize a man who thought pinning people to the wall was a natural response to being startled.

Nope, she refused.

The elevator slowed and the change in inertia had Casimir looking up, his expression clearing back to that arrogant look he wore so well. "Well, Olline Tavos, I do so hope to see you around." He exited the elevator first, as it took Olline a moment to remember how to move. She had been too unbalanced by the subtle change in his appearance when he didn't think anyone was looking.

Casimir's words lingered in Olline's mind long after she made it back to her apartment. She was unsure why someone who worked for an Under Senator would be in the sub-basements so late at night. Was he a personal assistant? But what personal assistant acted like *that?* Everything about him had her curious, which made her restless as she tossed and turned in bed hours later.

If there was one thing Olline was powerless to fight against, it was when her curiosity tickled her magic.

And she did love a challenge.

CHAPTER 4

Olline woke early the next morning. She blinked bleary eyes into the dim bedroom and murmured, "Good morning, lovely ladies." Her orchids rustled softly in reply.

Since Olline began her indoor flora-cultivating hobby, she had gotten into the habit of talking to her plants. Some people said it helped them flourish; she believed it was all her earth magic, but talking to them couldn't hurt. If nothing else, it made her feel less alone.

But on some days talking to her flowers was not enough.

Given the early hour, there was only one person she could talk to: her brother Lochan. He was a lab technician in the biomagitech and cybernetic research facility for the Hayashi Corporatocracy. The Hayashi Corp had dealings all over Audamar, and with the different time zones to account for, it meant her brother was an early riser.

Olline had enough time to pin the holo-video to show only her face when Lochan accepted the call. "Baby sister," he said in his normal, chipper sing-song manner. "To what do I owe the pleasure of seeing your face so bright and early?" Lochan smiled at her from where he was, making breakfast for him and his husband. Though she couldn't see her brother-in-law anywhere.

"Oh shit," she whispered, "Are we going to wake Goswin? I can talk to you later if this is a bad time?"

Lochan lazily waved his spatula, dismissing her concern. "Please, that man sleeps like the dead." Her brother winked a pale, lilac-colored eye at her, grinning good-naturedly.

The holo-projection shook as he readjusted his comm device to accommodate the twisting indigo horns protruding from the top of his head. Lochan's horns were taller than Darrin's, their oldest brother, and it was hard for Lochan to get the full length of them into any holo-call.

Olline had never met her brother's biological mother. Yet Lochan's horns, lilac eyes, and the dusky blue-grey of his skin looked identical to the few images she had seen of the seersha. Often, Olline looked for the little bits in Lochan that belonged to their father. They both had similar chestnut brown tones to their hair, but that was the only obvious similarity, and even that was mild, given the purple undertones of her brother's hair. Her and Lochan were both similar in temperament though, so she figured they both got that from Zachery Tavos.

"So," he continued, "you okay, little sis? Or was your first day just so amazing, and Antal so wonderful, that you couldn't wait to dish?" Lochan put a lid on the pan, and leaned on the counter, giving Olline his undivided attention.

Her stomach tightened, and she hesitated a moment. How was she supposed to tell Lochan about Casimir? Maybe she shouldn't. But that's why she had called him, right?

"I think," she began slowly, "that maybe someone tried to kill me last night?"

Lochan blinked slowly, face slack as he processed her words. "You think? Hold on," he sputtered. "What? You need to back up, Olline. What happened? Are you okay?"

Biting her lip, Olline wrestled her thoughts into submission and told Lochan what had happened when she left her office. Even as she recounted the surprise and initial fear, she couldn't quite smother the blush that inflamed every one of her freckles as she recalled meeting Casimir.

"So, wait," Lochan interrupted her. He massaged the base of his horns, mussing his short hair as if a headache were coming on. "Did you actually see a weapon? He didn't draw blood?" A pause, then, "Are you positive he meant to *kill* you?"

"I felt *something* sharp pressed against my abdomen," she explained. "And wait a second. Are you defending him? Even after I just told you he pinned me by the neck against the wall?"

"Hey, if you wanted a white knight to get on the next hypersonic plane and charge to Antal so he could beat this guy up, you should've called Darrin. That's his schtick, not mine." Lochan grinned at her, but the smile fell away as Olline pouted at him.

Lochan sighed. "I'm not defending him. But, sister," he said with tired patience identical to their father's, "government facilities *do* attract, purposefully, people like that. People who overreact first and apologize later. Antal may not be the corporatocracy Cyneburg is, but they operate the same when there are powerful entities with egos. They bring on people who'll protect the companies' assets at all costs. Think bodyguards, but specifically to protect against corporate espionage and to, sometimes violently, take new talent to help their employer's interests. I'm not excusing what he did, but if he didn't actually hurt you . . . I don't know. Sounds pretty normal from my experience in places like that. It sucks, but maybe don't take it so personally? And maybe carry more raw metal with you so you can use your magic on these guys?"

Olline huffed, annoyed that she could understand her brother's argument, and went about her morning routine. Lochan couldn't see her as she changed with the holo-call pinned to show only her face. "Speaking of which," Lochan prompted, still leaning on his kitchen counter. "Did your magic react to him?"

"Lo," she began, but he cut her off with a sarcastic eye roll.

"Yeah, I know. Your 'magic doesn't work like that', as you love to tell me. But humor me. Did you get any weird vibes from this Casimir guy?"

Clothes on and hair in place, Olline busied herself with her coffee maker. She tried to think back to the elevator ride out of the building and everything Casimir did and said. Had she sensed something from him? Any sign at all that he was lying? She had a gut feeling that usually bubbled up as a type of curiosity, but that was as far as it went. And clearly, it wasn't that trustworthy if she hadn't seen what a dick Achan was from a mile away, let alone Casimir.

Lochan was patient, waiting for her to sort it out without interruption. The sad fact was, she didn't. Nothing about what Casimir did *after* made her feel in danger. Maybe a little suspicious of why he'd offer to apologize with some grand gesture. But nothing . . . violent.

With a heavy sigh, she said, "The only feeling I got from the entire thing was my magic responding to the *mystery* around Casimir. That and curiosity over this politician he mentioned. Apparently, the same Under Senator was responsible for hiring me, too."

Lochan snapped his fingers and pointed at his comm device, which made it look like his holo-projection was about to poke her in the nose. "There you go! You can verify all of this. Look him up! If this guy works for a politician it could explain, not excuse, everything. And," he said, leaning closer, his horns now entirely cut off from view, "if it turns out he *wasn't* lying? Then you can totally take him up on an offer to see more of Antal."

"Lo!" Olline chastised, but a chuckle ruined it at the absurdity of his suggestion. Because it was absurd, wasn't it?

"What? With the way he was so quick to apologize by offering to take you out? He sounds *interesting*. I say, if he really does mean to make up for being a prick and *almost* hurting you, then let him prove it by groveling. There's nothing hotter than a man who grovels." He wiggled his dark brows knowingly, making Olline giggle like she was a little girl again.

"You're the worst," she said, but his suggestion was a good one. The looking up these guys part, not the taking Casimir up on his offer part. The leaves of her vines and ferns tilted toward her as she moved into the living room where her holo-tablet was waiting.

Olline powered on the device and pulled it into her lap, sitting cross-legged on the plush, taupe couch in one fluid motion. She was glad Lochan couldn't see more than her face; he would have teased her relentlessly about how many crates she still had to unpack. "All right, you want to hang around while I search? Or do you need to go feed Goswin?"

Lochan glanced over his shoulder, then shook his head. "I'll stick around for this scavenger hunt. Start with the Under Senator. He'll be the easiest to confirm Casimir's story around."

Under Senator Straub *was* easy to find.

"Well, shit," Olline murmured. Before her brother could ask, she explained, "He's exactly as Casimir said: the longest-sitting politician in Antal. The weird part is he doesn't seem interested in running for Senator."

"He's been an Under Senator this whole time?" Lochan asked, a hint of confusion in his airy voice.

Olline nodded. "Yeah. And get this, his name's attached to half a dozen different measures that benefit private infrastructure corporations. Sounds like your kind of thing, honestly. Maybe you should transfer from the Hayashi Corp to work for this guy, too. Then you can hang out with me all the time," she teased, but there was a hint of hope in her voice.

Lochan rolled his eyes, thankfully not catching her tone. "No thanks. I don't like being on the lobbyist side of things. Politicians," he said with an exaggerated shudder, "disgusting."

Now it was Olline's turn to roll her eyes. "Even though this guy is on a bunch of committees pushing for deregulating certain types of biomagitech?" She didn't wait for Lochan to respond. Reading ahead, she gave a low whistle. "This Etzel guy is really into pushing for some extensive cybernetic mods. The kind meant for body augmentation. It *really* sounds like your kind of thing, Lo."

He narrowed his eyes, all seriousness now. "Pass. Goswin can't leave Cyneburg. Seersha magic like his isn't as fun as your humani magic. He'll literally wither away if we leave the place where his magic was born. You, of all people, know that, Olline."

What she was reading distracted Olline too much to feel the full reprimand of his words. "Well, this is weird," she murmured.

When she didn't immediately elaborate, Lochan sighed loudly. "You do know I can't see what you see, right? Don't be rude. Dish, sister!"

"Right, sorry," she said, giving her head a little shake to refocus her thoughts. "For as much as he pushes for deregulating biomagitech in cybernetics," she explained slowly, "he's got no mods himself. At least, not from what I can tell."

"He's a full-blooded seersha, right?" Lochan asked. When she nodded, he shrugged. "Always hard to tell with some seersha if they have mods or not. Especially if the guy is old. Which, I'm assuming he is?"

Olline nodded again, reading him what she found. Etzel Straub was older than she would ever be—he was already three hundred and sixty-seven, though he didn't *look* old. Since seersha could live up to five centuries, aging took on a new meaning. Humani only lived a fraction of that, usually only up to two centuries, possibly three if they had magic—like Olline.

Changing the image setting on her wrist communicator, she showed her brother the images she found of Etzel. Outside of a few streaks of grey, his hair was still black as oblivion. There were no wrinkles on his sunset bronze skin other than a few hard creases between his brows and the frown lines that framed his black goatee. She supposed his eyes could have been cybernetic or biomagitech devices—they were a type of yellow diamond that seemed to glow—but Lochan didn't think so. Seersha's eyes were never subtle and most took pride in the bright, unique colors and wouldn't hide or change that with cybernetics, he explained. Etzel's rich cedar-colored horns had no magitech additions either, that she could see, as they protruded through his hair and curved down around his long ears—ears even taller than Casimir's sharp points.

Casimir.

Now that they had confirmed Etzel was who Casimir said, it was time to check if the mysterious seerani worked for the Under Senator as he claimed. Olline's stomach twisted as she searched, both dreading and hoping to find a reason to discredit everything he had told her last night. Which wasn't much, all things considered, but still. Lochan seemed practically giddy as she began combing through the digital feeds.

Olline found nothing, not even an image that would connect Casimir to Etzel. "But he *has* to work for Straub, right?" she said, hating that her voice took on a pleading quality. "He couldn't get down to the sub-basements otherwise."

Lochan gave her a sympathetic look. "Maybe he disabled the security?"

She shook her head, unsure why she was the one defending Casimir now. "He hadn't been sneaking around after. He just casually . . . sauntered out of the building. Even if you disable some of the security, backup droids would've responded. He'd have had to book it out of there."

Lochan nodded in agreement. "Keep searching then? Like I said, some CEOs like to have people off the books to prevent corporate espionage. Maybe your politician is the same when it comes to your mystery man?"

No matter where she searched, or the back channels she took through the Government Plaza servers, there was no mention of Casimir. Anywhere.

She found mentions of a Kullen Everhart though.

"A relative maybe?" Lochan suggested, trying to give her hope.

But outside of discovering that Kullen was a successful pleasure club entrepreneur, she couldn't find any connection to Casimir. "I can't even find a holo-projection of Kullen to see if they look alike," Olline groaned. She found it odd that someone in the pleasure club business was a ghost on every digital and virtual server she visited. Lochan didn't share her skepticism. He worked with enough business owners in Cyneburg to know that it was both common, and easy, to disappear digitally if you had the funds and knew the right people. A pleasure club owner like Kullen probably had both.

"Why do you even care about Casimir, sis?" Olline opened her mouth to remind him once more about how he accosted her, but Lochan rotated his hand flippantly, dismissing her. "Yes, he poked you and pinned you. But for as much as you remind me of that fact, it sounds more like you're trying to convince *yourself* of something, not me."

Olline came up short, her breath hitching in her chest. Was that what she was doing?

As she considered his words, she gently ran her fingers over her neck, where Casimir had pressed his forearm against her. It surprised her that there was not even the shadow of a bruise to be seen. More shocking was how crisply she could remember the feeling of his leather jacket, the warmth of his body beneath it, and the restrained power in his grip while he assessed her.

Her body was warming, her heart fluttering. Before she could embarrass herself in front of her brother, Olline made a disgusted noise deep in her throat. She jerked her hand away from her neck and glared at Lochan, glad once more that only her face was visible.

Lochan shrugged, laughing at her. "I just think, deep

down, you know that while his methods are questionable, he wasn't lying. At least about why he was there last night. And that he probably genuinely wants to make it up to you." He paused, letting her digest his words, giving her a knowing look.

"Don't bring up Achan," she warned, gaze dropping. Her chest tightened at the remembered embarrassment of how convincingly Achan had lied to her.

"Fine. But you know what I'm getting at, Olline. Wasn't one perk of taking this job the fresh start you'd get from it? So, start fresh!" Lochan looked like he was about to say more when something caught his attention off-screen.

"Got to go, baby sister," he said cheerily. "The husband is awake at last. Have a good second day, and," he said, tone becoming serious, "maybe this guy is just jumpy. You don't have to look so hard for an ulterior motive all the time, you know. You *are* worth getting to know outside the office. It *is* possible that this man wants to know you. The *real* you. Shitty first impressions aside. If nothing else, it'd be nice for you to make a connection out there. It doesn't have to be this man, but someone. As much as I love our early morning chats, I want you to have others to talk to, too. You deserve that, Olline."

Olline's thoughts drifted all day.

Through sheer force of will, she didn't dig deeper into the encrypted file, and thankfully she encountered no others like it as she went about transferring the old evidence files. It was boring work and, outside of one brief check-in from Karter once again in drone form, nothing remarkable happened. Well, except that Karter seemed surprised to see her, weirdly. But that may have been because he had heard what happened and assumed she would take the day off.

No one else had stopped by to introduce themselves yet again. Which gave far too much time for her traitorous thoughts to drift back to last night, and her conversation with Lochan. She was so frustrated by it, she took an actual lunch break. Though, she didn't venture out to make a "real connection" as her brother suggested.

She called her father instead.

Zachery Tavos answered his holo-wrist communicator before the loading screen fully actualized. "Olline, my girl, how are you? Is everything all right?"

There was a pleading quality to his voice, one that Olline knew meant he hoped things were going just poorly enough that she would want to move back home. She suppressed a huff and said, "Yeah, everything's great, Dad. Just taking a lunch break and wanted to . . . check in?" She cringed and wished the holo-projector had been turned off so her father couldn't see the expression.

He frowned, his blue-grey eyes narrowing in that knowing way of his. "You're bored, aren't you? Lonely too, I suspect. You always did work too much. Two days on the job and already on the path to burning out."

"Dad," she said, pinching the bridge of her nose, "please,

don't start—"

"Have you explored at all, Olline? Gone out to eat? Looked for botanist emporiums so you could share your hobby with others?" Olline didn't respond and her father plowed ahead. "Let me guess, outside of your home and work, you haven't been around Antal at all."

Again, she said nothing and her father let loose a heavy sigh that had his shoulders sagging like a balloon slowly deflating. "What was the point of going so far away, accepting such a huge bonus if you weren't going to enjoy it?"

Olline was starting to regret not leaving her office and knocking on office doors until someone answered. "Dad, I've literally been here less than a week. I've been busy. Besides, the city isn't going anywhere, there's no rush in exploring."

Zachery's frown deepened. "You know your mother would say that's you making excuses." Olline sucked in a sharp breath, her heart hitching like it always did when he brought her mother up in this way. He gave her an apologetic smile, waving the remark away. "I just don't want you to work yourself to death, Olline. I'm allowed to worry about you, you know."

"I know, Dad," she replied, her voice meeker than she intended. He continued to look at her with his judgmental gaze. With a deep sigh, she said, "I won't spend *every* moment working. Don't worry. I'll," she swallowed and took a deep breath before continuing, "go out and see what there's to do here."

His bushy ochre-colored brows shot up, his face brightening. "Promise?" He looked so hopeful that it nearly broke her heart.

"I promise."

"That's my girl," he said, nodding in approval. "I'll let you get back to your lunch break, sweetheart. Go use the time to meet the people on your floor!" Zachery suggested, eyes twinkling. "Stay safe, and I look forward to hearing all about the *fun* things you find."

Olline fought the urge to roll her eyes and, through gritted teeth, said, "Will do. Love you, Dad. Bye." She disconnected the line before he could comment on how tight her voice was and before she could make a snide comment about how he didn't even ask if she *liked* her new job.

She had called her dad hoping to take her mind off the mysterious Casimir, but all it had done was bring him to the forefront once again.

Maybe Lochan and her father had a point?

Casimir's offer to show her around fluttered through her mind, tickling her ribcage and making her heart slam against its confines. She had no way of finding him again, which made the whole thing too wild of a hope that he would return. It relied too much on coincidence, which she knew was pointless.

And yet, she hoped all the same.

CHAPTER 5

Olline didn't make good on her promise to her father that night.

She went straight home. Once there, to keep from going into a spiral, she dove head first into building the specialized data storage units she was constructing as part of her contract.

Building the hardware now was technically ahead of schedule, given where she was in the data analysis and transfer stage. But, well, she could start now, so why not? Theoretically, she would then have more free time later to enjoy the city!

She would stick to that story, should her father ask.

Hardware manipulation was a specialty of hers as an earth caster. She could manipulate the molecular makeup of the natural ore used to make the servers into something new. However, with the complexity and energy required, she could only use her magic in this way for so long without risking catastrophic results to her health. Olline had heard of casters overextending their powers, using too much and becoming a husk that would never wake again without a serious boost from natural power—usually their own stored somewhere else.

Olline eyed her plants as she arranged her materials. Getting that drained and pulling from the other places where a caster's power was housed was poor planning, in Olline's opinion. She shivered. She couldn't even bring herself to imagine using so much of her magic that she would be forced to take it back from her plant babies.

Olline lifted her head from her work, and it was only then that she realized how late it was. Exhausted and proud of herself that she hadn't thought of Casimir at all during that time—damn, streak broken!—Olline crawled into bed and passed out.

The next day, Olline was once again early to the Government Plaza. Her father, having taken her one afternoon holo-call to mean she was always free at the same time of day every day, was trying to get ahold of her again.

Guilt like barbed vines twisted through her stomach as she glanced at her wrist communicator, her father's grey eyes and shy smile glowing up at her from the caller ID image. But she knew what he wanted to talk about, what he wanted to ask her about, and it wasn't her job. The realization made the vines constrict around her stomach, and with a heavy sigh, she ignored the call. She vowed to keep her promise tonight after work, even if just for an hour. Then at least she would have something to tell her father when he inevitably called again the next day.

"An hour out wandering Antal won't be so bad," she murmured to herself, swiping more files into the transfer queue before clocking out for the day. "I'll have plenty of time to work a bit afterward." With that, Olline marched out of her office and left the building. Relatively on time, too.

She sighed, shoving her hands in the slouchy, metallic gold jacket she wore, and kicked at the pavement with her boot. "I'm not going to find anything around here," she said, eyeing the well-dressed office workers leaving from higher levels in the Government Plaza. Olline loved her work, but the people she shared an "office" with were decidedly not her scene.

What was her scene? She didn't know yet, but she convinced herself that finding out would be the adventure she needed.

Grinning to herself, Olline darted across the walkways to the first public access elevator she could find that would take her to the lower levels. The levels that weren't as artificially manicured, where the things that thrived were a little wilder and more carefree.

Or that was the hope, anyway.

Her hand hovered over the button for a moment, the hairs on the nape of her neck prickling. She had the oddest sensation she was being watched. With a quick glance over her shoulder, her eyes darted around, searching for the cause of her raised hackles. But nothing and no one looked familiar. She narrowed her eyes, then glanced up. There was a security drone hovering above her head. Olline sighed. Her magic was reacting to the pulses coming from the drone. Steeling her spine, she put the sensation from her mind and continued on her way.

Olline entered the elevator and picked a random location about three-fourths down into the center of the city. It wasn't the lowest location queued. She didn't dare study the others in the high-speed elevator to guess who was going farther down, but it was as low as Olline dared to venture.

She closed her eyes, battling against the inertia as her stomach struggled to keep up with the descending elevator. Thankfully, the doors soon opened with a trilling ping on the location she had picked on a whim. She inhaled the stale, slightly gasoline-tinged air as if it were a floral breeze, and paused at the threshold.

This low in the city, the air was heavy with a sticky humidity, clogged with the oil and grime from the aerial traffic. A mossy haze shrouded the sky, obscuring the sun and stars, with only the twinkling neon lights of businesses and signs capable of illuminating the gloom. The shadows hugged the mass of moving bodies, making the crowds appear to grow and swell in monstrous formations. Yet there was a vitality here that Olline could feel thrumming in her very marrow.

The earth far beneath her feet was polluted, yes, the soil not suitable for anything other than supporting the mammoth buildings that arched closer and closer to the stratosphere. But the loam had shifted, changed, and was still alive.

The earth thrived off a toxicity that permeated into the

people who lived lower in the city. It didn't feel poisonous to Olline. It held a frantic energy that buoyed her heart, an earthquake in her nerve endings that made her want to dance.

"Move it, bitch," someone growled from behind her, shoving her out on to the platform proper. Olline stumbled, blinking furiously, having forgotten where she was.

She looked for the person who shoved her, but the sea of people moving like opposing tides all around her made it impossible to find them. Some drifted toward the bars and clubs that were already teeming with activity, others flowed toward the hundreds of kiosks lining the walkways selling all manner of product for a fraction of the price as the same item higher in the city.

The rude shove would not intimidate her. Olline was too full of crackling energy to stand still.

Olline didn't make the mistake of closing her eyes this time. Focused on that small ball of molten energy in her core, the one that tugged her farther along the path, she headed deeper into the throng of people.

Twisting around the crowds, Olline didn't register faces or the smell of musky body odor as it flitted by her nose. She only paid attention to the tug in her core. But she was walking and walking farther from the public access elevators and fewer and fewer street lights were working the longer she meandered down the sidewalks, causing the hair on the nape of her neck to stand on end again.

With narrowed her eyes, she glanced up. There were security drones above her, even here. Old, clunky things, but they were there, so she pushed the uncomfortable feeling away once more. She was about to give up when the tug turned into an eruption, and she stopped abruptly where she was on the sidewalk.

Two larger buildings surrounded the club, with its door being almost too narrow to walk through. But the sound coming from inside . . . there was a band playing! Alongside a synth-bot to help the dancers keep going, but real musicians all the same.

Like her coffee and her plants, Olline was a sucker for things that were nurtured, created by living hands.

It was dark inside the club, or maybe it was more of a bar? Olline wasn't sure of the difference in this instance. The air was so gritty she could feel it all the way in the back of her throat. The red and yellow spotlights cut through the haze of smoke and heavy breathing, filling the room with shadows that concealed people as easily as alcoves. There was only one bar, the bottles of liquor suspended in different glass boxes that a robotic bartender called down as needed. It allowed the bar to be small and gave the raised platform off to the side those precious few feet with which to house the band.

She weaved her way to the center of the crowd, wondering if there was a caster on stage, using their power to draw people in. One had the horns of a seersha, but beyond that telltale sign, she couldn't tell if they had magic. All the others were humani and had holographic visors over their faces that obscured their eyes.

Olline's body moved, bouncing and swaying to the seductive pull of the singer's throaty voice. Her body rolled along with the heady beat coming from the drummer and the synth-bot that amplified it all. While most of the people on the dance floor were either shirtless or wearing tiny scraps of clothing, Olline didn't feel out of place. No one seemed to note her arrival, nor that she was one of the few people dancing without someone firmly pressed against her.

Olline lost track of time. A fine sheen of sweat coated her body, making her glisten. She kept her jacket on; the sleeves pushed to her elbows as she raised her arms and dipped her hips. Her bright purple crop top rose, showing off more of her torso and the curve of her wide hips around her low-slung jeans. That was when she felt a hand trail along the small of her back, sliding to her navel before the owner came into view.

Her magic hadn't even warned her that someone was that close.

A man with greasy blond hair that poked out from underneath the ratty hood he had pulled low over his forehead, obscuring his eyes, held a drink out under her nose. "Give that body a break, honey. Come sit with me a minute. I'll buy you any drink you want."

His voice was reedy, barely audible over the music. Her body recoiled against his touch, leaving a trail on her slick skin that made her feel clammy. "I'm good, thanks," she replied with an apologetic smile, twisting away from him.

But he moved with her, that glowing amber drink in his hand tilting up, like he'd force her to take a sip. "I'm just being nice, honey, no need to be so cold. You're too pretty not to have someone buying you a drink. Allow me. I'm a nice guy. You can trust me."

She moved away more forcefully. "No, I said I'm fine," she said again, putting more iron in her voice, letting the smile slip since he didn't seem to get the hint. "Leave me alone."

He moved to grab her arm, and she jerked away, glancing around at the other people on the crowded dance floor. None of them cared that she didn't want whatever this guy was trying to offer her. Plenty noticed, and were avidly watching the little drama unfold, but none stepped in.

Ice water filled her gut as she began backing her way out of the club, only to find a wall of moving bodies blocking her exit, trapping her with no way to navigate around them.

"I was asking you nicely," he said, his moist lips tickling her ear. Olline shuddered. She didn't know how he had moved so quickly or quietly to get around her so fast. "You shouldn't turn down a man who's just being nice to you."

Achan had said similar things to her. That he was being so nice to her, so she should do more for him. She should be grateful, because he was trying to help her. Her throat tightened, memories of Achan choking her until she swore she felt him breathing down her neck, his cold, deceptive touch sending a sickening chill through her once more. Panic threatened to overwhelm her, lost in a past she was working so hard to heal from.

Olline couldn't smile her way out of this or pretend that it would be easier to go along with it until she could disappear.

And she didn't want to, not this time.

She called her magic to the surface, let it coil around the iron in her piercings. Olline put steel in her spine and whipped around. "Back off, asshole!" Olline shoved the man as hard as she could. The sound of a grunt chased after her, but she didn't stick around to see if she had knocked him over. She turned to flee; she'd punch and kick the patrons blocking her path if she needed to, would let her magic clear a path if she had to.

"Cunt!" she heard the man yell. Then there was a whoosh of air behind her, and the firm grip of a hand around her wrist.

Olline clenched her free hand and spun, flinging her fist blindly and hoping it connected. She was lucky; her fist cracked against a sharp jawline as hard as granite.

A pair of familiar deep red eyes flared back at her.

Olline's stomach tightened, and she sucked in a breath. "Oh, shit."

WHEN IN HIS EYES

Casimir Everhart spent an agonizing couple of days puzzling over what had occurred in the Government Plaza. His actions, his very memory, was like a thick fog rolling in at dusk. Until the very moment his eyes locked onto *hers* outside a nondescript sub-basement office.

Olline Tavos.

The gems she called eyes were the first clear thing he could latch on to. Her fine lips were the second, even as they sputtered to, of all things, declare she had a *badge*. It would have been cute, unbearably so, if he hadn't been crushing her windpipe. His body still recoiled at the memory of how brutal that first encounter was. Which forced Casimir to consider: why had he regained awareness in the sub-basement in front of office two-hundred and twenty-three?

He had his suspicions as to why, but the mere idea was unthinkable. It would only birth hope and Casimir had learned decades ago that for a man like him, a thing like *hope* was best smothered in the cradle. That way lay only folly. Casimir had spent too long as madness's bedmate to so willingly hop between those sheets again.

Casimir would reach for the slight protrusion at the base of his neck, but stopped himself every single time, refusing to believe . . . What? That, Olline, of all people, stumbled upon something long hidden? Yet that little inkling that *something* had altered was the only thing that made sense, as mad as that was. Which meant only one thing: Casimir needed Olline. Which was a terribly uncomfortable realization made more so by the fact that the delightful woman had completely rebuffed him.

Which was . . . refreshing, if he were being perfectly honest.

For the first time in far, *far* too long, Casimir could follow a path of his choosing, and he wanted it to stay that way. Which meant his path *needed* to take him back to Olline Tavos. She had the very thing that could secure his new reality, but a life in Antal had taught him to be wary of people like her. He would need to keep his distance, well, his metaphorical distance, at least. Yet, showing back up at sub-basement thirteen was out of the question, and not because it would make him look like a stalker.

Casimir had other means, of course. Occupying his unique position in Etzel's menagerie of *employees* made finding people criminally simple.

He clenched his jaw and gave his head a sharp shake.

No, he wouldn't rely on Etzel for this. It was far too risky. Casimir knew where Olline was. He would simply find her at work and make some clever excuse that would ensure the pair of them worked together. He was good at those, even if he had bungled his first meeting with her by coming across too strong. Too *desperate*. Which, admittedly, he kind of was, but that was beside the point.

With a plan in place, he crept to the Government Plaza two days after that disastrous first meeting. Casimir stayed in the gloomy areas where the surveillance drones were intermittent with their sweeps, like he had done for decades. He found a patch of wall to lean against and waited.

And waited.

And waited.

Casimir sighed, annoyed that of all the people in Antal, he needed the one that was a workaholic. They were absolute bores to stake out.

Then Casimir saw her scamper from the building long after business hours, and a funny little flutter had his stomach tightening. She was so . . . animated.

Standing in the Government Plaza—dressed like some DJ in a club catering to the barely legal in her bright neon clothing, and not the brilliant magitech engineer he knew she was—Olline fidgeted like she had a delicious little secret. She kicked at the pavement, her stunning emerald eyes flashing. Her face scrunched and made her little nose twitch, the smattering of freckles on her rosy, bronze kissed skin darkened in a way that should not be as adorable as it was. She was obviously searching for something. It was the perfect opportunity for Casimir to step in and make himself useful. Olline wouldn't even question it, and yet his feet were concrete blocks at the base of his legs, rooting him to the shadows.

He was powerless to move, and for once, it didn't feel absolutely awful.

Olline was a spark of light in a world that had long since gone dim. All he wanted to do was watch her. How could he not? No one like Olline worked at the Government Plaza. Those peons were either beaten down by the drudgery or erroneously inflated by the façade of their miniscule self-importance. There was a lightness to Olline that Casimir wanted to hold on to and pray it could lift him up. She was a live wire that electrified him, and she had no idea.

That was all on top of the fact that Olline Tavos was resplendent. But surely, she had to know at least that much?

She had to know how her smooth skin begged to be revered. How people would fall into the forest of her eyes and stay happily lost for an eternity. How her earnest little smiles were so infectious they could make a statue grin. How her pink blushes matched her plush lips in a way that demanded they be kissed. How her glossy onyx hair with her moss green streaks encouraged someone to run their fingers through it until nothing else in the world mattered. Everything from her smattering of freckles to her rose neck tattoo begged to be tasted.

She had to know, because if she did, it would not be odd that Casimir noticed these things, too.

Casimir had been so captivated by her mere existence he didn't notice until it was almost too late that he had been trailing Olline, pulled along like she was the sun and he a moon in her orbit. Olline stopped, shoulders hunching. He had tailed people long enough to know when his presence was about to be detected.

He expertly slipped into the thick shadows just in time, Olline none the wiser.

Growling to himself, Casimir focused on tailing her, not on the seductive sway of her hips. Instead, Casimir fixated on what he would say to her, what excuse he would give for following her down into the bowels of Antal.

The sad fact of the matter was Casimir would have liked meeting Olline in another lifetime. Having an attraction for anyone, especially now, was not part of his plan. It couldn't be. It would be a death sentence for him. Shutting everything else out about Olline, Casimir followed her, silent and unfeeling as a tombstone. He puzzled over where she was going, and who she could be meeting in the cesspool that was The Pit.

Casimir stayed near the back of the shitty little dive bar, yet his eyes followed Olline no matter how much distance he put between them, or how many bodies swayed into his path. His lips parted slightly, a slow smile building even as she stole his breath completely.

The way she moved her body, the slow dips and turns of her hips, the way her tight pants clung to her round ass, the way her soft stomach rolled and her skin glistened caused an almost painful flutter in Casimir's chest. It was the kind of pain he wanted to bottle and get drunk off of when he inevitably looked back at tonight and thought:

What if, what if, what if . . .

In that moment, Casimir knew the plan he had meticulously constructed was in danger of crumbling and scattering like sand. He stamped down his want, his desire to hold this woman and let her speak for an eternity as long as she spoke to him. He had to, he had to, he *had* to . . .

Casimir had been so memorized by her, he failed to notice the repugnant little man approach until it was too late.

The cretin touched Olline as if he had the *right* to.

Casimir saw red. He moved through the crowd, a stalking shadow that had people cowering back before he even touched them. Casimir had murder on his mind as he watched Olline try to evade the lout, only for the disgusting male to play dumb. With pride, he watched her push him away, but his pride was swallowed by the dark mass that was his fury as the rat lurched after her.

In a breath, Casimir slipped between Olline and this sorry excuse for a man.

Casimir's fist was a hammer to the man's fleshy stomach. His knee was frozen concrete as he slammed the man's nose into it. Then he threw him to the ground like the garbage he was. He left the man writhing on the floor, all too aware of the weight of his mechanized stiletto dagger hidden at his side. Olline was fleeing though, and he couldn't lose her down here. Not now when The Pit's patrons were tracking her like a feast that had the audacity to not want to be consumed.

I'll gut you at a later date and time then, friend.

He darted after her, but made the same mistake as the rat whimpering on the sticky floor. Casimir grabbed for what was not his. The silky-smooth touch of her skin, her scent of fresh cucumber and mint, left him lightheaded. All of which was worth the punch she threw.

Her eyes widened, shining like the biggest emeralds he had ever seen, so instantly full of regret for something he very much deserved. It sent an electric jolt through Casimir that nearly cracked him in half. Olline was far too sweet for a place like Antal.

Which broke his heart, knowing what he had to do in order to survive.

CHAPTER 6

Olline was too stunned to stop Casimir from gently leading her out of the bar and out onto the sidewalk. As she passed, she glimpsed the creep laying sprawled on the tacky floor of the club writhing in pain. Olline hadn't seen what Casimir had done, but with how fast it happened and how much agony the man was in now, it spoke to an efficient ruthlessness that had no business making something in Olline's chest rustle.

So, she decided that nope, the fluttering was because of adrenaline and not because Casimir's hand was soft and firm like soapstone on her skin. Her arm was hot, her nerves sparking where he held her because Casimir was surprisingly warm. And she took deep breaths because she had panicked earlier, not because she wanted to be so easily calmed by his eucalyptus and lavender musk.

She didn't know how she hadn't seen Casimir before. His silver-white hair was hard to miss, despite being dressed all in black—this time his high collared leather jacket had red accents. Stares followed Casimir as he moved, drawn to him like plants to the sun.

Olline noted every single man and woman who paused to look at the seerani. But Casimir only ever looked at Olline.

Probably because I punched him, and now he's pissed he helped me out.

Casimir's nostrils flared, and he blinked his deep ruby eyes rapidly, as if his mind had been miles away and he was only now coming back to himself. He still held Olline; it wasn't an iron grip by any means and she could have wrenched her arm free at any time. Yet she was too stunned to remember that was an option. Casimir seemed confused by her, or maybe because long moments had drifted by between the two of them, observant and still, all over again.

It was the weirdest déjà vu Olline had ever experienced.

He dropped her arm. She could have fled if she wanted to, but she stayed where she was, curious about what he would do next. He lifted his hand, and Olline watched as he brought his large, open palm to his face and languidly used his thumb to wipe the corner of his lower lip, where a faint trickle of blood had collected. He dragged his thumb across his lip and she couldn't stop herself from lowering her gaze, tracking the slow movement as if her life depended on it. When his lips tilted into that amiable smile, her mouth went completely dry.

Casimir licked the blood from his hand in a motion that felt far too intimate for where they were and who they were to each other—which was nothing and no one—but sent a river of magma up her spine until her scalp was scorched.

"You're stronger than I gave you credit for." His voice was deep and rough in a way that was like a caress against her cheek, and made her heart race until her pulse flooded her ears.

She gave her head a little shake, told her heart to knock it off, and narrowed her eyes at him. "Yeah, well, I *am* pretty impressive," she said, crossing her arms over her chest. If she hadn't been flustered, and pouting because of an attraction that made no sense, she probably wouldn't have ever admitted such things aloud. But it was too late to suck the words back in.

"Aren't you just," he chuckled. But his smirk turned into a slow, lazy smile as he took a step back, appraising her.

She scowled, pretending a blush wasn't heating her neck, grumbling, "What're you even looking at?"

"I'm checking for injuries," he answered so automatically that his eyes widened, surprised by the admission. His chest expanded with a heavy breath he released slowly, the sharpness of his face softening at the edges for a second, before he seemed to catch himself. He cleared his throat and his deep red eyes landed on her face once more.

Olline licked her lips. "I'm fine, you know. You can stop staring now."

"Was I?" Casimir's eyelids fluttered. The movement was so subtle that she wasn't sure if she truly saw anything, but his smile slipped back into that unreadable expression. "Had you taken me up on my offer, Olline Tavos, you would've known better than to go to The Pit all by your lonesome."

She tilted her head up, finally spying the name of the establishment. The neon of the sign was a dull yellow, lost in the air's haze. She shrugged as if she were unbothered by it all, hoping to hide the slight shudder in her body as the adrenaline bled away.

"I was drawn by the music," she admitted, before narrowing her eyes at him once again. "Wait, how'd you even find me here? Antal may be smaller than Cyneburg, but it's not *that* small."

"Cyneburg, huh?" he said, his expression thoughtful. "Yes, I remember it being mentioned that the Department recruited someone from there." His voice was oddly flat in a way that made it seem like he was thinking of something else entirely.

He examined his graceful fingers as if bored. "You're lucky this particular stretch of Antal happens to be a haunt of mine, darling." She sneered at him, about to remind him how patronizing it was to call her that, when he rolled his eyes. Though there was a spark of humor in their red depths. "Me finding you here was nothing personal, Tav. Just stupid good luck."

A jolt went through her body, leaving her feeling weightless. "Tav?"

He shrugged. "Less condescending than 'darling', correct?"

The lightness instantly faded and her face twisted in annoyance, but she couldn't deny the fact that she rather liked the sound of Tav. Or, rather, she liked the way *he* said it. He said the nickname with such weight. Like he could see *her,* the whole of her. As if she were important. A sensation that had been stripped away after Achan made a fool of her.

"What's wrong with Tavos?"

"Nothing. It's as perfect as you are. But Tav rolls right off the *tongue,*" he said, voice lowering. Casimir took a fraction of a step closer and her breath hitched in response. "Don't you agree?"

She did, but he didn't need a bigger ego, so she said nothing and stood her ground. "Anyway," she said, glancing at the crowds that had not dwindled in the slightest, "that's my cue to go home. Now."

Olline turned and began heading for the public access elevators, not looking back to see if he was following. "At least I'll have one interesting story to tell Dad," she grumbled to herself.

"You ventured to The Pit to appease your father?" Casimir asked, a soft chuckle making his voice husky. "Bold of you."

Damn, he moves quietly! Does everyone in Antal take sneaking classes or something? But it didn't unnerve her as much as it had at first, now that she accepted her attraction as meaningless. "You don't have to walk me back, Casimir," she said, glancing at him over her shoulder. "I'm probably safer on my own than in your company, anyway."

"Recent history proves otherwise," he said, matching pace with her, the laughter in his voice more pronounced. "Can we move beyond that minor incident in the hallway, Tav?" Casimir said suddenly, his voice solemn. "I already apologized, explained I was merely surprised and doing my due diligence to my employer. And you've since punched me. We both reacted badly to the unexpected arrival of the other so, let's start with a clean slate, yes?"

There was an edge to his voice she couldn't decipher when he mentioned his employer. She slowed, glancing at him over her shoulder. "Funny you should mention that," she said. "I looked up your boss. Under Senator Straub? I couldn't find mention of you anywhere." Her eyes narrowed when he didn't immediately offer an explanation. "Who do you really work for in the Government Plaza?"

His face was like marble. Perfect, but emotionless. Even his eyes dimmed, no longer the deep red that sparkled like a ruby with mischief, but cold, a cooling ember. *Detached.* But before she could wrap her head around it, the expression was gone, and he lifted a shoulder in a half-hearted shrug.

"We've already been over this, you know. It's not my problem that you don't believe me." She frowned at him, and with a dramatic sigh, he continued, "I *do* work for Etzel Straub." She opened her mouth, and he stopped her words by raising one long finger. "Yes, I know you already went digging like the clever little cyber stalker you are. But you have to understand, Olline, not everyone in Straub's employ is, shall we say, on the record." He paused, letting his words sink in. They were so similar to what Lochan had mentioned that a chill had her chest tightening. He eyed her for a moment longer before continuing. "You won't find me mentioned in any official capacity. He has *people* who make sure of that."

He gave her a sidelong glance; the mischief returning to his eyes. "In fact, me telling you that violates at least a dozen secret NDAs. Don't you feel special now?"

She rolled her eyes at him. "You don't even know what kind of security clearances I have. It was Under Senator Straub who approved my job application. For all you know, *you* work for *me*."

"I assure you, I don't." There was a hint of a menacing rumble in his voice. "But very well," he said, his tone teasing again, his shoulders lifting, "I'll play your game, Tav. What're you working on that brings you to the Government Plaza, locked in one of those abysmal basement rooms where your pretty eyes can't even see the outside world?" He squinted at her, and she nearly tripped over her own feet. "You're an earth caster, if those flawless green eyes are any indication. Being in the sub-basement must be torture for you."

Olline shook her head automatically. Too used to people making the same assumption time and time again about what she liked because her eyes advertised her talents. Everyone thought they knew what an earth caster was like, that they were a monolith.

Hunching her shoulders, she shoved her fists into her jacket pockets. "Only one of those things is true. Well, one and a half. I am an earth caster. No, being in the sub-basement isn't torture. You don't know anything about me, Casimir, so don't pretend to."

Her breath caught in her throat. She hadn't even been this snappy toward Achan after, well, *after*. But tonight had been a lot, and she was tired and embarrassed, so she supposed it was all right to be grumpy.

To her surprise, and annoyance, because how dare he, Casimir took a deep breath and apologized. "You're right. I don't know anything about you and I shouldn't have assumed. I know I hate it when . . ." he trailed off and Olline stopped walking to look at him. Casimir caught himself and coughed awkwardly. "Enlighten me then, please. Tell me where I went wrong."

She looked away and resumed walking. "It'll bore you."

"Now who's making the baseless assumption?" Casimir chuckled like he could see the flush spreading over her cheeks. "Try me, Olline. I doubt anyone who's drawn to The Pit merely because it had a band could be doing anything remotely boring."

A smile threatened to brighten her face, make her steps lighter, despite herself. She always enjoyed talking about her projects, regardless of who she was talking about them with. And if Casimir said he wouldn't find it boring, well challenge accepted.

"I have a contract with the Police and Securities Department to move their oldest evidence files and cold cases into new servers. Servers I get to make and design the hardware for." She wiggled her fingers as if he could see the magic in her veins dancing on her fingertips. "It's my specialty. Manipulating the metals in tech so it does incredible things. Marrying the magitech hardware with my programming codes will make this the most secure server they've ever had, and, if they like what I make, they'll give me the contract for the *entire* Government Plaza. I, alone, will get to implement my code and hardware for the entire governing body of Antal!" She couldn't hide her smile as she turned to look at him, but Casimir had that emotionless look again.

Well, it was, technically, unreadable, not emotionless. But she took it to mean she was, technically, boring him and therefore, technically, hadn't been wrong in her assumption. But the realization hadn't brought her the joy she was hoping for.

Olline's smile fell away, and she hunched her shoulders as if walking into an icy wind. "I have pretty high clearance for that, obviously. I'm sure I didn't violate any of your precious NDA's." She meant it as a joke, but there was a bite in her voice that kept it from landing. "You haven't told me what you were doing down there, you know," she grumbled, pouting she knew, but she didn't care. "How do I know you work for who you say, huh?"

"If you're desperate for proof, just remember I was down in the sub-basement with you, left with you, not a single alarm was raised, and not a single security bot appeared to apprehend me." Casimir lengthened his stride to walk beside her. With a tilt of his broad shoulders, he seemed to shield her from being jostled by the thickening crowd as they got closer to the public access elevators. "If you want more proof, consider there were no disabled security personnel or bots. Which would've been too mysteriously badass for me to want to hide from a woman such as yourself. I just don't have a shiny little badge like you. That's really the only difference between your *contract* and . . . mine."

There was something in the way he talked, the way his face dropped and his gaze hardened that told Olline, without a shred of doubt, that Casimir did not like his role in Under Senator Straub's office. What that was, she couldn't say, but she believed he wasn't lying to her about who he worked for. Based on what Lochan had said, it was the simplest explanation for why he was in the building so late, even if she hadn't wanted to believe it at the time. She could feel the tension uncoiling slightly in her shoulders with the knowledge.

She was about to ask Casimir what it was he did for Etzel, and why he worked for the man if he disliked it, when he asked, "What truly lured you to a place like The Pit, Tav? I didn't peg you for the reckless type. Surely it wasn't really that awful noise you called music."

Olline couldn't stifle the sigh that escaped her. "It was the music." There must have been something about her wistful tone that caught Casimir off guard. His easy, confident stride faltered ever so slightly. Warmth spread over her cheeks, and she tucked her chin down, scratching idly at the braid on the side of her head. "I don't have the same empathic abilities a lot of earth casters do. I'm tied to plants and metals, sure, but not really the pull of people. But there's just something," she struggled for the right word, and with a sigh, said, "something magnetic about *live* music. It's real, created by flesh and blood. It has a *soul*. It just . . . it feels different."

Casimir didn't reply, and she rushed to explain. "Like,

have you ever had real coffee? Coffee made from beans grown in the ground and not the synthetic stuff a water caster can come up with in a shop? Most people swear blind they can't tell the difference, but I can. Same goes for music. I don't have any other explanation for it."

Olline stopped walking and shut her eyes, still floundering for words. Casimir stopped beside her. She could feel the warmth of his body shielding her from being bumped into. Her chin slumped to her chest, and she opened her eyes slowly. "As soon as I got down there, I felt the tug and I just had to—" she cut herself off abruptly, her cheeks flaming even more with awkward embarrassment.

Why was she even explaining herself to this man?

"Had to what, Olline?" Casimir moved to stand in front of her, and damn, if the look he gave her wasn't soft around the edges. His confident gaze smoothed out to something, almost . . . sweet.

Her brother's words tickled in the back of her mind. Reminding her that maybe Casimir was being honest, that he did genuinely wish to know her. Olline's stomach tightened, and she dropped her gaze to the pavement, shuffling her feet and ignoring the angry murmurs of the people they blocked on the sidewalk. "Had to move. To . . . dance to it."

She expected a man like Casimir to laugh. Most did. Achan would have. Casimir was so poised, effortlessly flirtatious in a way that confused Olline, and so painfully beautiful, that *of course* he would laugh at how childish she sounded. But he didn't. He remained silent, standing with a look of contemplative sadness on his face. That was the last thing she expected.

His plump lower lip turned down in a way that almost looked like a pout, and the infinite grief in his mahogany-red eyes cracked Olline's heart. The moment he noticed her gaze, the expression vanished. She couldn't say how it happened, but the hard edges were suddenly back, his sharp jawline a knife once more accentuating the curve of his smirk.

"You're precious, Tav. Don't let anyone rob you of that quality." Casimir was back to the charming rogue she had met a few days ago. While she didn't mind—she rather enjoyed being the focus of such charm, truthfully—she missed the thoughtful softness to his features. "Please, take me up on my offer to show you around properly. If you want to dance to something real and live and true, I can show you where. If you want to frolic around plant life, I can show you that, too. But please trust me when I say you don't want to get caught down here alone again."

Warm tingles danced across her skin with his full attention, and Olline could take no more of that. Lochan was proving far too correct when he said there was nothing hotter than a man who groveled. She grinned shyly, side stepped around him, and kept walking. At least the public access elevators were finally in view. She figured that, with her safely escorted back, Casimir would melt back into the crowed.

He didn't, and continued to match her stride. Her skin felt entirely too tight with his proximity, so, to distract herself, she asked, "Why not? You said this was your typical haunt?"

His shoulders stiffened ever so slightly, even though the

easy smile remained on his face. "My brother owns a slew of pleasure clubs around here," he answered, words clipped.

"Ah ha!" Olline said, grinning and forcing herself not to clap with victory. She skipped forward, walking backwards in front of him. "So that was your brother, then. Kullen? How come there're no images of him in the virtual forums? Does he work for Etzel too? Is that why you both are so hard to find any details about?"

Olline had completely forgotten she wasn't supposed to care or be curious about Casimir. Whoops?

"Questions, questions," Casimir chuckled, but his grin was wavering, and his eyes no longer twinkled. "Don't worry about Kullen, but yes, he's my older brother." She opened her mouth to press for more when he gently reached out, snaking an arm around her back, tugging her close as he reached out past her with his free arm. His eucalyptus and lavender scent flooded her senses again, and she fought the urge to lean in and sigh at the sheer comfort of the smell.

"Careful, Olline." He gently turned her, his arm falling off her back, not lingering like the creep's hand had done. Yet when his thumb brushed her bare hip, the electricity of his skin against hers was undeniable.

She blinked, noting that she was about to careen into the public access elevator doors. Too intent on watching Casimir rather than where she was going.

"Let's make a deal, my precious little caster." The words rumbled in his chest in a way that made her toes curl and completely forget that she should tell him not to call her "precious" or "little". "I will entertain every single one of your burning questions. But not here. Not right now. There's no fun in that." He reached around her and summoned the elevator, his scent caressing her senses again. "Say yes to meeting me again. Let me treat you. Be your guide. You clearly have no one else in Antal to show you its more tantalizing pursuits. Let me do that for you, Tav." It was taking Olline precious seconds to get her tongue to cooperate, seconds where the elevator sped to their location. "Or say no, and you'll never have to deal with me again." Casimir said when the silence hung between them like a blade. "Is that what you want, Tav?"

"No!" Olline responded far too fast and loud, given how close he was to her. Her cheeks burned, an all too familiar response around him, when she noted the laughter in his eyes. She gave her head a firm shake. "I mean, sure, ok. I'll take you up on your offer." Taking a deep breath, she forced her heart to slow its galloping beat. She lowered her gaze, voice dropping as she said, "I could use a friend here."

Casimir gave a sharp intake of breath and her gaze darted up. She couldn't see what had caused his reaction, but that slight languor had returned to his eyes and he tilted his head in her direction. "Friend?" He was looking up above her head at something Olline couldn't see. He jerked his head, seeming to come back to himself a fraction. "I . . . can do that."

Her chest suddenly felt too tight, but the soft *hiss* of the elevator doors opening saved her from rubbing the spot on her breast bone where his words struck her. She scurried inside, desperate for space. She wasn't a child that needed to have her hand held, even if the events of tonight *almost* told a different story.

"You know where I work, Casimir," she said, punching the closest location to the level of Antal where her apartment was. "I'll see you around."

There was a flash of fear across Casimir's face, quick as lightning. But the elevator closed on the expression—and him—too fast for Olline to continue studying this strange, yet unfairly confident and alluring seerani.

CHAPTER 7

Olline couldn't focus at work. Her thoughts were giving her whiplash, careening from wondering if Casimir would show up, to berating herself over what a colossal mistake this was.

With it still being early in the day, far too early to take a lunch break, Olline sent a message to Lochan. She was prepared to send whiny message after whiny message for the rest of the day. What she wasn't prepared for was her brother to send her a holo-call request.

Ugh.

For security, Olline again pinned the holo-video so the only thing Lochan could see was her face, and accepted the call. "What's wrong with texting?" she grumbled, queueing up another batch of files to transfer.

"Nothing." Lochan shrugged, dressed in his lab attire, getting ready to head to work. "But I've got the time to talk now, and I can't message in the lab. So why not? Besides," he said, leaning back and narrowing his eyes at her critically. "You sounded flustered. Even in writing. Which is quite the feat even for you, little sister. You okay?"

Olline blew out a long, exasperated breath. "It's because of Casimir," she whispered, like saying his name would somehow summon him.

Lochan's light lilac eyes remained narrowed. "What about him?" Careful not to be excited or have a reaction, in case it was the wrong one. Lochan was considerate like that. Quickly, she told him how Casimir had found her at The Pit. How she had taken him up on his offer to see the city, but didn't know if he'd actually show. She didn't bother with mentioning the creep who got too handsy with her or Casimir dealing with him. She still needed more time to process the fluttery sensations it prompted in her stomach.

"You're embarrassed," a rumbling baritone voice said off-screen. Lochan snickered, and a second later, the owner of the voice came into view.

Goswin loomed behind her brother, all dry seriousness. He was such a stark contrast to her light-hearted brother, and yet their marriage *worked.* Plus, they made a truly striking pair. One that, nearly a decade later, Olline still marveled at how their otherworldly beauty complimented each other.

A hulking figure, Goswin looked like he should work security somewhere rather than a professor of theoretical statistics at a private university. He was a good foot taller than Lochan, even with her brothers' twisting horns. Goswin had no horns of his own, but his ears were as tall and sharply pointed as daggers.

When Olline first met him and learned he was a caster,

she had assumed he had fire magic. Or maybe earth magic like her. But she had been wrong and learned an embarrassing lesson about assuming what power a caster had based on appearances. Goswin's skin was a soft, foggy green with eyes like brassy, golden ingots. His long brown hair had an ombre quality toward the end that reminded Olline of fire; the brown transforming to deep red, to orange, and fading to a light yellow at the tips. But Goswin was a water caster. His appearance and his vocation had nothing to do with his magic, and he seemed to prefer it that way. Olline loved that about her brother-in-law.

"I'm not embarrassed!" Olline squeaked. Goswin gave her a flat stare, and her brother tried—and failed—to stifle a laugh.

Goswin tilted his head. "Then what?"

Olline pushed another batch of files to transfer and rubbed her forehead. This was precisely why she wished her brother stuck to catty text messages. Now she actually had to figure out what was bothering her, and why. Olline rubbed at her sternum to lessen the burning pangs enveloping her chest.

Both Goswin and Lochan were silent, waiting for her. Goswin's steady golden gaze never left her face. Lochan glanced back and forth between the two of them like he wondered whose side he should take.

"When I got this job," Olline began slowly, piecing it all together as factually as she could for Goswin's sake, "I was free of the baggage I collected in Cyneburg." She took another steadying breath, distractedly swiping away a warning about the size of the files she was transferring. "Baggage that made me feel small and constantly in need of validation to take any space at all. The lightness getting this job gave me was something I didn't think I'd feel again after getting fired. Now there's Casimir showing up so often. First outside my office at night, then at The Pit? The last time someone was that attentive, who showed up randomly and pushed to spend time with me, to know what I worked on, it was Achan . . ." she trailed off.

That was what unsettled her. The old wounds Achan had caused were aching once more.

"Usually when someone shows interest, it's merely that. Interest. Has this person even tried to partner with the work you're doing?" Goswin asked. His expression was open, his eyes didn't narrow in suspicion or roll in chastisement like Lochan might have done. He seemed to genuinely want to know, which meant that Olline needed to seriously think about it. But of course, for once in her life, her mouth was faster than her brain.

"No!" she exploded. "But I'm worried that, well, what if he does start tampering with my stuff? He has access to my floor, clearly, since he was here prowling around the other night." Her chest tightened, her breathing coming faster and her words escaping in a rush. "What if that's why he's so eager to take me around Antal? So he can weasel his way onto my project? Then I'm right back working with greedy, small-minded men who let their jealousy over talent drive them to use their manipulative ways to blindside me. Like getting me fired for stealing work. Except the work in question is my programming language that I didn't a get a chance to license because I'd been too busy fawning over said small-minded men!"

She blamed her raw nerves on the ordeal from last night. The anxiety of not knowing if Casimir would appear, and the bitterness that no one seemed to care there was a new employee on their floor, as the reason for her outburst.

"I don't understand," Goswin responded slowly, looking from his husband to Olline. "That's quite the leap to think his access to your floor and his interest in making up for a bad first impression means he's trying to take credit for your work. Did Casimir do something you haven't mentioned?"

But she couldn't answer around her heavy breathing and the smoldering lava in her veins burning her up from the inside. Too worked up to formulate the right words, to even understand why this was coming up now, in this way.

The holo-projection shook. At first, she thought Lochan was readjusting the device, but it had nothing to do with him.

Lochan's eyes went wide. "Breathe, Olline," his voice was gentle, tone firm.

The magma beneath her skin was her power fastening on to her old hurt, her anger, letting it fuel magic she hadn't realized she summoned. She took several steadying breaths, letting the rage tremble through her fingers before it could latch on even more to her magic and shake the entire building down.

Blowing out a long, shaky breath, she said, "Sorry."

“Oh, little sister. Achan really messed you up, didn’t he?” Lochan said softly, sliding his fingers toward the comm device like he would reach through the projection and hold her hand.

Goswin’s nostrils flared slightly, his gaze sliding back and forth between the siblings when his eyes widened a tad. “Ah,” he said in his calm, dry way, “I see.”

He said nothing after that. Goswin merely gazed at them in understanding, like they all shared the answer now. This was the problem with geniuses, Olline figured. Lochan and Olline shared a knowing look, and he nudged Goswin with his shoulder. “Time to share with the rest of the class, handsome.”

“Hmm?” Goswin said, lost in her brother's eyes for a second. “Oh, yes. Well,” he continued, running a hand down his long, fire-like hair as he collected his thoughts. Goswin was often direct but, thanks to Lochan, had gotten better at delivering his thoughts in a gentler manner. “In my opinion, you’re putting a lot of assumptions on Casimir. You’re projecting your hurt from Achan onto this new character. It might be justified. It might not. You don’t know. The unknown makes you afraid. That alone isn’t enough to get your magic to act up, speaking as one caster to another. But a bigger emotion tied up with that could. Arousal, perhaps?”

Olline sputtered, choking on her own saliva while her brother laughed. “Goswin, stop,” Lochan gasped around bouts of laughter. “You can’t just say that to people. Let alone my baby sister!”

His brows scrunched as he regarded Lochan. "What? I'm simply focusing on what I know. This seerani's made a big show of wanting to make amends but hasn't set a time or made firm plans to follow through on that. And now he appears to work for a politician who also signs Olline's paychecks? It's confusing for even bright minds. No offense, Olline." She waved his concern off. Goswin saw things so clearly sometimes. It was refreshing to get his analysis. "What happened with Achan and your career in Cyneburg makes you question the purity of others' intentions. Couple that with this unknown entity working for the same politician when you're clearly the more tech-minded one. There are parallels to Achan. But," and he leveled his steady gaze at her once more, capturing her attention so fully she stopped casually working entirely, "consider if he'd have a reason to steal from you." He paused, and when she didn't say anything, added, "Does he?"

She gnawed on her lower lip, considering. In a huff of frustration, Olline dropped the holo-keyboard before she messed up her code. Casimir worked in the Government Plaza and could roam the sub-basements without issue. They technically worked for the same people. Which meant Casimir would have no reason to steal her ideas or sabotage her. It would just hurt him. Not that, that had stopped Achan.

With a shake of the head, she ran a hand over the top of her fluffy Mohawk. "Honestly? I don't know. Not really."

Goswin nodded, squeezing Lochan on the shoulder before moving away. "I'll leave you two to it. I should make a fresh pot of coffee, anyway."

"Use the beans I sent you!" Olline called after him.

He glanced over his shoulder, brow raised in confusion. "Why? Those are too precious to use on a random work day. I can make coffee myself that tastes the same," he said, wiggling his fingers to indicate his water magic.

Olline groaned as he walked out of frame. "It doesn't taste the same and you know it!" But Goswin was already gone.

"You know," Lochan said gently, getting her attention, "your mom would be disappointed you weren't at least giving this guy a chance. To either surprise you or prove you right."

Olline flinched as if someone flicked her in the chest. Out of her brothers, Lochan had been closest to her mother. He knew her well enough to make those kinds of statements and be right about them. She couldn't meet Lochan's eye as she murmured, "She'd also be disappointed that I'm even thinking about him. A lot rides on this contract, Lo. I literally can't afford the distraction. Mom would understand that."

The words were light enough, said with a forced bubbly attitude, but the admission still stung. She wanted to believe that maybe a guy like Casimir could want to be her friend, maybe more. But she had believed others' good intentions before and . . .

The simple fact was, Olline didn't have the luxury of being distracted by Casimir Everhart and his casual flirtations. Not that he was flirting with her. That would be absurd.

"You sure about that?" Lochan asked, smirking.

Olline groaned in frustration. "If Goswin were still here, he'd say that I've created a distraction loop caused by faulty data. That's all this is, Lo. Incomplete data."

"So, seeing him again would fix that." Lochan was quick to respond, fighting to keep the knowing look from his face. "That's why you're worked up. Why your magic lashed out."

She opened her mouth, and he flippantly waved his hand. "Yes, everything Goswin said, too. He made an excellent point. But you're agonizing on *if* he'll show up. So, you're trying to vilify him to make it easier on yourself if he just, poof! Disappeared." He propped his chin in his hand, and only then did Olline realize she was staring at him with her mouth agape. Her brother would have made an excellent earth caster with how well he could read her. "How close am I?" Lochan added, a chuckle making the words rumble in his chest.

Olline hunched her shoulders forward, stomach tight with embarrassment. "It's not bad logic." She reached for her holo-keyboard again, feeling heavier for having talked to her family rather than lighter.

Lochan gave her a sympathetic look, but she was done. Exhausted by the conversation and really, it wouldn't matter if Casimir never appeared. "I've got to focus, Lo. I'm sure you both have to get to work, anyway."

He glanced at the time and sighed. "Yeah. But keep me updated, all right? It's okay to be disappointed if this guy never shows. It's okay to *want* him to appear. Just don't let Achan make you scared and ruin something good before it can start, all right, sis? You—"

"Yeah, yeah, I deserve good things." Lochan winced at her biting tone, and her shoulders drooped. "Sorry. I'll talk to you later. Thanks, Lo. And thank Goswin for me, even though he's a dirty heathen for using magic to make coffee. Gross."

Lochan chuckled, waved goodbye, and the holo-projection flicked off.

Hunched over her work, Olline gnawed on the collar of her jacket as she lost herself in the data stream again. Refusing to put any more energy into her traitorous thoughts and redirecting that energy to her magic. Now she only saw code and metals and the molecular structures that made them all, bending them each to her will.

She was so absorbed, sucked into the gentle thrum of her minor magic, that the passing of time was meaningless. Before she knew it, the workday was done.

She poked her head out of the server room, seeing no sign of Casimir sauntering down the hall toward her. Disappointment cold as ice constricted her throat. Olline took a deep breath, told herself everything at The Pit had been meaningless, and ducked back inside. And yet, she decided she would stay a little while longer. Not to wait for him, of course, but there was more work she could do to get a jump start on tomorrow. To make up for her distraction today, obviously.

Two hours passed with still no sign of the seerani.

The relief she thought she would feel with knowing she could focus without pesky feelings distracting her never came. Instead, she was getting angry.

Olline could have spent the time at home, pouring her magic into the materials she was going to use for the server components. Instead, she had wasted time doing frivolous, busy work. It was draining, using her magic to manipulate materials on a molecular level, and she could only do it for so long before she became too exhausted to continue. She had to work on the hardware in small bursts for that reason. Pouring too much of her magic into the devices at any one time could literally drain her power and leave her life force no better than a shriveled husk. For casters, the risk of burning out was actually very, very high and could lead to death. A fact Goswin had cited years ago for why he didn't make his magic his job. Instead of waiting around for a mysterious, suave, devastatingly beautiful person, she could have spent the hours lingering on something worthwhile.

A soft knock against the door broke her silent tirade.

Olline couldn't quite stifle her gasp, and she took a moment to let the fluttery feeling in her belly settle before tip-toeing to the door. The anger and annoyance she had wanted to hold on to and wield against Casimir for making her wait evaporated before she ever could get a firm grasp on it. Her heart stuttered faster when her eyes landed on Casimir leaning against the doorframe.

His gaze slid down her, then trailed back up, only stealing quick glances beyond her. "You *do* actually work alone, don't you, Tav? I thought you had to be exaggerating. But here you are. Not a single person to help you move all these files or build . . . your server, was it?"

She shrugged, glancing at the room behind her. Olline couldn't tell based on his tone if he was trying to give her a compliment or teasing her. "It's not like I'm physically picking up and moving files. I'm just making sure they transfer correctly. A bot could do it, if Karter, my supervisor, wasn't worried about viruses or digital pirates."

She waved at her set up behind her. "This is like babysitting. But without the crying, or diapers, or playtime. So, not really like babysitting . . ." Olline trailed off when she realized she was babbling and was not even sure why she was trying to explain this. Hadn't she told Lochan and Goswin this was exactly what she *wouldn't* do? Give him the opportunity to get involved with her work? "Anyway, you get what I mean."

He clicked his tongue appreciatively, his gaze moving away from the room behind her to lock with hers. "You become more and more impressive each time we meet."

Olline's cheeks flushed, which grew more annoying each time it happened. "Yeah, well, I like what I do. I don't mind working alone. I kind of prefer it that way, actually." She bit off her words, in case she admitted something she wasn't ready to. She waved her hand a bit, shooing him back, so she didn't trip over his outstretched legs. "You know, work officially ended hours ago," she said as a way of accusing him of being late, even though they hadn't set a time to meet.

Casimir backed out of the room, hands buried deep in the pockets of his long coat. His shoulders were bunched up by his tall, slender ears, as if nervous that someone was watching. Which was silly. Someone was always watching. That was the point of the surveillance drones hovering, cloaked, near the ceiling.

"Yes, Tav, I'm aware. That was the point." His eyes darted around the hall once more, stopping briefly where, Olline assumed, the hidden security drones were. "I had a feeling you'd be here late again, and the first stop I want to show you of our charming Antal is best seen after hours."

She raised a brow in question. When he didn't offer more of an explanation, she hesitated at the door. *This is crazy, right? I don't even know him. What would Dad think if he knew I was following Casimir out into the night?* She wondered, gnawing on her lower lip.

He'd tell me to go out and have fun. That I deserved to have good things happen to me.

Casimir turned and curled his graceful fingers in a beckoning motion. "Come on, my impressive little caster, Antal is calling." He didn't wait for her, though. He was already taking hurried, silent steps back out the way he had come.

Lochan's words tickled through her, making her scalp prickle: *Your mom would be disappointed you weren't at least giving this guy a chance.* Deep down, she had wanted Casimir to appear, and then he had, and she was still debating going straight home instead? Because of Achan? She frowned, watching Casimir walk away. Lochan was right.

With a heavy sigh, to mask the excited thundering of her heart, Olline followed Casimir.

CHAPTER 8

Olline was getting nervous, tiny prickles teasing her scalp.

They hadn't taken a single public access elevator. Casimir hadn't led her toward any of the monorail stations that snaked up and down and through the city. He hadn't shown her to any late-night bistros. All things she would have assumed would be a top priority for her to know, that would be *safe* places to take a recent transplant. They were low hanging fruit in terms of locales for him to show her so she could get her bearings of where to go, where to avoid, and was the quickest way for him to "apologize" and then be done with her.

Instead, Casimir hailed a sky-cab as soon as they were clear of the Government Plaza, punched the coordinates into the automated driver, and then settled in directly across from her, grinning faintly as she squirmed. She wanted to ask him a million questions. Wanted to know more about what he did for Etzel Straub, if they were headed to one of his brother's pleasure clubs—because if they were, she would tell him ab-so-fucking-lutely not—or more about Casimir himself.

He seemed so effortlessly charming and confident. She was sure he knew how beautiful he was and that helped, but she was curious how someone like him became so comfortable in their own dangerous allure. Didn't it get exhausting?

The continued silence was clearly making her paranoid, a slight shiver tickling her spine and shoulders.

She could take it no longer and blurted out, only a faint tremor to her voice, "You're a seerani, aren't you? But not a caster?" *Smooth, Olline. You know better than anyone not to ask something like that.* She tried to hide her flinch of embarrassment by smiling at him as innocently as she could manage.

Casimir huffed. "Barely. I had a seersha grandparent. It's been humani ever since, though." His eyes slid to the window, that shadow of sadness creeping in over some memory before he pushed it away. "I assume none were casters, as I don't have a lick of magic. But I never met them, so I can't know for sure."

She couldn't stop her face from morphing into an aghast expression, her heart clenching in grief. "I'm sorry. I lost my mother about fifteen years ago. I understand what a loss like that can feel like."

He looked at her askance for a moment, then gave a flippant wave. "You can't mourn what you never knew you had, Olline. Don't pity me. Kullen raised me just fine, until—" He bit off his words, his throat bobbing as he swallowed. But the look vanished so quickly, a mask slipping off, or falling into place? She couldn't tell. Yet. But that coy smirk returned all the same.

"Until he didn't need to raise me anymore. Would have been nice to have power like yours, though." He gave her a wink and leaned forward, propping his elbows on his knees. "Now, usually the follow up to that is my age, with how long seersha lifespans can be and what not." Olline flinched again and he chuckled, his eyes twinkling, unbothered. "It's the natural curiosity you humani have toward seersha and seerani. I stopped being precious about the questions a long time ago. The outrage was too exhausting. So, let's get it out of the way, hmm? I'm a hundred-and fifty-six-years young. Beyond my good looks, that's the only gift my lineage has given me."

Now it was Olline's turn to swallow. He was over a century older than her. She wasn't young at forty-eight, not by humani standards anyway, but there was a certain power that came with age. She wondered if that was what she sensed about Casimir. "No, I meant merely because my half-brothers are seerani, too. They don't have magic, either."

Casimir huffed, but his eyes danced with humor. "That must gall them."

Olline shrugged, tugging at her fingers. "Not really. They care more about the fact that I'm closer to our dad, him being humani and all. The magic would be nice, but they'd rather look like my dad's kids. They both have horns, like their mom. It's really stunning, but it gets annoying for them to explain to people that, yes, that's in fact their father they're helping to the public transit depot."

"What a beautifully mundane problem to have," Casimir grumbled, but there was a faint look of yearning darkening his gaze. She didn't have time to be offended on her brother's behalf for the glib remark before Casimir was flitting to another topic.

"Ah," Casimir said, leaning back as the sky-cab slowed and came to a stop on the roof of one of the elite apartment complexes in the center of Antal. "Here we are." He pushed the door up, helped her out of the aerial vehicle, and stepped away before she could marvel at the soapstone feel of his soft, firm hands again.

She hesitated, looking around the aerial pathway that led to adjacent rooftops. It made a type of promenade platform exclusive to the rich and famous who dwelled on the top floors of these mega-skytowers. The sense of otherness crawled over her. Her anxiety became a roiling thing within her; unseen judgmental eyes piercing her, telling her this was the last place she should be. So why would Casimir bring her here?

The view was stunning, though.

The neon of the floating advertisements below reflected in the mirrored windows, and the inky indigo sky left her lightheaded. Like she could fall into a paradise of stars. So transfixed by the view, Olline didn't notice she had inched toward the protective plexi-glass barrier at the edge of the platform, or that the sky-cab had flown off, merging with the aerial traffic heading back into the major traffic lanes.

A gentle, warm hand was on the small of her back, not grasping, but soft enough to let her know it was there. "Careful, Tav. It'd be a shame to lose you so soon." Casimir's breath tickled the shell of her ear, the smell of him curling around her and encouraging her to lean into his chest.

Don't be ridiculous.

Olline moved away from his hand and the edge of the platform. She looked around the rooftop, avoiding his gaze. "Where are we? Do you live here?"

Casimir moved to her side, huffing in a way that was almost a snort. "Fuck no. I may be arrogant, but I'm not so entitled that I want my nose this high in the air." He glanced at her, at the wonder slowly bleeding from her expression, and his smile softened, almost . . . apologetic. The smug grin was gone, but he seemed to catch himself all too soon. He winked at her and gestured with his chin toward a glass dome on top of the building. "That's what I want to show you."

She kept her steps as light as possible, worried someone beneath would hear her. "Are we . . . allowed to be here?" she whispered, though there was no need. The sound of traffic and whistling wind between the buildings would keep anyone from hearing her words.

He laughed, looking over his shoulder with a devilish glint in his eyes. "Of course not. But I know people, shall we say? We're perfectly fine. Besides, the people who do have access to this place during the day won't appreciate it the way you, a bonafide earth caster, will."

A heaviness began settling over her body, her heart shrinking in her chest. She tried to hide her wince by rolling her eyes. Olline had a hunch about where Casimir had brought her. The location wasn't what disappointed her, but the *why*. At least, if she was right. "And how could you possibly know that?"

"Trust me," Casimir said, his eyes twinkling with a mischievous joy as he crouched in front of the door leading inside the dome.

Confusion washed over her, and she blinked, wondering why he was crouched. It wasn't until the door clicked open that she realized he had picked the lock. With his actual fingers. Who did that anymore? Every lock was digitized these days. Mechanical tumblers were terribly outdated in a world with casters. But Casimir had managed it, somehow. She didn't know if she should be impressed or horrified.

"What the fuck, Casimir," she hissed, pulling him away from the door. "You're going to get us arrested!" Then curiosity got the better of her and she crouched, peering at the lock. "How did you even do that?"

"You're precious when you're worried. Do you know that?" She glared at him over her shoulder, and he had the audacity to smile back. "Relax, I broke the lock the old-fashioned way. No digital alarms were triggered. And if something were to happen, I told you, I know people. We're fine."

She wasn't ready to stop glaring at him yet. "You've done this before, haven't you?"

He lifted a shoulder. "Yes. But not in decades. At least, not *here*. You'll forgive me when you see where I've brought you. You, Olline Tavos, will appreciate this far better than the petty celebrities below your darling little feet."

Olline didn't budge, but he gently reached a hand out to

her, giving her every opportunity to refuse. When she didn't, he gently tugged her inside, and she lost her breath completely, before that heaviness pressed down on her body a little more. Olline's hunch had been correct.

Vined, soft pink roses climbed the walls and beautiful, lush, green shrubs were all around her. In the center of the atrium was a jade green pool with massive lily pads gently swaying from a trickling fountain at the far side of the pond. Steam rose and curled off the water, making the leaves of the vines and the tall, thin shoots of young trees glisten with moisture. The entire room smelled like damp, freshly turned soil that Olline normally would find completely intoxicating.

Casimir had brought her to a rooftop botanical garden. Because she was an earth caster. It was a low hanging fruit location, no doubt, just not the kind she had hoped for.

Most people always assumed that earth casters wanted to spend time in gardens. True, it wasn't a *bad* assumption. Olline had mentioned that plants were a hobby of hers, after all. But this wasn't a place Olline could come back to, a place that would make her feel connected to Antal. This wasn't even the *real* Antal. She had hoped he would take her to *his* favorite haunts. Not places that, while breathtaking, told her nothing of this mysterious man and the city he so effortlessly traversed.

She took several deep, grounding breaths, letting the disappointment flow out of her with each slow exhalation. Olline shouldn't be disappointed that Casimir would bring her here. He didn't know her beyond the superficial.

I have no business getting close to a man like him. Casimir calling me "Tav" isn't because he sees me. He's just being a shameless flirt.

With that in mind, she tentatively reached out toward a massive emerald frond and rubbed the silky texture of the leaf between her fingers. A warmth, not unfamiliar to her, tickled her as the frond arched into her touch.

Oh, hello there.

The garden wasn't a product of her magic, but it originated from someone else's. The grounds keeper here was clearly an earth caster; their magic hummed within every leaf and vine, every delicate pink petal, every scratchy spiral of tree bark. Their magic twisted and curled along her own like a long-lost friend.

She giggled as more and more of the plants arched toward her, and she let a bit of her magic ebb out, feeding into their roots. Apparently, she was the stronger caster, if the flora's reaction was any indication. The leaves rustled in unison, creating a hum throughout the atrium. She smiled so wide, she thought her face would crack in half. "Looks like I've made new friends," she said, letting a few of the softer vines wind around her calves, getting the feel of her before slithering away.

Casimir's eyes were soft as he looked at her, his breath hitching slightly. Olline wondered what he saw when he looked at her like that. Casimir didn't give her the chance to formulate her words before he silently pointed up.

Her eyes snaked up the grey walls of the greenhouse,

dancing along every vine and rosebud along the way, until she was staring at the ceiling. From outside, it had appeared as no more than a plexi-glass dome. But inside . . . Olline's breath caught and she couldn't stop the little gasp from coming out as she lifted her hands to her mouth.

Stars. Thousands and thousands of stars twinkled above her.

Casimir moved to stand at her side, his hands buried once more in his long coat. "A very clever water and air caster came together to help make the glass," he explained, his voice a gentle whisper. "It dispels the pollution—light and otherwise—until all that's left is what should've been there all along. A crisp, clear night sky. This is what the people below will never see, why this whole botanical garden is wasted on them. They don't care for stars. They don't appreciate the *life* here. Not like you."

He wasn't wrong, her initial disappointment a distant memory. She was too full of wonder to make a sarcastic comment, trying to claim otherwise.

"Thank you," she said, her voice barely above a whisper.

He chuckled. "Ah, so you forgive me for breaking in then, my precious little caster?"

She whacked him good-naturedly in the stomach, trying not to notice how hard his abdomen was. He merely laughed. "Come on," he said, nudging her shoulder with his own. "Tell me what you, a hobby botanist and earth caster, see here."

Without thinking, she grabbed his hand. Pulling him deeper into the garden, she explained how the earth caster enriched the soil in one area in order to get the thin trees to grow as high as they did, and how they had to make the soil harsher for another plant that flourished best in dryer conditions. If Casimir found her explanations boring, or her rambling obnoxious, he gave no sign. He didn't ask many questions, but those he did showed he was at least listening to the explanations she was giving.

She named each type of bush, gave her theory why they used the feathery ferns to line the walls where the roses didn't grow—to keep people back while also encouraging them to trail their fingers over the tips, which she demonstrated—before taking him back to the pond at the center of the atrium.

"Oh, look!" Olline fell to her knees, tugging Casimir down with her. "See that?" She pointed to the lily pads. "They cheated to get them to float! The caster put a floating pad underneath. It's clever, but it's not how I'd have done it. They just needed to—what?"

Casimir was watching her with intense focus, and yet his expression was soft. There was no mischievous glint to his eye, no patronizing smile. He was looking at her like everything she was explaining was the real magic, not the tiny miracle that was tied to another's talent.

Right, he's impressed by the magic. Don't be silly, Olline.

He blinked slowly at her, and gave his head a little shake, tussling his silvered curls, seeming to catch himself. "You're just so passionate about this. It's . . ."

"Silly?" she offered. Olline meant it as a joke, but there was a tad too much bite to her words.

His eyes hardened. "No. Nothing you're passionate about is trivial and anyone who says otherwise is a bastard." He cleared his throat, his eyes losing the anger she saw briefly flash within. "I'm not used to being around that kind of passion. The sheer joy that something like this," he said, gesturing at the greenhouse, "could provide. It's been a century, at least since I've felt that for myself. It's refreshing. So, thank *you* for sharing that with *me*."

Olline's cheeks burned, but she waved the compliment off. "This sort of thing is a hobby of mine, remember? I love growing plants. Seriously, you should see my apartment sometime. It could give this garden a run for its money."

His smile was slow and roguish, his eyes half lidded, and Olline finally realized what she said. "Not that I'm inviting you to my place," Olline sputtered, leaning back from the pond. "Not that I'm not, *not* inviting you. Someday. But not like that," she stammered, trying to dig herself out of a hole.

But instead of laughing at her, Casimir simply sighed, his expression sobering. It was then that she realized, if she invited him to her place, for exactly that purpose, Casimir would have said yes. Olline wasn't quite sure how she felt about that yet.

"Oh, Olline," he whispered, and the way he said her name tickled down her spine like ice water. It was so . . . sad. Too sad, given where they were and what they were talking about.

She blinked at him, holding her breath as Casimir said, "I'm sorry. But you're too precious not to know the truth about what your contract with the Police and Securities Department truly entails."

CHAPTER 9

"What are you talking about?" Olline balked, leaning back, suddenly wary of being alone with Casimir. She shook her head and rubbed absently at her arms. "The terms of my contract were clear. I'd a legalese bot go through every line of fine print. I know exactly what my job—"

He cut her off with a long-suffering sigh. "Yes, yes. You're doing everything you're contracted to do. Correct. But do you know *who* is on the committee overseeing your department? The committee that decided, 'why yes, now would be a perfect time to overhaul our cold case evidence storage even though there have been no security threats to that department'?"

She narrowed her eyes at him. Her body tensed at his sarcasm, not appreciating it when he was, apparently, telling her she had been too trusting of a corporation to be honest with her. In trusting people to have her best interest in mind. Again.

His shoulders slumped slightly, and a hint of sympathy entered his voice. "Do you know the people on the board?

And who placed them there?"

Her body went stiff, guessing at what, or who, he would say, but hoping she was wrong. Casimir put his hands on his hips, shaking his head slowly. "This is precisely why they gave the contract to someone *not* from Antal, Tav. You already knew Etzel Straub was involved. But I assure you, he's much worse than a shadow figure who merely signs your paychecks. Etzel has his fingers all over the department you're contracted with. He's used them for over a century now as his own private blackmail racket. How else do you think he's guaranteed that he stays in power for as long as he has? You didn't truly think he'd been elected honestly all this time?"

Olline's jaw dropped slightly, grasping for words as the picture Casimir painted came into focus. Lightheadedness overwhelmed her. Her stomach dropped as dread rose in her. She had done it again. Been gullible enough to believe the job of her dreams hadn't been too good to be true. But if Casimir was right . . . and why wouldn't he be? Karter had confirmed it already: Etzel had been the one responsible for hiring her, even if his name had appeared nowhere in the document itself. Her spine bent, shielding her as she shuffled to her feet, trying desperately to hide her embarrassment.

"Oh, my dear," he said, clicking his tongue in pity, misreading her discomfiture. "You really are an idealistic creature, aren't you? No politician is so popular, so committed to their district within any city-state, that they could manage to remain undefeated over decades of election cycles. This is especially true of Etzel. He's remained in power this long by corrupting every system and influential person around him. Etzel is too old and too cunning to leave an election up to *democracy,*" Casimir said with a bitter laugh. "He is, after all, the only seersha in all of Antal's long history that will *save* this city-state. From what, only Etzel seems to know. Regardless, Under Senator Straub has created a system where Antal will be a utopia or some nonsense, but only as long as he can be the one to shepherd us plebeians into a new biomagitech age."

Olline crossed her arms over her chest and squeezed, digging her fingers into her ribcage. "Don't talk to me like I'm some naïve child, Casimir," she snarled. "Of course, I know there's corruption in every system." And she knew that, she honestly did. But she had *hoped,* and had let that hope bloom so big it overshadowed her common sense. She needed to stop doing that. Stop being so dazzled and trusting.

Olline gave her head a little shake, trying to banish the chill of dread. "But the whole point of bringing *me* in was to ensure that those who were taking bribes weren't involved in transferring the old evidence and cold case files over."

"Perhaps on paper," he breathed, a mean little glint in his eyes. "Security theater is very important to Etzel, after all. Bring in an outside party to look above reproach," Casimir continued, waving a hand, the motion dripping sarcasm. "When in reality Etzel has already bribed the people who drafted your contract, who monitor your payment. All probably long before he even had the listing sent out." Olline stared at him blankly. Everything he said felt real, but her mind rebelled against it, refusing to believe that she had been duped into playing a role in someone else's scheme.

Casimir took a step closer and moved like he would hold her hands. Perhaps he meant it to be comforting, but the last thing Olline wanted was to be touched by someone patiently telling her she had been an unwitting fool. She recoiled, and Casimir stopped moving so fast it looked like someone had pulled the plug on him.

He lowered his hands slowly, his eyes dropping to the ground a heartbeat later. "Those files? That evidence you're moving into a secure, fancy new server? They'll be transferred directly to Under Senator Straub as soon as you're finished."

"No," she said, shaking her head as her mind reeled. The gorgeous view of the stars above and the greenhouse around her losing their magic with every breath she took. "That can't be true. I'm going to upgrade all the server rooms—"

Casimir wagged a long, elegant finger at her. "No, Tav. You *could* have your contract extended if this first 'trial' goes well. Those were your words. But I know for a fact that won't happen."

She turned pleading, disbelieving eyes on him. Her expression screamed "how", even though her throat was too tight to choke the word out.

He ran a hand through his hair, his wavy curls twisting around his fingers, and he had the grace to look away in shame. "Sub-basement thirteen, server room two-hundred and twenty-three, is where Etzel stores his personal files." He noted her look of disbelief, and his tone became gentle once more. “Think, Olline. Why have you start there? Why that room? Why give such a large contract to one person? Why claim there’s room for extension when that job would be far too large for a lone contractor, no matter how brilliant and talented that freelance contractor was?” Casimir took a deep breath and murmured, his voice strangled, “Why else would I have been there on your first day?”

Olline’s stomach sank, pulling her down until her knees wobbled. Casimir was there in a flash, silent as ever as he moved. He eased her to the ground and Olline had to fight back hot tears of frustration. Once again, she and her work were being taken advantage of. Once again, she found herself in a position where she would be discarded once she delivered her beautiful project over to someone who had lied about its true purpose.

She licked her lips, trying to force moisture back into her mouth, and pushed away from Casimir, scooting back on her hands to put distance between them. “How could you . . . How could you know all this for certain?” She couldn’t keep the plea from her voice, desperate for him to say that maybe, just maybe, none of this was true, even when her gut said otherwise.

“You know exactly how I know all this, Olline,” he whispered, his arms limp along his side, his face downturned, red eyes hazy. “I know him better than maybe anyone. I can see his handiwork from the stratosphere. And you, Olline, are exactly the kind of person he’d bring in to hide his messes without them—you—ever knowing."

"Someone like me?" She shook her head, and she fought the urge to pull at her hair. "What does that even *mean?*"

There was a fleeting look of pity in his gaze that Olline absolutely hated. "Someone sweet and kind." Casimir's words trickled over her, chilling her to the marrow. After the revelations he had dumped on her, shattering the façade that she and her work were finally getting the accolades it deserved like thin glass, his kind words left her speechless.

Casimir took her silence for incredulity, as he was quick to continue, filling the void her silence birthed. "He needed someone so in love with their work that they would relish the challenge and not look beyond that. Someone who is, at their core, *good* and wants to give people the benefit of the doubt. Unless I'm utterly mistaken, and I don't think I am, that's the kind of person you are, Olline." He reached out, and this time, when she didn't back away, he gave her shoulder a gentle squeeze. "Etzel specializes in using people like that. Like you."

Olline blinked slowly at him, a sour tang filling her mouth. "How could you work for someone like him, knowing all of that?"

A muscle along his perfect jawline ticked, and his deep red eyes lost their sparkle. "I don't have a choice. Or didn't. I don't expect someone like you to understand."

Her mind was still spinning, trying to accept his words as fact. "What am I supposed to do?" she whispered to herself.

"You leave. You take your brilliant devices, you sabotage

the files, and you leave Antal."

All the air fled her lungs. The contract she had so lauded as being perfectly fine came into clear focus. All the stipulations around her signing bonus, the clauses she couldn't break without legal ramifications. The perfect apartment she wouldn't be able to keep if her contract wasn't extended like she had planned.

"I can't," she said with a dejected sigh, a numbness enveloping her body. "I can't break my contract until the work is done or there will be, well, *consequences.*" Olline rubbed a palm into her forehead, feeling a headache threatening. Cyneburg may punish breaches of contract with death occasionally, but Antal was severe in its own way. "I can't run. Not without being dragged to court." She shook her head, hugging her arms around her a little tighter. "The sad thing is, that's not even the part that upsets me most. My apartment . . . It seems so small in the grand scheme of things, but I'd lose it if I don't complete the job. There's no whistleblower safety clause. I didn't even insist on one because, well, why would I?" She laughed bitterly. "It's the first place that's truly felt like mine and if what you say is true and they were never going to extend my contract . . . I'll lose my *home.*"

Olline took a deep, stabilizing breath. She had been blindsided before; this was nothing new. The difference this time was she didn't have any pesky emotions conflicting with her options. Not that she could see what those options were yet, but that was beside the point.

"No, there has to be another way besides running." She

lifted her chin and met Casimir's gaze. His look was unreadable as he studied her, but she didn't care to analyze what that meant. "I'm not going to let anyone—corporation or politician—steal *my* work and throw me away after. I'm *brilliant*. I should be able to, I don't know, find a loophole or something." She snapped her fingers, smiling broadly and willing the rest of her body to feel the optimism she was projecting.

Casimir continued to stare at her. The moments flittering by felt like an eternity as her heart continued to hammer in her chest. Slowly, ever so slowly, Casimir seemed to come to a decision and nodded his head. "There may be a way. It's risky, but it's possible that we could keep your extraordinary work from being used for nefarious purposes. We just have to be clever about it. Beyond stealthy. Etzel can't know I'm involved or—" he sucked in a breath, cutting himself off. "He just can't know."

Olline gave him a sarcastic smile, pushing up to her knees. "Are you thinking we blackmail the blackmailer?" She shook her head, but there was an ironic chuckle bubbling in her chest. "That sounds just as wicked as what Under Senator Straub is doing."

Casimir's coy smirk returned as he too got to his feet. "Well, that would've been the simplest course of action, yes. But, fine, we can try to be all noble about it. It just requires more thought, more time." He gave a heavy sigh again, but his look was playful. "It sounds awful. Are you sure you don't want the quick and dirty way?"

His words had her toes curling and Olline glanced away

before the blush of her cheeks could betray her. It wasn't Casimir's fault that she could interpret his words another way, even if his knowing grin said otherwise.

She studied the surrounding plants, letting their earthy power and aromas clear her mind of the panic that had been clouding the edges of her focus. She hadn't been looking into any of the files she was transferring, she had wanted to respect the privacy of those victims and families she thought the files pertained to. None of the documents had seemed like anything other than what they claimed to be.

Her previous concerns with Goswin and Lochan came back to haunt her. Had she been right? Was this how Casimir weaseled his way in so he could attach himself to her work? Or maybe Casimir was lying? Was he trying to undermine the Police and Securities Department? Or had she merely not found the documents Casimir claimed hid in the servers?

The encrypted files.

Olline groaned and buried her face in her hands, startling Casimir. "I can't believe I forgot about those!"

Casimir tilted his head, his expression confused. Olline took another deep breath to keep her words from fumbling over one another. "I found a weird encrypted file my first day that didn't seem to belong with the others. I was curious, so I used my administrative privileges to tell the server that particular folder needed an update and to accept it without question." Casimir raised a brow at her, still confused. She cleared her throat, explaining as simply as she could, "Basically the fake update I created made a backdoor into the system, which let me take a peek into the folder and I found all these . . . chips. I don't know what they're for, but there's dozens of them. Maybe if I can crack into them and we corrupt what's there, that'll be all we need to safeguard my contract while also exposing Etzel."

"This fake update you pushed," Casimir said slowly, as if picking his words with care, "did it already corrupt the chips?"

She scrunched her face in thought for a moment, then shook her head. "No. As long as the server and the clients—the chips in this case—are synced, it wouldn't have done anything. Assuming all the chips are viable, so they aren't excluded from the update anyway," she added with a shrug. "But given the security around that encryption, I couldn't imagine any of the chips being that old."

"And if they *were* out of date?" Casimir asked, his voice a gravelly whisper.

Olline rubbed the back of her neck, considering. "Well, I guess if the server couldn't communicate with the chips, they would probably just continue to do what they were last told to do and wouldn't get any new instructions. Why? Does it matter?"

Casimir's face remained as stoic as ever. If he was excited or worried about something, he didn't share it vocally with Olline. "You truly are a brilliant little caster, aren't you?" he said eventually, a slow smile brightening his face until it morphed into his customary smirk.

She didn't blush this time, which was an awesome development, but smiled at him in return. "I already told you I was impressive."

Casimir chuckled and said, "Well, Tav, I think the answer to our problems lies in that encrypted file you found. Dismantling that will be the key, and while I'm not as technically savvy as you are, I think I can help."

Olline pressed her lips into a tight line, a knot forming in her belly. "Why would you even want to get involved?" she asked slowly, carefully. "Why tell me this at all? What's your angle here? You have to have one. From my experience, no one helps anyone for nothing."

Casimir's head jerked back a little, his linen white skin paling slightly, which was actually kind of impressive. Less impressive was the way his throat bobbed before he shut his eyes and gave a slow, disbelieving shake of the head. "I told you that my involvement with Etzel isn't exactly voluntary. I want him stopped. His web of pain and deception ripped apart forever. And if I can keep a sweet woman like you from being destroyed by Etzel at the same time? Well, the good karma certainly won't hurt."

Her heart sank.

He had said that, hadn't he? That the work he did for Under Senator Straub was not by choice. Of course, he would want to help her under those circumstances. He was helping himself as much as helping her. Somehow, though, it didn't make the sting in her chest ease any to recognize that none of this was even truly about her or keeping her safe, despite what he said. They were strangers. He had no reason to actually care about her.

"So," she whispered, giving him a tentative smile, "should we go back to the office and bring the bastard down?"

Casimir laughed, full and deep, making his whole chest rumble. The sound was like music played by a live band, more comforting than even the swish of hundreds of leaves. "Even if we could, from a technical standpoint, dealing with Etzel still requires a delicate touch."

"But we don't have time," Olline argued.

Casimir cut her off with a long, drawn-out sigh. "We have a little time, my dear. Etzel's at a conference. While the monster's away, the children will play or some garbage. What we *can* do is begin to strategize. Now won't that be fun?"

Olline couldn't hide her earnest expression, the excitement of a challenge. The thrill of bringing down a bad guy like a hero in a classic virtual simulator had her body humming with electricity. But all Casimir did was sit down, and lean back until his elbows propped his torso up so he could look at the magically enhanced stars above.

"But not tonight," he stated. "Tonight, you are going to enjoy this. Enjoy Antal. I have a promise to keep, after all."

CHAPTER 10

Going to work the next morning had Olline's body doing funny things. There were the heart palpitations that rattled her chest like a rockslide, the slightly nauseous feeling which was super fun when all she wanted was to enjoy her coffee in peace, not to mention she was certain everyone could see her clammy hands.

She wasn't a naturally paranoid person, but she felt like everyone could see the revelations of the other night flashing on her face as obviously as the neon advertisements on the mega sky-towers. But Brayden and his trusty security bot merely waved her on like they did every day, his sleepy, bored expression never altering. He merely grumbled once again about "fucking morning people".

Was she disappointed? Maybe a little.

She had never been involved in something like this, and the virtual simulators made it seem so romantically daring. But mostly she was relieved no one noticed her.

Olline scurried to her office, tossing furtive glances over

her shoulder with almost disastrous results. “Excuse you,” a soft, but curt voice snapped just before Olline collided with the woman who worked next door to her office.

“Oh! Sorry, I wasn’t looking, my bad.” Olline twisted, her feet skidding on the floor, making an obnoxious squeaking sound. To her credit, the woman didn’t bite back on how obvious it was that Olline hadn’t been paying attention. The woman tilted her head, eyes trailing over Olline, as she planted her fists on her hips. She was a pretty woman. Smooth black skin, warm brown eyes, and a delicate septum ring in her button nose. She had diamond dimple piercings that sparkled when her full pink lips tilted up in a smile. “You’re the new girl?”

Olline bobbed her head. This would have been great any other day except today. All she wanted to do was dive into her office and hide lest she say something that could alert the ever-present security drones to what she now knew. “Olline Tavos,” she said in way of greeting, hoping the woman would leave it at that and let her go.

“Briallea Jensen,” she said, and stuck out her hand. Olline hesitated before quickly shaking it, hoping Briallea couldn’t feel the sweat on her palms. “Sorry for not saying hi sooner. No one sent a data package telling us you were even here. Management can be shitty about stuff like that,” she said, chuckling good-naturedly. Olline nodded again, but before she could even wonder if it was odd no one was told she was working here, Briallea tilted her head, and a flash of silver illuminated her eye. Her gaze became hazy as Briallea absently scratched at the tight, ebony curls hugging her skull. Olline wondered what kind of cybernetic modification she had that connected her to the building, but it would be rude to ask.

With a huff, Briallea refocused her attention on Olline. "Sorry to cut this short. Meetings first thing in the morning are the absolute worst. Am I right?" She gave little laugh that reminded Olline of wind chimes, which was impossible not to like. "Let's grab lunch sometime, okay? Us girls have to stick together down here. Goodness knows there's precious few of us in the sub-basements." Briallea stepped away, waving over her shoulder. "Nice to meet you, Olline."

Was it nice to meet me? Was it really? Olline wondered viciously. She had barely said a word! Under different circumstances, she would have been mortified by her manners, but the panic to get inside her fucking office was still too strong. Her hands were still shaking as she waved her credentials in front of the lock. When the door slid up, she all but flung herself inside.

Only when the door shut behind her did breathing get a little easier. Which was silly. There were cloaked security devices monitoring every office, including hers, but she felt . . . safer here. She wasn't sure if that was her magic, not sensing anything from the devices in the room, but she wasn't going to question it.

Sinking into her chair, Olline powered on her devices, cracked her knuckles—that's what all the hackers in the holo-vids did—and got to work. She was hoping she wouldn't need Casimir's help the way he insinuated she would. She was determined to figure out what Under Senator Etzel Straub was hiding, and how he was getting all these powerful people under his control, all on her own. Not that Olline didn't *want* to work with Casimir, but, well . . . all right, she didn't want to work with him. But oddly, not because she didn't trust him.

The last person she had worked with had crushed her, destroying a confidence that had just begun to grow. Working alone was the only way she knew to prevent a repeat of Achan from ever happening. Not that she and Casimir were even close to what she and Achan had been, even before she knew what was really happening with *that*. She didn't even like, *like* Casimir. He was just attractive and . . . where was she going with this again? Oh, right: proving that working with Casimir wasn't necessary.

Olline shook her head, tried to focus, but all she could think about was last night. Before he had dropped his bombshell, the night had been lovely. She would have been happy to tell her father and brothers all about it. Then, well, then nothing made sense anymore.

If she hadn't found those files, would she be where she was now? Would it have been better to remain ignorant of what was happening? Knowing she was aiding in a coverup . . . well, now she felt responsible for the mess. She should clean it up herself, and more importantly, she *could*. For all his cool charisma, Olline knew that, on a technical level, Casimir could not help.

The only tricky part would be breaking the encryption, so she could actually access the chips.

"It sounds so easy when I think of it that way," she murmured, grinning to herself. Olline leaned over her keyboard, finally able to focus. The first thing she needed to do was to pull up her administrative prompts and search for another sneaky way around all the layers of encryption encasing these chip files.

Olline had, long ago, devised her own decryption software. Not for any malicious purpose, just for fun and to prove she could. And it had worked great! Not that she could show it to anyone without actually breaking into a secure file. Until now. Loading her software into the administrative prompt, she let it get to work while she sat back and, once more, absently gnawed on the collar of her jacket.

The process was slower than she expected. As the minutes trickled by, the lines of code her software was detangling flowing by like a waterfall, Olline wondered if she should keep working. If the rest of the files she was moving were as full of potential corruption as this one, would she make things worse if she did her "job"? Or would it help her keep some semblance of a cover? Which made her wonder if everyone on this floor was part of the scandal. Was Briallea? Karter? She didn't think so. The bigger a secret got, the harder it was to keep, but you could never really be certain where power and politics were involved. That line of thinking was making her dizzy though. It was better to focus on what was right in front of her for now. Which was the lines of code her decryption software was going through. Fun . . .

She sighed, boredom about to win out, when the door to her office slid up. Olline jumped, grasping for her magic out of reflex, letting it tug around the iron piercings.

The piercings morphed in less than a microsecond, sliding out of the holes in her ears and eyebrow one by one, until they spun like a tornado in her palm. She was ready to throw the projectiles, her paranoia already expecting the worst, when a pale hand curled around the doorframe and stopped her cold. Casimir poked his head inside and stared at her wide eyed with such a look of panic on his face that Olline stopped breathing for a second.

"What're you doing here? I thought being seen together was dangerous." Slowly her surprise ebbed away to suspicion and, narrowing her eyes at him, she released her magic. Her piercings reclaimed their shape and hooked back into her ears and brow once more. "Wait, did you have a key pass to my office this entire time?"

Casimir stepped into the server room, his movements stiff, shoulders tight with fear. He took a deep breath. Casimir had always appeared so in control, so unconcerned, that the hairs on Olline's arms stood on end, a chill raced up the back of her legs to tickle her neck. She looked behind Casimir, but she didn't see any danger that would warrant him coming here, let alone with such open alarm.

He blinked rapidly at her from behind his opaque protective visor for a moment. "I opened it the old-fashioned way. Everyone puts too much faith in technology, especially here," he said quickly, his words clipped. Casimir took a step toward her, his eyes darting about the room as if looking for an assailant. When they settled on her holo-tablet and the string of code still scrolling through the projection, he froze. "Whatever it is you're doing, you have to stop it. *Now*."

Her heart thundered against her ribs with renewed vigor. Icy dread poured through her chest. "What? Why?"

His forearms were strained as he leaned down on the table next to her, his mouth so close to her ear that the tickle of his breath had her shivering for other reasons entirely. "I'll explain once we're safe," he said, his words a shaky whisper. "But you—we have to leave. Immediately. Whatever you're doing tipped the wrong person off. Security's on their way. Right *now*."

Olline's mind couldn't keep up, but there was no mistaking the urgency in Casimir's rigid posture. She killed her decryption software, aggressively swiped her screens off, and began unplugging everything. "What are you doing?" Casimir fumed, watching her pack up. "There's no time for that!"

"If I don't take my stuff, Casimir," she snapped, "then we're truly and deeply screwed. Okay? You can go if you're so worried, or you can help me pack up so we can both get out of here together."

That gorgeous bastard actually hesitated at the door, the muscle along his jawline flexing, as if he were truly considering leaving. With a growl, he said, "Fine."

Casimir moved surprisingly fast. Well, it wasn't that surprising. She had seen him move quickly. He just wasn't as stealthy about it now. Under different circumstances, Olline would have been bothered by how roughly he handled her devices. As it was, she cringed each time one of the holo-tablets cracked against a keyboard. Objectively, they had everything disconnected and put away within twenty-seven seconds. Subjectively, it was twenty-seven years.

They left room two-hundred and twenty-three and nearly barreled into Brayden and his little bot. Only this time, he didn't look sleepily exasperated to see her. The puffy little man was all business and steel and glaring at them like Brayden had never seen Olline before in his life.

Briallea poked her head out of the office next door at the commotion. She glanced from Brayden to Olline, and frowned. Olline swallowed, thinking she had lost yet another potential friend before she could properly start. Only Briallea's warm brown eyes settled on her instead of Brayden, and she mouthed: "all good?"

Olline did not know if it was "all good". If Casimir's panic was any sign, they weren't. But whatever was about to happen, Olline didn't want Briallea to be a part of it. Discreetly, she gave her neighbor a thumbs up and a little nod. Briallea still frowned, eyes narrowing, unconvinced. Eventually, the woman shrugged and ducked back into her office as Brayden came to a stop in front of Olline and Casimir.

She swallowed and met the security guard's gaze, forcing a smile despite his suspicious glare. Neither she nor Casimir said anything to Brayden as he continued to block their path in chilly silence, his hand gripping the butt of his pulse-pistol on his hip. Her eyes bulged at the sight. *Why is Brayden holding on to his gun?*

The sound of her heartbeat thrashed in her ears, black

spots danced in her vision. Reflexively, she reached for the comfort of her magic, but no sooner had it curled around the natural metals in the room than the security bot trilled loudly. It must have a magitech sensor attuned to casters pulling on the raw materials they needed for their magic. Olline's ethereal fingers dropped the tendril of magic as if scorched. Brayden, reacting to the sound, widened his stance, readying for a fight.

Shit, shit, shit! Deescalate this, now!

Olline didn't know what was happening, or why the guard's response needed to be violence, or how Casimir had gotten there so fast, but she did her best not to show it. Her life depended on convincing Brayden that whatever he thought was happening was definitely not happening.

Casimir kept his face obscured in shadow behind the high collar of his black coat. The visor, now darkened instead of opaque, shielded his unique eye color. Olline thought it was unnecessary at this point. So many of the spy-drones along the ceiling would have already caught sight of him and run his face through facial reconditioning software. Whatever made him feel safer, she guessed.

"Oh hey," she fumbled, trying to sound nonchalant. "Is uh, everything okay?"

Brayden glanced from her to Casimir and back again, the security bot vibrating at his side. But something about her earnest expression seemed to soften Brayden.

"Got a call from the big wig IT guys," Brayden grumbled, his eyes narrowing. "They got a notification about something fishy getting installed. Didn't seem to know what it was, but they're too busy to check it out themselves." He didn't elaborate further, merely shifted his glare from Olline to Casimir. His fingers curled even tighter on the butt of his pulse-pistol and inched it out of its holster.

The guard seemed to lose focus. Something in his eye went hazy, and with dawning clarity, she realized he was running facial recognition software through a biotech chip installed in his eye.

Olline and Casimir didn't have a plan for what to do about Etzel and his encrypted files and the chips yet. But the cornerstone of whatever plan they would devise had, and would always be, that Etzel couldn't know Casimir was involved. If Brayden did flag him well, Olline didn't know exactly what would happen, but she assumed it would result in the guard pulling his gun completely free of his holster.

She would have to use her magic then, to hurt people. The thought stabbed at her gut, a million tiny thorns curly and squeezing. That wasn't the point of magic. A sour taste coated her mouth over the utter shit they were in.

Think, Olline! Think faster!

"Oh, that!" she blurted, the glint of metal from the gun forcing Olline to run with the first thought she had and pray it worked. "Someone was bored and installed something dumb on their rig. Some bootleg virtual card game to help pass the time. They didn't realize it was full of junk code that left the system vulnerable. You know how it goes."

Brayden's eyes remained narrowed, but the hazy quality

was gone so at least he had stopped using his cybernetics. Olline laughed nervously, running her hands along the sides of her head, smoothing her hair to hide how much they were shaking. "This um, intern," she said, putting a hand on Casimir's tense shoulder. "He saw it and didn't know what to do about it." Brayden seemed dubious of this, so Olline quickly amended, "He went to Camirin first, but she didn't want to bother with it. You know how Camirin is." Well, she hoped she knew how Camirin was. The IT woman had seemed bored, not really wanting to do more than necessary for her job. Or that was the impression Olline had gotten from their one not-quite-meeting.

Apparently, she was correct, as Brayden's stance relaxed some, and his brows pinched in annoyance. *Sorry for throwing you under the bus, Camirin,* Olline thought, and quickly pressed on before Brayden could ping the woman. "So, the intern came to me. It was a nasty little virus, let me tell you!" Olline shifted the satchel that held all her gear. "I managed to isolate the program in my system, but it'll take some time to erase and make sure no backdoor was opened to let hackers in through the junk files."

The guard's gaze lost focus as she babbled. Olline's explanation had, like it usually did with non-tech minded people, begun to bore him. "Someone downloaded a game with a virus?" But Brayden's eyes remained narrowed in suspicion.

She nodded enthusiastically. "Yup, happens all the time! I really should have notified IT. I'll be sure to do that. No worries," she added hastily, actually full of worries. "But I figure it's best I take this all back to a clean room and wipe the system where it can't do any damage." She waved at her satchel again and gave Brayden the brightest smile she could muster, and hoped it didn't look like a grimace. "All good? Can we, uh, go now?"

Brayden glanced from Casimir to her once more, his hand still poised on his pistol. *Why is this, whatever this is, something to get* shot *over?* "You're taking all your equipment out of the building. To wipe it of a virus. That someone got from downloading a game. Because they were bored." Brayden parroted again, his tone flat. Olline got the distinct impression he didn't believe her, and fear made her legs shake. This was about to get messy . . .

"Yeah, exactly," Olline tried to say brightly, like none of this was a big deal. "Better safe than sorry and all that, right?" Brayden dropped his gaze to the security bot at his side. It still vibrated and hummed in place, but no longer trilling an alarm as long as she didn't call for her magic.

Finally, the bot stilled completely, and Brayden lowered his hand, giving a long-suffering sigh. "You tell them IT nerds it's handled then, and to not bug me with this the next time some old-timer gets bored, got it? Fucking, lazy-ass Camirin."

Olline bobbed her head. Before she could say anything else, Brayden was toddling back down the hallway, all steel and malice gone like it hadn't ever existed, and into the elevator bays. He didn't bother to offer an apology for being a heartbeat away from shooting them.

Casimir was so deathly still at her side, she wasn't even

sure he was breathing. He didn't move until the guard was out of sight and the murmur of people at work filtered out through the closed doors again. "We have to go," Casimir whispered urgently. Without being fully conscious of the action, she found herself walking as quickly as she dared toward the elevators, Casimir a half step ahead of her.

It wasn't until they were clear of the Government Plaza, its hulking height fading in the distance, that Olline felt safe enough to speak. "What just happened?"

Casimir slowed, finally stopping and giving her his full attention. "Whatever program you were running got flagged through the system's security." He ran his fingers through his hair, twisting them around the curls and tugging as if that would ground him. He took a deep breath. "I know one of those bored IT personnel you mentioned that would pass off a security flag to literally anyone else, so they didn't have to deal with it. Not Camirin, but good to know that she's the same way."

"What would have happened? If you weren't there to warn me?" Olline whispered, afraid to know, but she *had* to.

Originally, she thought this would be a fun little challenge, well, a *dangerous* challenge, but Olline happened to find those fun. She was weird like that. But if this, whatever they were attempting to do, could elicit a reaction where someone tried to shoot them first, apprehend them second, well, she should know that, right?

"To you? That depends on your termination and non-disclosure clauses." She could feel the color leach from her cheeks and Casimir continued, "By your expression, though it seems like your termination clauses are less than ideal. I'm sure that was by design, Tav. Dazzle you with the offer, so the fine print didn't seem so ominous." He didn't even bother to try and grin to lessen the bite in his words.

"For me? You'd never see me again," he said matter-of-factly, and her heart sank to her stomach. "I'd be erased. No better than a broken tool to be discarded. I'd be removed so thoroughly that no one would ever even know I existed. Shall I go on?" She swallowed, not saying anything, her eyes wide in disbelief. "I mean death, Olline. They would kill me," he snapped, as if she didn't understand that well enough already.

"Yes, I got that!" she bit back. She placed her hands on her hips to keep her fingers from trembling all over again, her thoughts racing. She thought her decryption had been too obscure, too well made to have tripped any of the security protocols. Had she been too confident in her abilities? No. But that didn't matter when, regardless, her actions had almost gotten Casimir killed.

"I'm sorry," she murmured, the dullness spreading in her chest doing nothing to untangle her knotted belly. "I should've known my program could've been flagged like that. I won't be so careless again."

The hard edges around his eyes softened and the firm line of his lips relaxed ever so slightly as he looked at her face, heard the regret in her voice. "You covered it well though, I have to say," Casimir said, his tone gentle. "It was brilliant, truly. It buys us time and another crack at Etzel's entire operation. So, well done there." She raised her eyes, trying not to be as comforted by the compliment as she was, but she couldn't stop her core from warming all the same. "There's just one problem with your cover."

Instantly, her stomach fell again, and she licked her lips nervously. "What's that?"

"Intern?" Casimir took a step back, waving a hand down his hard and lean body, and Olline did her best not to notice how well the lines of his tight-fitting black attire hugged every dip and curve of muscle. "Do I truly look like an intern to you? I'm far too magnificent to be so low on the corporate totem pole." Casimir scoffed and Olline couldn't help but laugh.

"You're such a drama queen," she said, her laughter dying off. "Come on, I was able to isolate the files we want before the shitshow started, so there may be a way for me to fix this that doesn't risk your life again."

WHEN IN HIS EYES

After showing Olline the garden, and having that marvelously backfire, he had modified his plan and steeled his heart accordingly.

Casimir's problem was how ridiculously cute Olline was when she got animated over something. How her smattering of freckles darkened each time she got excited, the rosy tones to her bronze-kissed skin deepening with her obvious enthusiasm. She practically radiated light and warmth, and he could not handle it. He had then panicked and blurted out more about Antal's political machinations than he had planned—or was ready—to reveal. Hence the modifications to his initial plan.

Yet, there he was in the Government Plaza the very next day, closing the literal distance between them once more. What he was doing now was reckless, perilous, and plain stupid. He knew that. Yet if Casimir could spare Olline, he would. He still had that much of his soul left, and it was worth clinging to, even if it got him killed.

His one consolation was that Etzel was not currently in the building. The seersha was at a weeklong conference about deregulating biomagitech, or something. Casimir didn't care as long as it meant Etzel wasn't nearby. While the distance between him and his boss was a help, he knew that if Etzel wanted to find him, no amount of distance would matter.

Casimir had needed to make sure Olline was safe where she was, ensconced within enemy territory. He kept his presence hidden behind his biotech visor so he could slip by undetected until he got to the hidden service hallways meant for the robotic staff. From there he could get anywhere in the building the old-fashioned way: by walking.

Which was usually a pain in the ass, but he found he didn't mind. Not when images of Olline's utter delight at seeing stars filtered through his mind. She was so open about her joy that it made her even more adorable each time he saw her.

He had to constantly remind himself that the stars were fake, that her delight was over something false and he, therefore, shouldn't take pleasure in it, either. He wished the dullness that settled heavily in his chest was the familiar numbness he usually embraced, but this felt . . . different.

In the privacy of the service corridors, Casimir let his shoulders sag, his feet drag, and the fatigue of the pretense take over. If Etzel didn't kill him, his plan to secure his freedom may very well do the trick.

Under normal circumstances, that alone would have been enough to get Casimir to turn around and get the fuck out of there. But Olline Tavos was a decidedly not normal circumstance. She was the spark in the dark, drawing him deeper and deeper into places he never thought to venture again. So, he had trudged through the service hallway tucked behind her shitty little office and scoured the space for what he knew was there: the surveillance chip that had led him to her.

Casimir may not be a savant with technology the way Olline was, but he had picked up enough over the past century to get the job done. Besides, he didn't need to be clever in order to be efficient. But no sooner had he identified the chip, then he picked up a signal.

His muscles clenched, terror like frozen nitrogen rooting him in place. For a heartbeat, he thought . . . no, best not think of it.

But the signal hadn't been about him at all. Which he would have preferred once he realized that what he found meant *Olline* was in trouble. Because of course she was. The woman was brilliant, but she was as subtle as a grease fire.

He hated that he didn't hate that about her.

He crushed the chip beneath his heel, told the persistent fatigue to politely fuck off, and darted out of the service corridor as fast as he could while remaining stealthy.

That had been the easy part. Even lying to her after he had gotten her to abandon what she was doing had been easy. He had gotten good at lying over the years. It was second nature to him now.

The complicated part was the guard who had shown up with his pesky gun.

Casimir knew he would have to kill the man and disable

the bot before they could haul Olline and him away. The killing wasn't what bothered him. Killing was easy now, and after so long, he was numb to it. One cannot be part of Etzel's menagerie without learning to disassociate. Casimir had been slower than some to learn that trick, but now? It was as easy and second nature to him as lying. Funny how deciding murder was the best option came to him so quickly these past decades. What bothered him was how much he looked forward to dismantling this puffed-up security guard and his bot for scaring Olline in the first place.

Casimir had nothing but his mechanized stiletto with him, as always. Guns were loud and terribly inelegant, but he wished he carried one now. He did rapid calculations of what to do first, where to strike to bring the man and bot down, and how to move in order to shield Olline from getting wounded. That was an extra complication, one he wouldn't have even considered before. Yet the mere idea of that precious caster getting even a scrape made his hands flex, ready to strangle anyone who dared lay a finger on her sweet, cheerful face.

Casimir had just figured out the best way to get them out of danger when Olline began to speak so rapidly, he couldn't follow any of it. Except the intern part. That was absurd, but it worked so, bravo Olline. She hadn't even used a lick of her power. If Casimir had her magic, he didn't think he would ever *not* use it against people who threatened him. That was another difference between them. Olline was objectively a good person, and he was, well, not. Not anymore. There had been a time when Casimir despised so-called good people, kind people. Those people had never bothered to be good or kind to him in the past. But Olline . . . her goodness had his insides going soft and warm at the absolute worst times.

Here he was, agonizing over how he was going to get them out of there, how he would explain the murder and hope that maybe it wouldn't be too traumatic for her, and instead she was smoothly getting them both out of peril with that delightful mouth of hers.

Which was another problem. Because now he was thinking about other uses for that sweet mouth.

Stick to the plan.

Being angry with her didn't help him stick to the plan as much as he had hoped. Her help had nearly cost him everything. Had she been anyone else, he would have killed her for that. The realization chilled him, because she wasn't anyone else. She was painfully easy to forgive, just as she was easy to flirt with. Her blushes were a balm to everything and Casimir found himself wanting to get her to blush and smile at every chance he got. He wished she weren't so fun to tease. It would have made it easier to stick to said strategy.

When Olline decided that the best place for them to go would be back to her apartment, he wished she were wrong. He wished he could maintain enough distance that he wasn't at risk of failing at his own fucking plan . . . Funny, Casimir had stopped wishing for things a long time ago, and a few days with Olline had changed all of that.

Oh, this was bad.

Despite still being slightly pissed that she almost compromised his very existence, Casimir trailed behind Olline. Helpless to do anything else, even if he had wished to.

CHAPTER 11

No matter how she tried to steer away from mere feelings and veer toward logic instead, there was still this graceful danger to Casimir that sent electrical jolts tingling over her skin each time they touched. Olline knew better than to find such danger appealing. Yet she couldn't stop herself from stealing long looks at him as he strode beside her.

The problem was, her plan was good. Okay, *that* wasn't the problem.

The problem was that the plan required her to bring Casimir to her apartment. The apartment she had confessed to loving, admitting she would be more devastated by its loss than incarceration. After what happened at the Department, saying such things about an apartment she hadn't even lived in a full month was juvenile of her.

Which was the last thing she wanted anyone to ever think of her again. Especially Casimir. A realization she blamed his attempted heroics on, even if he was cagey as to what he was doing nearby.

Oddly, she wasn't nervous about him being in her apartment specifically. Which, come to think of it, was probably the correct reaction to have. Yet, when she was with Casimir, the last thing she felt was nervous.

Curious.

What she was anxious about was what Casimir would think of a space she had made so uniquely hers. Would he think her plants were a waste of power like Achan? A silly little hobby no respecting earth caster would waste their time on? Would Casimir look at her space and decide it was unstylish, or worse, childish? All of which was an absurd thing to worry about *right now*. She didn't—or shouldn't—care about that when there were far bigger things to concern herself with. Like all the documents she was going to have to decrypt.

After she told him she had a safe place to go, they didn't speak again until they were on the pedestrian promenade leading to the mid-level entrance of her building. It would have been faster to take a sky-cab, but Olline was nervous it would make them easier to track and trap—if they were, in fact, still being monitored. Recent evidence said they were better safe than sorry, and Casimir had agreed.

Well, he had said nothing, so Olline took that as agreeing with her.

Casimir stopped beside her, collapsing the holo-visor he used to conceal his eyes, and craned his head back to see the top of the building. Exhaust shrouded the mega sky-tower, making it difficult to see the level where Olline's apartment was located. His jaw tensed, the muscles in his neck flexing, and he gave a little shake of his head, but whatever thoughts were churning behind his deep red eyes, he kept to himself.

Olline darted inside first, ensuring that the front desk clerk was occupied elsewhere before guiding Casimir into the high-speed elevator bay. It wasn't until the doors finally slid closed, Olline took a deep breath and leaned against the wall of the mirrored elevator, letting its coolness soothe her hot skin.

"You know," Casimir said, his tone lazy despite the stiff way he stood across from her, "for someone who ventured down into the bowels of this city looking to feel a real connection to Antal's heart, you live rather far from its core, don't you, Tav?" He lifted a steel-colored brow at her, a type of judgmental amusement flashing in his eyes and evident in the grin he awarded her.

Olline shrugged, fidgeting to hide her worry. "Despite what my previous actions show, I do actually care about my safety. And living that far down in the city wasn't a good idea—a smart idea." Now it was her turn to flash him a mischievous smile. "Besides, I make up for being so far above the core of Antal in other ways. You'll see."

She had let no one see her hobbies since Achan, and the sting of that disastrous show of vulnerability still lanced through her heart. But Lochan was right. Her mother would want her to give Casimir a chance. He wasn't Achan. And yet apprehension flooded her system as soon as the elevator opened on her floor.

None of that stopped her from opening her apartment

door and ushering Casimir inside.

Olline shut the door behind her and whipped around, running smack dab into Casimir's back. He barely even swayed with the collision. She rubbed her nose, trying hard not to inhale his comforting scent, and walked around him. "What's wrong now?"

"Did you buy all these?" He waved a hand at the plants clustered on every table, ignoring the plastic crates she still hadn't unpacked. The vines, with a few days of being fed magic, grew so thick you couldn't see the walls they were crawling up. Splashes of orange, red, magenta, and lilac blooms poked out of variegated green fronds at every entryway, her latest additions. His expression was that unreadable mask again, but his tone was free of sarcasm, so that was . . . good?

Casimir hadn't moved. The heat radiating from his back, the electrical jolts of the contact shooting down her abdomen. She had to fight the sudden urge to wrap her arms around his waist, to bury her face in his chest and hug him until he had forgiven her for the mistake she had made.

Hug him? Ugh, stop that.

Olline chuckled nervously and scampered to the low table in the middle of her living room, one of the few surfaces completely free of greenery. "Why would I buy them when I can do this?" Her eyelids drooped as she tugged at that warm tendril of power in her core and reached out for the vibrant, verdant life around her. She wiggled her fingers and every single plant rustled as if a gentle breeze wafted through her apartment.

Casimir sucked in a breath and Olline let the magic go, worried she startled him. "I send away to the agricultural colleges for seeds and scavenge the discarded soil from herbalists' shops when I can. But sometimes it's just easier to make my plants from scratch." She glanced around the spacious apartment and pride swelled in her for all the florae that were thriving because of her. "I haven't lost a single plant in years, even with relocating."

The leaves rustled again, arching, reaching toward her, and her swell of pride turned softer, warmer, stronger. "They're my friends," she admitted before she realized what she said. Olline snapped her jaw shut before she could confess that they were her *only* friends, the only things that drove away the ache in her chest born of an intense longing for—

Focus on work, Olline.

She cleared her throat, avoiding Casimir's face. Olline didn't want to see the pity he surely felt for her. Because it was sad, wasn't it? To admit that plants, of all things, were her friends. She knew she should embrace her hobbies, the things that brought her joy, and to do so unapologetically, but she wasn't there yet.

Olline removed the tech from her satchel and plugged in her hastily shut down holo-tablets and laptops. Casimir still hadn't said anything, and heat began crawling up Olline's neck until it reached her hairline, her breaths coming faster. She couldn't bear to look at him now, too afraid to see the amusement in his gaze.

After another heartbeat of silence, a ragged sigh came

from where Casimir stood, still unmoving at the threshold of her apartment. Olline quickly looked up, she couldn't help herself. Her heart tripped over itself at the wide-eyed look of wonder on Casimir's face as his eyes trailed over every one of her plants.

The heat turned into a buzzing warmth spreading throughout her body as she took joy in *his* joy. But as quickly as the look was there, it smoothed into stone. His eyes hardened and the muscles along his neck flexed as he clenched his jaw. Olline's chest tightened, mourning the loss of something she didn't fully understand.

He glided from the threshold to stand near where she sat on the floor, and she pretended she saw nothing and had been too busy with her devices. "Your talents are wasted on developing magitech, Olline," he said. His tone was, dare she say, kind, despite his stoic expression.

Olline sucked in a breath. Of all the things she had expected him to say that hadn't been on her list, not even in the top twenty. She blinked rapidly, too stunned to look at him.

"You could be creating real life with nothing more than the wiggle of your charming little fingers. Why in the world would you," Casimir stopped himself, taking a ragged breath. "It would've kept you from getting tangled with Under Senator Straub, if nothing else."

The heat crawling over her body turned into a river of lava at his words, and she tucked her chin against her chest. She booted up her devices to hide the flush in her cheeks and to give herself something tangible to focus on.

"I love my plants. They bring me peace no matter where I live. But my flowers are . . ." She stopped, considered her words with care as it suddenly became very important that she explain this right. "It sounds silly, I know, especially coming from an earth caster, but these plants? They're mine and *for me*. If they were my job, the serenity and joy I feel in having them in my home would be, I don't know, spoiled somehow."

A heavy silence fell, then Casimir finally sank down beside her. "It doesn't sound silly at all," he said, his voice a breathy whisper that sent a tingle down her spine. "I understand wanting something to have just for yourself and wanting to keep it sacred."

His words tickled something in her mind, and her brows pinched together as she gave him a side-long glance. But he was moving on before she could turn over his words further.

"That rooftop garden," he said, a chuckle making his voice a void she wanted to sink into. "It was a mistake, wasn't it? Not the going after hours part. That was rather fun. But the gesture of taking you to a place like that. It was a staticky holo-vid compared to what you've done here. Clearly, I didn't think it through." His words became halting toward the end, as if he was thinking of saying something else, or something more, but couldn't.

He gave her such a bashful look, a faint flush going from his cheeks all the way to the tips of his pointed ears, that Olline couldn't help but give him a sympathetic smile in return, even as her heart ached to do more. "It wasn't a *bad* idea, just," she paused, her fingers flexing like she could pluck the word she was searching for from the air. "It was a safe one. It was very lovely though, don't worry! I really did appreciate the effort you put into it."

Casimir ran his hands through his curls and Olline couldn't help but wonder if they felt as soft as they looked—like silken strands of silvery moonlight. He shook his head, an ironic chuckle making his words light. "Safe? No one has ever accused me or my ideas of being 'safe'." He flashed her one of his rare, relaxed smiles, his eyes dancing with mirth. "You're entirely too polite, you know. I promise to do better next time."

Her heart stuttered over the "next time" part, the rumble in his voice as he said it. Her words were heavy on her tongue, her mind spinning, which was unfair. Olline shouldn't let a pretty face catch her off guard like this, especially when it had such a smooth tongue. Without a single doubt in her mind now, she knew that should she make a move, Casimir would take her to bed. But after Achan . . . was casual sex even something she wanted? Even if it was with—

Nope!

Thankfully, Casimir was already moving on, and she could only hope he hadn't noticed how flustered she was. "So why magitech then?"

She shrugged, glad for the change in topic, and pulled up her files again, even gladder for something to focus on that had nothing to do with how close he was to her. "It brings me joy, too. A different kind, but still joy. Working with the metals, crystals, and alloys in technology and manipulating them to go above and beyond what they're supposed to? All to *help* people? That's my definition of magic." She couldn't stop the smile from tugging at her lips as she finally got the courage to look at him again.

"Take this server I'm making. But remove the whole, I'm accidentally making it for a corrupt politician part," she added quickly with a nervous laugh. "When I'm done, the new magitech hardware I'm assembling will remove all those old devices from that room. It'll free up that entire space so *people* can work there again. I'm helping people. Or I thought I was." Her shoulders slumped, but she shook the defeat away before it could weigh her down and drown her. "Anyway, when done right, my magitech helps on a scale my little plants never could."

His face was that stoic mask again. The one Olline was beginning to understand was the look he had when he wanted to hide what he truly thought. Something in her chest cracked, and the desire to rip his mask away was so overwhelming she was sure it showed on her face.

"Never underestimate the help, the *power,* something you cultivate through joy can bring to Antal—or Audamar, or even the whole of Eerden." His tone was firm but a little rough around the edges with an emotion Olline didn't want to analyze for fear of the hope it might give her. A tentative smile grew as the surprise of his words sank in, her breath catching slightly in her throat.

"Look, I know I'm impressive, but I'm not . . . nothing I can do is all that remarkable," she said, her voice shaky, which wasn't aided in the slightest by her disbelieving, high-pitched laugh.

She looked away before Casimir could do the nice thing and pepper her with more compliments or reassurances. If he did that, she was certain she would immolate them both with the fire of her unease around praise.

"We should get to work before the IT guys decide to look at what was actually flagged in their program security. Or worse, someone tells Camirin that I threw her under the bus for something she has no idea about. Although, maybe she wouldn't care." Her face scrunched up as she looked at the folder containing all the chips in it. A heavy sigh pulled her shoulders down. "I'll have to figure out the passcodes and enter them in slowly, so I don't raise any other flags." With a groan, she threw her head back on the couch behind her, staring at the ceiling. "I don't have the time to crack it, not when I have the pretense of a job to maintain."

"Does it help that Etzel is preoccupied for the week?" Casimir offered, and she rolled her head to look at him. "He's at a conference trying to get other Senators to deregulate the restrictions around certain kinds of magitech. He's still in Antal, of course. But he's not at the Government Plaza and won't be for another six or seven days. Does that help?"

Olline considered, and then slowly shook her head. "Not really. I mean a little, but we'd have to get really, really lucky, too." She groaned again. "This is going to take forever."

"Sounds like you have to do things the old-fashioned way," Casimir said. The amusement in his voice had Olline squinting at him. He grinned down at her. "I did tell you I'd be able to help you. This is how. I *know* Etzel. The real Etzel. I'm sure I can help you pick these locks, as it were."

Leaning forward, she lifted a shoulder, reluctant to tell him how many potential password combinations there could be, and how they couldn't get a single one wrong. Preoccupied or not, if they tripped a security sensor, she didn't doubt Etzel would send someone after them. But Casimir wanted to help, and looked so sure of himself, that Olline was reluctant to shatter that so soon.

She pulled open the file and the first password prompt, fingers poised over her holo-keyboard, and said, "If it keeps more security guards from pulling a gun on us, it's worth a shot. No pun intended."

The first file was titled "Everleigh.Maldonado". It was meaningless to Olline, though she guessed it was probably someone's name. Casimir's eyes narrowed on the file and a corner of his lip twitched into a sneer. After a moment of study, he said, "Try Gold, with a capital G."

"You're sure? We can't guess or, well, you know what. Are you positive?" Olline cringed at how shrill her nervousness made her voice, but she really, *really* didn't want any armed guards showing up at her complex.

Casimir titled his chin down, bringing his face a fraction closer to hers. Her breath caught, snagged on a ribcage that was too tight around her racing heart. Casimir still had a slight sneer on his lips, but his eyes were twinkling with a kind of calm happiness that made her heart feel light enough to float away.

"Trust me, Ollie," he said, his rich deep voice reminding her once again of satin sheets rustling in the dark.

Her mind snagged on the new nickname, and her fingers tingled with the need to touch him, to pluck the name from the air and hold it tight. She looked away and typed in the passcode instead. Because the truth was, she did trust him. Lochan would be so proud.

Casimir didn't have to warn her she was about to be caught. He could have washed his hands of her right then and there and not risked his exposure. But he hadn't. He had come for her, and that had to be worth something.

Olline held her breath as she hit enter. And the file opened immediately.

It worked. Holy shit, it worked!

She didn't know why she was surprised; this is what they wanted. But something about Casimir getting it right on the first try . . . Something tickled in the back of her mind, but she soon forgot about it when she saw what the file contained.

Her stomach went into freefall. These weren't just blackmail files. There were dozens of those, too, pictures and videos, scraps of holo-messages, and transaction records that were incriminating. But the main attraction of each file was access to the chip that collected all these pieces of evidence. It wasn't a simple administrative bot chip, a program whose sole function was to keep the incoming data organized for the main user.

No, these chips were *control* chips. Control chips implanted in living, breathing, *people.*

Then the tickle became a painful scratching, and she leaned back, removed her hands from the keyboard, and leveled her full scrutiny at the seerani next to her. Casimir had taken one look at the filename and had known the password. It wasn't a guess. He *knew*. Which should be impossible. She didn't have to be a theoretical statistician like Goswin to know the odds said it was impossible and yet . . . She silently tugged on the power in her core, ready to summon her plants if need be.

"You knew what these chips were this whole time, didn't you? That it wasn't simply blackmail we were dealing with here." Despite her words, they weren't questions.

Casimir didn't so much as flinch, even as his gaze dropped away from hers. "Yes," he admitted quietly.

"How?" she demanded. "What do you do for Etzel Straub where you could just *know* his passcodes?" Her green eyes narrowed on him. "Who're you really, Casimir? How are you tangled up in all this? Tell me now, and tell me the truth, or else." The leaves rustled ominously around her, the vines slithering closer, bearing down on them, making her threat clear. She wouldn't hurt him, not purposefully, but she could restrain him easily until help arrived.

Their gazes collided, a silent explosion as his stare bore deeply into hers. Finally, he said, "Because one of those chips is mine."

CHAPTER 12

"Yours?" Olline's heart stuttered in her chest, and she could barely choke out her words. "You have a control chip. Implanted in you?" Her mind spun, a chilly numbness spreading through her limbs, unable to accept his words.

A control chip was the darkest side of biomagitech. Completely able to override a person's mind, body, and free will, the chip would, essentially, allow remote access to the person being controlled by the chip's owner. It was a violation on a scale Olline couldn't fully comprehend. Yet here was Casimir, calmly sitting beside her, saying that he had such a device *implanted in him.*

Suddenly his statement from earlier, of not working for Etzel willingly, made much more sense.

Casimir nodded slowly, anger flashing in his eyes. He blinked, and his mask of nonchalance fell back into place. "I didn't lie to you, you know," Casimir began, a vicious sneer pulling his face into severe lines. "Etzel has ensured that, at least where he's concerned, democracy isn't an issue. He's found a way to guarantee his complete control lasts for centuries. The power he's cultivated is untouchable. All because of these tiny little chips."

Olline struggled for words, wanted to reach out and comfort him or . . . But his body was so tense, every muscle flexed like he was ready to defend himself, that she didn't think he would appreciate even a comforting touch. "Casimir," she started, her voice raw with disbelief and pity.

His head whipped toward her. "Don't," he snapped. She startled, and he blinked, taking a deep breath. "Now is not the time for pity, precious Tav. I've survived, on my own no less. I will continue to do so regardless of the outcome of this little misadventure. Save your pity for someone more deserving, hmm?"

She swallowed the heaviness in her throat and nodded, sitting on her hands lest she reach out to smooth away the lines of pain, making his beautiful face so severe. "Why," she began again, then shook her head. The *why* of it didn't really matter, now did it? "How did this happen?"

He laughed, harsh and low, his hands flexing, then clenching. "Ironically, I was trying to help someone. I learned my lesson very fast about the cost of doing the right thing. I had minor influence because of Kullen and his pleasure club enterprises. Nothing spectacular, nothing like what Kullen had—has." He couldn't keep the anger from his voice, with how clipped his words were, though Olline knew he was trying. "It was enough for our businesses to catch the eye of Etzel and, well," he flicked a silver-white lock of hair off his forehead, masking the cringe, but Olline noted it all the same. "There was an issue I needed—*wanted* to take care of. For my brother. Turns out this *issue* was orchestrated by Etzel. He wanted someone with my *look,* with my access to places where, if other important people in Antal were seen, it would be more than just a tad embarrassing. So, I was lured to a place I shouldn't have been."

Casimir's words cut off abruptly. His jaw shut with an audible *snap,* and his throat bobbed as he swallowed whatever emotion sharing this history brought up for him. Olline was about to tell him to forget it, that it was okay, that he didn't have to continue, when Casimir took a deep, ragged breath.

"Etzel doesn't ask for the things he believes are his right to take, and I fit that mold. Thanks in no small part to Kullen. Simple as that. I was knocked out, and when I woke up, I had this . . . control chip." He gestured vaguely to the base of his neck. "Etzel stood over me, explaining exactly what our *relationship* would look like going forward. How I'd be the first of many to help him create and mold Antal into his version of utopia with none being the wiser. A long game, he claims. But at some point, you have to wonder," Casimir grumbled, then shrugged. "A century of this shit seems more than merely a 'long game'."

A million things ran through her head at once. Horror and disgust for what Casimir must have undergone, that someone could even do that to another person. A sick curiosity about what he had to do in order to . . . what? Collect blackmail from his brother's clubs? The fun Olline thought she would have dismantling a corruption ring was utterly and completely quashed. Icy terror washed over her skull, sending a shiver throughout her body, when a terrifying thought occurred to her. "You're still implanted? Is this a trap, too?"

Casimir's shoulders sagged, his firm body deflated, making him look smaller, somehow. "I am, but this is no trick of Etzel's, Olline," he said gently. "I was his first, you see. My chip? Little better than a working prototype from my understanding. When you did your fancy little back door peek into that file, it did something to my chip. It's not connected to what Etzel uses to control—give me assignments anymore. I'm, temporarily, free."

Olline sucked in a breath and would have covered her mouth with her hands if she wasn't still sitting on them. "My fake update," she murmured. Casimir raised a brow at her, and she hastily added, "It's what I used to look at the files initially, remember? I knew at the time that if one of those chips was a different version than the rest, it may not sync properly. I just didn't think something with that level of sophistication would even include an outdated device." The more she spoke, the quicker her words came out, the full scale of what she had accidentally done clicking into place. "My update made it so the server Etzel uses can't communicate with the client. Your chip can't receive instructions, basically."

Casimir grew still. His eyes widened slightly as she spoke, drinking in her words. Finally, he asked, "Ever?"

She bit her lip, not willing to go that far, but not wanting to destroy whatever hope he may have. "I don't know," she said slowly. "I need to dig around more. We'd have to find the schematics of your particular chip so I could make it inert permanently. But, if nothing else, no new actions will make it to you. I just don't know how long that'll last." She leaned forward, glancing at all the files within the folder containing the chips. "There's so many of these, Casimir. So many people, all enslaved by one crooked politician. And you couldn't tell anyone this was done to you?"

"Etzel is, unfortunately, clever. He took such things into consideration. The chip, dear Tav, isn't the only means of control he employs over his *thralls*." Casimir's smirk was as vicious as a serrated knife, and Olline figured it was best to move on. For now.

Casimir needed help. Not just with his chip, either, though that took priority. Olline may find him incredibly alluring, in a poisonous flower kind of way, but the ache she felt toward him now was something else. No one should experience what he had undergone. She didn't need to know the specifics to know that much.

"So that's how you know so much, right? Like with this?" she said, moving her hand to wave at her holo-tablet and the file they had opened.

Casimir laughed, but there was no mirth to it. "You mean with Everleigh's file? Yes. Etzel is a crafty bastard for most things, but he's like any old seersha when it comes to passwords." He examined his nails, as if bored, but there was still such a despairing look in his gaze that Olline wondered if he truly believed he was fooling her. "It's like you said. There are too many of us for him to get cute with naming the files. But being Etzel's first has its advantages, I suppose. I got to see behind the curtain, so to speak." He waited, as if waiting for her to say something. When she didn't, he continued, "The man has hobbies. Hobbies that are tangentially related to his business interests." Olline stared at him, a blank look on her face, and he sighed, dropping his hands. "Etzel collects beautifully rendered paintings of the elements and periodic tables. All the things that go into making his evil little contraptions." Casimir paused, unable to hide the contempt from his voice, the scorn from his face.

"He gave us little pet names based on them. I heard him once, commenting on one of my *coworkers*. Called him as 'interesting as carbon', which is to say he's rather boring. He laughed while he said it, put something into his holo-tablet, then seemed to remember I was in the room and sent me off on an errand. Ever since then, I had a hunch as to how to get into the files. I just couldn't access them." His words drifted off, and his face smoothed enough to give her a tired grin. "Until now."

Olline tried to smile back, but the coldness throughout her body and the heaviness in her chest made that impossible. She swallowed, hoping her words didn't sound as scratchy as her throat felt. "Why gold for Everleigh then?"

Casimir's gaze took on a far-off quality, his smile slight and private. "She's beautiful, rare in that she's an upper class humani, making her worth a lot to someone like Etzel. But Everleigh is . . . soft. So, gold."

"So, it's not like you knew-*knew* the passcode, you still just . . . guessed?"

He shrugged, his head hanging slightly, as if embarrassed. "In a fashion. But I've been one of Etzel's thralls for a long time, Olline. I know all these people. Some I even *recruited.* With enough time, I can figure out the elemental code name Etzel has for all of us."

Each time he revealed a little more about the chip and what he had done, a million little fault lines splintered through her heart. But if she wanted to help Casimir and all the other people under Etzel's thumb, she had to be smart about this. Or *smarter,* really. Smarter than she had been when she had first casually approached the issue, and now smarter than a seersha politician who literally had centuries on her. Failing to silence an alarm quickly would not only reactivate Casimir's chip, but it would also mean that she would never discover the identities of his other thralls, leaving them enslaved indefinitely. Then there was, of course, that in failing to help, Olline would place herself in the crosshairs of a dangerously powerful man. If Under Senator Straub found her? Well, *at best,* he would kill her.

No pressure.

Olline shut her eyes and took a deep breath, letting it out slowly. "Okay, so we have a time limit here. Probably. There's no telling how long we have before Etzel tries to give you a command and notices it hasn't worked, even while at this conference. What I did wasn't obvious, but it will be if he wants you to do something. Not to mention that if we want to really ensure that this practice of using illegal biomagitech in people is shut down for good, then we . . ." she trailed off, her heart sinking to her stomach with the realization. "Then we can't shut the other chips down. Not yet. Etzel will notice and he'll just start the program up again."

Casimir clenched his hands, the only sign of his agitation. He leaned closer to her, and despite his white knuckles, there was curiosity sparkling in his deep red eyes. "What are you suggesting we do then, Tav?"

She scrubbed her hands over her face, fingers digging into the base of her Mohawk, disheveling the jade and ebony strands. "We have to collect the information from the chips first, divert everything into a clone program. Then we need to get access to wherever those contingency plans are stored. They aren't in here, from what I can tell. We need all that in a safe location first before we find someone not in Etzel's influence to give it to. Someone who can and will use the coercion and blackmail to dethrone Etzel and not further their own political agenda."

Olline groaned. She was too new to Antal to even make a guess who to go to, who to trust. She couldn't even be sure if she could trust Casimir. What if his chip reconnected? She would need access to more of the schematics before she could even attempt to dismantle the chip with her magic. Biomagitech was tricky; it was practically a living thing and required delicacy and finesse to dismantle without causing irreparable harm to the person the biomagitech device was implanted in. The last thing Olline wanted was to cause Casimir even an ounce more pain or discomfort.

"Not to mention I still have a job to do, even if it's a farce." She scrubbed her hands over her face until she saw spots. "If I'm supposed to be making a new server and moving all this over, it's because Etzel needs it moved and he'll be monitoring my progress. Probably through Karter, given he was so anal about me clocking in and out. If I stop doing that to focus on this, he'll suspect something, and I'm assuming that kind of attention will be a bad thing. And all this has to happen in the week before Etzel comes back to the Government Plaza." The amount of work was staggering on its own, but that's not what made her breaths come in shallow bursts. It was the ticking clock that made her heart race, her vision blur at the corners, as she fought to keep from getting overwhelmed.

"Look at me," Casimir said. "Ollie, look at me," he said again, his tone gentle and coaxing as if he were wrapping her in a warm blanket. "I'm here. I have a vested interest in your success, don't forget. I'm going to help you. Just take a deep breath. You can always give me the files and I can use the power that gives me to keep us safe."

Olline couldn't tell if he was joking, merely saying something so outlandish to get her to smile . . . or if he meant it. He took her hands in his. The gentle, soapstone feel of his powerful hands, the tenderness in which he looked after her when he was the one so abused that Olline couldn't phantom his hurt, left her lightheaded and her chest aching anew.

He studied her a moment, letting her breathing become deeper, then gave her a sad smile. "Let's break this down into manageable bites, all right? Let's spend today getting as many passwords figured out as possible. That is within *my* power to give you. While you do your magic with cloning files and what not, I'll look for the right person to give this information to. I've spent enough time crawling through the shadows of this city to avoid Etzel's detection for as long as possible. If that fails, we still have options we can discuss."

His thumb ran over her knuckles, once, twice, and then he was carefully putting her hands back in her lap. Without his warmth, Olline felt oddly cold, the familiar pang of loneliness ready to strike. She was so focused on the sensation, she almost missed Casimir's words as he said, "We will divide and conquer, my dear. But you have to recognize the things we can't control and let them go."

She narrowed her eyes at him, but his sad smile remained as he moved a fraction closer to her, dipping his head a little closer. "I have too much practice in relinquishing control, and you don't have enough, for good or bad. If Etzel figures out my chip is disconnected? We can't control that. All we can do is work as fast, and as long as we can, until that happens."

"*If* that happens," Olline was quick to add.

Casimir lifted a shoulder. "I'm too jaded to have hope, but I'll borrow your optimism. If the chip is reconnected, I'll have mere moments to alert you. That's how you'll know to avoid me at all costs. Until then, I'll help you look for the contingency plans. I don't have your expertise, but I'll recognize the files when we find them."

Olline took another deep breath; it helped to compartmentalize the way Casimir suggested. It helped her see the building blocks making up the tower of things they needed to do and take them apart one by one. Wiggling her fingers, Olline leaned over the holo-keyboard once more. Offering Casimir a sly smile, she said, “Let’s bring this system to its knees, shall we?”

His smile was a slow, seductive one that made every one of her nerve endings tingle. “Oh, Olline, I like the way you think.”

CHAPTER 13

They took their time with the passcodes, neither wanting to risk entering the wrong element in case that sent an alert to Etzel. Which meant that, frequently, they took breaks so Casimir could focus and put himself in the mindset of Etzel. Every time he had to stop and consider what cruel, inside joke Etzel would have for each of the people he enslaved, a bit of the light went out of Casimir's red eyes.

She wished she had a password hacking program, or that her magic could somehow crawl through the wires to dismantle the passwords from within. But her skill and magic could not help in this instance. Each time she watched Casimir struggle to return to himself after another knot twisted in her belly.

Olline tried her best to distract him with pleasanter things in those moments, stories about Lochan and Goswin, and what an adorably odd pair they made. Or little anecdotes about Darrin and her father and how Darrin desperately wanted to follow in her father's footsteps in literally everything—from where he worked to even how her father dressed. Casimir would smile, ask what her brothers and father did for a living, even chuckle over Goswin's dry humor. Sadly, those stories were only effective and grounding for so long.

They were, perhaps, a quarter of the way through when Casimir squinted at the screen. He mumbled the file name quietly to himself, then shook his head and shot to his feet.

She watched him from where she sat on the couch, her feet tucked under her as she worked on writing the code for the clone program. It was something to keep her hands and mind busy, to keep her from feeling too helpless while Casimir tortured his mind. He raised his arms over his head, stretching and curving, easing the tension in his arms and back.

His form fitting shirt rose a fraction with the action, showing the irresistible muscle that peeked just above the belt line of his pants. His muscles were taut, his skin so smooth that Olline had the sudden urge to run her fingers over every contour, curious to see what kind of touch would make a man like Casimir squirm.

Olline sucked in a breath, startled by the thought and the delicious, tingling warmth it had spreading out from her core. *Get a grip, Olline. It hasn't been that long since you touched someone. The man has been through enough without you ogling him.*

And yet, Olline couldn't help herself.

Despite what he had gone through, Casimir was still so magnetic, a powerful allure born from assurance. Confidence in his appearance, in his skills, in himself. Olline suspected, whether or not Casimir was aware, that it was those qualities more than his connections that put him in Etzel's crosshairs. It was the quality that, the longer Olline remained in his path, pulled her closer and closer. It was an attraction, no, a *distraction,* she couldn't afford, and that was before she found herself coiled up in a blackmail scheme.

But maybe . . .

With how Casimir flirted with her, she knew he wouldn't be opposed to a casual fuck. Clearly, there was *some* mutual attraction there. But they were working together now; it changed everything. What if the sex brought them closer and then *something* happened? That was a complication she didn't want again; she knew from experience.

Her gaze lingered on the muscles of his back as he twisted again. When, suddenly, there was this *tug* pulling at the molten core of her magic. Her attention snapped up to the base of his strong back, to the curve of his neck, where the tug was strongest. Her eyes widened as she realized it was her magic reaching out to the control chip buried in his spinal column, as if, now that she knew it was there, her subconscious activated her power. She had to stop herself from rubbing the base of her own neck in sympathy. Olline had experienced hurt and betrayal, yes, but Casimir's reality was on a scale that went beyond comprehension. On a scale no one should ever experience.

No one should feel such lacerating anguish from someone they trusted.

"Like what you see, Tav?" Casimir said, voice low and inviting as he looked over his shoulder and caught her staring.

Her cheeks were instantly hot, her lips parting as she tried to find the words to explain her thought process and how yeah, it started as ogling, but that wasn't why she was still staring. Or not the only reason. They didn't have that kind of relationship—they had no kind of relationship, more aptly—so she couldn't just explain herself. That would be *mortifying*.

So instead, she blurted, "I think that goes without saying. You know exactly the effect you have on people, Cas. You're distracting me. So can you," she waved vaguely, gesturing up and down his lean body, "stop doing whatever that is."

He chuckled, low and deep, like his whole chest was rumbling with a pleasure he was trying to contain. Then, abruptly, he stopped. Raising a brow, he turned to give her every ounce of his attention. "Cas, huh?"

A scorching heat filled her, and her mouth was suddenly dry. Olline was too breathless to answer. Too late, she realized she had given him a nickname. That was too intimate, wasn't it? Too casual for what this was? Which was nothing. Absolutely nothing and it would stay that way. She was a professional, dammit.

He stalked closer to her, sinking to his knees at her side, close enough for her skin to prickle with the warmth. His enticing scent of eucalyptus and lavender tickled her nose, and she had to fight the urge to close her eyes and inhale, savor his heat. This was neither the time nor the place—for either of them.

Olline's tongue felt heavy in her mouth, but she couldn't

take the way he was looking at her with that burning gaze. "If you're going to call me Tav, or Ollie, I reserve the right to call you Cas," she answered, her words wobbly as she tried to sound playful. But then she remembered who she was talking to and her heart sank. "Unless you don't like the name?" Olline stammered, her breathing becoming rushed. "I should have asked. If you don't like it, or don't want a nickname, that's okay! I just thought—" she cut herself off, noting the way his smile changed while she stammered through her apology.

His smile started slowly, but it grew until his pale skin was flushed. He moved even closer, so close to touching, and yet there was that made Olline's chest and joints ache. Electricity crackled between them. How did he not feel that? Or was he just messing with her for fun? Was she going crazy?

Probably. That seemed the safest explanation.

"You're sweet, Ollie," he said, his mouth parting ever so slightly, and Olline wanted nothing more than to rub her thumb over his full, lower lip.

"And brilliant. Not enough people mention that about me," she said, losing her inhibitions. And she hadn't even had anything to drink! She licked her lips, trying to get control but failing miserably. Maybe she didn't want control to begin with. Maybe it wasn't a bad idea to fuck and get it out of her system . . .

"Well, they should. You're absolutely magnificent, my dear." He let his words hang in the air. His eyes flicked to her lips, before he leaned back a breath. Olline already felt a chill without him near, and reminded herself that sleeping with a *coworker* was a very bad, no-good idea. "Don't worry, you can call me Cas if you wish. It's nice you wanted my consent to something so trivial, Tav, but don't worry about it."

Her brows pinched together, her mouth falling slightly, hurt that he could even say something like that about himself. As suddenly as it had washed over her, the fiery desire that had her nearly feverish was gone, replaced with a yearning to hold him and throttle Etzel.

"Consent is never trivial." This time, she did reach out and put her hand over his. She felt his hand stiffen beneath hers for a fraction of a moment before he relaxed. Casimir glanced away briefly before his gaze landed on her fingers, then trailed up to her eyes, as if he couldn't look away for long. "Your consent matters to me. It will always matter. You never deserved to have it taken away, Cas, okay?"

His face adopted that mask of stoicism again, and Olline desperately wished he hadn't buried whatever emotion he didn't want her to notice. His nostrils flared, and his throat bobbed as he swallowed, before abruptly shaking his head. That coy smirk of his returned, and Olline would have given almost anything to bring back that glowing smile from before. "You didn't know who I was before the control chip. Perhaps I deserved all that came after."

"You didn't deserve it, period," she said without hesitation, emphasizing every word. "No one does." It was then she noticed she was still gripping his hand, noticed that he was holding hers in return. His gaze remained fixed on her. Something about having Casimir's complete attention made her dizzy, made her wonder what it would be like to truly have him all to herself.

She sucked in a breath, forcing air into lungs that wouldn't fill properly in a chest that felt suddenly too tight. He seemed to do that to her a lot, and she wished she minded more. She cleared her throat, moving her hand back to her holo-keyboard with more effort than the action should have required. "Ready to keep going?"

Slowly, Casimir turned his attention back to the holo-screens in front of them. He frowned at the blinking curser that waited for them to input the next password. He sucked in a deep breath, shutting his eyes for a moment, then shook his head slightly. "I don't know if you've noticed, but it's incredibly late. We should take a break."

Panic had her eyes going wide. "We can't! There's still too much to do and not enough time to do it in. I've no way to tell if new commands have been issued to you, or any of the other chips. What if Etzel is already on to us?"

He rolled his eyes. "You're an absolute workaholic. Has anyone ever told you that?" She frowned at him, and he sighed. He tapped something into his wrist-comm and a moment later, a live feed of the committee meeting blinked in front of her. "Until now," Casimir explained, "all the people Etzel was meeting with were in discussions. From the commentary, the discussions weren't going terribly well, keeping every ounce of the Under Senator's attention on those talks. Now," and he pointed to an imposing seersha with cedar-colored horns and flashing yellow diamond eyes, "Etzel is not preoccupied with those discussions. We shouldn't risk poking into a system he can pay attention to now."

Casimir's words reminded her they were now down one more day, creeping closer and closer to when Etzel would return to the Government Plaza. Her chest constricted as if there was a vice around her ribs, slowly crushing them. But the smile he gave her at seeing her reaction . . . It was so tender it hurt just as much. "You've given me my freedom already, no matter how fleeting. You've given me a gift, even if you didn't know it at the time. I won't forget that. So let me thank you, truly, while I have the freedom to do so."

"But I can keep working," she said, reaching for her holo-keyboard again.

He snatched at her hand, catching her wrist before she could even blink. She sucked in a breath. But Casimir didn't seem aware of his reflexes. His eyes were wide, linen white skin pallid with panic. A second later, he dropped her wrist, gave his head a slight shake, and forced a mirthless chuckle. "My apologies, my dear." He cleared his throat and stood up. "I'd really rather not take the risk, and besides, I did promise to do better after taking you to that garden. Please. Let's stop for the night. Let me treat you properly."

Olline eyed him suspiciously for a moment. The paranoia she could understand. But the pleading to take her out again? Why do that now rather than get a good night's rest instead? But Lochan and her father and even Goswin's words tickled through her mind again and she no longer felt like arguing.

In truth, she wanted more time for her and Casimir. More

time to figure out if the desire was simply that or something . . . more. "There's more I can do to protect you. To safeguard everyone else trapped under their chips' influence." But her words held little of the conviction she had earlier in the day.

"Running yourself to the bone won't help. We both need to approach this with clear and fresh minds." When she still didn't immediately shut her devices down, he gently started doing it for her. "It's like you said, too much is at stake for us not to be careful and meticulous. We can't afford mistakes. Working all night and then doing it again in the morning? It's a guaranteed way to ensure a mistake happens." With her devices powered down, he reached a hand down to help her up. Olline merely stared at his open palm.

Her mind flashed back to Brayden appearing at her office door because of her decryption program and a lump lodged itself in her throat. Casimir was right, even if she hated to admit it.

Swallowing to ease the tension constricting her throat, Olline took Casimir's hand, ignored how it wrapped around her own with a tenderness that felt as natural as breathing, and let him pull her to her feet. "Maybe you're right," she admitted reluctantly. "And I'm kind of curious to see the *effort* you'll put into showing me other places in Antal that'll top the garden."

His flirtatious smirk turned a bit more sincere with his excitement, and she couldn't help but grin back at him. "Show me *one* amazing thing," Olline declared. "We shouldn't stay out late. There's a lot to do tomorrow, but you have a point. A little break wouldn't be too bad, right?"

He tugged her toward the door, mischief dancing in his eyes. "You'd be surprised how productive a little fun can be, Ollie."

CHAPTER 14

She was half expecting him to break them into another garden. Instead, he led her to the public monorail that twisted through Antal, heading for the outer city limits.

Casimir didn't tell her where they were going. Normally, Olline didn't like surprises after the nasty shock Achan had given her. Yet there was such a . . . *sweet* quality to Casimir's joy, that she was starting to love surprises all over again.

The monorail stayed within the mid-levels of the city, so at least she knew they weren't going to any of the rich and elite areas again. She pressed her face to the plexi-glass of the monorail, trying to see where they were going, and being dazzled by the glittering lights of the city that gave all of Antal a glowing mauve hue from this level.

They pulled into the station and departed with a handful of other riders. Casimir tilted his head, indicating the way they were to go. When not a single other traveler headed in their direction, Olline's heart ticked up in its tempo.

But it wasn't in fear, not anymore.

After Casimir shared what Etzel had done to him, even without the full scope of the details, well, she had started to trust him. He was more than the raw sex appeal that had sparked her initial attraction, more than the handsome face he showed the world—even if it was an incredibly handsome face. He was also an active listener and was incredibly sweet and gentle when he didn't have to worry about survival constantly. Casimir *cared;* about her and her comfort, and about the others trapped in his situation. There was layer upon layer of mystery to this man, and it sparked a curiosity in her core, one that tickled her magic, one that she wanted to unravel in whatever way she could. Even if it was just as a friend.

Better for everyone if it was as friends. If he was being nice to her only because she was doing him a favor, then once that was done, his interest in her would . . . change.

Yeah, definitely better for us to be friends when that happens.

Olline's gait slowed as her mind slammed against that sad truth. She enjoyed working. Olline felt safe immersed in her code and hardware, and would gladly stay there. She liked small crowds and preferred the company of her plants to most people these days. She was *friendly,* and being friendly in a city like Cyneburg—and now Antal—seemed like a strange thing to be. A dangerous thing to be. Dangerous for her, anyway.

And yet Casimir hadn't scoffed at her the way others had, for being an earth caster who preferred to keep her plants a hobby and specialize in metals instead. He seemed determined to make up for his safe assumptions about her and her magic. So, maybe . . .

"Careful, Olline darling," Casimir said, his hand on the small of her back as he gently maneuvered her away from the railing of the platform she had been heading for. "You're liable to fall."

Warmth blossomed from where his hand lightly touched the bare skin of her midriff. She had to keep from leaning back against his fingers, wanting to feel the whole of his hand on her and not just the delicate brush of his fingertips.

She cleared her throat and shot him a side-long glance. "Where are we going, anyway? Maybe it'd help if you shared a bit more, so I didn't wander too close to the edge or something."

"And ruin the surprise?" he said with a little chuckle. "I think not. But we're almost there. It's just over here."

Olline glanced around and frowned. They were on a residential level and she couldn't see any businesses nearby—at least none that she particularly wanted to wander into. "Are we going to your place or something?" Olline said with a grin, trying to hide the nervous fluttering she felt moving through her. "I think I said to take me somewhere amazing, Cas."

He turned, giving her his full attention, and pulled that delicious lower lip between his teeth, releasing it slowly. Olline forgot how to walk for a moment as her eyes locked on his lips, her breath hitching in her chest. "Tav, if you wanted to go home with me, you merely needed to ask. My flat may not be amazing, but I can think of a few things we could do there that would be mind blowing."

It was like walking on gelatin as her legs went wobbly, her lower abdomen clenching as if in anticipation, daring her to imagine what he meant. *Stop it. This would be a bad complication and you know it. I bet it would be amazing, though . . .*

"No! I mean, I didn't . . . That's not what I meant. Not that I'd say no to that with you, but . . . wait. That didn't come out right," Olline stammered, her mind too foggy to think coherently. Words were beyond her skillset at the moment. Her face was so hot she was positive her cheeks would burst into flame any second.

Casimir laughed, a full body laugh with his head tilted back and everything. It would be humiliating if it wasn't such a sweet sound to hear. Plus, it didn't seem malicious to her. Though that could be wishful thinking on her part. Again.

"You're adorable, do you know that?" Shaking his head, he motioned her to follow him again before they attracted unwanted attention, standing around as they were in a residential block. "Trust me, Olline, if I invited you to my home, there would be no ambiguity about it."

She was still too flustered to say anything as she trailed behind him. One glance over his shoulder, at the look on her face, must have told him how embarrassed she still was. "All friendly flirting aside, my home is probably not the safest place for us to visit. Etzel owns my flat and I can't promise that he doesn't have the building under surveillance. But where I'm bringing you is amazing, trust me."

He turned a corner and went up a twisting staircase to the next level before he stopped and looked around. She wasn't sure what he was looking for, but he found it before she could ask.

"Ah, here we are. I knew my memory hadn't failed me." He ushered Olline into a darkened, narrow doorway between two apartment complexes she swore was an alleyway access. At least until her eyes adjusted to the dim light, and she picked up the sound and vibrations coming from the walls and floor.

It was . . . music.

There was no electronic thrum going through the music like with a synth bot. It tugged at her core and rattled her bones, seizing on to the latent part of her magic that had led her to The Pit. She stepped around Casimir, the pull of the music guiding her along. She tilted her head, trying to make out the instruments and voices. Finally, her feet led her to another narrow staircase that ended in a steel door.

"Allow me," Casimir whispered, his breath tickling the shell of her ear. Her posture relaxed and her knees went weak all over again. Olline could only hope it wasn't as obvious to him as it was to her.

He glided around her, his hip lightly brushing hers as he stopped in front of the door and knocked. There was no secret knock, no sliding panel in the door, and no exchange of code words, which was a tad disappointing. Someone simply opened the door a crack, looked at Casimir, and then flung it open, welcoming them both inside.

Casimir leaned back, allowing Olline to go in first. She was far too aware of where their bodies brushed against each other. No matter how briefly or lightly. It caused a spark of electricity to race through her, had her steps slowing to savor the moment for a millisecond longer.

But the shock of his touch wasn't what caused Olline to suck in her breath.

Casimir had brought her to a venue that had clearly been someone's home once upon a time. Most likely abandoned and repurposed by the people who ran it now. Long, narrow windows took up the back wall, giving a view of the advertisements and other shops on this level of the city, the neon flashing and twinkling like the stars Casimir had shown her. The small kitchen had been gutted to make a bar. A string of blue lights dipped and curved around the shelves, holding the bottles of liquor, making the liquid shimmer and twinkle. There were a few people perched on barstools, but no one was dancing, despite the band against the far wall.

Live music.

While some people had their heads tilted toward others in soft conversation, most were listening to the humani woman singing a soft, almost melancholy tune alongside two seersha with a guitar and giant bass. The effect was haunting and had tears prickling Olline's eyes for reasons she couldn't put into words. It was a feeling, an overwhelming sensation of connection that ignited her neurons in a way that gave her a sense of hope mixed with catharsis and contentment. It was confusing as fuck, but she loved the sensation.

She felt his hand on her back again, gently pulling her inside and toward a pair of empty barstools. They didn't speak, Casimir didn't even offer to get her a drink, as if he knew better than to break the spell surrounding her. They simply sat next to each other, Olline engrossed in the music, and Casimir captivated by her open enjoyment of the musicians.

Unfortunately, they arrived at the end of the set and soon the trio was standing, accepting the applause of the meager crowd, and retreating to an alcove where they could enjoy their break. Olline remained speechless for a minute, holding in the lingering beauty of the music as long as possible. She didn't care that the smile she gave Casimir next was so big it made her cheeks hurt.

"That was incredible, thank you, Cas," her voice was breathy, catching on the lingering emotion stirred by the melody. He dipped his head in response, shifting in his seat. She twisted around on the barstool, facing the bar in case that helped him feel more comfortable. "What is this place? How did you even find it? You'd never expect to find a bar like this in, well, *here*."

Casimir waved for the bartender, who was finishing up making a cocktail, and said, "For as long as this place has existed, it's never had a name. And I'd know, this was the first club I . . . well my brother and I founded well over a century ago. The buildings were different then, of course. But this apartment had been abandoned, and we scooped it up thinking this level of the city could use a little fun." He looked over his shoulder, his eyes glassy, as if what he was looking at was the bar as it had once been, a long time ago. "It didn't turn out how we envisioned. Well, how Kullen envisioned. He wanted to abandon this place, but I kept it. Turned it into an artist's haven of sorts. When Etzel got me, I made sure he never got to this place. It needed to remain protected, so I sold it, and the others like it. They're community owned and operated now. Safe from me—well, safe from Etzel using me to taint this place." He sighed blithely. "This place, dear Tav, is to me what your plants are to you. A thing to be kept sacred."

Olline was utterly speechless. The bartender appeared by then and Casimir gave her an expectant look. She was too flustered, moved by Casimir's admission, to think clearly. "I don't know much about drinks. I'm fine with whatever's good here," she said, giving the bartender an apologetic smile.

Casimir ordered something with a fancy name and turned his attention back to her. "Everyone here is employed in one of my brothers' more profitable clubs. But here they can follow their passion without having to worry about pesky things like tips and a paycheck."

Olline blinked slowly at Casimir. That . . . had not been what she was expecting. She smiled at him, raising an eyebrow. "I didn't take you for the anti-capitalist type, Cas."

"Does that bother you?"

She shook her head quickly. "Not at all! I'm just surprised. The way you hold yourself, I just assumed you enjoyed the finer things in life. It's refreshing to hear you say otherwise." He didn't look convinced, and she placed her hand on his forearm, ignoring how she would rather trail the line of his jaw with her finger instead. "I mean it. This place is incredible. It's sweet that you made and preserved it when your brother would've thrown it away." She turned slightly, a fire caster moving to the stage, taking the flame from a tiny candle and turning it into a burning tableau of the more recognizable buildings in Antal. "Thank you for bringing me here. I mean it."

He awarded her with a smile that slowly spread, highlighting the sharp angles of his face in a way that made her want to trace them with, well, *not* her finger. "Does it satisfy your desire for something amazing?"

Olline pressed her knees more firmly together, trying to bury the heat building between her thighs. Casimir had this infuriatingly irresistible way of speaking in double entendres that left Olline reeling. Left her wanting to erase every bit of distance between them.

At least until the reality of what tomorrow was going to bring settled over her like a moist blanket.

The bartender slid their drinks over and Olline raised hers in a toast, hiding the frown creeping over her lips, the stoniness she felt her face settling into. "Yes, it does," she answered quietly, hoping her voice didn't betray her.

Olline turned away. It suddenly hurt too much to look at Casimir anymore. She watched the fire caster with an intense focus, hoping to get absorbed in the dancing flames as they morphed from buildings to plants. The flames shifted in hue from red, orange, and blue as the heat intensified.

She noticed Casimir's lips tilt up with suppressed joy from the corner of her eye and something in her broke a fraction. This, whatever *this* was inside of her, felt as sharp as a cactus's barbs, and yet Olline couldn't stop from reaching out, even if it pricked her, the barbs implanting in her heart. It was insane to have these feelings for a man she barely knew, but they were there and all Olline could hope to do was survive being in his presence long enough to truly, and permanently, free him and everyone else. After that, Casimir would disappear again as quickly as he had appeared in her life and . . .

She shut her eyes tightly against the spiral. The images made with the flames burned behind her eyelids and somehow morphed into Casimir's burning gaze. An ache of longing squeezed her ribcage so tightly it had tears prickling the corners of her eyes.

Olline took a deep breath, then forced a smile on her face as she clinked her glass against Casimir's. She downed the drink before she could taste anything. She doubted it would have tasted like much given the sourness suddenly churning in her stomach.

"It's a beautiful reprieve from what we'll face tomorrow," she murmured. She turned back to the fire caster, telling herself that she simply imagined the way Casimir's hand flexed beside her. And Olline buried the futile wish that he would pull her to him.

CHAPTER 15

Olline had to go back to her office the next day. If she didn't, the chances that Karter would think something suspicious was going on would go up exponentially. Casimir hadn't liked it, but there was no help for it. At least it gave them the excuse to exchange wrist communicator information without it being awkward—or it didn't feel as awkward to Olline. Casimir merely seemed amused by her stammering shyness.

The man had to know the effect he had on people. He *had* to. So why did it amuse him when she floundered around him, her blushes uncontrollable when he flirted with her? Though she suspected that was the way he showed his version of friendliness. Through flirting. She didn't mind if that was the case. No matter how many times he called her darling, or his precious little caster. It didn't mean anything, or shouldn't.

"Ollie" was what tripped her up.

There was something about "Ollie" that felt different. It made her stomach tighten in a way the other names didn't, and she couldn't put her finger on *why*. It was merely another puzzle piece Olline was going to ignore.

Olline was still thinking about it when she entered the Police and Securities Department. She was early—she was a morning person and refused to be apologetic about it anymore—and Brayden was behind the desk like always.

He looked up at her with bleary eyes and she flashed her badge at him like always. His expression was blank, simply going through the motions, until his mind seemed to catch up with what, and who, he was seeing. His gaze narrowed, his puffy cheeks pulling down in a frown, and Olline had to swallow the dryness building in her throat. Her hands were clammy, even as she sent her ethereal fingers to coil around the piercings in her ears and brow, just in case.

Olline had never altered how she greeted Brayden, and she knew if she started now, it would most likely set off some alarm in his head. She wasn't *that* forgettable. With a wiggle of her fingers in a wave, Olline strode down the hall, her heart hammering the entire way.

Once she got to room two-hundred and twenty-three with no issue, she sent a quick message to Casimir:

I'll sneak out to you. Security guard is still weird.

The door to her office was still open, she had forgotten to close it in her haste to get in and message Casimir. Before she remembered, Briallea Jensen walked in. She was in a tailored purple jumpsuit so dark it looked nearly black. Her hands were in her pockets, her lips tilted in a friendly smile that made her diamond dimple piercings twinkle. "Hey, Olline," she said, her voice light.

Olline jumped in surprise and Briallea swayed back, her warm brown eyes widening. "Oh, shit, sorry. Did I say that wrong? It is Olline, right?" Her smooth, black cheeks darkened with a blush of embarrassment.

Taking a deep breath, Olline shook her head. "No. I mean, sorry. Yes, that's right. You just spooked me, that's all." Olline took a deep breath and hoped her smile wasn't quivering. "Do you have another early meeting? Or are you a morning person too, Briallea?"

She winked and readjusted her obsidian septum ring. "Guilty. Say," she said, leaning closer, "since we're going to be neighbors for a bit, want to grab lunch today or something? There are too few of us breathing people down on this floor. Mostly bots and they're no fun to talk to. Us organics need to stick together. You down?"

Her spirits lifted, the fear of who she worked for momentarily forgotten. It had been a long time since someone invited her to lunch. Someone who wanted to talk. Someone maybe a little lonely too, if Briallea's quip about the bots was any indication.

"I'd like that!" Olline answered brightly, before she remembered her message to Casimir. Her shoulders dipped slightly. "Maybe not today, though. Tomorrow?"

Briallea bobbed her head in a nod. "It's a date," she said, a kind of relief making her usually bright smile even warmer. She fluffed up her short, tight black curls and looked about ready to say something else when something in the corner of Briallea's eye caught her attention.

"Creepy fucking Karter," she growled. Briallea turned her attention back to Olline, while already backing out of her office. "Gotta split. Karter's coming and his stupid drone gives me the creeps. Later, Olline!"

She frowned, watching the shorter woman leave. With a shrug, she waved her hand, motioning for the door to close, but a drone zoomed in before she could. Karter was back, still as a holo-projection via a drone.

"Olline, good," he said, though it sounded anything but. Karter seemed flustered, his scared cheeks flushed, even with the soft filter over the projection. "We want to make sure things are moving on schedule, so here." He glanced away, and then Olline's wrist-comm buzzed. Before she could ask, Karter explained, "We've got a quota system for you to adhere to for number of files moved. Just a way to measure success should they extend your contract."

The hairs on Olline's arms rose, staticky suspicion danced over her skin. The way he kept saying "we" and "they" without ever revealing who these people were reignited her paranoia.

"Who—" Olline began, only to be cut off.

"Log the number of files moved whenever you clock in and out. It'll flag the system should you fall behind on the quota." Karter barely paused for breath and when he did, his drone was already maneuvering out of the door. "Understood? Excellent. If you need help, ask Camirin. I've got another matter to attend to."

Olline glanced at the quota, and her stomach fell. It was an absurd number of files and raw data to transfer, even if she wasn't worried about a corrupt politician using chips to enslave people. Which gave her the sneaking suspicion that this mysterious "they"—though it was most likely someone in Etzel's entourage—wanted to keep tabs on her. They wanted her where they could easily find her.

Her flight response had sweat collecting behind her knees. But she couldn't run. If she did, and it tipped off Etzel, what would happen to Casimir? What would become of everyone else he enslaved?

So, Olline did the only thing she could: she got to work.

As she transferred data, she also put out digital feelers, looking for strange documents or hidden folders within the server that could be the "contingency plans" Casimir mentioned. He hadn't said exactly what those plans were, so she didn't know what to look for, but she hoped it would stand out in some capacity, like the folder containing the chip information had.

Three hours later, while hunched over a holo-tablet, her wrist-comm buzzed and startled Olline, nearly causing her to topple out of the chair she had been perched on. She glanced down and grinned, a flush warming her cheeks.

Sorry, dear. Had to make the rounds to avoid Straub getting suspicious and sending anyone looking for me. I'll send you the location of a place to meet. I'll bring coffee to apologize for my late reply. Lots of coffee.

Olline could practically hear Casimir's slow, deep, sensual voice even through a holo-text. Almost like he had run a feather light finger down her spine. The message had her toes curling in her boots and her nipples hardening as if his breath brushed against the sensitive skin.

What was happening to her? She hadn't even been this giggly around Achan when things had been, well, not *great,* but at least decent. Before things went to shit.

The buzz of her wrist-comm with the location notification brought her back to her senses. She had a few more search queries to run, and needed to finish moving over one more program, and then she was free to duck out for a bit. Hopefully, the security guard took breaks occasionally. That way she wouldn't have to see him as she slunk past.

Olline wasn't that fortunate.

There was, at least, a crowd heading out for lunch at the same time that she could hide in. Spotting Briallea, Olline nearly ran to catch up with her. The shorter woman grinned, but she narrowed her eyes. "I thought you couldn't do lunch today?"

Olline angled her body to avoid Brayden seeing her face. She hated using Briallea as a cover, but desperate times and all that. She didn't need the man tattling to anyone that she hadn't clocked out when she left. "I can't. Well, I mean, I am. But I'd already made plans. That's why the raincheck." Her voice was a shrill whisper as they walked past the desk, and Olline prayed Brayden hadn't been told to explicitly monitor her.

Briallea gave her a funny look and then chuckled. "You're kind of weird, aren't you?" Olline didn't have time to so much as blink before Briallea added, "Me too. I dig it." She waved in farewell and said, "Enjoy your lunch, Olline." And just like that, they had made it past security without a single alarm going off.

Stealthy as fuck.

She was proud of herself for only getting turned around twice as she attempted to find the coffee kiosk Casimir had picked. Even so, she was a few minutes later than she said she would be, but she thought that wasn't *too* bad.

Olline nearly tripped over her feet when she saw him.

Casimir stood casually leaning against a pillar, holding two of the biggest cups of coffee she had ever seen. He wore a loose-fitting long-sleeved black silk shirt with gold trim, which he tucked into pants that hugged his muscular thighs and calves. His shirt was open to his sternum. The hard curve of his pectorals and smooth skin captured the entirety of Olline's attention. Walking and breathing at the same time was a skill she suddenly struggled with. His dark holo-visor concealed his piercing gaze, so she had no idea if he saw the effect he had on her.

The man should come with a warning label of some kind. He really was unfairly beautiful. Surprising everyone, but mostly herself, Olline had not tripped over her feet and made it to Casimir without incident. Thank goodness for minor blessings.

She glanced over her casual attire and suddenly felt woefully underdressed as she approached him, reminding herself for the umpteenth time that they were only friends.

Olline gratefully took the coffee Casimir offered, even

though it was late afternoon. The fact that he still needed coffee was kind of cute. Until she noticed he seemed to be waiting for her to take a sip first before he would bring the cup to his mouth. She stopped the coffee millimeters from her lips. "What is it now?"

Casimir startled slightly as if he wasn't aware of his own immobility. "Nothing," he blurted. "Take a sip. Tell me what you think."

She scrunched her brow in confusion but did as asked. There was a warm, roasted explosion on her tongue that had her moaning involuntarily. "You found it," she said, her words so full of bliss she wasn't even embarrassed by it this time. "*Real* coffee!" She wheeled toward the coffee kiosk, ready to ask a million questions about their supply and process, only to have Casimir catch her arm and draw her close.

The jolt that went through her from him simply touching her arm did more to electrify her senses than the coffee did. His feather light touch made her remember how her body reacted to simply reading his holo-message. She had to bite back a gasp as her nipples became painfully sensitive once more.

"Not here, Ollie. I know a place, and I wasn't going to risk bringing you there if it turned out you actually hated their brew." His fingers slowly uncurled from her arm, and his chin was tucked against his chest as if he were . . . bashful? No, that couldn't be right. "You do like it though, don't you? This is what you meant when you said you like real things, grown by hand?"

She blinked slowly. That—recently—all too familiar fluttery feeling returned to her stomach. "You remembered that?"

It was Casimir's turn to look at her with confused surprise. "Of course. I remember everything that slips out of those lips of yours." Her lips parted unconsciously at his words, and his nostrils flared, but he hid his face behind his own coffee cup before she could see whatever it was his expression was doing. "Your verdict?" he pressed.

Olline had almost forgotten what they were talking about when the delectable scent of coffee tickled her nose again. She couldn't hide her delighted smile, even if she wanted to. "It's perfect. You didn't have to go through all this trouble for me, Cas."

He shifted his weight slightly, before giving himself a little shake and taking a step back, gesturing for them to move away from the kiosk. "How long do you have before they notice you're gone, Tav?" Casimir whispered in her ear, his breath tickling her earlobe, as he maneuvered them through the milling crowd toward an empty bench.

"I didn't clock out. I don't want Karter tracking me." With a snort, she gave her head a slight shake. "I doubt anyone would even notice if I didn't come back at all if it weren't for the new quota system." She meant the words to be teasing, but it was impossible to bury all the bitter baggage that came with self-depreciation.

Casimir stiffened, and he turned to look at her sharply. "Don't do that, Olline. Someone would notice." He lowered his head, his eyes twinkling like rubies over his visor with an honest sincerity as he reached out like he would take her hand before stopping himself. "*I* would notice if you disappeared, my precious little caster." She opened her mouth to remind him about calling her that, when he grinned and held up his hands in a peace offering. "Apologies. But what I said stands." He moved to the bench, sitting down, and then patted the seat beside him. "How much time do we have, truly?"

She took a sip of the coffee to give herself something to focus on rather than how touched she was by his words or the electricity thrumming in the minuscule space between their thighs. "Let's say an hour, hour and a half, tops. It'll let me blend in with the crowd returning. Just to be safe."

Casimir nodded and, with a last glance around to make sure no one was overly interested in them, rolled his hand in a gesture of 'let's get started'. Olline took out the portable drive she had put the next few files they needed the passcodes for on, and offered him the device. That left her free to savor the deep, roasted flavor that only came with hot coffee grown from real beans.

With fresh eyes, it didn't take Casimir long to figure out the first two of the seven passwords—mercury and argon. Olline was hopeful they could get this batch done during her lunch break so she could sneak back in and keep Karter from flying his drone down to check on her.

"Casimir?"

Olline jerked her head up. "Where have you been hiding?" a gruff voice said a second before a shadow fell over them. Casimir became still as death beside her.

She blinked at the man who loomed above them. Casimir's face was as smooth and emotionless as ancient stone as he subtly swiped the files off the holo-tablet they were looking at, and tilted his chin up at the newcomer.

"Bode," he said, his voice far lighter and friendlier than Olline thought possible given how tense and motionless Casimir had gone. "What brings you crawling up from the depths of the city? Finally need a gulp of fresher air?"

"Charming as ever," Bode said, a forced laugh making his voice grate against her ears.

The man was a humani like her, but that was where the similarities ended. He had so much visible biotech augmentation that most government classification forms would consider him a cyborg. One eye glinted silver as the iris twirled and twisted like the lens of a camera, a metal plate covered half of his bald head, one of his legs was completely robotic, as were his middle two fingers, and that was just the mods Olline could see. Who knew what other hardware and software made up the entirety of this man?

"Come now, Bode," Casimir drawled. "You know I save my charms for those who're truly interesting. And you, my *friend,* are far from worthy of that accolade." The corners of Casimir's eyes twitched, and he glanced at her so briefly that she wasn't sure if he had actually looked at her at all behind his visor.

Bode didn't miss the movement, however, whatever it truly was. The lens in his biotechnological eye whirled, focusing in on Casimir with such an intensity that Olline was eighty percent sure he had x-ray capabilities.

His real eye—a rich, deep brown a shade darker than his skin—settled on Olline. Bode's thin lips curved into a mean smile that had her wanting to shrink in on herself. "Is this the one?"

Ice pumped through her veins at his words. Olline didn't know how it was possible, but Casimir stilled even further. Fear tickled her nerves, and she reflexively reached out around her for the natural materials she could use should her magic require it.

The one? Was Casimir sent to get her? Or was he out on assignment when she disrupted his chip? That would make Bode one of Etzel's thralls. The implications made her tremble, an action not missed by Bode's electronic eye.

Casimir scoffed. "Don't be so dramatic. 'The one'? You know better than anyone that there is no *one* for me. That's not the game, Bode."

Bode raised a bushy black eyebrow, and his smile turned . . . charming? "Then I suppose you won't mind me cutting in then, old *friend.*"

Olline blinked rapidly, certain it was a trick of the light but nope. Bode's smile was so completely pleasant, it even created a little dimple in his cheek. Olline would have been completely taken with such an attractive grin if she hadn't seen the vicious sneer.

Casimir shot her a quick glance. The opacity on his visor was clear now, though it didn't help in her deciphering his look. His throat bobbed, and he grumbled, "Bode, don't. Not here. She's not part of that old bet. You know I already have you beat in the charm category. So why not let it go, hmm?"

Bode laughed, taking another step forward playing a game Olline didn't know the rules to. Casimir leaned back on the bench and put his arm behind Olline's shoulders. The move could have been friendly, except the tension in his muscles made his arm as hard as granite. "Have it your way," Casimir said, his tone oddly light once again. "Olline, my dear, this here is Bode Collins. One of my *coworkers* I've told you so much about."

The emphasis was light and totally unnecessary. Olline may be confused by the dick-measuring contest they seemed to be waging, but she already knew *what* Bode was. She knew the danger that accompanied his sudden appearance, even if it was coincidental—especially for Casimir.

She tuned out the men's verbal barbs and let her eyes race over all his mods and what she knew of the control chips in him and Casimir. Which was still very little without access to the schematics. But she knew she had to stop this man from getting close, or *closer* rather. If Bode hadn't already alerted Etzel that something was amiss, if he hadn't actually been sent here to seize Casimir, then Olline had to make sure he didn't report back to the Under Senator.

Casimir looked like he would happily murder the man. Even if they hadn't been in a very public thoroughfare, Olline didn't want blood on her conscience, let alone Casimir's. But Bode had so much tech on him, and she had brought so little of hers . . .

She couldn't keep her eyes from widening slightly as an idea struck her.

Thankfully, Bode was squinting at Casimir, as if trying to sus out what was different about him, perhaps wondering why their game wasn't playing out like normal. She used the momentary distraction to let her fingers slide along her wrist-comm and attach it to the small holo-tablet and drive she had smuggled out of the sub-basement. By memory alone, she pulled up her decryption codes and the killware she was working on to shut the chips down once it was safe. It was nowhere near done; she didn't even know if it would work—she hadn't spent as much time on it as she had her cloning software.

Now is as good a time to test it as any.

Bode was swaying back on his heels, frowning at Casimir. Shit, she hadn't heard a word they said to each other. Had one of them asked her a question? Whoops. At least Casimir would forgive her lapse in focus once she saved him. She kind of liked this white knight stuff. Outside of the ever-present threat of enslavement and death, that was.

Casimir's muscles went taut as a metal wire pulled too tight, ready to snap. Olline saw the flash of something silver at Casimir's side, the same glint of silver she remembered seeing when he first found her after work. She knew what that glint meant, even if she didn't know what it was. Her heart raced as fast as her fingers as she sprinted through the wireless networks in their immediate area, looking for anomalies, made infinitely harder by trying to be both subtle and systematic.

Olline needed more time. There were too many networks! Too many people leeching from network to network, hiding their own activities all piled on top and below each other as Antal stretched down and above them. There were too many to go through, too many to narrow down, to make sure she didn't waste her one shot.

"Something's changed with you, Casimir." Bode scrutinized him more intensely. When, without warning, he gave a sharp inhalation and jerked back. "What've you done?" Bode growled, and Casimir leaned slightly forward. Olline saw the flash of silver again as he palmed a blade in preparation.

Holy shit, this was going to end in murder in the middle of the walkway.

She couldn't even use her magic to stop it without making the scene even worse. People got weird when there was a crime involving a caster. Their fear wasn't unwarranted, but it was going to make the scene far more memorable than a simple brawl turned murder, as twisted as that was. Olline swallowed, but the distress wasn't for her safety. It was for what would happen to Casimir if this played out to its inevitable end.

Her wrist-comm pinged.

Bode swung his head toward her, as if he could sense she was bearing down on his internal schematics. Olline wasted no more time and sent a silent prayer that this would work. She pushed her decryption and killware toward Bode.

The man froze, his body going stiff as his electronics and biomagitech cyber devices fizzled. His fingers splayed wide, his jaw clenched as he gritted his teeth, and his mechanical eye rolled uncontrollably in his head. It was painful to watch, and for a heartbeat, Olline thought she had killed him. A moment later, Bode's body relaxed, his vitals stabilized, and his head lolled to his chest, even as he remained standing.

Casimir moved fast and deathly quiet as he got up and placed Bode on the bench instead. Olline scooted away from the man, her eyes wide as disbelief over what she had done washed over her.

"Explain what you did, Tav. I need to know if Bode sent anything back to Etzel," Casimir hissed, tilting his head as if he were listening for security bots and drones to descend on them at any second.

Olline shook her head, pushing down her panic to latch on to the facts, the logic of what she had done. "I isolated the signal that connected all his," she floundered for the correct term, "cyber-enhancements. I told it to go back to factory settings. His memory will be wiped in the process. I hope. Maybe." She frowned, looking at Bode, who looked like he was sleeping. "I don't know! I panicked. I may have wiped everything about him with how much hardware and software he was packing, but there definitely weren't any outgoing messages in his queue when I shut it–*him* down." She was hyperventilating, the weight of her potential consequences sitting on her chest and making it hard to get enough oxygen into her lungs. "Oh, fuck! What if I made him a vegetable?"

Casimir knelt in front of her, taking her clammy hands in his own. "You haven't. Bode has survived worse, Olline, we both have," he whispered. "I know that from experience." His thumbs brushed over her knuckles, and instead of the thrill the action would normally give her, all she felt was a dull numbness.

"You did what you had to," Casimir continued. His words washed over her, but barely reached her. "If he'd figured out what had happened to me, what we were doing, he'd have had no choice but to tell Etzel. Bode wouldn't have even been thanked for the information. Worse would have been waiting for both of us when we returned." When she still couldn't tear her gaze from Bode's unconscious form, he gave her hands a gentle squeeze, moving his face so it was directly in her line of sight. "You saved me again, Ollie. Thank you. You really are making quite the habit of it, you know. I'm going to have to start repaying the favor." His voice had a kind of purr to it that finally focused Olline's gaze, bringing her back to the present.

"In fact, let me start now," Casimir said, pulling her to her feet. When she didn't move, Casimir huffed and lifted her arm so he could access her wrist-communicator. "I'll get Bode help, all right? I'll use your wrist-comm," he explained slowly, giving her time to process, "to anonymously summon biomagitech disaster services. They'll be best equipped to help Bode, and there'll be no chance for Etzel to trace it back to me if we use your device." Olline watched him do exactly as he promised, and while the vice in her heart released slightly, she still couldn't bring herself to move.

"Come, my precious little caster," Casimir said, giving her a gentle tug that finally propelled her into motion. "We've only moments before others catch on to what happened here and realize our dear friend Bode isn't, in fact, having a midafternoon nap. Let's make the most of our escape, hmm?"

CHAPTER 16

Olline was positive Casimir's chip was still offline. She felt no trace of it when she shut Bode down. Casimir couldn't say for sure if Bode had found them completely by accident. He was leaning toward coincidence, as Bode wasn't acting like he was on assignment. Which left only one other explanation for how Bode found Casimir to begin with: there was something in his apartment that alerted Etzel to Casimir doing something unscripted.

If their plan was going to succeed, Olline needed to dismantle whatever tracking device may be hidden in Casimir's home. Never mind that Casimir had already told her his place was most likely being watched, so it wasn't safe for her to be seen there. Forget the possibility that it was Olline who tripped something, who Etzel had sent Bode to find. Those were details Olline was trying to pretend were small and didn't matter as much as they most certainly did.

Olline's stomach was already churning. Any more anxiety and she was liable to puke. So, ignoring certain things seemed like a great idea.

"Are you certain you don't need to get back to the sub-basement?" Casimir asked, looking at her askance, his hands clenched within his pockets.

They were idling on the sidewalk a safe distance from where Bode remained on the bench. Olline refused to move farther away until the emergency services team arrived to ensure no one took advantage of Bode while he was vulnerable. Even this high in the city, there were plenty of people who would scavenge tech right out of an unconscious body. So far, the steady stream of business attired people hadn't stopped. They were too focused on their own wrist-comms, or their gaze hazy as they watched something from an ocular implant, but guilt kept Olline rooted nearby.

Olline shrugged, tugging the strap of her satchel higher on her shoulder. "It doesn't really matter now. Either this thing with Bode was completely accidental, in which case, no, I don't need to get back to the Government Plaza. I never clocked out, remember? Or this thing with Bode wasn't random, which means the bigger threat is to *you*. Either way, this is the smart play."

She wasn't about to tell him how nervous and wary she was about this. Casimir would just do the nice thing and tell her to forget it, and his freedom. His life mattered too much to her to allow him to do that. Even after such a short time together, she found she enjoyed his company. Perhaps it was because she knew no one else, but she found she looked forward to his easy, dry sarcasm, even his effortless flirting. Especially the flirting, actually, despite her constant flushing.

Casimir was still frowning, trying not to glare in Bode's direction, but his body still tensed whenever someone got close to the man. She bumped his shoulder playfully to distract him. "What's the matter, Cas? You afraid to bring a lady to your home?"

He gave her another sideways glance, but this time amusement danced in his deep red eyes. "Quite the contrary, Tav. But I wanted your first visit to my humble abode to be a bit more *carnal* than this."

His words had Olline choking on the air in her lungs, coughing and sputtering at his side. Which made Casimir chuckle, watching her with a devilish smile on his face. Olline wasn't sure if he had simply been teasing, he enjoyed getting a rise out of her, but with how his eyes lingered on her lips . . . Her core turned to liquid and her cheeks blazed like a wildfire. She grappled for some witty retort, but couldn't think around the possibilities his words brought up in her mind. She was positive she would think of the perfect reply the next day, when it was too late to matter.

The biomagitech disaster services saved her. Their drones appeared almost out of nowhere to hover over Bode Collins. The few people glaring that this lone man was taking a whole bench to himself scattered as the drones zipped in. Yellow light washed over the inert Bode, scanning him as the drones established a perimeter, pushing those who craned their necks to see what was happening out of the way. A second later, the wailing sirens cut through the din of traffic and the pedestrians as the main response team arrived.

Casimir tilted his head, tracking the sound. When the blaring red lights became visible, bouncing off the glass and polished steel mega sky-towers surrounding them, he gently put his hand on the small of her back and turned her away. "Come, we can cut through here and save some time. I know all the shortcuts. Here's hoping none of my other *coworkers* decide to surprise us." He didn't bring up the whole carnal thing again, so Olline decided he was simply teasing her. It was better for her sanity to believe that, anyway.

He insisted on taking the automated pathways and high-speed elevators to get to where he dwelled, lower in Antal. There was less risk of getting stuck in a sky-cab where Etzel could override the robotic driver. The way Casimir was leading them was meandering—to better see if anyone else was following them—so it took what felt like forever to get anywhere in the city.

Antal pulsed with life everywhere they travelled. The dim mauve tones shifted to blue as they went higher, and a copper-green when they descended lower once again. The megalithic towers showed their age with cracked plexi-glass and rusty splotches that the cruel blare from the neon advertisements highlighted. No amount of work from a maintenance bot could repair some of the rust or the damage from centuries old gang wars. One day, developers would strip these buildings and replace them with new businesses and coffin-sized apartments void of personality. But for now, even in their disrepair, there was an almost cozy quality to them with how lived in they appeared, how they seemed to sag closer together for comfort.

Throughout their meandering flight, not once did Olline spy anyone who looked like they were following them. While she appreciated the tour, she was getting antsy and uncomfortable with the silence. It didn't seem to bother Casimir, though.

Perhaps the thing Olline was uncomfortable with wasn't the silence, but her own growing attachment to a man who seemed to know more about her than she did about him.

"Can I ask you something?" She skipped closer, making sure she was at Casimir's side so she could observe him better.

He smiled at her, dipping his head. "You're rather adorable when you're thinking of what you want to say. Ask away, Tav."

Her heart tripped over itself, and she tried to stop being moved by his compliments. He was so casual with them; he couldn't *really* mean them.

Focus, Olline.

"You said something about Bode. That he's endured worse? That you know he has based on experience?" She saw the slight stiffening of his shoulders and licked her lips, deciding to press on anyway. "What did you mean? Was that how you got . . . captured by Etzel?"

His stride slowed, but then Casimir seemed to catch himself and picked up the pace again, his expression shifting into that all too familiar granite mask. "I suppose it's only fair for you to know the whole story, since you're trying to ensure my freedom." He shrugged like it didn't bother him, but the muscles in his neck and jaw were tense, making his words slightly clipped.

Casimir eyed the people around them for a moment before turning down a sloping alley between businesses, thick with the smell of soggy refuse. "For any of this to make sense, you have to understand that I idolized Kullen. He took care of me when we had no one else. He was my flawless big brother. I'd have continued to follow him blindly if he hadn't sold me to Etzel."

Olline couldn't suppress a gasp of horror. Her chest tightened, her heart squeezed too tight, and her gut fell through her. She couldn't imagine someone selling another person, let alone your very own brother. She'd had her own issues with her brothers. Their family was a complicated one given she was their humani half-sister, but even in those darkest moments when she was still a child, she would never even think that they might do something so unforgivable.

Casimir shifted, as if uncomfortable with her horrified reaction, and quickly pressed on as if he didn't want her to apologize on his brother's behalf. "In order to rectify his own mistakes surrounding his . . . vices, my brother made a deal." He sighed heavily, turning her down another narrow walkway next to a service road, this one managing to smell even worse. "Kullen loved the pleasure club scene. The sex, booze, and debauchery of it all. He had no business sense. But I did. We made a good team in that regard. Then Kullen let his taste for narcotics get the best of him."

Olline sucked in a breath, ready to tell him how awful addiction was, because it was, when Casimir shot her another sidelong glance, and snorted. "Oh, I didn't care what he consumed. Narcotics shouldn't be illegal. Regulated, yes. But illegal? All it does is ensure that recreational drugs remain unsafe. It doesn't, and won't, stop their production." He shrugged off her scowl, then shook his head. "But I digress."

He was silent, which worked well for Olline because she really couldn't think as she hopped over one questionable oily puddle after another. Once they left the alley behind, Casimir found his voice again. "His penchant for drugs, he took too many for me to remember them all now, got the best of him. He was caught in several *compromising* positions with men and women who shouldn't have been in his clubs. I had cleaned up his messes before. I didn't mind doing it even though I told him time and again his vices would be the death of him. Of us. But I'd no idea that he resented me the way he did."

They walked down a cracked and uneven side-walk giving the few people huddled on the street a wide-berth. Soon enough, Casimir stopped and squinted up at the decrepit, mega sky-tower in front of them. The building was dull with age, several windows were broken, or replaced with flimsy tarps. Rusty oily stains trailed down the side of the building. The longer Casimir peered up at the complex, the more Olline worried he would change his mind about sharing his story with her. But with another little shake of his head, he waved for her to follow him.

"I didn't know that Kullen begrudged the fact that it was *me* that made our club enterprises as successful as they were. If I'd known his jealousy had begun to fester. . ." He sighed, pushed open the grimy door to the complex, and ushered her inside. "It doesn't matter now. Kullen got himself entangled in another mess. But instead of going to me, he turned to the Under Senator who'd given us our latest business license."

Casimir trailed off, his gaze going distant, lost in a memory. He moved on autopilot, leading Olline through the shabby lobby marked by unidentifiable stains and the stale smell of smoke. Olline's skin crawled like little bugs were all over her with how filthy everything around them was.

He summoned the elevator, his eyes blankly settling on his reflection. She reached out and gently put her hand on this taut shoulder blade. She wanted to make sure he knew he wasn't alone, not anymore. With a slight shudder, Casimir came back to himself. He didn't shake her hand off. In fact, he seemed to lean into it ever so slightly, and her heart clenched.

"I never learned the details of their deal. Etzel never cared to tell me. At first, it was too heartbreaking to ask, and now, well, it hardly matters. I can see the results clearly enough without knowing how little my life was worth to my brother. Kullen operates our businesses with impunity now. And Etzel has—*had* me," Casimir said with a mirthless laugh, cut short by the elevator doors opening.

They stepped inside, and Olline was slightly comforted by the high floor number Casimir pressed. He wasn't buried in the toxic underground of the city-state, at least. "All I know is why I was such an attractive offer. Etzel *loves* to tell that story." Casimir couldn't hide the sneer in his voice as he glared at the elevator doors, staring at something she couldn't see. "Etzel had a million ideas for how to *utilize* someone with my looks, charm, and intuition for finding the right clientele for our businesses. It'd have been a nice boost to the ego if I hadn't been strapped naked, face down on a table with a surgical bot above me, poised and ready to install the control chip."

"Oh, Cas, I'm so sorry," Olline murmured. She couldn't stop herself. His voice wavered with so much repressed emotion that he tried so desperately to hide behind his nonchalance. He had been pretending, hiding, for so long that Olline didn't think he knew how to stop. She hated that his tenderness, his need to help his older brother, had backfired so cataclysmically that Casimir tried to bury that side of himself so thoroughly now. She looped her arm through his, at a loss for how else to comfort him.

His gaze whipped to hers, fury making his eyes flash like emergency lights, but then he seemed to remember it was *her* that held his arm and not someone else. "I don't need your pity, Olline," he said, words clipped as he jerked his arm free. "It is what it is. I managed to survive and I'll continue to do so, regardless." Olline winced, his words a sharp barb straight to her breastbone. Casimir cringed. He licked his lips, and watched the numbers blip by as they raced up the building, and Olline tried to ignore the chill spreading through her arm from where he had shaken her off. Worry prickled at her scalp. Had she messed everything up?

His face fell briefly, and he ran a hand through his silvery-white hair, dropping his gaze to the elevator floor, and mumbling, "I apologize. I didn't mean to be an ass. Not to you." Almost shyly, he took her hand. "I'm sorry." It wasn't until Olline gave him an encouraging squeeze that he relaxed again.

After a moment, he shrugged, still trying so hard to appear unbothered by what he was sharing, and Olline wished she could tell him it was okay to not be okay. But Casimir didn't seem to want to hear that, either. "Etzel primarily uses me for luring people involved with the business and government panels in charge of his campaigns—or in opposition to his plans—and get them into compromising positions. He records the blackmail, stores it on the server, probably the one you're digging through, and ensures that no one can oppose his power."

"When you say he uses you," Olline began, but trailed off while she searched for the right word.

"Oh, I mean that quite literally I'm afraid," Casimir said, forcing that same mirthless chuckle in an attempt to make light of the situation. "The chip allows him to use my body. When he's in control, I'm no better than a puppet. I have no idea what happens when he takes control anymore. I've gotten very good at disassociating, you see. I'm still left with the aftermath when Etzel's grip loosens. It gives me a good idea of what kind of evidence Etzel collects. Sometimes I awaken covered in blood, not always my own. Other times, I wake up covered in the aftermath of some orgy. Occasionally, I'll be standing in the operating room where I have led his next victim. I've been through the gamut. So, when I told you that I know Bode's endured worse, it's because we all have. Every single one of Etzel's thralls is used similarly."

Olline was speechless. At least when the elevator slowed to a stop, and Casimir led her out into a grim, grey hallway, it gave her an excuse to remain silent, to come to terms with everything he was saying. She couldn't in her wildest nightmares imagine someone so willingly collecting living, breathing, people and using them in such a way. And for what? So they could remain in political power? It was so . . . small, so unimportant, for what Etzel Straub was doing to people like Bode, like Casimir.

Mutely, she followed him down a narrow hallway, stopping in front of what she assumed was his apartment door. "The thing that's kept me sane the century I've been his slave," Casimir said, his voice barely above a whisper, "is the knowledge that it's not *me* doing these things Etzel forces my body to do. That each time I have to do something horrible, I get to use this." Casimir pulled out a mechanized stiletto. The long-bladed knife unfolded in his hand, flashing such a bright silver it looked made of liquid. With a tiny gasp, Olline realized this was the blade he had almost used on Bode, the one she had, most likely, felt pressed against her own skin.

He tucked it away quickly, still staring at his front door. "Kullen gave me this when we opened our second club. For protection, he said. I never got to use it for that. But I use it now when Etzel forces me to do violent things, as a way of transferring the blood on my hands to Kullen's instead." He hung his head, sighing. "I know that's not how that works, but it does let me sleep at night occasionally."

Olline's stomach was rolling, vines of bile crawling up her gorge, and her eyes stung with unshed tears. Casimir had been through so much, had survived everything that Etzel had forced him to do, and he seemed so . . . functional despite it all. Or perhaps it was in spite of what he had survived, the betrayal he had endured.

If Olline had been in Casimir's shoes, she would have turned into a crying blob on the floor decades ago, unable to function at all. Casimir made the choice every day to accept that he wasn't the one responsible for the reprehensible things he did and had done to him. It made her feel even more childish for having run all the way to Antal to get away from the mistakes of her misplaced loyalty.

"I'm going to free you. I'm going to help you get back to the man I know you are, the one who cares about people like me not getting caught up in stupid shit. I'm going to make sure no one uses you again, Cas." Olline's voice was steady despite the revulsion still coating her tongue. Casimir blinked slowly, mouth slightly slack, his posture slumping forward, heavy with disbelief. She didn't blame him. Hope would be a deadly thing for someone in his position.

"I'm impressive, remember?" Olline murmured. "Let me do more impressive things, and watch as I save you." She squeezed his hand, taking a step closer, wanting to cup his face in her palm and smooth away some of the sharpness.

"I'm going to save all the people Etzel's trapped. But," she said, frowning at the apartment door that Casimir had yet to open, "how come you haven't been able to go to anyone and tell them what Etzel was doing? With as many chips as he has, he can't monitor you all every minute of the day." Casimir narrowed his eyes, and she held up her free hand, adding quickly, "I'm not judging or blaming you! I need to know so I can get countermeasures in place for when we do pull the plug on everything. I need to know what Etzel does to keep you, and everyone like you, from alerting, well, anyone to what he's up to."

Casimir waved his key fob in front of his apartment, his locks and security system clicking, and his door opened a crack. He took a deep breath and said, "I don't know exactly what it is, but we've tried." He pushed open the door and entered, letting Olline follow in after him. "Something about our brain chemistry when we're about to alert someone literally shuts the thought down. It's similar to a thought you have, and the moment just before you can share it, you forget what you were about to say. After we've gone home or left the situation, the thought returns. By then it's too late. It reinforces the idea that we're powerless around Etzel, which I'm sure is by design," Casimir growled, flicking on the lights. "But the specifics of what or how that process is triggered, I haven't the faintest idea. I just know that since my chip stopped talking to his command center, I haven't had any such restrictions or lapses in memory. If it weren't for Etzel's hands on so much of the Department's inner workings, I'd have gone to the authorities properly, but with his control system still technically active," Casimir trailed off, waving his hand vaguely.

"I can work with that," she said, trying to sound more optimistic than she felt. "Because I meant it, you know. I'm going to free you. You won't ever be controlled like that again."

Casimir huffed out a sound that could have been a sob of relief, or a snort of disbelief. He didn't turn to look at Olline, so it was impossible to tell, especially when he deadpanned, "You're sweet to want to try."

Well, fine. He could doubt her if he wanted. She would take that much more joy in proving him wrong.

Olline was puzzling over what in the biomagitech chip could force such a response, when Casimir's apartment came into focus, the lights bathing the space in comforting periwinkle and azure. He had no windows, but a holo-projection screen that displayed a view of the city not dissimilar from her own. His apartment was a standard cramped little studio with barely any space to maneuver between the bed and minuscule kitchen island, and the small pathway to the bathroom. Even this small space that Etzel "gifted" Casimir, was another thing the Under Senator could rip away at a moment's notice. As she blinked at the surrounding space, she got the feeling she had been here before.

Then it hit her like a speeding sky-cab: Casimir outfitted his little apartment to look almost identical to the artist's haven he had taken her to the night before.

The barstools tucked under the kitchen island looked like

the bar they had sat at together, and the art on the wall were prints of performers that had been at the space. Even the lighting was the same. The biggest difference was the enormous bed taking up so much of the room that there was no space for much else besides one tiny bedside table, with nothing on it. Everything in the room had an oddly antique feel to it, something old and worn in, but looked new still. Despite not being given any kind of additional compensation for his work by Etzel, Casimir cared a great deal for his few comforts, if the bed and emulating the performance space were any indication.

Olline tried not to let her gaze linger on the bed with its plush, stone-grey comforter. Or the black silky sheets she saw peeking out from underneath.

She could feel Casimir's gaze on the back of her head as she took another step into the room. The intensity of his stare made her skin prickle. But she wasn't sure what to say, too torn with a desire to comfort and save him while being all too aware that they were sharing a small space with a massive bed between them. Because she was Olline, nervous laughter won out.

With a giggle that sounded shrill even to her own ears, Olline slipped her satchel off her shoulder. "Shouldn't take me long to clear you of any spying devices. There's only so many places someone can hide them in such a small space."

Casimir chuckled, and Olline flinched at how poorly her words came out. "I've had no complaints on the size, or what I can do given a few . . . inches."

Olline rolled her eyes, dismissing his flirtations as a way to move them past the horror he had shared with her. She cleared her throat and silently got to work. True to her word, it didn't take her long to clear Casimir's place for spyware. She only found one, and it was a simple motion sensor of sorts. She was able to subvert the signal with help from her earth caster abilities, ensuring the device appeared to be working, without accurately telling Etzel when Casimir came and went.

It didn't make sense that there was so little here with how Etzel controlled his people. Olline had expected even such a small apartment to be full to bursting with covert surveillance.

Olline bit her lower lip, turning to face Casimir, whose gaze locked instantly on her lip and the indents her teeth made. She sucked in a quick breath, but there was no denying the hunger that flashed in his eyes ever so briefly. She gave her head a little shake, focusing on the task at hand. The task, ironically, was safer territory than anything to do with that look.

"Is there another place you frequent where Etzel may be monitoring you?" She waved her hand at where the bug was, which she put back so nothing would be out of place. "Hard to believe that's the only external method he uses for watching you."

Casimir leaned against the wall closest to his door, idly watching her as he thought. After another moment, his eyes widened and his coy smirk returned in force. Leaning toward where she was sitting on his bed, he said, "There's one place.

I haven't visited since the chip stopped working. Perhaps my absence triggered something? It's where Etzel has me keep an office, for lack of a better word. I'll take you, but first," he said, beckoning her forward, "you'll have to go home and change. You can't go where I'll be taking you dressed like that, my dear."

CHAPTER 17

Olline had two hours to "wear something scandalous," as Casimir put it. He put a lot of faith into assuming she had something that would fit that criterion.

She finished putting the final touches on her lips, a metallic deep purple lipstick with bronzed gloss that would keep it from fading or getting on her teeth. It matched her eyeshadow, minus the smoky fade she added that made her bright, emerald-green eyes sparkle like gemstones. Even Olline found herself mesmerized by the effect, even though she had long ago become accustomed to the uncomfortably bright hue of her eyes.

While Olline was tucking the last pieces of her hair into the twin buns on either side of her head, twisting the deep, mossy green locks so they weren't completely lost in her ebony hair, she heard the buzzer at her door go off. She glanced at the guest's name and immediately granted him access to her floor.

Her heartrate ticked up even as she forced herself to act

calm. Forced herself to *walk, dammit,* as she grabbed a thick gold chain adorned with a large gold ring on her way to meet Casimir at the door. The necklace wasn't just a pretty bauble; part of her time while digging through her clothes had been spent using her magic to hide her scanning equipment within the necklace. The necklace wasn't subtle, but it was smaller than most of the accessories that were in fashion. Olline had taken pains to be sure it would not rouse suspicion.

Olline snapped it around her neck and opened the door without looking.

Casimir was leaning against the door frame, effortlessly breathtaking as always.

He had kept his form-fitting black pants but had traded his shirt for a sheer black top. The material was like nothing Olline had seen before. It shimmered like silk but had thick veins, akin to marbling, curving throughout, hugging every line of his muscles: his pectorals, his abs, and hard V-shaped line that disappeared at his belt line that Olline couldn't look at too long without her gaze drifting lower. Over the shirt was a chain that reminded Olline of a spider with long spindly legs with how the multiple chains wrapped around his body. The material of the metal was enhanced to give it the appearance of liquid silver.

Olline wanted to tangle her fingers in the chain, pull Casimir close, and let her fingers dance over the defined lines of his muscles until he was weak in the knees. The same way she felt when his quick, easy smiles were aimed at her and her alone.

The fantasy was easy to build on, but not in the lusty way she had first imagined. It was startling easy to picture what it would be like to be with Casimir. The playful teasing and the flirty barbs as he took her down to the coffee shop that used real beans. Her dragging him to all the greenhouse flower shops they could find, and Casimir pretending there were better places to visit but secretly relishing it all the same. Them cuddled up on a barstool watching a musician sing in one of his little artist havens. His attention never straying, always on her, even as he trailed his fingers up her thighs . . .

But was that how it would end?

When the excitement of freedom wore off, when their shared experience wasn't new, and all the places they visited became second nature, what then? A pang twisted her heart because when that happened, Olline couldn't imagine him sticking around, at least not in a way that had them sharing a bed. No, better the fantasy remained just that. If she never crossed that line, then at least they could stay friends and he wouldn't leave her life entirely.

With a sharp intake of breath, she realized she had been staring at him. But Casimir hadn't seemed to notice. His eyes weren't on her face at all. They were sliding along her body, his gaze like beads of ice water trickling over every inch of her.

Her body tingled under his attention like she wasn't wearing anything at all. To be fair, she did feel practically naked in the neon green micro-dress she wore. It was skin tight with a black and silver pattern along the front that sparkled like fish scales. She had gotten the dress for a holiday party she thought she would attend with Achan and then . . . never wore. If she so much as leaned forward, the outline of her ass would peek out, so she had put on a pair of sheer black stockings that went up to mid-thigh. It didn't help with the leaning aspect, but it helped her feel a little less exposed.

"Is this okay?" Olline asked hesitantly. "I wasn't sure what 'scandalous' meant in your context. I can put tights on underneath. Or I can put a nicer jacket over my usual crop top and jeans if that's more the vibe," she babbled, plucking at her necklace.

Casimir's eyes snapped up to hers. They were dark pools of blood with a primal twinkle that tightened her stomach. His chest was rising and falling quicker, and he licked his lips, taking a step toward her like he couldn't help himself, couldn't stop himself. Olline held her breath, wanting him to close the gap between them, to shut the door behind him and throw her on the bed, to mark every inch of her body with his lips and teeth.

Which was, wow, a really intense thought about someone who only recently got their autonomy back. About someone who would never under normal circumstances look at her twice.

And that's all Olline wanted it to be, too. Casimir was fun to be with. He was a good friend and she wouldn't risk losing that over some passing . . . *thing* between them. Truly!

Her eyes widened, and something about her expression—perhaps it was shock, fear, or disappointment, she really did not know what her face was doing—stopped Casimir in his tracks. He leaned inside the doorframe and that easy, casual smile returned as he met her gaze. "You're temptation incarnate, Tav." He took a deep breath, and said on the exhalation, "You're perfect."

His words left her feeling weightless, a leaf buoyed on the wind. Olline wasn't sure he meant what he said, or . . . but what if he did? What then?

Maybe that's not a bad thing? It would be less complicated than what happened with Achan.

She clenched her jaw. Achan was the last person she wanted to think about—ever again. Achan had never said such kind and romantic things to her, *ever*. The realization made her bold, far bolder than she had been so far. Instead, she returned Casimir's smile with a playful grin of her own.

Grabbing the clutch that held the rest of her equipment, she slid past Casimir. Her hips brushed his, a firestorm raging over her skin and tingling between her legs. She blamed that scorching heat on her sudden loss of inhibition, letting her fingers trail over that seductively smooth and chilly sheer material he was wearing, giving the spider chain the lightest tug. Olline couldn't help herself; she had been dying to know how it felt. It was probably a stupid idea, or she thought it was until she felt his breath hitch under the feather-light touch of her fingers.

Her brain refused to process that response, but her body . . . well, it was doing funny things to her. If she acknowledged how tight her nipples became or the sensitive tingle between her legs, she might die of embarrassment.

Without looking back, she said, "Come on, Cas. We've work to do."

"Welcome to Refractory, my dear."

Olline shouldn't have been surprised by where Casimir took her. It was one of the pleasure clubs that he had once co-owned with his brother. Kullen had long since taken full ownership, making it the perfect location for Etzel to plant Casimir in. Olline hadn't been to a pleasure club since she left grad school, and that had only been as the dry chaperone for her friend's birthday party. That experience had been blurred out with her trying to herd her friends away from one mistake after another, so her memory couldn't be trusted. This club was more . . . hedonistic than she was expecting—or prepared for.

She assumed the club, Refractory, was mainly designed by Kullen. Nothing about the space *felt* like Casimir.

There was no live music, just dueling synth-bots on either end of the cylindrical space. Refractory was all mirrored surfaces, so you could see everyone and everything, no matter where you were. Especially the dancers on their platforms that moved up and down, going from the ground floor to the top of the four-story club. Two of the three were women wearing some sort of thin, micro-bikini made of tiny lights that barely covered anything but had the effect of stars collecting at their most intimate places. They moved slowly in a sensual dance that was both captivating and mouthwatering.

The other dancer was a man, but he was wearing only metallic body paint from what Olline could see. His role seemed primarily to be taking different patrons on to the platform and transporting them up to the higher levels. The patrons didn't come back down with him. Which would have been ominous until she saw what the higher levels contained.

The main floor was rather traditional; people were simply dancing, even if some of them looked like they were doing more than that, despite the clothes. But the upper floors . . . Olline wasn't an exhibitionist, but watching the club goers being fucked so publicly and *so thoroughly* by pleasure workers and other patrons alike had her nipples hardening and her core turning to liquid all over again.

Casimir gently led her away from the entrance toward the bar where a steady flow of servers was coming and going. They wore leather from head to toe. Chains around their waists allowed for patrons to pull them close to make their orders, and not all requests were for liquor. It was obscene and yet . . . *And yet* Olline was hot as magma, the pressure between her legs begging for release.

Casimir ordered something for them from the bot-bartender, the only thing here not available for pleasure. Olline wasn't sure what he ordered, too absorbed in the surrounding people. "Tav," he whispered in her ear, his lips a breeze on her earlobe, "you're going to need to focus a little harder if you want to find whatever bugs Etzel has here to spy on me before he spies us."

Her breathlessness had nothing to do with the task she was here to do. She tilted her chin up—she told herself it was to hear him better, but it was a flimsy lie at best—exposing her neck as if in offering for him to kiss her instead. His gaze trailed over the curve of her neck, and his eyes glossed over briefly before he blinked the look away.

He handed her a crystal glass with amber liquid instead and stared intently at the bot-bartender. But she had seen him look at her, and it had to mean something, didn't it? She twisted the glass, letting the liquid catch the light. "If you want me to work, you probably shouldn't be plying me with alcohol," Olline said, desperate to say something, anything, but having to almost shout to be heard over the thumping music.

His thigh brushed against her, and she could practically feel him rumble with a chuckle. "If we aren't going to dance or fuck, Tav, we have to drink. Can't look too conspicuous, after all."

She nearly spit out the tiny sip she had dared to take.

Olline refused to let herself think too long on his words, lest she get lost in the fantasy again. Because the fantasy wasn't just sex anymore. Granted, *a lot* was, and she wasn't exactly proud of that, knowing what she did. But, well, Casimir had this effect on her and she was tired of pretending he didn't because her body liked to betray her at every turn. Which was rude, but she wasn't entirely mad about it. The whole thing was confusing. But his words, the way he stared at her, the way he listened to everything she said. How could she not fantasize about this, whatever *this* was, of becoming more? Maybe it didn't have to end when the job was done?

And maybe, just maybe, it would work and continue to work long after the shine of a new relationship wore off. Once they finished freeing the people enslaved by Etzel Straub, of course.

Priorities.

Something in her chest suspiciously close to her heart shifted, and she found herself smiling at nothing. She shook her head and, looking anywhere other than Casimir, she brushed her fingers over her necklace, turning the scanner on. The necklace would pulse as it searched for any signals that linked to the offline control chip in Casimir's spinal column, intensifying the pulse as she got closer to wherever the surveillance equipment was hidden. It took her device a moment to orient itself, to weed through the various signals from cybernetic biotech clogging the local data streams, before honing in on a familiar frequency.

The pulse was faint from where they stood. The main device hid somewhere near the top of the club and to their left. Because, of course, it would be on the more salacious levels if its purpose was to catch Casimir leading a target into a compromising position.

Olline turned in the correct direction and, taking another sip of her drink, flicked her eyes meaningfully in the direction they needed to go. Casimir followed her gaze and, with a deft nod, led her away from the bar and through the undulating horde.

Hands reached for her through the crowd. There were too many bodies for her to see who was grabbing her, who was trying to tempt her into a dance before taking her upstairs. But before their hands could connect with bare skin, before they could pull her into the crowd to be swallowed by the collective desire of the patrons that made her skin feel too tight and her pussy throb, Casimir intervened.

He captured her hand and pulled her away, his face set in a hard sneer for anyone who tried to pull her deeper into the mass. He pulled her against him and she felt the rumble of his chest as the man practically growled at everyone around them. His hands fell on her hips, his fingers digging in slightly with an unspoken claim to her that kept others away. It shouldn't have been as hot as it was. Shouldn't have made her want to run her hands over her own skin to get some relief. It definitely shouldn't have made her want to turn around and kiss the hollow of his collarbone until he stripped her naked.

Olline was light-headed, her blood scorching where his fingers pressed into her hips. Yet she still followed the pulse from the tech in her necklace as it grew stronger as they headed for Refractory's top floor.

The higher they went, the more sensuous the club became. They never stopped for long, though, and Olline only caught flashes of each floor. Some had people tied in elaborate silken binds to be teased by anyone willing, unable to respond to the pleasure. Other sections had vats of hot wax that people poured on exposed nipples, their cries of painful ecstasy not completely drowned out by the music.

Soon, the pulse in her necklace brought them to a mirrored panel. Olline would have missed it without the magitech device; just another panel of polished mirror in a sea of glass. Along the wall close to them were people in blindfolds being pleasured by men and women. Some wore masks, some didn't, but most used toys to tease their blindfolded partner, keeping them guessing what exquisite device was pleasuring them. Their moans blended until it sounded like a never-ending orgasm that had Olline so wet she was sure Casimir could see the moisture on her legs. She knew this was a natural response to have, given everything she was seeing, but still.

Olline gave her head a little shake, determined to *focus,* and opened her clutch to bring out the mini holo-tablet she'd brought, as well as a few magitech drive sticks in order to block and divert the signal like she did in Casimir's home. The wall of bodies around them swayed and moved, coming closer before pulling away a bit, but inching closer all the same. No one seemed to pay attention to them, but Olline didn't know what would happen should the mass of bodies reach them, and neither she nor Casimir participated in their anonymous orgy.

Casimir seemed to read her mind as he put his hands on either side of her, framing her between his powerful arms, barely a breath between their bodies. The heat was a tangible thing that had Olline wanting to arch into him and—

"I'll protect you, darling," Casimir said, his voice a husky promise that broke her train of thought. "But work fast."

"What?" she said, her voice a breathy gasp. "Why? Don't

you own this place?"

Casimir chuckled low in his throat that almost sounded like a growl. "Not for a long time. This place is technically Kullen's, but in actuality is a front for Etzel's blackmail schemes. Hence why he has me frequent the place." He shifted against her, shielding her, and Olline could barely contain herself from leaning into his embrace. "There are workers in the crowd." His breath tickled her ear, making her shiver. "They'll know we aren't participating and, well, we don't want that, now do we?"

Olline swallowed, fighting the urge to turn around and trail her lips along the sharp line of his jaw. Which was insane! All of this was crazy. Ugh, stupid, sexy club making her want to do stupid, sexy things to this stupid, sexy man . . .

Shutting her eyes, Olline took a deep breath and forced herself to focus. "Yeah, we definitely don't want that," she said, her voice smoky. She forced a chuckle, hoping to bury the desire in her tone.

But if the way Casimir's elegant fingers flexed against the mirrored wall was any sign, she wasn't fooling anyone.

Shit.

CHAPTER 18

The monitoring device hidden within Refractory was much more sophisticated than the one in Casimir's home. It wasn't surprising but, given the locale, Olline had hoped this would be a quicker job. Unable to plug any of her devices in, Olline chewed on her lower lip, tracing the mirrored panels with her fingers, trying to find some way to form a connection so the tech she brought could get to work. Finally, she felt a small indent, and pressing it revealed a tiny port with which she could covertly stick one of her magitech data sticks in. It wasn't much, but it would have to do.

The initial scan was not promising. Olline blew out a frustrated breath, glaring at the tiny holo-tablet hidden in her clutch and the tangled lines of code it showed her. She liked a challenge, but this . . . the security here was so advanced she almost considered it to be biotechnology. It avoided her hacking, as if it was alive. The complexity of the device wouldn't have normally been a problem, but all the people enjoying each other's bodies around Olline distracted her. And, of course, Casimir.

Maybe she could have ignored everything and everyone else. But she couldn't, and frankly didn't want to, ignore how he pressed against her, his tight pants leaving nothing to the imagination, less so with the pressure of his cock against her lower back. It was impossible not to be aroused by all the low moans and sighs of pleasure, but having Casimir so close at the same time . . . she was nearly undone.

"Tav," he whispered, voice tight. His cheek was nearly flush against hers as he leaned ever closer. "We've been noticed, and not in the way I'd like."

"How can you even tell?" she snapped back, more flustered than she meant. "Besides, what can they do to us, really, other than ask us to leave?"

"We're clothed, for one," he said, voice thick. "For another, we aren't doing anything nearly as fun as the rest of the people here. We stand out." He took a moment, as if composing himself, then added. "To protect the people who come to enjoy themselves anonymously, it's policy that the staff don't simply *ask* you to leave," he said like he was reading a script. "They're trained professionals, usually with some kind of biotechnology that will zap us until we're unconscious. They'll confiscate our devices to make sure we haven't recorded anything, and that's *before* they turn us over to the Police and Security Department. Which, in case you've forgotten, my precious little caster, is precisely the thing we're trying to avoid."

"You couldn't have told me this sooner?" Olline usually enjoyed Casimir's dry sarcasm, just not at the moment.

Her fingers couldn't move fast enough against the holo-tablet in a way that wasn't obvious. "I need more time," she said, her heart racing for less pleasurable reasons now. "The surveillance and tracking system he's installed is giving me issues. I have to use my magic on it." With a tug at the power in her molten core, her ethereal fingers slithered through the mirrored panel in front of her. Her magic was quick at isolating the chip within its copper encasing until each one of the device's metals shimmered in her mind's eye. Closing her eyelids, she extended tendrils like snaking vines into each of the components, allowing her to see exactly what each piece was made of and where it linked to.

"Time isn't our friend," he answered, bringing her attention out of her magic. Casimir's fingers flexed again on either side of her, his arms tensing until she could see the veins on his forearms through his sheer blouse. Her magic hummed around her, stalling as she lost focus. He took a deep breath, his chest brushing her back, the bulge between them more obvious now. "Do you trust me?"

If Olline reflected on how they met, the odd way he spoke when dealing with Bode, even the control chip—regardless that it was currently offline—Olline knew she *shouldn't* trust him. But, regardless of how infuriatingly unreliable it was, her gut told her she could. Even if that was insane and would only get her in trouble. Again.

But maybe not? If she wanted something beyond a casual fling, something the way Lochan suggested she deserved, then maybe Casimir was worth risking her heart for.

"Yes," the answer was a whisper, a prayer of hope, escaping her lips before she could think better of it.

"Good," he said with a sigh. "I can help us blend in. I won't do anything like what's happening around us. But I'll need to make it look convincing. I'm," his words cut off as he swallowed heavily behind her, his neck brushing the back of her head. "I haven't done this voluntarily in a while, let alone with someone I," he cleared his throat, cutting himself off. "It's hard to remain in the present," he added with a forced, nervous chuckle.

Her heart shriveled with anguish for Casimir. This must be so triggering for him . . . there had to be another way. She twisted around, the bulge in his pants pushing her micro-dress up an inch, and stopped him cold with a trembling hand to his chest. She risked the little time they probably didn't have, but this was too important. "This isn't about me," she said, drawing him close so he could hear her soft words. "I don't want you to feel like you have to perform, that you don't have a choice. You get to say no this time."

"I'm not saying no. Not to you," he replied so quickly that even he seemed surprised. But then his eyes darted away, and he frowned at someone slinking through the writhing crowd, their trajectory leading them to only one place: where they huddled against the wall. Casimir's throat bobbed as he swallowed and slowly turned his attention back to her. "If you don't want this, Olline, we can figure something else out. We'll find another way. Just say the word and we'll slip away," he murmured, his hand moving like he would brush a loose strand of hair back, but stopping himself.

She hated that he stopped.

"Is there a way of coming back when the club is closed?" Olline asked, before gnawing on her lower lip, torn by what she really wanted.

He was silent for a moment, then, "Theoretically. But it'll take time to find a way back in."

"Time we don't have. Etzel will be done with his conference in a few days," Olline said the words he left unspoken and stared at the devices hidden around her.

His smile was as easy as it always was, but there was a gentleness to it that went against the way he held himself, tense and hovering above her, giving her space while still trying to make it appear like they belonged there. Belonged together. "This place has a way of making your body respond in ways you weren't prepared for. We can pretend what happens next is just a result of the sex in the air seeping into every inch of us. Or we can go. Whatever *you* want, Olline, is what we will do."

Pretend?

As quickly as her mind latched onto the word, she forced it away. She didn't really believe that. Not when it came to Casimir, not with how he was looking at her right now.

Olline shook her head. "No, we'll stay. We can't squander this chance to get you free. I just need a little more time, is all."

"You're a treasure, my dear," he said with such relief that Olline's head spun. "I promise to do my best to make it so you can still work. But this has to be convincing." He smiled, but his eyes were soft with a kind of longing, as he asked, "Ready?"

Olline nodded, and Casimir inhaled sharply, his nose running along the side of her neck, nipping her rose tattoo lightly with his teeth. "You're going to have to blindfold me in order to sell this, Tav. And then do your magic." He dropped a hand, releasing her from the cage of his arms, to drag a silky white blindfold between them.

"Shouldn't I be the one blindfolded?" Olline asked, her eyes flicking to the people around them.

"I'd love it if you were," he said, a husky growl in his voice, putting the blindfold in her hand. "But I'm assuming you wouldn't be able to work with one on. I, on the other hand, am perfectly capable of selling this ruse quite convincingly, without having to see everything I'm doing to you. A pity, really."

Olline licked her lips, her clit throbbing at his low, sensual words. Which was not conducive to what she needed to focus on. She needed to reclaim the power she left waiting for her in the system, and then chase down each component used to make up the surveillance network. Which meant hunting through all the wires and isolating all the signals in a way that she could divert to her other magitech data sticks. By doing that, she could ensure Etzel would never know she disabled the devices. If she was successful in dismantling and diverting the magitech spy devices, the Under Senator would believe Casimir was back at work per usual, that he was still one of his thralls.

His eyes dropped to her mouth and stayed there, his breathing slowed, and she saw a little hitch in his chest, and heard a quiet gasp. She reached up, her hands brushing his long ears, the silky feel of his hair tickling her fingers. A low sigh of pleasure escaped his lips as she secured the white piece of fabric firmly over his eyes—eyes as bright as embers burning with lust before they were covered completely.

She took a quick, sharp breath and turned around. Funny how easily Casimir made her forget she had a job to do, that his very life depended on her success.

Reclaiming the magic coiled around the copper wires, she closed her eyes. The glow of the surveillance network flashed behind her eyelids, and she used the very metals in the wall to alter the pathways within each wire as she went back to spoofing the network monitoring Casimir. If she didn't have to occasionally check the holo-tablet in her handbag to ensure the functionality of the electronics in the wall and that no alarm had been set off, she could have easily done this blindfolded. With her eyes closed and so engrossed *in* her magic, the swaying bodies around her disappeared entirely.

But she felt *everything*. Casimir's hands floated down from where they were on either side of her face. A feather-light touch of his fingertips brushed along the sides of her neck.

His movements were agonizingly slow, barely brushing her flushed skin, like he was memorizing the feel of her, every dip and contour of her soft body. Olline found her ethereal fingers mirroring his movements through the circuit pathways. Her power skimmed over the components she was stalking, almost languid. Her magic twisted and curled, perfectly in sync with Casimir's caresses. Which slowed her pace significantly, but it was hard not to be swept up in his touch.

Casimir's graceful fingers fluttered down her shoulders, dancing along the bare skin. The soft touches had her skin burning so hot his fingers were like drops of ice water that had her gasping for breath. Her stomach tightened with want. His lips followed his delicate caress. Just the merest brush of that plush lower lip and she nearly dropped the clutch concealing her holo-tablet so she could grab him and press her lips to his.

Through a herculean force of will, Olline kept spoofing the network. The tendrils of her power played a game of chicken with the security software that was trying to catch her at the same time. For each pathway that blinked out in her mind's eye, a new one was diverted toward her. She thought she was making good progress, mostly by ignoring the way her nipples ached as they pressed against her dress and the wetness that coated her inner thighs as a pulse throbbed in her pussy in time with her thundering heartbeat.

Until Casimir's hands drifted along the outer curve of her breasts.

Olline shivered, and it was like all her clothes had disappeared. The glow behind her eyelids that showed the zigzagged pathways bent and became curvy until the outline of her naked body shimmered before her and her ghostly skin sparkled from the circuit pathways. Her magic latched on to her desire, and now she was the network, and her magic transformed into Casimir's fingers as they hunted across the pathways to make sure nothing was missed.

Casimir's touches were so, *so* soft, almost reverent and worshipful like she was a treasure to behold. Her power pulsed, showing her the exact path he took across her skin. His touch tingled through the fabric of her dress each time she successfully avoided detection within the network. A reward for doing her job that had her arching into him, straining in a way that begged him to touch more, to cup her breasts and make her scream his name. Olline was getting too swept up in her own magic, fueled too much by the desire that had leached into every molecule of Refractory. She leaned back, using one hand to cup the back of Casimir's head and pull him closer.

She shouldn't have done that.

Because Casimir didn't pull back, didn't shake her hand off. He didn't reject her at all. It was the opposite, really.

Uh oh.

Now she knew how impossibly thick and silky those soft, silver-white waves were. Now she no longer had to wonder what his hair felt like slipping through her fingers, didn't have to imagine the response he would give her if she tangled her fingers in those locks and pulled him down, directing that wicked mouth to kiss her senseless. Because now she knew and she could never forget.

Casimir responded eagerly. Her magic flared, a white-hot glow behind her eyelids as she struggled to keep control of the power and her desire at the same time. She pulled him closer, feeling his chest vibrate against her back as he groaned—before he growled and pulled back a fraction. He whispered so quietly that she wondered if his words were meant for her at all: "Not like this. Not here."

Or she thought that was what he said.

She didn't have time to question. His hands began moving again, this time down to her waist where they curved, framing her lower stomach and pressing her back into his hard body. He walked them forward, his erection pulling up her micro-dress, getting them closer to the panel again, a subtle reminder to them both that this fondling business was a cover for their real mission.

It was *such* a bummer. But a bummer that let her reclaim focus and start the transfer like she had done in Casimir's apartment.

Casimir nuzzled the side of her head so he had better access to the hollow behind her ear and the sensitive skin of her neck. His teeth found her earlobe, teasing the skin on the right side of pain, and Olline sucked in a breath.

"Darling," he murmured in her ear, "we're still being watched." How he could possibly know that she couldn't tell and she squirmed for another reason entirely. "No, no. Don't look. The fact that we are still very much clothed is a hindrance. If I . . . do *more,* will you still be able to concentrate?"

Fat-fucking-chance, she thought, even though that was the wrong thing to say. She *really* didn't want him to stop touching her. The bigger issue was that if she wasn't careful, someone would notice her hacking, which would be worse than a suspicious worker inching closer and closer to them.

Olline loved a good challenge, but this was decidedly *not* it.

"Do what you have to. Just give me more time," she said, her voice so breathy she was surprised he heard her at all.

Casimir stilled behind her for two heartbeats, then asked again, "You trust me?"

Normally, having to answer the same question multiple times would annoy her, but with Casimir, knowing what she did, she found him seeking that reassurance endearing. Sweet, even. Though she didn't think he would appreciate her saying so.

"I do," she said, her voice firmer. "Of course, I do."

"You're a gift," he said, before dragging one hand up her torso, snaking between her breasts to lightly grasp her throat, a tender echo of his rough treatment when they first met. Even with the firmness of his grip, Olline never felt forced or scared. The intimate possessiveness had her pressing her body back against his, giving him access to more of her. Whatever he wanted, whatever he could handle. She perfectly nestled against him, feeling his own desire so long and hard between them. His lips moved from her ear to her neck, his kisses sharp, his teeth nipping the skin, his tongue poking out and tracing the sensitive curve of her neck, as if he were trying to outline her rose tattoo from memory. As if he wanted to do more than merely taste her.

Olline bit her lip, hard. Hard enough for the faint taste of iron to fill her mouth. She needed to keep some semblance of control, of focus. She put her hands against the mirrored panel as if willing herself to feel what was beneath rather than the places on her body Casimir traced.

While Casimir's lips continued to tease her neck, his hand still firm around her throat, his other hand moved from her stomach. Sliding down until those graceful, strong fingers found the hem of her dress. He began moving then, rolling his hips, pressing firmly into her in time with the music. The tips of his fingers brushed the sensitive skin of her thighs, exposed beneath her dress. Her hands clenched against the wall. The sparks of the magic behind her eyelids showed her where he was touching again. Her ethereal body glowed brightest in the places she wanted him to touch, where she wanted him to slide his fingers into.

Olline held her breath, wondering if he would do more, kind of sort of hoping he would, but too shy to ask for it. Especially when she was actually trying to save him at the moment.

His hands stayed where they were. One holding her chin, elongating her neck and giving him access to where the curve of her neck met her shoulder, his sharp teeth nipping until she was practically vibrating with desire. His other toyed with the hem of her micro-dress, his fingers dancing up and down, and slightly between her thighs at random intervals. She wondered if his little shivers meant his fingers trailed closer to her aching clit when he could no longer contain himself.

All Olline knew was *she* couldn't contain herself. As her

magic latched on to the decryption code, she flicked from her holo-tablet hidden in the clutch at her side to the system behind the panel. Her magic showed her what Casimir finger fucking her would look like. Each time she envisioned his fingers sliding into her wet pussy, her magic diverted another attempt at the security system to stop her. So, she had her magic move faster and faster. All the while her flesh prickled where Casimir's fingers trailed across her skin.

She rubbed her thighs together, clenching them closed, desperate for the release of orgasm—

Then the mirrored panel flickered slightly, like there was a light behind it, before stabilizing. There was a nearly imperceptible vibration that Olline hadn't even noticed until she disabled and rerouted the surveillance and monitoring system. She blew out a breath of relief, releasing her magic at the same time before she did anything she would regret. At least now Etzel could not monitor Casimir from the Refractory.

For as much as she enjoyed his attention, this wasn't the way she wanted to enjoy him. She didn't want any pretense about what they were doing, no pheromones to cloud their judgment, no public sex acts from others to make their bodies respond. If she was to ever have Casimir, she wanted it to be for real, not like . . . this.

Slowly, Olline turned around and gently undid his blindfold, letting it fall to the floor between them.

For a moment Casimir looked at her, his eyes half-lidded in a type of relaxed bliss. Like he found harmony and ecstasy and was blinded by the sheer peace of it for the first time in his life. The lines around his mouth and eyes were soft, his expression unguarded. But in the blink of an eye, it was gone, and he was staring at her with concern.

She lightly tapped him on the nose, hoping it looked playful to fool the club worker, who she could feel staring at them from within the moaning crowd. "We're good," she whispered in his ear. "Etzel can't track you from here anymore. You're safe, and, even though it's weird, thank you for trusting me to handle, you know, all of this." She flinched slightly, her words not quite coming out the way she wanted, but she had meant them all the same.

Olline stepped back, and Casimir's face dropped slightly. Regret flitted through his gaze before he blinked, and it was gone. He was good at that; his emotions flickering by too fast before he shut them down completely. It was tragic, really.

He snaked his arm around her waist, and began leading her back out of the club as he murmured, "It was my pleasure, my precious little caster. *You* are my pleasure."

WHEN IN HIS EYES

Casimir had known, had *known* with piercing clarity that taking Olline to Refractory was a colossal mistake. Not because she couldn't find what Etzel used to keep track of him. No, Casimir had absolutely no illusions that his brilliant little caster would find and dismantle any device used for spying on his activities.

His?

That was where the first mistake lay.

The second mistake was opening his mouth and telling her to wear something scandalous when he knew full well he needed to be cautious with the flirting.

What had he truly thought would happen after telling Olline something like that? That she, a luminous humani, would then answer her door in something drab? Perhaps he had wanted her to surprise him in a way that made keeping his distance easier. It was wishful thinking on his part, something he hadn't been prone to in such a long time that he thought, well, that went without saying, didn't it? Because, of course, Olline wasn't going to answer the door in an oversized black plastic bag. She had answered her door in that incredible tiny dress which showed off her long rosy-bronze legs, the very ones that he wanted to spend the next decade memorizing. Keeping her from noticing the effect her mere appearance had on him was such a force of will, he thought he deserved an award.

The third mistake, and far, far from his last, lay in him simply not telling Olline where they were going and what she would see there.

He knew what the Refractory was, what went on there, but he hadn't told Olline any of that because he wanted to see . . . what exactly? What her reaction would be? What she would do around all that sex and debauchery? For that matter, what had he wanted her reaction to be?

Disgust, probably.

That would have made things easier. Would have certainly let him act the part without complication. Instead, Olline was so achingly *nice*. She was so clearly turned on, and so embarrassed about being turned on, and yet she went along with it all so she could unravel one more rope that kept him bound to Etzel.

Casimir knew he should be honest with her. He should honestly disclose every little thing he knew to her and bare what was left of his soul to this perky, perfect woman. But a century of torment kept him at a distance. A distance, he told himself, that was for their collective good.

Regret warred with longing until his limbs were concrete

blocks, weighing him down as he sat on the edge of his bed. He wasn't one to brood, not usually, but Olline had him thinking and feeling so many inconvenient things as of late.

Thinking of her now, hours after leaving Refractory, with the surveillance rerouted and a distant threat, brought the same heat and electricity snaking through his limbs all over again. He couldn't forget the feel of her soft, flushed skin, or how it trembled beneath his fingertips. Casimir couldn't ignore the yearning to taste the moisture between her legs like it was nectar from the stars. He couldn't pretend she hadn't shivered and arched into his touch, so pliant and trusting beneath hands that she knew had taken lives. Casimir couldn't disregard how she had allowed him to touch her to begin with.

Even now, he could feel her fingers tangle in his hair, pulling him closer until her musk of cucumber and mint made him drunk with need. Her little gasps made him want to drop to his knees and sink his teeth into those lush thighs of hers. He wished, like nothing he had ever wished for before, not even his own freedom, that he could have seen her divine face while he memorized the contour of her curves. That he could have seen what he was doing to her, that he could have tasted her lips after she had tasted him.

He wanted to kiss her senseless, make her cry for more, and beg for mercy, all in a single breath.

Casimir couldn't ignore Olline and the effect she had on him—and his cock. His erection was getting painful, but he refused the release because that would mean . . . That would mean . . . No. Best not to go down that road. For Olline's own good. Casimir had tried to have lovers and relationships after being chipped, and while Etzel hadn't made Casimir hurt any of his partners, the threat was always there. Knowing that Etzel knew who they all were, as intimately as Casimir did, all because of that fucking biomagitech device buried in his marrow, had poisoned all those relationships before they could fully begin.

But he also knew the truth now; of why he was at sub-basement thirteen, room two-hundred and twenty-three. He had no right to know the things he did about her. The weight of his own reality dragged him down. Yet Casimir couldn't predict what Olline would do or say if he fucking told her the truth. Better, safer maybe, for them both if he kept his mouth shut for once.

So, for Olline's own safety, he wouldn't, he couldn't . . . Not until he had the leash Etzel used to tether him firmly in his grasp. Olline wouldn't like him then, he knew, so it was best he kept to his original strategy.

Casimir merely needed time and distance so he could forget how perfectly she fit in his arms, how the curve of her back lined up so achingly *right* against his chest. He would distract himself with the task at hand, uphold his end of the plan to find someone they could rely on, if only so he could have a bit more time to get Olline to come around to his true plot for Etzel.

Casimir couldn't sleep, so he got to work searching for someone they could, well, not *trust* exactly. But someone who wouldn't want to benefit from Etzel's files, at the least.

Despite the late hour, he sent Olline wrist-comm messages to make sure she was all right. He received no answers to those, which he told himself was fine. They were pretending and all that nonsense. She was probably sleeping like a baby.

Then, the next day, his search bore fruit. Casimir checked the live feed from the biomagitech conference Etzel was attending, to make sure they still had the five days to work without his attention. Muscle memory had Casimir flinching when he caught sight of the seersha. He was speaking heatedly to a lobbyist, which Casimir took to mean things weren't going great and Etzel would not return soon. The fist around his chest unclenched and he pulled up his search results again to share with Olline.

He needed to talk to her because the sooner they got moving on this, the sooner he could get the fuck out of Antal. So, of course, he had to message her again.

Olline didn't respond.

He tried sending her a holo-call request even though he detested calling people. Still no response. It was now creeping close to two days since he had heard a peep from that friendly earth caster. Which was what he wanted, right? Distance? But the silence left his heart sluggish in his chest, his fingertips cold and tingly, with a weight on his sternum he couldn't banish with a hot shower or booze—and he had tried both.

Casimir tried getting her on a holo-call again. And again.

His heart started racing, a dizziness so profound he could barely stand. He paced his studio apartment with jerky movements, trying to calm himself, trying to be rational and think of the plethora of logical reasons Olline would answer none of his messages. She knew the time constraints they were under. If she wasn't answering, it was because there was nothing to worry about, no reason to rush into something. The safest option was that she was merely ignoring him, even though that option felt like someone stepped on his chest until it splintered like thin ice.

Casimir shouldn't care the way he did but, well, the thought that perhaps they hadn't escaped Refractory as smoothly as they first thought . . . "This is fucking ridiculous," he growled to himself. Olline's technical skill was the one thing in this awful world he didn't question. They were safe, they had gotten out clean.

He told himself that fact again and again. Yet, as the silence stretched past thirty-nine hours and forty-six minutes—Casimir hated he knew the precise minute he had last heard Olline's throaty voice—he stormed from his home.

He wasn't worried. He really wasn't. Still, it would be better for everyone if he verified Olline was safe and sound. She had to be. Because if she wasn't, Casimir was going to burn Antal to the fucking ground and bathe in its ashes.

CHAPTER 19

Olline was not avoiding Casimir. Nope, definitely not. She was just busy.

That was, mostly, not a lie actually, so that was a pleasant surprise.

With the last of the files in the transfer queue, she needed to assemble the new server. It didn't matter anymore, the new server, but pretenses were vital at this stage. Moreso after the plethora of threatening messages Karter had sent about her not logging out when she left, of falling dangerously behind on the quota system. The excuse of staying home and using her magic to make the hardware was the only thing that kept him from sending someone like Brayden to her home and dragging her back to the office. Regardless, she did like using her magic on hardware components, so it was win-win. Well, except if she were to walk away from all of this corruption, they would strip her wages, take away her home, and she would be jailed if she couldn't pay the bonus back, making her an easy target for Etzel to scoop up once again.

Minor details.

Olline's chest tightened with guilt about not going to the office. She would miss out on lunch with Briallea, but hopefully the woman would be forgiving. Of course, it was possible Briallea was part of Etzel's schemes, but she really hoped not.

Taking a deep breath, Olline sunk down to the floor of her living room to work. She needed to focus on the task at hand, and that meant pretending that everything was normal and fine. It was tricky, convincing the elements to do what *she* wanted, and not what nature made them. Moreso when she was drained from using her magic at Refractory, and distracted by the bleak reality of her and Casimir's situation. Which meant, Olline decided, that she could not see or speak to Casimir. She couldn't, not if she wanted to have any hope of doing her job. With all her communication devices switched to privacy mode, one holo-tablet set to the live conference feed to monitor Etzel in the background, she attempted to sink into a creative hole.

She had hoped that her focus would become sharper as time put a healthy distance between her and the . . . *act* Casimir had performed at Refractory. By the next afternoon, however, a whole thirty-six hours and some change later, her focus was no better, even if she had forgotten to switch her devices off privacy mode.

Olline could still feel the pressure of his hips, the phantom caresses of his hands and fingers, the sharp scrape of his teeth against her skin. If she let her mind wander, her day would be spent in bed, curled around the fantasy with her hand between her legs.

Whenever that urge hit, and it was embarrassingly often over that day and a half, she switched gears. If she couldn't avoid thinking of him, she might as well be practical about it. She set her mind and magic to working on a secret gift. When she would give it to him, she didn't know. That partially depended on when she finished with its creation (she was pretty much done, but she liked being *positive* about such things first), and partially on their circumstances. For now, it stayed hidden in her room where she could work on it in spurts of activity when her imagination and the memory of the club got to be too overwhelming.

Which was a totally normal reaction to have. And she would tell herself that, repeatedly, until she believed it. It wasn't working yet, but she was optimistic.

The jade and lime green philodendron and moss and emerald pothos around her apartment rustled as if rolling eyes they did not have. Olline glared at the verdant vines. "Hush," she snapped. "I refuse to be judged by things *I* created."

With the last of the passwords cracked, outside of Casimir's, Olline could start disabling the chips and move the files she had access to, to a safe location. But she didn't know what to do with those files once they had them all. Or, Olline didn't, more aptly. Casimir still brought up the possibility of using the documents for himself, in order to take Etzel's influence and use it for good. But that wasn't an *actual* option for Olline. She didn't want to risk transferring and spoofing the chips and their attached folders until they had that part of the plan established.

She needed to get her priorities straight, but she couldn't. Not when it came to Casimir. Much like her contract, Casimir seemed too good to be true. Yet that didn't stop her from wondering what would happen next. If there could be an *after* for them. Because, with a sinking clarity that had her body buzzing, Olline knew she wanted to be more than friends.

As she began connecting the wires for the new server, she went back to their first meeting. How he had been outside her office door not long after the chip had stopped receiving a signal. Then there was what Bode said, too. Something about it itched at the back of her mind, and she tried to remember exactly what he had said, and Casimir's response. Perhaps it was finally time to ask Casimir more about Bode. Without looking, Olline took her devices off privacy mode . . .

Buzz! Buzz!

She glanced at her wrist-comm, expecting it to be Casimir, but it wasn't, though she noted the alarmingly high number of missed calls and messages. It was her father trying to reach her. Olline winced. She never responded to him after she promised she would enjoy Antal and not spend all her time tied to her job.

Her stomach twisted into knots, guilt clawing at her ribs. Olline closed her eyes, took a deep breath, and answered.

Zachery Tavos's face winked into view, a hazy holo-projection over her wrist-communicator. He blinked, orienting himself with where to look. When his gaze settled on her, his usually solemn face split into a wide grin, making his grey-blue eyes twinkle.

"Olline, sweetheart! There you are! I was starting to worry. How is everything? Are you ready to come back home yet?" He meant it good-naturedly; a typical joke fathers were supposed to make when their last child left the nest. But there was a genuine kernel of hope humming through his tone that he couldn't completely mask.

Olline had to stifle a sigh before replying. "Everything's good, Dad. I'm good, Antal's great. I've only been here like a week. I'm still settling in."

Saying it out loud, Olline had to suppress a shiver. They had three full days left before Etzel returned to the Government Plaza. Three days for Olline to crack Casimir's file so she could finally see the blueprints of his old chip and could, theoretically, make it permanently inert, like her killware would do for the newer devices. It was possible they wouldn't even have that time, if Etzel got what he wanted from the other board members early. She didn't bother to mention any of that though, nor the details of her contract that made leaving and moving back home impossible, even if she had wanted to.

Even considering the danger, she didn't want to leave. If Olline was being perfectly honest with herself, Casimir was a big part of that desire to stay, but not the entirety of it. She had made Antal into a place where she put herself first for once, and she wasn't willing to sacrifice that. But she didn't think she could tell her father that, or about Casimir yet. Not when she was still trying to make sense of her own feelings.

"Well, then, I hope that means you've at least taken my advice," Zachery responded, unable to hide the slight huff in his voice. "I hope you've ventured beyond that posh apartment of yours and carved out more spare time for yourself. Time," he added quickly, "spent on something *besides* fiddling with your little plants."

This time, Olline did roll her eyes. "For the record," she said in the bored tone that had become a habit each time he made an offhand comment about her plants, "working on my plants is important to me. I enjoy it. It makes me feel good, Dad. We've been over this."

He waved her comment off and motioned for her to continue. She sighed, and carefully told him what she had done, what she had seen since the last time they spoke. She left out all mentions of Etzel to be on the safe side, and she absolutely did not mention a single word about the club she and Casimir went to almost two days ago.

She couldn't avoid telling her father a little about the mysterious seerani she met, though. Of the magical places he had taken her to that were safe to share with her father, at least. She found that the longer she spoke, the more she shared, the more she smiled, the more her skin tingled, imagining Casimir's arm around her waist.

She trailed off, lost in the memory of the artists' club Casimir had taken her to, the one that looked so much like his tiny apartment. Her father's low chuckle snapped her out of it. She blinked, slowly returning to the present, to see her father beaming back at her from the holo-projection.

"My little girl's found someone. You truly like this boy, don't you, Olline?" Zachery said, nothing but happiness in his words. "So, when do I get to meet him? And what's his name again?"

Olline's cheeks burned. She had purposely not told her father Casimir's name.

She rubbed the back of her neck, gnawing on her lip as she thought. With a shrug she said, "He found me, is more like. But I don't know if you'll ever meet him, Dad. Things are . . . complicated, I guess."

"Anything worthwhile is always a little complex, sweetheart," Zachery said, his tone just shy of patronizing. She narrowed her eyes, and his shoulders slumped in response. "I merely mean that you shouldn't question your heart when it comes to joy. I know from experience. My marriage with your brother's mother no longer brought joy, had turned toxic." Olline's eyes widened to hear her father talk so candidly about his first wife, but he waved her surprise away. "I've made that no secret, especially to your brothers. It helped explain the pleasure I found in your mother and my decision to remarry. I think, anyway. But my relationship with your mother was complicated. How could it not be? I was the humani father of two infant seerani boys whose biological mother would outlive us by centuries. But what your mother and I had was special. She was worth all the . . . complicated days and feelings we had over the next few decades of our lives together. Even with your mother gone and at peace now, I love her still. She's my joy."

Her father trailed off, staring into the distance before he gave himself a shake and came back to the present. He smiled at her a little sadly and shrugged. "My point, sweetheart, is this person has brought you happiness through these excursions. If he's found a way to connect to your soul through the things you enjoy most, then perhaps he's worth all the difficulties he comes with?"

Olline chuckled dryly. "That's a bit idealistic, Dad. And that's saying a lot coming from me. It removes the weight of those so-called difficulties, ignores all the baggage and what that heaviness could do to any potential future." She sighed, shaking her head. "It's a pretty idea, Dad. But that's all it is. It's a fantasy. Unfortunately for me, I'm stuck in reality."

Zachery frowned, his bushy brows pinching together, ready to argue, when there was a knock at Olline's door. An actual knock. Not a buzz on her wrist-comm or on one of her tablets asking to be let into the building. But someone outside of her door. *Right now.*

Olline's face went slack, her heart racing. "Olline?" Zachery asked, suddenly worried by her expression. "What's the matter?"

She didn't know. No one should have gotten to her front door without alerting her in some capacity first. So, whoever was there, whatever they wanted, it couldn't be good. But Olline also didn't want to worry her father.

"Nothing, Dad. It's nothing. I've got to go. Work stuff."

"Are you sure everything's all right?" Zachery pressed.

The mystery person knocked again. Olline shook her head

and forced a grin she prayed was enough to fool her father through the holo-projection. “Yup! All good. I’ll catch up with you later, Dad. Bye!” She disconnected before he could interrupt her again, before she had to lie to her father even more.

Olline stared at the door, hoping that maybe, just maybe, whoever was there got the wrong apartment and had learned their mistake by now and wandered off.

The knock came again, three loud taps, more insistent than before.

Trepidation coursed through her as she slowly got to her feet and padded toward the door, her magic prepped and humming beneath her skin. It had been over forty hours now since they left Refractory behind. Surely, if she had tripped some alarm, Etzel’s muscle would have come crashing down on her before now?

The purple passion plant by her door arched its jagged, spade shape leaves forward, the purple hairs hardening and ready to strike should Olline command it to. Swallowing the boulder in her throat, she flipped the opacity setting on her door, letting her see who was there without them seeing her in return. Her heart lurched into her throat, replacing the boulder, and her breath hitched in her chest.

Casimir was gripping her doorframe.

She disengaged the locks and threw her door open, staring at the seerani with wide eyes. “What? How?” Olline stuttered, quickly looking up and down the hallway, hoping no security drones or delivery bots noted Casimir. She grabbed his arm and pulled him inside. Kicking the door shut behind them, she prayed no one noticed the world-endingly attractive man hanging around outside her door, knocking of all the inane things. "Do you know how risky it is for you to be here? So soon after," she trailed off, her skin scorching in the places he touched not even two days ago.

Casimir brushed past her, prowling through her apartment, movements jerky like he was looking for something. He went to the kitchen, sniffed at the old coffee in her antique coffee-maker, shifted one of the many cups around, rotated the jars with her gem-colored succulents, huffing and mumbling all the while. Finding nothing, he stalked back to her and gripped her shoulders, searching her face as if making sure she was truly there. Her chest heaved, unable to breathe through her confusion and rising anxiety around his sudden appearance.

He tilted his head to the side, his gaze sliding from her face to settle on her plants—which quivered in response to her agitation. Casimir inhaled deeply, his hands flexing on her shoulders, gripping her tightly before letting his hands slide away. Her plants calmed, the leaves gently swaying, and it wasn't until everything settled down that Casimir diverted his attention away, rubbing his face with his trembling hands.

"Why weren't you answering my messages?" Casimir bit out, voice dark with quivering anger.

She flinched. "Sorry, I had everything in privacy mode so I could focus. But you didn't have to risk exposure coming here, Cas."

"I was careful. But I couldn't . . . I *had* to risk it to check on *you,*" he said, voice tremulous.

Her breath hitched a little. She had never seen Casimir this unsettled before and she didn't know what to do, or really understand it. She waved her hand at the devices on the floor. "Karter was acting suspicious, so I had to do work or else, well, it's fine now. I didn't mean to worry you." Olline brushed invisible dust off her clothes, hoping that would remove the warmth she felt from him worrying over her safety. Casimir's shoulders lowered as the tension bled away from him. Crisis averted; she narrowed her gaze at him. "How'd you even bypass the building's security?"

He walked away, his movements becoming more graceful as he went. The manic energy from before was gone by the time he got to her living room, where he plopped down on her couch. Casimir lounged with his arms spread along the back, his body angled as if inviting her to curl up in the crook of his arm, sprawled against him.

"You, my dear, put far too much faith in your front desk clerk. Really, one little smile, and the man probably would have gotten on his knees and sucked my cock if I'd asked. A few suggestive words and he let me come straight to you all on the sweet little lie that I wanted to surprise my darling Olline. Well, it wasn't a lie, but I wasn't going to clarify the specifics to *him,* now was I?"

Olline's heart fluttered, but she forced it to settle lest it trigger her magic and make the plants react once again. Besides, he hadn't really admitted to anything, just a sweet half-truth, like what he used to get up to her floor. Her eyebrows pinched together, her mouth set in a thoughtful line as she looked at him, still sprawled on her couch.

Olline refused to move closer. She refused to be the one to bring up all those gentle caresses, his erection against her back, the flirting and desire she saw that looked and felt too real to be part of a cover story. She figured that, if it truly meant more, he would say something.

She refused to acknowledge how badly she wanted him to say something.

He watched her in return for a moment before he sighed. "I did tell you that was one reason I was attractive to Etzel all those years ago, Olline. My *charm* has always been a part of me. But a century of using it for manipulating others . . . well, it's second nature now."

Olline's heart cracked a bit at that, and she lowered her arms. She took a step closer, but stopped. That itchy feeling in the back of her mind returned, wanting her attention, for her to focus on something, though she couldn't quite grasp exactly what. It was on the tip of her tongue—

"But, like I said, the reason I'm here right now," Casimir drawled, interrupting her train of thought, "is you weren't answering your wrist-comm. At best, you wished to avoid me, which would have crushed my ego but would be much preferable to one of Etzel's goons visiting you instead." His gaze became slightly pained again, softening the edges of his face. With a start, she realized it was *relief* she was seeing. It was only then she fully realized how worried not answering his messages had made him. Warmth was flooding his eyes even as he asked, "You are all right, aren't you?"

She felt the tension unwinding from her body. Olline moved to the couch, perched on the edge, and resisted the urge to lay against his side. She put her hand on his knee. Even through his clothes, the feel of his muscles was electric, and she wondered if he felt it too as he sat up straight and faced her.

"I'm fine, Cas. I didn't mean to worry you. I was just . . . busy." She glanced again at the hardware strewn about her living room table and hoped he didn't notice her hesitation.

His eyes flicked to the table briefly, a slight frown on his face. "I was worried I'd chased you away. That the other night was, well, it goes a bit without saying, doesn't it?"

"Oh, I don't know about that," Olline said with a playful grin. "I think you could say it. Just for clarity."

Casimir chuckled. "You need me to tell you what is painfully obvious, my dear?"

Heat crawled up her neck, her hands suddenly clammy as her heart lodged itself in her throat. "We're still getting to know each other, Cas. I wasn't going to assume anything."

Her breathing was rushed, her ears impossibly hot, and she realized her hand was still on his leg. Could she remove it without it being awkward? He hadn't exactly moved her away, he didn't even seem to notice. The placement of her hand suddenly felt much safer to think about than what she had said.

Olline wasn't ready to have this conversation. But maybe her father's words had gotten under her skin more than she realized. Maybe she was no good at staying busy enough not to want the bliss that came from having someone at and on her side.

"I don't want you to . . ." He trailed off, a flash of worry shooting through his deep ruby eyes. Olline leaned forward, hoping he would continue, a silent plea in her gaze.

Either Casimir didn't notice her look, or he ignored it. He shook his head, running a hand through his silver-white hair, and the moment was gone. Olline's heart sank, her lungs shriveling, mourning the loss of something that never even took its first breath. Slowly, she pulled her hand back into her lap.

"The other reason I was so insistent on speaking to you *now,* Tav," he said, a forced levity to his voice that brought back that slight manic tinge, "is that I believe I've found the perfect person to take Etzel's horde of corruption and use it to end his career." The subject change left her numb, blinking in confusion.

This expression, Casimir did apparently notice, as he grinned at her, almost hopeful. "Unless you've changed your mind about giving me access to it instead?" Casimir suggested. Olline sucked in a ragged breath, ready to bring up her now old arguments once again, when he held up a hand, stalling her. "Fine. Well, I suppose this is a fine enough option."

He sat up straighter; the twinkle returning to his eyes. "I believe she'll be the perfect person to ensure my—and all my *coworkers*—freedom. Permanently."

CHAPTER 20

The ride that was Olline's emotions was chaotic.

Olline's heart was in freefall, taking her stomach with it, her body heavy with an aching disappointment. Then, within the next breath, elation washed over her, and her body felt light with relief. Being in Casimir's orbit certainly wasn't boring, that was for sure.

"That's fantastic!" She leaned closer, the pressure in her chest gone. "So, this means I can finally move the files and control commands we found? I can set the killware timer, right?"

Casimir crossed his leg at the knee. His own look of excitement faltered. "Soon. I haven't made contact with this woman. I've merely identified her as a suitable candidate to help us, assuming she's willing."

"Oh." Olline couldn't stop her shoulders from slumping in response.

"Look, Olline darling, this is a far second choice for me. So, of course, I haven't done more than identify someone we could hopefully, maybe rope into this scheme. I'd much rather we use the information from Etzel for our own gain. Specifically, mine. I'd really rather not be anyone else's pawn ever again. Having the plethora of blackmail I alone have collected for that bastard would ensure both you and I were untouchable." He shrugged, trying to make light of the monstrous thing he was suggesting. "I'm doing this to protect you as much as to protect myself. I want to keep *you* safe, Olline."

For as touched as Olline wanted to be, the idea of Casimir continuing the work Etzel started when he didn't have to, made her sick to her stomach.

She was tired of having this conversation. Shaking her head, she said, "No, Casimir. I think you're confusing power with freedom. You don't want to turn into someone as bad as Etzel. That isn't freedom. That's not safety. This is your chance to break the cycle! Don't squander it."

Pure anger darkened Casimir's pale face for the briefest of milliseconds before it was gone and his mask of nonchalance settled back into place. But not before cold fear pierced her. Before she could voice her concern, he gave her another shrug and said, "Just keep an open mind to it. That's all I'm asking. In the meantime, there's always Plan B." Casimir waved toward the holo-tablet.

"Yeah, assuming this person would even be willing to dirty their hands with this, as you said," Olline grumbled, trying to think of yet another alternative in case this didn't pan out. But she came up with nothing. She was still far too new to Antal to know where to even start looking for potential allies, but she would scour the bowels of this city-state if it meant Casimir had no reason to take control of the information they had unearthed.

"Cheer up, darling," Casimir said, but even he didn't sound as confident as he normally did. "Part of why I picked her is because she is exactly the type to *want* to help."

Olline tried to be optimistic, but she couldn't help but be wary now. So much had seemed too good to be true from first glance and it had gotten her—and Casimir—into trouble. Olline was all too aware that one misstep would alert Etzel to what he had lost, and what he could still lose if he didn't regain control of Casimir. Her eyes flicked to the small holo-tablet she had monitoring the conference's feed. The attending lobbyists, committee chairs, activists' groups and Under Senators—including Etzel—were sitting down to debate once again. At least Etzel seemed as busy as they were.

Straightening her shoulders, she asked, "Right then, tell me about this person." She pulled another holo-tablet toward her, ready to research the woman as Casimir spoke.

"Under Senator Delora Peralta," he began, his eyes twinkling with pride. "She's very much a junior in the realm of politics. Still in her first term, eager and unjaded by the old-guard types like Etzel. In fact, she often opposes him on, well, most things."

Olline did a quick search on Delora, confirming what Casimir was saying, but also delving deeper into her past to see who she was before she was elected. From what she could tell, she was exactly as Casimir described her—perfect.

Delora was an attractive woman with smooth, ebony skin, short poofy midnight black curls framing her head like a halo, and warm, smoky quartz eyes. She was purely humani, with no magic in her background, on either side of her family, but she had always been a vocal advocate for the humane treatment of casters when they were arrested. The common practice was still stripping them of their magic through biomagitech devices, which many suffered mental breakdowns from afterward. Delora had an arrest record for protests turned riots advocating for more regulation on the megacorporations and developers of biomagitech devices meant to shackle casters—and through Etzel's backroom deals, people like Casimir.

Casimir confirmed everything Olline was finding, and she began to nod, bouncing her leg absentmindedly. "The problem," Casimir said haltingly, "is that I can't approach her. The pesky fact is that I *am* Kullen's brother, and that connection isn't something that would endear me to Under Senator Peralta. His shady reputation proceeds him, even if Etzel shields Kullen from legal ramifications. She's a typical politician in that regard, I'm afraid."

He looked at her meaningfully, and Olline huffed. "You need me to do more of the heavy lifting? Typical."

Casimir laughed at her reaction; his face unguarded for one blessed moment. Olline wanted to bottle that expression and keep it close to her heart. "I promise it'll be easy, Olline. Unless, of course, you'd rather not? We can stick with Plan A and keep all the files and Etzel's dirty empire for ourselves." That mischievous glint and smirk reappeared on his face at the suggestion.

Olline glared in response, and Casimir shrugged. "All right, we'll try it your way. In the meantime, approaching Delora won't be much of a challenge for you. With your clearance and the real evidentiary files you're transferring, it wouldn't be odd for you to request a meeting with her regarding the file storage of something tangentially related to something she was involved with." He rotated his hand, as if searching. "Maybe a protesters' arrest that's similar to her own record. She seems the type to want to be involved and help with such things," he added with a slight sneer.

Olline chuckled, and his face fell, as if he had been unaware of his expression. "Have a thing against do-gooders, do we, Cas?"

Casimir leaned forward, propping his elbows on his knees, hands dangling between his legs, his eyelids heavy with defeat, and Olline had the urge to reach out and take his hand with how vulnerable he looked. "In theory," he began slowly, "I'm all for them. The idealism of someone trying to do 'good'? Absolutely adorable. But none of those so-called do-gooders ever seemed to look my way. In that first decade of my forced servitude, I often tried testing the boundaries of the control chip's power. Tried to push past the boundaries of Etzel's influence. No one I encountered even tried to meet me halfway, to expend any extra effort to see what I was trying to hint at. Ever. Perhaps I was never worth their attention, their help. Looking at idealists, even back then, it merely confirms that my life is nothing but a waste now. They're what made giving up, *giving in,* so much easier."

Olline leaned forward, her hands pressed into the space between them on the couch, and before she could think better of it, she threw her arms around Casimir's neck and hugged him.

Casimir stiffened briefly, his arms tensing, his fingertips as rigid as if they were blocks of ice. "Life is never a waste. *Your* life isn't a waste," she whispered, still hugging him. "You aren't a bad person, Casimir. You never were, even if Etzel took advantage of your natural charisma. You needed help, you *deserved* it. I'm sorry you didn't get support when you most needed it. But you have me now. And friends help each other."

He shifted slowly, tentatively, nervous that his movements would scare her away. Casimir reached his arms around her and she felt the heat of his hands hovering over her back for a moment, as if he was afraid to touch her. Finally, he snaked his arms around her, his hands splayed across her back, as he returned her hug. Casimir was stiff for a second, then his entire body seemed to melt, sinking into her.

"Thank you, Ollie," he whispered. The softer nickname made her toes curl in her shoes, and she hugged him tighter, realizing that it had probably been a century, at least, since the last time anyone had shown Casimir even such simple kindness. "A friend . . . I can't remember the last time I've had one of those."

Her stomach felt like it was dropping through her all over again. She had wanted to be friends, right? That's what she had told him. So why was she disappointed in his confirmation? Being more than friends was part of that fantasy she had told her father about, nothing more. It was *idealist.*

Casimir needed a friend. A real friend. One who was going to put him first and take care of him and show him that the world didn't have to be so cruel. Shit, Olline needed a friend like that, too. If they could be that to each other, and only that, she would seize it with both hands and cling to it fiercely. And yet she still couldn't deny she wanted more, and maybe she needed that too. She *deserved* that, even without having been through what Casimir experienced. But could she wait for Casimir to feel the same?

That was too big, too depressing to think about. Especially when all Olline wanted to do right now, in this moment, was to hug Casimir until they both felt safe enough to let go.

Casimir settled his head against hers. Their breaths slowed until their chests were rising and falling in sync. Olline could get comfortable like this.

More than his expert caresses, *this* is what she wanted. What she had always wanted and people like Achan had fooled her into thinking she had; someone safe to be with. Someone she could be vulnerable with, who she didn't need to hide from. Someone who she could be a safe harbor for in return.

He inhaled deeply, and pulled away enough to study her, her emerald green eyes reflected in the deep garnet stones of his own. He removed one hand from her back so he could cup her chin delicately in his elegant hand. "I wish I'd found you so, so much sooner," he murmured, his lips parting slightly, his nose gently brushing the side of hers.

All Olline had to do was lean forward and press her lips to his. More than that, for the first time since Achan laughed in her face and she was fired from her job, she *longed* to be kissed. She wanted to be kissed stupid by Casimir, and Casimir alone.

Surely, he must have been aware of their breath mingling, that her natural cucumber and mint scent was melding with his own lavender and eucalyptus. His hand tightened on her cheek for a fraction of a second, before he put his forehead to hers, sighed, and leaned back.

Olline blinked rapidly, wondering if she had done something wrong, but Casimir's smile was thoughtful, his gaze slightly somber. "Unfortunately, my dear, we have a long road still ahead of us. I can't . . . I won't risk Etzel using me to hurt you. My life, and whatever it may or may not be worth, is still not fully mine."

"Not *yet,*" she responded quickly, the sting of him pulling away salved by his words.

"As you say, my adorable little do-gooder." He reclined back on the couch, a playful challenge in his gaze. "Shall we get to it? Come tomorrow, you should try to make contact with Under Senator Delora Peralta so we can be done with this Etzel business once and for all."

Olline could not agree more. And in the chaos of all their revelations, Olline completely forgot about the gift she had hidden away in her bedroom.

CHAPTER 21

"You don't have to stay, you know," Olline murmured, as she watched Casimir pace from her kitchen island then back to where she sat on the floor. His fingers twitched occasionally, flicking imaginary loose threads off his clothes or drumming on a crate she hadn't unpacked yet as he passed by.

He stopped mid stride, blinking at her like his mind had been galaxies away. Casimir scoffed and straightened his shirt, eyes downcast; he seemed embarrassed despite the coy grin. "My dear, if it's all the same to you, I think I'd rather stay. As a precaution. After the heart attack you nearly gave me, it's really the least you can do."

Suspicion trickled under her breastbone like icy water. Olline had seen how much more frantic he had been when he first arrived, and this . . . this wasn't that. She narrowed her eyes, looking up from the devices she was idly fiddling with. "Something's bothering you. Something *else*. If you're going to stay, you might as well spit it out." His eyebrow raised in amusement and she rolled her eyes. "Don't be gross."

Casimir chuckled but didn't immediately answer. So, Olline connected remotely to the servers back in the Government Plaza. After finding the type of evidence files she could use as a ruse to reach out to Delora, she queued a message request to send later in the afternoon. Statistically, Delora was more likely to be at her desk then. With two more flicks of a finger, Olline was able to take all the passcodes Casimir had provided, copy them, and begin the true cloning process. She wouldn't delete the files until Delora was well and truly on their side, but Olline was feeling, if not confident, at least hopeful.

He seemed to sense she had finished a task as he came to perch behind her on the couch. "If you must know, your little stint of silence has made me more, shall we say, anxious about everything," he said haltingly. "For as much as I try to keep up appearances by haunting the usual places Etzel leaves me, making the rounds with the few thralls I do interact with so we have no more surprises like Bode, I've no real proof that Etzel hasn't tried to command me to do something nefarious." He exhaled loudly through his nose, examining his nails, feigning at being unbothered despite the sharpness in his tone that betrayed his fraying nerves.

A vice squeezed her heart at his words. Olline swiveled around so she could look at him, and gently placed her hand on his knee. She wished she could do more, she *wanted* to do more to comfort him. But with the way Casimir's muscles tensed beneath her touch, she couldn't help but wonder if perhaps she was reading too much into the way he worried for her safety. "If it'd make you feel better," she offered, leaving her hand where it was for the moment, "we can focus on your files for a while? Maybe if we can crack it, that'll give you some peace of mind?"

The muscles in his jaw flexed as he clenched his mouth shut. Despite that, his eyes were soft on her face and she had the sudden urge to reach up and cup his chin. But then his gaze slid away and focused on the holo-tablet in her lap. "Have you finished then?" he asked, gesturing to the files currently loading. "With identifying all the documents and whatnot connected to Etzel and the chips?"

She lifted a shoulder in a light shrug. "Almost. But it's fine, I can come back and finish later if it'll help you—"

Casimir cut her off with a sharp shake of the head. He gave her fingers a squeeze, holding tight for one breath, then two, before relinquishing his grip and moving her hand off his knee. She expected that to sting, but the movement had seemed so bittersweet that, instead, there was an ache of longing deep in her core.

"No, best you stay focused, darling." His voice was so dead that she didn't have the heart to give a sarcastic retort about not calling her "darling", even though, truthfully, she was starting to like the nickname. Well, she liked when *he* said it. He noted the pained look in her gaze and his eyes flicked away as if burned. "Finish finding all the files that this Under Senator may need," he said, moving off the couch and resuming his slow pace around her kitchen and living room, her giant monstera idly tracking his movements by tilting its leaves. "I've waited this long; I can certainly wait a bit more."

Frowning, and not sure what else to do, Olline went back to the task at hand. Her thoughts were elsewhere, though, as she mechanically moved everything over. Distracted by why Casimir didn't seem interested in cracking into his own file. Whether because he didn't know the element Etzel used to designate him, or he didn't want Olline to see that side of him, she didn't know.

She wished she respected that decision more.

Eventually, she would need to get into that folder despite Casimir's reservations. Until she accessed his file, she couldn't use her magic to dismantle the chip currently embedded somewhere in the spinal column at the base of his neck. They needed those schematics or the risk to Casimir should she tinker with the chip . . . She shuddered, unable to think about it in more detail. With a heavy sigh, she turned away. For now, she supposed, it could wait. After all, Etzel was still distracted elsewhere.

Come the early evening, Olline had done everything she could. "I'm done," she said to Casimir's back, as he was still prowling her apartment, rechecking places as if he expected spy devices to have suddenly appeared. "Do you want to try to crack open your files now?"

He hesitated for a moment, opened his mouth, and then closed it with a snap. "No, best not. We need to keep up pretenses still. Your supervisor, Karter, was it? If he's suspicious, best you pretend to be working on that project for a bit." He forced a smile that quivered at the edges. Before she could reassure him it was fine, he had resumed his pacing. "I can wait, remember? Besides, I do so love watching you work."

And he had been content to watch her for a time, but eventually he moved off to one of the large windows where her vine plants crawled up the panes, soaking in what they could of the sun. Much like her plants, Casimir stood in the beam of light, eyes closed, relishing the feel of the sun on his skin.

She watched him as she worked, a lurch of sadness twisting her heart. Where Casimir lived, where the clubs were that he had to frequent, he rarely got up high enough in the city to see actual light, to feel a breeze that wasn't caused by buzzing bots and aerial traffic. She didn't blame him for wanting to stay in the window, in the natural light.

If their places had been switched, Olline would do the same.

Maybe we aren't all that different, after all.

"See something you like, Olline?" Casimir said with a chuckle, studying her from over his shoulder.

She blinked rapidly, unaware that she had been staring so obviously, her thoughts having drifted a thousand miles away. Almost without thinking, she responded, "Maybe. Do you see something *you* like?" she asked, gesturing vaguely at the window.

He turned to face her; the light making him glow like some sinful god. He tilted his head as he watched her. "What's not to like? You have the whole package, my dear. Oh, and the view out the window isn't bad either."

Olline couldn't help but chuckle despite the burn of her blush. "You overhear that line at one of your clubs?"

She decided Casimir flirted because it was safer than anything real. He'd had a chance to say what he truly felt, shied away, and came back to his lines. The trench he was digging between them, that kept her at arm's length, was becoming a chasm. If Olline didn't do something about the distance soon, something as silly as bluntly telling him how she felt, then eventually it would become an abyss she could never cross. Even though his words tickled her core, this wasn't the version of Casimir she craved.

Then he smiled.

His lazy smile was heart meltingly slow and sweet. He studied her, as if drinking in her laugh. "How could I not use that line after you queued it up so perfectly?" he chuckled, and took a few steps toward where she was sitting on the floor. "Doesn't make it any less true, though."

Despite the heat she felt spreading from her cheeks to the tips of her ears, Olline rolled her eyes and went back to work. She heard him shift, going back to the window. Each time there was a pause in her work while she waited for something to generate, she would steal glances at him. Each time, her core melted all over again.

In need of a better distraction, she flexed her fingers over the raw materials, the wires and minerals, and called to the magma deep in her core that was her magic. Olline was powerful enough in her specialized version of earth magic that she didn't need to twist her fingers and hands in order to shape the magic at her disposal, but she did need to shut her eyes and visualize what she was doing, what she wanted to happen. Not dissimilar to what had occurred at Refractory, minus the lust taking over. She envisioned the result, the elements before her lighting up until, in her mind's eye, she was seeing in ultraviolet. Once she could see everything, she began shuffling the molecules that made up the ores and minerals before her to bring the final result to life.

Her plants fluttered in response. Whenever she drew on her power, her plants, tied to her and her magic, responded in kind. It could be interpreted as fear, the plants she had created worried that she would take the magic from them to accomplish her goals, though Olline would never do something so heartless to her friends. She liked to think they knew that, but that was giving the plants more sentience than even Olline was willing to do.

Regardless, the background sound of the swaying leaves and quivering vines was soothing, creating a sort of white noise hum accompanied by the fresh scent of newly turned soil that filled the apartment. It was loud enough that she didn't even hear Casimir creep closer until he stopped nearby, sinking to the floor at her side.

She stiffened, her magic stalling for a moment, but he didn't interrupt her, didn't even sit close enough for her to feel the crackle of his presence. But she knew he was nearby all the same. When nothing happened, she continued her work, picking up flawlessly from where she left off.

Olline was a slow eruption, pouring her warmth, her

power, into her task. But eventually, the fuel for that magma dwindled. Her ultraviolet vision faded. The molecules blinked out one by one until all that was left was the glow of the raw elements, and even that disappeared soon enough. Her plants stopped swaying, and the heat in her chest, her arms, all the way to the tips of her fingers, dissipated until her arms trembled with exertion. She wasn't done with what she was working on, but she was closer, and that was good enough for now.

With a deep breath, she lowered her arms, her eyes slowly fluttering open. Once her vision could focus again, the first thing she saw was Casimir.

Whatever he had witnessed, it had captivated him.

Olline shot a quick glance down at her computer components, but besides a faint glow around the materials, nothing looked different, at least to the untrained eye. Nothing had moved, nothing had morphed and transformed into something visible. Olline had been manipulating the ore at a molecular level. There was truly nothing to see. Her eyes darted back to his face, but the look remained.

There was an air of contentment around Casimir, an ease that she had never felt from him before. The raw sensuality of him was gone, replaced by this softer version, the version she imagined he had been before his brother sold him to Etzel: easily captivated by the magic around him, taking joy from others enjoying what they were doing. Olline had little experience in connecting to the empathetic pull that most earth casters had, but in this moment, Casimir's feelings were so obvious that they felt like her own.

Olline held her breath, desperate not break the spell. As the last of her plants settled down and the glow faded from her materials, Casimir blinked slowly and, with a little shake, came back to himself. Immediately, the feeling of serenity that had enveloped him was gone, replaced by that vague, coy grin he always wore. Olline reached out, wondering if she could touch his face and feel the Casimir of before lurking within, but she stopped herself.

She imprinted the memory of his expression, the sensation of him, into her very bones so she could always hold it tight. It was only then that she remembered what she had created for him. Excitement rippled through her. It was a long shot, or maybe it wasn't. She didn't know, but she hoped that maybe this was the way to keep the version of Casimir she yearned for as the default instead of the mask he wore.

With a little gasp, she shot to her feet, startling Casimir. "Don't move," she called, darting from the room and into her bedroom.

The orchids straightened their curved stems in welcoming when she entered. She greeted her creations distractedly, eyes wide, as she glanced around the space. She may have forgotten her gift in the chaos of Casimir showing up like he did, but she knew right where she'd left it. Gently, she scooped up the little pot and the deceptively resilient bloom she had coaxed to grow. Cradling the flower in her hands, she marched back out into the living room and said, "Close your eyes."

She waited for Casimir to comply, grumbling all the while, before sinking back down onto the floor next to him and putting the plant carefully on the table in front of him. She didn't have to be so cautious with the plant, she of all people knew that. But she was so proud of this creation that it elicited a reverent response from her all the same.

Taking a deep breath, she placed her hand on his shoulder and positioned herself so she could see his face. "Okay," she murmured, "you can open them now."

Olline wasn't worried about giving him a gift like this. With how he was around her plants, and how hypnotized he had been by watching her wield magic, she knew he would at least take care of the plant. The trick was making sure she got it right.

There were hundreds of plant types, hundreds more when magic was in the mix. It would be so easy, nay, *too easy,* for her to have made something that didn't fit Casimir. The probability that she had gotten it wrong was high given the small window into Casimir and his life she had been gifted. Yet, Olline had a good feeling about this.

Casimir gave a sharp intake of breath. His garnet red eyes widened, and he hesitantly reached out toward the blooms, afraid to touch them. A tentative smile slowly built as the surprise settled in.

"Did you," he began, voice halting and raw, before clearing his throat and taking a deep breath. "You made this?"

Olline nodded enthusiastically, the hesitant grin she had before stretching into a dazzling smile. "It's a black orchid, but I've modified it for you." She rotated the pot slightly so he could better see the long stem clustered with blooms. The flowers were blacker than the void with a faint, feathery indigo hue on the underside of the petals. The stamens were a bright yellow, framed by soft peach, white, and deep red hues on the surrounding petals. "I made sure it doesn't require any light. Well, not any sunlight. It'll thrive with the bulbs you have in your apartment. And you don't even need to water it! Well, you won't have to water it very often. There's only so much I could do with the soil, unfortunately. I've been calling this variation a 'night orchid', but you can name it whatever you want. It's one of a kind." She cut herself off before she could add "like you".

She straightened her shoulders, pointing at the top bloom. "Orchids are my favorite. Both as my favorite flowers, and favorite to work with." The fronds of her ferns rustled angrily, and she murmured, "Sorry, you know I love you all."

Olline quickly glanced at Casimir again and noticed that his jaw was tightly shut, his eyes focused on the flower, and his expression suddenly became impossible to read. Her heart sank, her limbs almost too heavy to lift. Was she too presumptuous that he would even want the responsibility of a plant? Even one as changed as the night orchid? Maybe she had been wrong in assuming he would want even more dark colors in his life?

"But if you don't like it," she added quickly, "or-or have a different plant you like, I can change it. I just figured, well, you have that little table by your bed with nothing on it and it seemed kind of lonely. You've been so nice to me, and well, I guess it's no secret that I *like* you, so I wanted you to have something nice in return . . ." She trailed off once she realized what she said. Heat flooded her cheeks. She hadn't meant to admit liking him, and now he wasn't even speaking.

Shit, shit, shit!

Casimir may not say what he claimed was becoming obvious between them, but Olline could. Furthermore, she needed to. If she said the words out loud, then the ambiguity was gone, for better or worse, and she could better deal with the consequences. But the grey, liminal space they had found themselves in was one Olline could not thrive in.

The longer the silence stretched, the more oppressive it became, until her chest ached with fear. Casimir was going to react the same way Achan had: turning the plant around in his hands before laughing. Telling her this was cute, but what was happening wasn't special. All he wanted was to get a closer look at her work, not her. This was the moment she was going to discover Casimir was the same, wasn't it? He was close to her because of the control chip and what she could do to get rid of it and the damning files tying him to Etzel. Olline tried to keep her breathing steady, reassuring herself that, at least, the ambiguity would be gone and that was what she wanted, after all.

Casimir shook his head in disbelief, and Olline's breath caught in her throat. "You made this. For me?" He drawled the words, emphasizing each syllable, like he couldn't believe what he was seeing.

Olline nodded hesitantly, reaching out to take the plant back, but he stopped her by capturing her hands in his, cradling them as if they were the delicate blooms instead. "You beautiful creature, you," Casimir whispered, dipping his head toward her. "Why would you expend your amazing power on *me?* I've . . ." Casimir trailed off, taking a deep breath, before starting again. "I've hurt people. Hundreds if not thousands of people. People I can't even remember. I'm not deserving of such a gift. For this is a *gift,* thank you. To share your favorite bloom with me is, I don't know what it is. You, darling Ollie, have left me speechless."

Olline gripped his hands in return, leaning toward him until his breath tickled her face and she could see the watery sheen over his eyes. "You weren't given a choice, Casimir. If you had been, I know you wouldn't have done any of the things Etzel forced on you. I've seen the real you, despite you trying to hide it. And yeah, I've noticed you doing *that* a lot, too," she said with a light giggle. Olline took another deep breath, her voice softening with sincerity. "You love creation! That artists' club you showed me is evidence of that. I wanted to give you something to show you that I, well, I understand."

Casimir took a deep ragged breath, his eyes moving from the black orchid on the table, to their clasped hands, to her eyes, before flicking to her lips briefly, and then dragging back up to her eyes where they remained. "No one has ever cared about me like you have. In over a century, you're the only one. Other people don't have a soul like you. You're . . . *you.* No one is like you, Ollie."

Olline tilted her chin up, searching for the lie. The deception. Searching his face for some sign she was misreading. But there was nothing there. Casimir's eyes were heavy with emotion, a happy sadness softening the sharp lines of his face. His tone was husky when he called her "Ollie", but not honeyed in a way that masked any sort of trick. She removed one of her hands from his and gently traced the line of his chin, making sure this was *real.*

He leaned into her palm, melting into her light touch. Olline's stomach flipped, her chest tightening as Casimir relaxed. It was nice to fantasize about his impeccable body, those devilish lips on her neck, those sinful fingers tracing her skin, but the Casimir that was enamored with creation, with life, who could be vulnerable and open . . . Why couldn't he be like this all the time?

Olline ran her thumb along his jawline, brushing the underside of his lip with the tip of her finger. He met her gaze again, his eyes still vaguely forlorn, but his face was so relaxed that Olline couldn't help it. She leaned toward him, her lips parting. She moved slowly, letting him decide if he wanted her to kiss him or not.

The corners of Casimir's lips tightened briefly, before his eyes widened slightly, and he tilted his head toward her. Olline leaned closer, her breath caressing his face, the tip of his nose brushing hers. Her eyes fluttered closed—

Her wrist-communicator pinged.

Olline was happy to ignore the summons, but she felt Casimir pull back slightly. She opened her eyes and her lungs shriveled until she could hardly breathe with the ache in her chest. His mask of nonchalance had slammed down over his face, the lines of his jaw becoming sharp enough to cut her teeth on once again. His eyes weren't on her though, firmly fixed on her wrist-communicator instead.

Under Senator Delora Peralta had responded to her message request:

Let's talk.

She glanced back at Casimir. He was grinning faintly, and while getting a response was a good thing, a great thing, even, Olline feared that the fragile moment that had started to take shape had crumbled like a dry, brittle leaf and she would never be able to piece it together again.

CHAPTER 22

"Are you *absolutely* sure you don't want to be on this call with me?" Olline asked for the third time.

Casimir stared back at her with his customary stoic expression, hands buried deep in his pockets. And yet he kept taping his foot and shifting slightly from side to side. It was the only outward appearance he gave of any kind of edginess or worry. He nodded curtly and lifted a shoulder in a stiff shrug. "Yes. It's better this way, trust me. Best not to give Ms. Peralta even a crumb to chew on about any of Etzel's actual thralls."

"Suit yourself," she relented. Olline let out a long, shaky breath and set up a secure channel.

Before she had even finished, Casimir was peering over her shoulder. "Be sure to obscure your face, darling, and your voice. Delora seems clean but better safe than sorry, as they say. Just in case—"

"In case she's actually on Etzel's payroll?" Olline snapped back, squirming. "Yeah, I know," her tone was harsh with sarcasm. Nervousness made her nerves tingle painfully and her stomach twist into knots. More hovering was certainly not going to make that better.

Casimir huffed and stepped back, moving out of sight of the holo-projection. Olline winced, rubbing at the back of her neck. “Sorry. This is all just . . . They make it look so exciting in the virtual thriller vids. The reality is anything but.”

He awarded her a faint, understanding smile in response, but the corners of his eyes remained pinched with tension. With a sigh, Olline could delay no longer. She hit enter, connecting her to the Under Senator.

Delora sat at her desk, the holo-projection giving her cool, black skin a mesmerizing glow. “What do I call you?” Delora said, her words crisp in her deep, smoky voice. “You didn’t provide an alias.”

Olline swallowed, muted her sputtering, and then said. “Just call me Sub-thirteen.” It was the only thing she could think of under pressure: the floor she worked on in the Government Plaza.

Delora folded her hands on her desk, her expression serious as she nodded. “Fine. Let’s get to it. What’s this *really* about?” She didn’t bother with pleasantries, and so Olline dropped the pretense of why she reached out immediately.

Olline explained the situation, what she found, and how her contract was a lie. Delora didn’t react beyond leaning slightly forward, her attention on Olline with an intensity that could put Casimir to shame.

She moved her hands out of view of the holo-projection

so Delora couldn't see how Olline twisted her fingers. Thankfully, with the privacy filter on, the Under Senator couldn't see how Olline kept stealing glances at Casimir, or the dewiness collecting on her brow as her nervous sweating got the best of her.

So far, Delora hadn't said anything, which made Olline worry she wasn't explaining the situation well. "They're all thralls," Olline said, her impassioned plea coming out deadpanned with the voice filter on. "I can't . . . I don't want to be complicit in Etzel's corruption. He's controlling innocent people, *enslaving them* to do his bidding. They have to do whatever he commands. Murder, rape, and everything in between."

Casimir made a halting motion on the other side of the projection. Olline glanced up, and he motioned for her to mute the channel while Delora digested her words. "Don't tell her I'm free," Casimir whispered unnecessarily. She arched a brow in question, and he narrowed his gaze at her in return. When she didn't immediately speak, he crossed his arms and drummed his fingers on his biceps. "Best she not know a single one of Etzel's people is free. We don't want that bastard to start sniffing around should Delora's office be compromised."

Olline blew out an exasperated breath, then glanced down quickly to make sure Delora was still contemplating the details of what Olline said. "Yeah, okay, that makes sense. But Cas," she said, her voice softening, "the time of you lurking in the shadows is at an end. You don't *have* to hide. At least not for much longer."

"Maybe. But maybe I like the shadows," he mumbled. She

frowned, but didn't have time to respond as Delora let loose a heavy sigh. Olline had to rush to unmute the channel.

"Unfortunately, Sub-thirteen," Delora said slowly, her smoky-quartz eyes locking onto Olline's face with a resigned sort of dejectedness, "I've expected as much for a while now."

Olline couldn't stop from giving an audible gasp as her stomach went into freefall. There was a sputtering sound behind the projection. Glancing up, Olline looked at Casimir, and her eyes widened. Fury as intense as a grenade flashed across his face to where even Olline imagined she was scorched by its intensity, her face burning.

There wasn't time to mute the channel, so Olline could check in with Casimir, as Delora was quick to clarify, "Or, not *this* precisely. But it makes sense for Straub. He's kept such firm control on his seat, his committees. Even the experts or witnesses I bring in to challenge him on the insane deregulation proposals suddenly have a *perfectly logical* change of mind." She rolled her eyes like what Olline had outlined was . . . tedious. "There've been far too many measures that've benefitted him personally, pushed through our offices for corruption not to be at play." Delora grinned; a triumphant gleam making her eyes twinkle. "Glad to know I was right. In a sense."

Casimir started pacing in quick, little jerky circles. His arms were no longer wrapped around his chest but were down at his sides, straight as iron. He clenched his hands into tight fists, and Olline was worried he may lash out in his scorching—and justifiable—fury. The ferns nearest him trembled, as if afraid to get burned.

Olline swallowed the lump in her throat and asked, "Why didn't you do anything? Investigate his offices or look into his aids and the people working for him?"

Desperately she hoped that Delora's answer would dampen some of Casimir's rage. But when Delora gave a delicate shrug, idly patting her halo of poofy black curls, Olline knew she had been wrong to even ask. "The resources I'd need to launch an investigation like that would require I bring in other Under Senators, probably even a few Senators as well. This is a reelection cycle for me. I need my name to be the one people remember. Not just one of many."

"You didn't investigate obvious corruption," Olline said slowly, too stunned by Delora's words to fully register the piercing disappointment, "because you didn't want to share the spotlight for freeing people controlled by illegal biomagitech." Her breathing was coming faster now, unable to get enough air around the jagged hole in her chest from her despondency.

Delora gave Olline a flat look. "Politics is cutthroat. I can't do *anyone* any good if I lose my seat in the Government Plaza."

Casimir was livid and could remain silent no more. With a strangled yell, he punched the wall. Her vines curled out of the way just in time. Olline jumped in surprise, fumbling to mute the channel, and held up one finger in the universal "just a second" sign.

He faced the wall, huffing. Tiny spiderweb cracks fanned the fist Casimir kept against the wall. Olline couldn't see his eyes, but his shoulders shuddered with the realization that Delora, or someone in power, could have freed him decades ago. That people suspected Etzel of misconduct but still did nothing. Something inside Olline splintered and cracked like her wall. A bubbling hatred for Antal—and Eerden as a whole—where people could so willfully let something like this happen.

Hearing Delora's admission must be like getting victimized all over again to Casimir.

Olline's heart ached to go to him, to let him rage and scream, and maybe punch another wall—one free of her plants. But Olline couldn't move, she couldn't go to him and risk Delora realizing someone else was in the room if she hadn't guessed it already. "Cas," she whispered, her voice strangled with her own heartbreak on his behalf.

"*Of course,* Delora wants to benefit from this," he said with a bitter laugh. "Why would I ever expect anything less from these so called, idealistic 'do-gooders?'" Despite his words and his spiteful tone, his shoulders slumped, collapsing under the weight of his misery. The twinkle was gone from his eyes. There wasn't even fury there to create a smoldering ember in his gaze. Replaced instead with a flat hopelessness.

"What do you want me to do, Cas?" Olline murmured, her fingers aching with the need to grab him and hold him tight while she promised to . . . what? Make it all better? Olline was out of her depth here, but she needed to do *something*.

"I haven't got all day, Sub-thirteen. What is it, exactly, you're offering and want me to do here?" Delora said, her husky voice deepening with impatience.

“I should sneak into his estate before he knows I’m free,” Casimir seethed. “I could kill him and take his power and *save myself* once and for all.”

“Cas, no,” Olline gasped. “You aren’t the only one suffering under Etzel. We’ll free them all alongside you.” Casimir still glowered, and Olline was running out of time. She wished she could reach out to him, in lieu of that, she said, “You don’t need to be Etzel to be free. I’m not asking you to trust Delora. I’m asking you to trust me.”

Casimir opened his mouth, and then snapped it shut, avoiding Olline’s gaze. He sighed and turned away so he could brace himself against the wall again. “I trust you, Tav.”

And yet Olline hesitated; her finger held over the screen to unmute the holo-tablet. Her chest squeezed with indecision. With a heaviness weighting her stomach down, she licked her lips, and unmuted the channel. But Olline could not completely ignore the defeated, rough sigh Casimir made.

“I want you to end Under Senator Straub’s enslavement of people,” she said, putting authority in her voice so it wouldn’t quiver. “I want you to bring justice to all his thralls. And I don’t want you, or anyone else, to use or abuse these people again. They’re innocent no matter what Etzel made them do. Destroy every shred of blackmail and other evidence, so it can’t be used by anyone. The people who benefited from Etzel’s blackmail schemes must face justice, along with the Under Senator," she added sternly, but the voice modulator ruined the effect. “I’ll give you everything you need so you don't need to bring other Under Senators in on this."

Delora drummed her immaculate red nails on the desk, her gaze calculating. "It's true," she began slowly, "that I've no interest in continuing anything Straub's doing. It's unequivocally repugnant. Politics aside, I'd personally delight in dismantling those chips and have all the developers who crafted them stand trial alongside Straub. Assuming all your information is verified, of course."

The woman paused, and her fingers stilled in their tapping. Olline's eyes narrowed, suspicion making the hairs on her arms stand on end. The unsaid "but" hanging over them like a bladed pendulum. "You do realize," Olline said, her tone biting, "That *you'd* be taking all the credit here. I don't want anyone knowing I was involved." Delora perked up, leaning forward slightly, no longer seeming to hesitate about acting on what Olline was offering.

A muscle in Casimir's neck bulged from clamping his mouth shut as he watched the exchange. It didn't stop him from rolling his eyes and shaking his head before mouthing, "I told you so."

Her muscles tightened, and Olline fought to keep from withering visibly. She hated Casimir was right. That even the best option within Antal's government was unwilling to free Etzel's thralls unless they could take *glory* from it.

Olline felt sick to her stomach on Casimir's, and all the other thralls, behalf.

"You can have it all," Olline spat, which caused Casimir to still in his fuming and study her with a curious glint in his garnet eyes. “All the accolades, all the power that comes from doing the right fucking thing. I just need you to *do it*.”

Faced with her own callousness, Delora had the grace to look contrite as she lowered her gaze and slumped ever so slightly in her seat. “What can I give you in return,” Delora murmured gently, her ebony skin flushed with shame. “For doing the hard work I was too selfish—no *cowardly* to do myself.” She sounded genuine in her remorse, in her earnestness to do the right thing, but Olline could no longer trust the woman.

Outside of Casimir—and maybe Briallea—she no longer trusted anyone in Antal.

Olline barely needed to think about what she and Casimir needed. Want was a silly thing to hope for when up against someone like Etzel. “Immunity,” she answered. “Total immunity and protection against retaliation for me and anyone who helps me get this info over to you,” she added quickly, stealing another glance at Casimir, who nodded curtly in agreement. His naturally pale face was still flushed and his lips pressed into a thin line from his sizzling anger, but at least they were moving in the right direction. It just went to show that no one in a seat of power was truly altruistic, and despite the disappointed anger still radiating from Casimir, protection and immunity were all they needed from her.

Delora nodded; her gaze still thoughtful. “Absolutely. Consider it done. Once you send me everything you have, Sub-thirteen, I’ll need,” she trailed off. The Under Senator glanced to the side as she figured out the logistics, her lips moving slightly as if counting. "Ten business days at a minimum to bring charges against Straub."

Olline blinked, her stomach sinking. They only had a day left before Etzel returned to the Government Plaza under the best of circumstances.

She sputtered, and Delora gave her a pained look, Olline's fear obvious despite the filters. "You have to understand," Delora said gently, "that these things take time even with ironclad evidence. I have to get my staff in position to take legal measures, judges and barristers not on Straub's payroll will need to be brought in simply to identify the dozens of laws and regulations Etzel violated. Not to mention securing outside witnesses, as in people who aren't chipped, merely to corroborate all the blackmail."

Olline was too stunned to speak, her eyes wide as the sinking feeling she had before threatened to drown her. The flush Casimir had before was completely gone now. He was so pale he looked sick, which was not helped by his harrowed expression.

Delora sighed. "I sympathize with your fear, your desire to get this done quickly. But if we don't do it right, no charges will stick. Straub's an oily son-of-a-bitch." She paused, letting Olline speak, but she couldn't get enough moisture into her mouth to croak out any words. "I'd understand if you didn't want to go through with this." The Under Senator's words were gentle, judgement free, but there was no way, in no scenario, that neither she nor Casimir was going to back out now.

Panic entered Casimir's gaze then, his fingers flexed as he

took a half step toward her. Was he afraid she would drop the matter? Or afraid she would agree?

Taking a fortifying breath, Olline said. "No. Let's do this."

Olline broke down the plan of how she would get everything to Delora, and Delora told her when to deliver all the evidence. They would trap Etzel in one fell swoop before he could bribe or weasel his way out of anything.

During that time, the control chips would need to remain active. Casimir didn't look pleased about that. Shit, Olline wasn't happy about it either. But she didn't think anything would make Casimir happy at the moment.

Once everything was agreed upon and Delora provided Olline with a secure virtual drop box to put everything in, Olline disconnected the line and deleted their holo-meeting room. She had to assume Etzel had some kind of spyware in the Government Plaza system and she wanted to make sure nothing could be linked back to her when they were getting closer and closer to achieving their goals.

The glow from the holo-tablet had barely faded before Casimir was pacing in agitation, each lap taking him closer to Olline's front door. "Etzel returns from his conference tonight. We're out of time. I'd assumed Delora would act with a bit more haste than this, given the severity of Etzel's crimes."

"Faster, maybe," she said cautiously, "but not safer. This is the better plan, Cas. Etzel isn't exactly alone in all this. He has partners, biomagitech engineers and developers giving him the means to run his scheme. If we don't take that side of his business down, there's no guarantee he can't start it up again in the future, or worse, continue to run his racket from prison."

Casimir was still frowning, so she held out her hand and whispered, "Do you still trust me?" Olline didn't want to sound like she was taking Delora's side over his. She wasn't. The situation was truly fucked, and she didn't want to risk all of their work being for naught.

He stopped in his tracks, surprised by her outstretched hand. "Olline, you're probably the only person on this whole rotten planet I do trust. But my faith in you doesn't change what I—"

Casimir cut himself off abruptly, his eyes widening a fraction, like he was about to say something he hadn't meant to. Olline sat up straighter, suspicious. He shook his head and moved back to the table where his black orchid sat. "I don't trust that something won't go wrong before Delora can pull the plug on Etzel, as it were. It's *her* I don't trust."

Before she could press him though, Casimir carefully picked up the flower, cradling it as if it were delicate glass, and said, "I've been here too long. I need to make my rounds in case any of my other coworkers are looking for me." He shifted the orchid gently and made it to the door before Olline could even rise to her feet. "I'll let you get back to work in peace, Tav." His hand hesitated on the door, his shoulders rising and falling in a heavy, silent sigh. "*Thank you,* truly. For the night orchid, for everything. I won't forget it."

He was gone before she could make sense of his cryptic parting words. It sounded like he was saying goodbye.

She shook her head. That line of thinking would only depress her when, all things considered, she should be celebrating. Delora's involvement meant safety was within reach at last! So why did she feel so hollow inside?

Everything was happening so fast, almost too fast for Olline to make sense of. One minute, she and Casimir are finally having a moment—a moment she had wanted since before the Refractory job if she was being honest. The next, she's dealing with a selfish Under Senator, followed by Casimir storming out as if danger lurked in *her* home instead of out in the wider city.

Maybe something's wrong? She tried to shake the thought off, but it wouldn't leave. Without another plant to pour her energy into, and still too depleted from manipulating the elements to do real work, Olline pulled up Casimir's password-protected file.

She chewed on her lower lip for a moment, considering. Casimir had never guessed his password, had never even suggested they try. Yet if Olline wanted to ensure that, no matter what came next, Casimir was safe, she needed to crack it. Her stomach churned, bile coating her throat as she tried to think like Etzel. Especially when it came to Casimir, but then . . . Well, did she really need to think like a monster to break this code? Didn't she know Casimir too? Better than a bastard like Etzel, certainly.

Fortified with that knowledge, Olline wracked her brain over the periodic table. As an earth caster, she was intimate with most elements in a way most people could never be. Taking what she knew, and what she had discovered of Casimir, she scoured her memory, staring at the screen until her eyes watered and the holo-projection blurred.

Then it hit her. Hesitantly, she entered the element and . . . It worked. Holy shit, *it worked.*

Floating on a high like no other, she moved the files she had found linking back to Casimir onto their own mini-stick without looking at a single document beyond the chip schematics. She separated his out from everyone else's, allowing Casimir to do as *he* wanted. She knew Casimir, she didn't know the rest of the people Etzel had chipped. Olline could only imagine how Casimir would feel if she went snooping at his files without his permission, and she doubted he would want yet another Under Senator to have access to them.

She flipped the mini-stick over her knuckles and wondered if maybe she should have taken a tiny little peek, if that would have calmed the insistent scratching in the back of her skull. Then she would be positive that everything Casimir had told her was true.

Maybe she was still looking for something to be wrong because of her experience with Achan, simple as that. The more she thought about it, though, the more she didn't think that was the case. With everything prepped, the clone files moving to the secure drive, and her spider program locating every bit of blackmail Etzel had on those he controlled, Olline had a spare moment to think about Casimir without interruption.

Her mind kept latching on to their very first meeting. Why was Casimir even outside her office door to begin with? Her brain was trying to get her to focus on *something*. A missing detail that continued to slip past her mental fingertips every single time. She stopped playing with the mini-stick, clutched the device in her fist, and formulated a plan.

Because if there was one thing she hated above all else, it was allowing herself to feel shitty and paranoid over something she had the power to fix.

The way Olline saw it, there were two options. Best-case scenario: Casimir realized the depth of her feelings and didn't return them and wasn't sure how to let her down easily. The worst-case scenario: he was still in Etzel's control, and this had been an elaborate ruse. She desperately hoped it wasn't the latter, even if that killed her.

What Olline needed to do was talk to Casimir, openly and honestly. And maybe, if she did that, the thing clawing for attention in the back of her mind would finally be satisfied and they could move on. Move on to what, though? Olline didn't know, but anything had to be better than this stagnation.

She knew what she had to do, and yet she hesitated. Her skin prickled, her nerves sending sparks through her. If she was wrong, she would be stepping into the home of a man controlled by someone objectively evil. And if that was even a remote possibility, then she shouldn't do it.

But it was impossible for her to believe that. Not when Casimir looked so touched, so enchanted by the night orchid and by the sheer fact she had used her magic to make him a present.

Olline completed her transfer sequences, shut down her

holo-tablet, and shoved the mini-stick into her pocket. After she sent an innocent enough message to Casimir and confirmed he was headed home, Olline headed out.

CHAPTER 23

Three hours after their meeting with Delora, just as the night put the city in a choke hold, Olline was standing at Casimir's apartment. Her legs were tense and her hands curled into fists, as she convinced herself to stop being a coward and knock on the damn door.

The ease with which she could retrace her steps from only one visit mildly impressed herself, but it wasn't enough to steel her nerves. Taking a deep, ragged breath, she screwed her eyes shut and knocked. She shifted from foot to foot, her heart racing, as she waited for Casimir to open the door.

The seconds trickled by. Hours seemed to pass as she stood there, convincing herself that he wasn't home despite hearing the faint rustle of movement from inside.

Maybe he has company.

Her heart tripped over itself with the thought and she was about to scurry away, the weight of the mini-stick heavy in her pocket, when Casimir opened the door a crack. "Olline? What're you . . ." he trailed off, frowning, and opened the door a bit more to look up and down the vacant hallway. "Are you all right?"

She nodded and said, "Yup!" far too brightly. She cringed and rubbed the back of her neck. "Can I come in? I have something for you and I want to . . . I need to talk to you. Is now a good time?"

He blinked at her slowly before opening the door wider, allowing her inside. She tried not to sigh in relief at seeing his apartment empty. "Another gift? Really, Olline darling, you're far too kind." When she flashed him a smile that was more grimace, Casimir asked again, "Are you sure everything's all right? If you wanted to talk, you only needed to message me. You didn't need to trudge all the way down here."

She lifted a shoulder in a shrug, but stopped when she saw the black orchid on his nightstand. It was so perfectly in the center of the table that she imagined him painstakingly placing it with care. Warmth bloomed in the center of her chest, calming her nerves. "It's not really a gift, so don't get too excited. Besides, that's not really the reason I'm here. It was just a nice excuse to talk to you. Or, really, to explain in person. Because if I don't get this off my chest now, I'm going to go crazy and, honestly, I'm tired of always being the one chasing people."

Already off to a great start, way to go, Olline.

He gestured for her to sit, his expression slightly bemused. She perched on the edge of his bed, and tried not to notice how smooth and cool the fabric was. Olline locked her gaze on her hands, which was safer than Casimir's face by leagues. She couldn't bear to look up and face his mask of marble right now. "I need you to know why I keep trying to get you to say, or admit, to this feeling between us. Or acknowledge if it's all in my head, because who knows, it may be. Which is why I'm here." She couldn't believe she was actually saying this, but she was here now and if she didn't get it all out, as fast as possible, she never would. Wringing her hands, Olline took a deep breath. "But first, for you to even know why this is so important to me, given the shit ton of drama we've going on around us, you have to understand why I took a contract in Antal. You know, beyond the obscene amounts of money they threw at me."

Casimir moved so he was leaning against his little kitchen island, giving her enough space to not feel crowded. It felt like a kindness of sorts and she appreciated the consideration.

"There was this guy, Achan," she began, her words stilted, slowly gaining strength. "I liked him and thought the feeling was mutual. I shared . . . everything with him. Showed him all the secret projects I was developing for our supervisor. I even showed him my garden. Tried to give him a plant and everything." She jerked her chin at the orchid, letting her gaze rest there instead of her hands. "Turns out, he already had a girlfriend. All he wanted from me was my work. He thought my hobbies were silly and a waste of time and talent. He stole more and more of my magitech programs, my codes. Each time I brought him into my home, he stole a little more and I was too enamored with the idea of him to want to see all the red flags he was waving."

There was a ragged breath, a thump like Casimir bumped into something, but she didn't dare look up and meet his gaze. Olline sighed, balling her hands into fists, refusing to let the memory make her frayed and raw all over again. That was the past. She was only looking forward from now on.

"I was heartbroken. I felt so stupid. But that wasn't even the worst of it." She cringed; she was more annoyed by what happened then hurt by it now. "Achan took my work, shared it with his girlfriend, and together they passed it off as their own. They stole it and cut me out and went to our bosses and said I was the one trying to cut *them* out of what I'd spent so long developing. I was so blindsided, so hurt, that I guess I didn't make a compelling case to corporate. They fired me on the spot."

She heard Casimir shift, moving closer. Olline stalled him with a sharp jerk of her head. She needed to finish. If she didn't get this all out now, she didn't think she ever would.

Olline kept her eyes firmly on the orchid as she pressed on. "To be rejected like that, to have my loyalty so misplaced and to have my work stolen . . . It's made me want to hide from everyone. To throw myself into work because it's safer than needing anyone else. I'm sure I was partially to blame for it all, being that gullible isn't anyone's doing but my own. But since then, I look for signs of betrayal in others so I can leave first."

She took a breath, ran a clammy hand over her thigh and the slight impression of the mini-stick in her pocket, and finally met Casimir's eyes. They were watery, fixated on her as if he hadn't even blinked while she spoke. "Something feels off. There's this distance and I need to know if it's because you don't see me in any kind of special way or, I don't know. This sounded better when I was practicing what to say on the way here," she said with a forced little laugh. Casimir didn't respond, and she cleared her throat, tilting her face away. "I need to know before I start really falling for you, Cas. Because that's what's happening. You can blame Achan for how incredibly awkward this all is, but I can't go through that kind of humiliation again. I need to know if what I'm feeling is one-sided, because I can't trust myself anymore."

She shut her eyes for a moment, put iron in her backbone, turned to face Casimir, and opened her eyes. The pain she saw in Casimir's gaze gave her hope, so she pressed on quickly before the iron in her spine melted away and she pretended none of this ever happened. "There're things that don't make sense about how we met, why you were at my office to begin with. About what you said to Bode when he thought I was, well, I don't know what he thought I was, but we never got a chance to talk about it, either."

Taking one last fortifying breath, she said, "Before things end with Etzel, I need to know what's happening between us. I don't want to waste my time, wreck my heart, over a fantasy again."

Casimir didn't respond for a second, every muscle taut as he remained leaning against the counter. He took a deep breath, and something seemed to break as his shoulders slowly sagged. Yet he remained silent for a moment more.

The iron in Olline's spine finally crumbled, and she shot to her feet. "It's silly, I know. I'm being overly dramatic. You've dealt with so much, and so much worse than anything Achan ever did, so it's not fair for me to put you on the spot like this. I'm sorry, I'll just . . . I should go."

He stopped her with a gentle hand on her shoulder before she could dart past. He carefully pulled her back to sit on the bed where he lightly held her arms so she could wriggle away if she wanted to.

She didn't want to, but it was nice that he gave her the choice.

"It's not a contest, you know," Casimir said with a sad smile, "between who has gone through worse. Emotional wounds bleed all the same." Casimir searched her eyes, but for what, Olline wasn't sure.

She bit her lip, silently withstanding his scrutiny, waiting, hoping, when, with a heavy sigh, Casimir said, "There's something I need to confess to you, too."

CHAPTER 24

Casimir released her, his arms heavy at his side. His shoulders slumped, yet he still met her gaze. Deep red eyes searched hers, flicking back and forth until the corners of his mouth turned down and his normal smirk was gone. The firm lines of his face smoothed, pulled into a kind of remorse that made him look . . . well, *lighter*. She couldn't find holo-images of Casimir as a teenager, before Etzel gotten a hold of him, but she imagined this is what he looked like before: earnest and eager to please the people he looked up to.

There was still an easy confidence, a raw pull of charm that so easily turned toward an undeniable sensuality. In this moment, though, there was a vulnerability to him, a slight fissure of fragility that Olline wanted to patch and protect. She reached out toward him, but stopped when she caught the harrowing look in his eyes.

"I didn't meet you by chance," Casimir said, his words low and slow, as if he spoke them with great reluctance. Suddenly, the tiny device she had brought with Casimir's files felt like a lead weight in her pocket.

"You have to understand, it took me a little while to piece it together," Casimir continued, running his hands through his silvered hair, his fingers tugging at the soft curls. "When Etzel gives my chip a command, I rarely remain aware of what the command is or what my body is doing. This didn't start out any differently. But then you found the chips, you curious, precious thing." He trailed off, the ghost of a bittersweet grin tugging at his face before fading. "The first thing I saw when I came to was you, Olline. Turns out, the order Etzel gave was to abduct you. To take you. To add you to his sick collection of mindless peons." Casimir laughed bitterly, gesturing at himself. "It's probably why he relocated someone here rather than hire locally. By the time anyone noticed anything was wrong, it'd be too late."

Olline's throat was a dry desert, her tongue coated in sand. She couldn't force enough moisture in her mouth to even squeak, let alone scream the way she wanted with the utter sense of terror of almost becoming a thrall. What would have happened had Casimir been mere hours earlier? Would she have ever seen her father again? Her brothers? What would become of her work? What would Etzel have used her magic for? Icey fear lodged itself around her heart; her breathing was fast and labored.

That was before the betrayal crashed through her.

And yet . . . and yet she clung to the hope that maybe Casimir had just now figured out what he had been ordered to do. That he hadn't purposely lied to her and hidden the truth all this time. The dread of being fooled by him, like Achan had fooled her, made her want to curl into a ball to better shield her cracking heart.

"It wasn't until you explained about the difference in control chips that I figured it out," Casimir said, dropping his hands back to his sides, flinching away from her. "I completed the order to find you and grab you. When the chip refreshed, to get the next step, the next instruction, it couldn't connect anymore. That's how I knew I was ordered to get you at Etzel's command. The rest, I surmised on my own from past experiences. If Etzel wasn't preoccupied with his conference . . ." he faltered, unable to continue.

Her heart sank, falling through her body and crumbling to dust. She had explained those technical aspects of the chip what felt like so long ago now. He had known who she was. He had known Etzel had wanted to enslave her, and instead of telling her, he feigned ignorance. The conversation with Bode and all those little things that had tickled in the back of her mind from the onset crashed to the forefront, finally making sense.

"That's why you were there that night at The Pit, how you got there so fast when that prick wouldn't leave me alone. You were following me. Nothing about that was a coincidence at all." She couldn't stop the tremble from entering her voice. A ragged gasp escaped around the sharp, broken edges of her chest where her heart had once been, and she said, "That's why you always stopped us—me from decrypting your files. You didn't want me to see what Etzel had ordered you to do to *me.*" The horror of having a control chip in her, forcing to her be someone else, to do terrible things, to maybe even hurt her family, threatened to shatter her into a million pieces.

As she swallowed to strengthen her resolve, another realization slammed into her with the force of a runaway cargo truck. "That's what Bode meant, wasn't it? When he asked if I was 'the one'? He was asking you if you'd fulfilled your assignment in getting me." Casimir raised his head, and the look in his eyes was the only confirmation she needed. He twitched, like he would move closer to where she sat, and she lurched clumsily out of reach. She bumped into the table, nearly knocking over the night orchid, but Casimir was quick to save the little plant.

Something broke inside of her, a strangled whimper escaping. "Why didn't you tell me?" Olline cried. Time seemed to stop as the force of the betrayal made her nauseous, and black spots flashed in her eyes.

"I didn't—" Casimir began, but cut himself off with another heavy sigh. "The truth? I didn't *want* to. At first, I simply needed you to like me. I didn't know if you were already working for Etzel or my brother. If you were compromised. I hoped if you liked me enough, you wouldn't hand me over to Etzel again. After I realized you were, well, *you,* I didn't want to change what you believed of me."

Olline stared at him, brows furrowed in confusion. Casimir looked up briefly before dropping his gaze, as if it physically hurt him to look at her. "This, Olline, is the truest part of my confession." Casimir's back straightened, but he still wouldn't meet her gaze. "Once I knew what Etzel wanted, and that I was free, I decided that you, my brilliant Olline, were going to save me. I decided that it wasn't a choice I could risk giving you, whether or not to help me. To do what I consider—*considered* to be the right thing. 'Do-gooders' are terribly unreliable, after all," he said, attempting a weak smile, but the effort was halfhearted and the expression soon evaporated.

"I fell back on a century of experience. I let the things Etzel commanded me to do become instinctive, and it was *easy.* So terribly easy." He took another deep breath, his face hardening again into a type of anger laced with disgust. "I needed you to like me, so I manipulated your feelings. I needed you to care about me so you would do what I wanted and set me loose in order to usurp Etzel and take his power and influence and claim it as my own. It was the only way I saw to save myself, protect myself, and keep me safe. Forever."

Olline's chest constricted even more; her worst fear come to life: she had been taken advantage of and would be abandoned *again* by a man she had feelings for. *Unlovable, unlovable, unlovable* . . . the vicious voice in her head whispered over and over until it drowned out every other virtue she believed she possessed.

She didn't know when she stopped breathing, but her lungs were on fire as she took a shaky breath. Everything around her was disintegrating, her vision blurring at the edges with darkness. Her gaze flicked to the exit, then back to Casimir, then back to the exit, but she couldn't make her feet move. The mini-stick weighted her down, still tucked in her pocket, the thing she had so foolishly brought as an excuse to talk to him and see if Casimir *liked* her.

"I was right all along," her voice as broken and strangled as her heart.

The realization stung even worse than it had with Achan.

A thousand tiny needles of molten steel pierced her soul, and she couldn't understand *why*. Why did Casimir's confession hurt so much when they weren't anything? The attention, the flirting, the soft caresses were all a momentary ruse. All to help him get what he wanted.

The memory of his soft, elegant fingers trailing over her skin made her nauseous now.

For as much as she tried, she couldn't push that dalliance into the meaningless rendezvous category she desperately wanted, if only to save her from the crushing weight of heartbreak. The thundering pulse of her heart nearly drowned out the rest of Casimir's so-called 'confession'.

"Seducing you was my plan to achieve all of that, to ensure your cooperation and that you would never betray me while allowing me access to the control chips. It was the natural thing for me to do." His words were gruff and low, but Olline could no longer tell if it was remorse or something else at play. "Frankly, seducing you was the easy part."

Olline could take no more. She would listen to no more of this. Her heart hurt too much as it was and rubbing at her breast bone wouldn't ease the pain this time.

Her hands were trembling. The black orchid, the only

real thing in Casimir's shitty apartment, began to vibrate and shake, practically bouncing on the table as she tried to control herself. Casimir jumped a little, eyes widening in terror as he watched the little plant threaten to break apart. The room vibrated, the metal and stone cracking, breaking free from their fabricated constraints beneath their feet. Bending and twisting, screaming to be unleashed and to rip everything apart until Olline didn't *fucking* hurt so much.

Instead of obliterating the orchid and throwing the pieces at Casimir's stupid, gorgeous face, Olline shoved her hands in her pocket, fingers wrapping around the mini-stick. Gripping it tighter and tighter until the room no longer buzzed around her.

She clutched it so tightly in her hand she thought it would crumble. She pulled it out and stomped toward the door, shoving the data stick into his chest as she passed. Casimir moved to grasp her hand. But she tore her fingers away before he could, leaving him fumbling to catch the mini-stick before it fell to the floor.

Olline stormed to the door, and before her tears could make her voice catch, said over her shoulder, "Congratulations, Casimir. You got everything you wanted. You played me for the gullible little fool I am *and* got your precious file." She took a shuddering, steadying breath, and wrenched open the door. "That's all I was to you, a means to an end. So, here it is: the end. Your *freedom*. You can go and fucking choke on it for all I care. *Alone*."

She didn't hear any movement from Casimir as she

forced herself to tear away, slamming the door behind her. She didn't hear it open again, not as she fled down the hall. No tall, imposing figure followed her to the elevator bays, or called after her as she raced out of the building.

A small, quickly dying part of her *wanted* him to chase after her. But he didn't.

Casimir Everhart let Olline flee, alone, into the night.

CHAPTER 25

Olline stayed locked up in her apartment, unable to sleep. Each time she tried to close her eyes, Olline saw Casimir's slow, unguarded smiles and her heart would fissure and crack apart anew. Tossing and turning, she gave up once the early morning crept around. With a shuddering breath that tugged at her frayed emotions, Olline decided she might as well make herself useful instead of drowning in the events of the night before.

She pulled out her holo-tablet and connected it to the laptop on the table. "Last time I take Dad's advice about stupid, gorgeous men being worth their baggage," she grumbled, angrily swiping a stray tear from her cheek. "At least he'll be happy with me coming home."

Olline hadn't planned on moving back to Cyneburg. Ever. But she didn't see an alternative now. Once Etzel wasn't a problem, her contract would be voided, and Olline didn't want to start over in Antal, not when the pieces she had seen of it held too much of Casimir's touch on them. Her plants rustled around her, their leaves shaking in reproach, as if to say: *your father would rather see you happy far from home, then miserable back in Cyneburg.*

She sneered at the foliage. "Hush. You don't know this wasn't Dad's hope all along. For me to put myself out there just to get hurt and come crawling back home."

It was easier to blame her father than Casimir. But no, that was wrong, wasn't it? Her father did truly want the best for her, even if he was bad at showing it sometimes. Casimir, he . . . he just wanted to make sure she liked him enough to go along with his plan for revenge. That sharp, icy pain in her chest was fucking Casimir's fault, and his fault alone.

"Well," she said, glancing at her vines and trying to sound more confident than she felt, "I rebuilt my life once. I can do it again." She sighed, looking mournfully at the home she had built for herself. All she could see now were the echoes of Casimir gently rearranging the succulents tucked around her kitchen island. The view she was once so dazzled by seemed muted now that he wasn't there to bask in the sunlight. Even her ferns and giant monstera plants appeared listless now that they weren't arching toward Casimir as he prowled her living room. With a shake of her head, she looked at the computers in front of her. "Focus, Olline. You're not out of this yet."

Casimir now had the freedom to do whatever he wanted, but the others, such as Bode, remained trapped. If nothing else came from Casimir's deception, at least Olline knew he wasn't lying about the control chips and what it made the others like him do. Casimir may not be interested in helping anyone but himself, but that wasn't her style. It didn't matter that they would never know what she had done for them. That wasn't the point, it was simply the right thing to do.

No one should have that kind of power over another person. Ever. And with Etzel's conference wrapping up that afternoon, Olline had precious little time to secure Bode and the other thralls' freedom while Delora worked on all the lawsuits.

There was a mountain of work waiting for her, but her thoughts were spiraling and the ferns and vines clustered around the room had already cast judgment on her situation and therefore could not be trusted. There was only one answer now for her situation: time to chat with her family while she worked. But her finger hesitated over her scant contact list. True, her father and Lochan knew about Casimir already, knew her complicated feelings around him, but they were too sentimental—no, too *romantic*. An industrial sized shredder had torn her heart apart, reducing it to a pulpy fertilizer. Olline didn't want understanding, or even pity. She wanted to rage and fight—metaphorically speaking.

Which meant she could talk to only one person: her oldest brother, Darrin.

Darrin didn't answer the first time, allowing Olline to code the killware for the remaining control chips and setting it up so that, once she handed the data packet over to Delora, all the Under Senator would have to do was hit "enter" and all the people Etzel had infected would be free. By the time she had finished, Darrin finally returned her holo-call request.

"Olline," Darrin answered, wiping his face with a towel. She must have caught him after a workout. His skin, a dusky bronze tone, was flushed and dewy, which made his grey-blue eyes, the same shade as their father's, pop all the more. For a seerani, Darrin looked more obviously like their father than Lochan did. Except for the short, twisting indigo horns that poked out of the top of his fluffy, dark teal hair. But Darrin and her father had identical solemn expressions, though her father had earned his with loss, and Darrin was born with a bit of a stick up his ass.

"Darrin," she responded in kind while putting a similar killware program in the blackmail files Etzel had on his thralls, and had them gather. "Are you busy? Because if not, I'd love it if you came to Antal so you could kick someone's ass for me."

To his credit, Darrin merely blinked back at her. His lips didn't even twitch in humor or surprise. He ran the towel over the top of his damp hair, his nostrils flaring as he inhaled deeply. "Right then," his tone resigned, as if Olline often called him requesting he pummel someone—she did not. "What's happened that'd require me to come down there and protect you?" She shook her head. "Okay, beat someone up for fun on your behalf. Details, Olline. If you want me to put in a PTO request for this."

Bless Darrin and his machismo sometimes.

"Hypothetically speaking, let's say there's this guy that tried to use me to gain access to some pretty powerful biomagitech chips—"

"Did he succeed?" Darrin interrupted.

"Well, no," she began hesitantly. "He came clean about it. But only after I confronted him. He was . . . in a complicated position," Olline reluctantly admitted. "But he still hid the truth from me longer than he should have and I—"

"Caught feelings for him," Darrin interrupted again. This was the problem with talking to a hyper-sonic plane mechanic. Darrin wanted to diagnosis the problem and fix it *fast*. Olline never remembered her father being this way when he had been the lead mechanic at Darrin's company, but Zachery had retired while Olline was fairly young.

Glaring at her brother, Olline needed a moment to remind herself why she called Darrin and not Lochan. "Yes, fine, I caught feelings." Olline rolled her eyes, hoping that would hide the tears prickling in the corners that blurred her vision. "That's not the point, Darrin. He lied and hurt me. Like Achan." Saying her not-quite-ex's name had the desired effect. Darrin's lean face hardened as he clenched his jaw, his body tensing. "So, will you come down here and beat him up now? Lochan keeps reminding me the white-knight business is your deal, not his." Olline didn't really want Darrin to beat Casimir up. But it would be nice if someone was willing to protect her heart, and out of all her remaining family, she hoped Darrin would be that one.

Darrin pinched the bridge of his nose. "Sure, Olline. But can I ask you something first?"

She narrowed her eyes, suspicious. Quickly finishing the

code she was working on, Olline nodded, already dreading where this was going.

"This guy in your hypothetical scenario, did he want this powerful biomagitech to help him get out of this complicated situation you're alluding to?"

A shudder raced down her spine, and she nodded again. "Kind of. He claims it's ensuring his safety, but power like that . . . it corrupts everyone eventually. Cas—this guy would become no better than the person he's trying to escape from. I know it."

Darrin's eyes narrowed, and she got the distinct feeling he was seeing more in the holo-projection than she intended. Both her brothers had an uncanny ability to read her. It was annoying, especially in moments like these.

"You sure about that, Olline? And I mean one-hundred percent sure."

Her heart twisted, her mind flashing through those moments where Casimir seemed so sincere, so vulnerable. Those sleepy half smiles that were so different, so open and honest compared to the coy little smirks. Olline tried to convince herself that the flirtatious version, the master manipulator, was the real Casimir. Not the vulnerable man too scared to have anything for himself, too worried for anyone to even see his authentic smile.

"Nothing is a hundred percent like that," she grumbled. This conversation was taking an unexpected turn. Where was the brother who would gladly beat up all the bullies who teased her? Who had threatened Achan with castration when she came home crying after getting fired?

"Right," Darrin agreed. "But you're saying this guy hurt you like Achan?" He waited for her to nod before continuing, "Okay, but Achan was using you to launch his career. This guy sounds like he's in a jam, probably suspicious of everyone, and then he met *you.*" Darrin's lean face rounded slightly with the ghost of an affectionate smile. "Your . . . niceness was rare in a corporatocracy like Cyneburg. I'd bet it's not that much different in Antal. It's hard to know if that friendliness is genuine. You should know how hard it is to trust again after being put in a *complicated* situation."

She squinted her eyes shut, took a deep breath, and mumbled, "I trusted him, Darrin. I did nothing but prove I was trustworthy and he still . . ." She choked on her words. With a sharp shake of her head, she waited a beat before continuing, "I did the right thing saying goodbye. Nothing could've ever come from that . . . infatuation. Nothing good, anyway." Olline blew out a shaky sigh, the air catching on her ragged, raw emotions. "So, will you take my side on this already? I should feel good that I got rid of him. It's a *good* thing he's gone. Hypothetically speaking."

Her plants swayed again, as if shaking their leafy heads. She glared at them, then dropped her gaze to her work, not wanting to meet her brother's eyes. Instead, she sent a quick message to Delora Peralta and set up the final meeting. Unfortunately, it was still nine days away, as Delora hadn't finished getting all the legal documentation set up.

Darrin gave an exasperated sigh, rubbing at his forehead

before smoothing his dark teal hair around his short indigo horns. “Can we stop with the hypothetical shit, Olline? It’s giving me a headache and I’ve work later that I’d rather not be pissed off for.”

Olline huffed, snapping her gaze back to her oldest half-brother. “Fine. Someone I worked with used my access to get what he wanted. *Just like Achan.*”

Darrin drummed his fingers around where he had his holo-projection set up. “I don’t know, Olline.” She balked and Darrin rolled his eyes, tossing his towel off to the side and out of view. “Achan had a lot of red flags from the start. But you liked him, so I kept my mouth shut. So far, from what you’ve told me, this guy had a reason—which doesn’t justify lying, I get that,” he added quickly before she could cut him off. “But you know what I’m saying. Look at what this guy did and said, and what Achan did, and then honestly tell me they’re the same. Because if you can, I’ll catch the first flight out in the morning, I promise.”

Her gaze drifted away, unable to look at her brother’s serious expression as she considered his words. Idly, she picked up the materials she had been manipulating for the hardware portion of her contract to give her hands something to do. The last time she had touched these metals was when Casimir observed her while she manipulated them with her magic. A sudden vision of Casimir telling her what a wonder her power was left her gasping with a sudden chill.

“Talk to me, Olline,” Darrin prompted gently. “That’s why you called me, right?”

"I think," she began, only for her words to break against her emotional wounds. She swallowed the complicated feelings, the hurt and hope, and began again. "He did lie. He did manipulate my feelings. That's a *fact*. But I think . . ." she paused, a sob threatening to crack her voice in half as she remembered how Casimir's eyes widened to behold the world when he wasn't worrying about being so guarded. She blew out a shaky breath and said, her voice soft, "I think he was only able to charm me because, well, because . . ."

When she trailed off, Darrin finished for her. "Because parts of what he did and said were real? Were genuine?"

Swallowing the whimper clawing at her throat, Olline nodded. There was no stopping the tears from escaping now. The one thing to have come from Achan deceiving her was that she could tell the difference between true and feigned interest in her and her work. Maybe she should send Achan a fruit basket in thanks.

Darrin's expression remained mostly serious, but there was a softness in the corners of his eyes that made Olline feel safe to ugly-cry in front of him. Not that she would, but it was nice knowing she could. "Tell me more," Darrin murmured. "What's real about this guy when you compare him to Achan?"

Olline cradled the devices in her hand, imagining it was a holo-screen displaying every single interaction she ever had with Casimir, and put it side-by-side with her experience with Achan. Slowly she explained that each time she had tried to downplay her own accomplishments, Casimir had stopped her, reminded her of the minor miracle her power was with her creations. Achan had agreed with her self-deprecating comments, made her believe he was above her and she should feel lucky to be in his orbit. Achan had discouraged her hobbies as useless, no better than pretty baubles, and Casimir . . . Just recalling his face, the bald marvel he had when looking at all the thriving greenery, made her heart ache anew.

Darrin rubbed his chin as she spoke, listening intently. When she finally finished, her voice hoarse with the hurt she tried so desperately to smother, Darrin nodded. "Sounds like this new guy needed *Olline*. Achan had wanted *your work* for his own gain. You see the difference, right?"

Oh, she certainly did. And it was world altering.

Tears streaked down her cheeks, and she leaned back, her head resting on the couch cushions behind her. She stared at the ceiling, feeling broken inside. "His interest in my work and hobbies may have been real," she conceded, "but nothing else was. He could've been honest with me, told me everything from the start, Darrin," she said, voice brittle. "I would've," a hiccupping sob interrupted her, and she bit her lip until she had better control. "I'd have rearranged the sky if it meant his freedom. But no. He'd been too broken to trust me or my intentions."

Darrin narrowed his eyes at her. "That's not his fault though," his voice was gruff for the first time since their conversation began. "If what you're implying about his situation is even *half* as bad or complicated as you're alluding to, it's not his fault he didn't immediately trust you. Sounds like this guy has been seriously fucked up, Olline. Cut him some slack."

Olline scoffed, "Typical guy defending his fellow man." Darrin rolled his eyes good-naturedly, and she added in a quiet voice, "You sound like Lochan."

"You take that back," Darrin growled, but couldn't look menacing with the humor twinkling in his eyes.

Olline sighed. An empty resignation had her retreat inward once again. "It doesn't matter. Someone like me and a person like that? In no reality, does it make sense." With a violent shove, she pushed all her hardware away from her, jostling her holo-projection and making Darrin's face contort briefly with static. "I love magitech and using my magic to grow pretty plants. I love wearing bright colors and dancing alone to music made by real, breathing people. Cas—this guy is dangerous, mysterious, and so terribly beautiful it hurts to look at him sometimes. He flirts so casually that anyone would feel special in his presence, even if he doesn't feel the same. Meanwhile, I," her throat tightened, choking on emotion. She swallowed the heart-shaped lump down and said, voice throaty, "I don't know how to love someone without it being with my whole heart and soul."

"If all that were true, Olline, then why does saying goodbye to this guy have you asking me to kick his ass?" Darrin's tone, despite his playful words, was gentler than she was used to hearing from her oldest brother. The last time he had taken such a tone with her, it had been shortly after her mother passed away.

She licked her lips, considering. "He still lied and used me." She cut herself off before she mentioned Casimir had been sent to abduct her and didn't think that was something she should know. Telling Darrin that would ensure he came racing to snatch *her* away himself before she could put an end to Etzel's schemes. "He didn't *trust me* to do the right thing. That's why," Olline said, trying not to pout.

"Yeah, he did do that." Darrin shrugged, his tone matter-of-fact. "And that's shitty, no doubt. If I ever meet this guy, I'll rough him up a bit for that, cool?" He winked lazily at her. "But you've said he had a reason. He fucked up, sure, but it wasn't malicious like Achan. I think, Olline," he said, leveling her with a piercing stare so like their father's that it had her shrinking back, "you're more upset at how you reacted. And, if that's the case, maybe you should talk to him again? Clear the air when you aren't, you know," he gestured vaguely at the holo-projection, *"emotional."* The way he said it made the word sound like a dirty curse. Olline chuckled dryly, which allowed her to stifle her wallowing enough to consider her brother's words.

Casimir stalked the shadows, reveling in the more debaucherous side of life. Olline thrived in the light, craving an emotional connection. Plain and simple.

And yet . . .

The one person Casimir had looked up to his entire life deeply betrayed him. She couldn't fathom her brothers, whom she *adored,* doing to her what Kullen had done to Casimir and even surviving that initial treachery. He'd had his consent taken away for a century and found a way to endure that every single day. He was strong, a survivor, and his instincts were to make sure he used everything he had to seize his freedom when it was presented to him so unexpectedly.

"He opened up to me, and I slammed the door in his face for it." Olline's voice was little more than a pained whimper. Her plants didn't even sway in remorse, their silence a heavy judgment in the air. Darrin, for his part, merely nodded. A slight, sympathetic smile twisted his lips.

At least Casimir has his files, she thought, trying to put a healing balm over her hurting soul. *He can flee and start over, free of Etzel.*

"I think you know what options you have here. And none of them includes me coming out there and pummeling some guy."

Olline sighed again; her chest heavy with dejection. "Yeah, probably. But why don't you make yourself useful and tell me what my options are, anyway?"

Darrin chuckled, the sound rough with disuse. "The way I see it, you can go back to this guy, forgive him for over relying on survival instincts around the one truly genuine person he's ever met—"

"Even though he didn't need to," Olline interjected, her words harsh. "Even though it broke my heart and violated my trust."

Darrin shrugged. "You said it yourself. He was doing what experience told him he had to in order to survive."

Olline grumbled unintelligibly for a second. "What's my

other option?"

Darrin rolled his eyes. "You take a page out of my book. Let it all go. Forget he exists and focus on something else."

There was plenty for Olline to focus on beyond what she and Casimir never really had. She could spend her time and energy focusing on covering her digital tracks so Etzel couldn't discover what she had done, what she had given to Delora. Olline could take the time to clone and hide her kill-ware in the Police and Securities Department so there could be no risk of anyone, including Casimir, creating backups of anything she discovered. She could spend this time ensuring that she was as safe as Casimir was now, because if she didn't, who else would?

"Thanks, Darrin," she mumbled, mind made up. "I think I know what I need to do."

He narrowed his eyes suspiciously at her. "Do I want to know what that is?"

She laughed humorlessly. "Probably not."

Darrin stifled a sigh, bracing his thick arms on either side of the holo-projection device. "Fair enough. But, for what it's worth, Olline. This guy really doesn't sound like Achan. Do with that as you will. In the end, I know you'll do the right thing." She opened her mouth to argue, but Darrin spoke over her. "It's in your nature to do the right thing. That's just who you are. No use fighting it. I trust you to do that here." Darrin glanced off to the side, frowning at something she couldn't see. "I'm going to be late for work, but keep me posted? I need to know if I still need to fight someone on my baby sister's behalf."

Olline grinned faintly and rolled her eyes. "Jerk."

"Love you too, Olline," Darrin said with a slight smile, and disconnected the call.

Olline sat motionless on the floor for a minute before pulling her holo-keyboard toward her and scrubbed her digital footprint from every server she had flitted through, making sure Etzel Straub couldn't find her. She rationalized Casimir was long gone from Antal by now, fleeing both Etzel and Kullen in one fell swoop.

It's what she would have done in his place. She had done it before.

With a sigh, Olline forced Casimir from her mind with considerable effort, starting by deleting and blocking all his contact information. With that done, she hunched back over her rigs, her fingers flying over the keyboards, swiping through the screens, hunting for anything that could lead back to her. Like always, Olline was the picture of focus while she worked. And, for a moment, she wasn't so lonely.

CHAPTER 26

Olline wasn't sure how many hours or days passed as she worked.

Just kidding, she knew it was about twelve hours, but it felt like years were crawling by.

She had severely underestimated how large her digital trail had been. On the bright side, working non-stop meant she had no extra capacity to think about Casimir. She was determined to be too exhausted to even dream of him or to remember the feel of his hands on her.

That was the hope, anyway.

His phantom touch still haunted her. Her magic tickled over her skin as if retracing the path his fingers took. Olline did her best to ignore the tingling sensations in order to secure her freedom. At that twelve-hour mark, Olline took her first break to indulge in a home brewed cup of coffee. The mug barely brushed her lips when a memory nearly had the mug tumble from her hands.

The newer control chips, similar to the ones Bode had,

could not be reactivated once the killware was triggered as planned. But Casimir's device was old, little better than a working prototype, he had told her. His could be manually restarted if someone were to get their hands on him. It was why she had needed access to his files to begin with, to find the schematics, and she had stormed off before ever taking care of the problem.

Even though he had left Antal and was probably halfway across Audamar by now, if Etzel sent a bounty hunter after Casimir and dragged him back, he could be enslaved all over again.

Maybe Casimir will go into hiding and Etzel won't be able to find him once Delora has him arrested.

She tried to calm her annoyance with that thought, but Olline's hands still shook.

What if he hadn't fled Antal yet? What if he was still securing a safe way out of the city? What if Casimir stayed?

What if, what if, what if?

There was no way for Olline to contact Casimir now, not after she deleted him from her wrist-communicator. Even if she could unblock him, there was nothing left to unblock. Her breathing started coming in fast little bursts and she put her coffee down on the table so she could shake out the anxious energy collecting in her fingertips.

It didn't help.

Casimir may have crushed her heart, but that didn't mean he deserved to be enslaved again. Throwing her disheveled hair in an even more disheveled bun on her head, Olline grabbed her favorite turquoise jacket, slipped on her black boots, and ran out of her apartment. She didn't bother changing out of the little crop top she had been in the past two days. Her leggings were stiff on her skin, but she had no time to change. Olline may not know how to contact Casimir, but she knew where to start: right back where she had last left him.

His apartment was abandoned.

Well, not entirely, but Olline thought it was pretty obvious her first instinct had been correct. Casimir got out of Antal at the first opportunity, taking only the essentials with him.

Casimir left the door unlocked, as if he didn't care who came looking for him. His closet wasn't empty, but he probably left with just the clothes on his back. Why would you take your dishes or the framed prints of musicians if you needed to get out of the city as fast as you could? Why would you take the plant that the girl you manipulated made on the run with you?

She hesitated in the middle of the room, tugging on her fingers. It seemed like a defilement to be in the apartment without Casimir, without being invited. Olline didn't know why she still cared; he hadn't taken even that miniscule level of consideration toward her. But that was the difference, wasn't it? Olline wasn't like Casimir; she couldn't even pretend to be.

She sighed and pushed her feelings away; she wasn't here

to snoop for fun.

As she began picking through his place, it amazed her all the tiny, personal touches she had missed the first time. Or maybe she knew Casimir better now and she could see him more readily in everything. That, however, would require her admitting that not everything was, or could have been, faked or a lie between them.

There was such *care* put into the few things Casimir had. Aged frames that had been patched, the fake wood repainted and smoothed out a dozen times at least. His clothes weren't new, but they had been treated with reverence. Tiny stitches could be seen along the seams, repairing them and altering the fashion to remain chic even decades later. The furniture, at first glance, had looked like a matching set, but now that Olline was looking for any sort of communication device Casimir may have left behind, she could tell that they weren't. Casimir had taken discarded stools and painted them and changed the upholstery, anything he needed to get the stools to look like they matched. That they belonged together.

Her chest tightened, her throat constricting as hot tears prickled in the corners of her eyes. Casimir had made this tiny studio a home, a haven for himself when he wasn't allowed sanctuary anywhere else. He showed the world a facsimile of who he was, but here? Here was the real Casimir. And he had invited her in willingly.

"It doesn't matter," Olline said with resignation. "He's gone." She took a deep breath, looking around one last time for anything she could have missed. The tears she had banished returned with a fury.

The room still smelled so strongly of Casimir. Like she had *just* missed him. The musky eucalyptus and lavender scent coiled around her, stronger now that she noticed it, and Olline mourned. She grieved for what might have been, what could have been, if a few things had been different. Running a delicate finger over the night orchid, she lost herself in the fantasy of what being with Casimir would look like:

Her dragging him to every little coffee kiosk that made real coffee, him grumbling about it through the ghost of a smile, garnet eyes twinkling at seeing her delight. He would surprise her by taking her to secret garage band practices on a random work day afternoon. Even the mundane things like grocery shopping would be a fun little adventure, with the two of them teasing each other up and down the bread aisle.

She clenched her fists and screwed her eyes shut again. "Stop it, Olline. Focus. Casimir still needs help."

There was nothing in his apartment that would help her find him. So where could she go?

Definitely not Refractory, that was too close to Etzel for Casimir. Same went for the Government Plaza. Maybe that private garden he had snuck her into? It was late enough he could sneak in . . . "But why would he go there?" Olline murmured. "There's nothing there for him." Perhaps he had gone back to The Pit? But no, that didn't make sense either, because he had only gone there when he was stalking after her.

Her eyes trailed over the pictures on his wall, and her breath caught in her chest. "That's it!" The little artists haven

Casimir had made and kept after Kullen abandoned the club, and Casimir. She doubted he was there, but someone there might know how to get in contact with him.

If nothing else, it was the best—only—lead she had, and Olline was going to follow it.

In theory, it was a great idea, the perfect plan to start with. In execution? Olline did not know where she was going.

Unlike Casimir's apartment, the tiny little club he had converted from a residence was well hidden. Antal had morphed and grown around the location over the years to where it wasn't obvious or easy to retrace her steps to. Casimir had taken her on such a convoluted, winding path she was already disoriented.

Olline thought she was in the right area, but she wasn't positive. A lot of lower Antal looked the same: shrouded in an oily dusk, the neon lights around the businesses creating hazy shadows to light the pedestrian pathways. There were hundreds of tiny alleys and alcoves that led nowhere, dozens of street vendors all hawking the same knock-off magitech devices or street food block after block after block.

Ducking down a side street that looked familiar, Olline tried to stay in the light as much as possible. It *looked* like the same alley Casimir's club was tucked into with its cluster of tiny homes. She decided to check the closet sized residences to see if she could find the right door again, when the alley abruptly ended in a greasy wall.

"Dammit," she growled. Olline turned to leave, only to find her path blocked by a burly figure that hadn't been there a second ago.

Olline moved to the side to get around the person standing in the middle of the narrow path. There were homes in this cramped alleyway, after all. It was possible she had surprised someone by being somewhere she shouldn't have been.

But the person stepped in her path as she tried to move around, and Olline realized she was only half right. This was definitely not somewhere she should be.

Olline pulled on her power, reaching out to the natural elements, and even her own piercings in her ears and eyebrow to aid her should it come to that. She couldn't see the person's face, so she didn't want to rely on her tech skills if this person didn't have biomagitech in them like Bode had.

She tried to step around them again, murmuring, "Excuse me," in case they were merely rude, only to be blocked again. By then, she had identified the pieces of real stone in the walls around her and was ready to pull them toward her, to bundle them around the sharp steel she would free from her own skin, when the figure spoke.

"Olline Tavos." They're voice a raspy, wispy whisper that brought her up short. They said her name without question, and the magic fizzled in her fingertips in her surprise. "You've been a busy woman. Too difficult by half to track down." There was a grating rumble that Olline too late realized was a laugh as they captured her wrists in their enormous hand. "Lucky me, I've found you. The boss will be pleased."

CHAPTER 27

Olline tried to wrench her hands free, but it was no use. She dug her heels into the slick concrete and pulled every ounce of her magic from her core, reckless in how quickly she coiled the ethereal tendrils around the raw materials at her disposal. With a wordless yell, she flung her magic outward, commanding it to bind her assailant and pin them to a wall.

Air *whooshed* out of Olline as if she had been punched in the stomach with an iron fist.

Sputtering, she twisted her wrists, called to the power she could feel bubbling and earnest deep inside her. But as it boiled to the surface, like hitting an invisible lid, something blocked it once again.

Then she saw it. A quick blink of purple light, nearly lost to the gloom, coming from the fleshy part between her assailant's thumb and pointer finger. Seeing that, she knew. She *knew*. They were equipped with a piece of magitech specifically used to block a caster's magic.

Only qualified security and police were equipped with

such magitech, in order to apprehend casters before they could pose a threat to public safety. The person who held her now was in no discernable uniform and even if they had been, they had zero reason to be treating her this way. They were clad in a smoky grey coat, covering them from head to toe, making it impossible to see who they were.

Olline opened her mouth to scream, only to have the goon violently pull her forward and twist her around. They slammed a hand over her mouth and face with such force she was surprised hot blood didn't spurt from her nose.

Horror settled in, and Olline fought to suck in enough air to stay conscious. The massive figure moved, dragging her out of the alley. She knew with a sinking certainty where she was being taken: to Etzel. To be implanted and enslaved for the rest of her life. Only the hand over her mouth kept her from spewing on her attacker's feet in terror.

She was choking, kicking wildly. Desperately she stared at the darkened doorways around her, silently screaming, praying for anyone, *just one fucking person,* to come outside and help her.

They were almost out of the alley now, almost to wherever the figure had come from. She lurched and struggled for all her worth. The person holding her was too massive, too strong for her to break their hold on her hands. Her magic kept far away.

Then they stopped moving altogether.

There was a wet gurgle, the trickle of something hot that smelled metallic dripping onto her shoulder. Her attacker stumbled a step, and then she was falling. Her assailant still held her in a vise, and was falling forward, so she would be the one to cushion their fall.

Perfect. Just perfect.

The filthy street rushed up to meet her before she was savagely pulled free. Her magic returned to her in a rush, and she was crushed against someone else's very solid chest. She gripped the magic in her fingertips, had it rip the metal piercings free from her skin, and took a deep breath, ready to unload on yet another person who wanted to abduct her. Then she recognized a familiar scent.

Eucalyptus and lavender.

Not even the metallic musk of blood could mask it completely. Olline pulled her head back and stared into panicked crimson eyes. "Casimir?"

"Ollie," he said, breathing her name out like it had consumed all his oxygen. Her skin prickled, and she tried to pull back, to truly look at him, but he held her tightly, crushing her to him.

"I'm all right, Casimir. I'm okay," she reassured him. It was a lie, but she couldn't handle his fear and him being here and what it all meant. Not right now. She focused on returning the piercings back to their original form, putting them back in her ears and eyebrow, and hoped they didn't look like a mess. It was frivolous, but it was a safe task to distract herself with.

Yet he still held her, cradled her to his body, buried his nose in the top of her hair.

It took him a minute before he finally seemed to accept

that she was here with him. That she was safe-ish. That it was really her he held in his arms. "What were you thinking?" Casimir said at last, his voice shaky.

"I was looking for you." Olline tried to yell, but as the adrenaline bled from her system, she could manage nothing louder than a heated whisper. "I was thinking that I had to find you and warn you about your chip. It's still possible for Etzel to reactivate if he ever catches you." She took a choked breath that burned all the way down and said, "I was thinking I still had to help you."

She was shaking now, her teeth clacking as shock settled in. His hands supported her, kept her steady. She tried to turn, to see what Casimir had done to Etzel's thrall, but he stopped her. "You don't want that image in your head, my sweet," he murmured, gently leading her away.

His hands were sticky, the metallic scent suddenly overpowering as she realized there was blood on them. And now on her, too.

"Did you kill them?" she whispered, her steps uncertain as he supported her.

"Yes," he answered sharply. Then hissed out a breath. "No. They would need aid *right now*. They're as good as dead, which is better than they deserve for touching you."

A calming warmth blossomed in her chest. Still, they couldn't leave them there. The person had been following Etzel's command, no better than a puppet. They didn't deserve to die for that. Despite her vision going fuzzy at the edges, the nausea returning as the blood dried on her skin, Olline sent an anonymous request for immediate medical attention from her wrist-comm like they had done for Bode.

Casimir huffed as he noticed what she was doing, but he didn't stop her. "Your kind heart will be the death of us." But there was no heat or reprimand in his words.

Us.

Quickly, but still careful of her unsteady steps, Casimir led her out of the alley. To distract herself from the shock, she asked, "What were *you* doing here?"

He gave her a sidelong glance and his throat bobbed as he swallowed. His eyes trailed over her, lingering on the tender bruises slowly emerging on her wrists. His jaw clenched, the muscle in his neck feathering, but his grip on her remained gentle. "Let's get you somewhere safe first. We don't have much time before Etzel sends another one of my colleagues after you. Best we're far from here when that happens."

Olline nearly tripped over her feet at his words. Her steps were already sluggish, but the terror of her close encounter rushed back all too eagerly at the idea that there could be—no, *were* more people out there that would come after her.

Casimir, seeing her stumble, wrapped an arm around her waist and practically carried her. "I have to ask," he said, and Olline was positive it was simply to get her mind to think about something beyond what had almost happened. "How did you crack my file? Was it another clever decryption program of yours?"

"No," she croaked. "I figured out the password like you, the old-fashioned way."

She may have imagined it, but she swore his steps faltered. "Dare I ask," he murmured, "*how* you figured it out?"

"Like it was hard?" Olline responded, trying to be playful, but her shrug, her words, everything felt stiff and forced. She sighed; her limbs were still shaky as they moved through the city. "I didn't have to think like Etzel. I just . . . thought like me and what I knew of the elements, and then it was kind of obvious. You're Uranium."

He huffed. "Radioactive?"

"Not . . . exactly." As she spoke, the panic bled from her. "Purified Uranium isn't the natural state it wants to be in, it's the state *we want* it to be in, the state we find most useful. Well, not *we,* but you know, scientists who like bombs and pustulant dickheads like Etzel." She paused; her explanation was about to get more technical than she intended. "Point is, Etzel made you into something you weren't, something radioactive because it suited him. So, Uranium." A chill settled over her as the hot fear left her cold, her skin prickling. Rubbing her arms, she said, "I don't think Etzel intended for the double meaning with purified Uranium but that's how I like to look at it."

He was quiet, thoughtful for a moment. "You figured all that out, and it was correct? How?"

"Because I know you—*knew you,* better than either of us thought," she whispered mournfully.

Casimir let the matter go. Instead, he idly chatted with her to keep her thoughts far away from the attack. He asked about how her half-brothers and her father were doing, to tell him funny stories of growing up with seerani brothers. He seemed to enjoy the fond snippets she shared more than he wanted to admit, and even chuckled when she told him Darrin owed him a throttling for hurting her. Casimir shared a bit of his life before Etzel ever came into the picture; the scant memories he had of Kullen before addiction transformed him, and even where that delicious coffee cart was located that provided real coffee beans. It was . . . pleasant, all things considered.

She was sure getting to her place must have taken a while. Neither of them could risk taking any automated transportation for fear of being tracked. She was certain that people noticed the blood on both of them, but they continued to whisper to one another as if in a dream. They were never stopped, and while Olline didn't exactly like how all of this came about, she wouldn't have traded that meandering conversation for anything. They arrived at her place without further incident, and Olline wanted to believe it meant their luck was turning around.

He helped her inside and only once Olline inhaled the clean, earthy scent of her apartment and all her plants did she risk asking, "Are we safe here?"

Casimir locked the door and lifted a shoulder in a shrug before gently nudging her toward the couch. "Safer than anywhere else I can think of. For as ostentatious as this place is, my dear, it works in our favor this time. Etzel would have to be very, very careful with getting to you in such a well-to-do mega complex, not to mention on a floor so high up."

Olline's hands trembled with mini earthquakes as she worked on releasing the anxiety still pumping in her veins. Casimir grasped her hands in his, his long elegant fingers still encased in flaky, muddy blood, but Olline didn't mind. In the warmth of his hands, she felt safe.

After another moment of breathing deeply, letting his presence comfort her, she asked again, "How?"

Casimir swallowed, and he shifted on the couch next to her so he was facing her. Their knees brushed, and even now Olline could feel the electric heat sparking from such casual contact, sending tingles down her calves to curl her toes.

"I was looking for you. I came here. Your doorman recognized me and let me back in, but you never answered. I didn't know where you could've gone, and I feared Etzel had completed the job he'd programmed me to do from the onset. That's how I found you. I figured that, if Etzel was impatient with me, he would send Wolfe." His lip twitched into a slight sneer, but he shook the expression away. "That's who grabbed you. Wolfe is . . . they're the hammer Etzel sends when his more finessed tools aren't working at the speed he desires."

Casimir sighed, dropping his head slightly. But was that regret she saw in his gaze? "Wolfe is never hard to find. After so many years working together, I can track pretty much any of my colleagues without issue, but Wolfe's always been particularly easy. It would've been better if I'd gotten to you first, but, well, at least I wasn't too late."

He freed one of his hands so he could cup her cheek, gently running his hand over the tender flesh of her jawline.

"Why would you *ever* come looking for me after I betrayed you? You had no reason to."

Olline's shoulders slumped, exhaustion catching up with her in a rush. "Your chip. It could still be reactivated if Etzel got to you again. It's why I even needed access to your file to begin with, to get the schematics. Your chip is *so old* that I couldn't risk tampering with it until I had those outlines, and once I got them," she left the rest unsaid, clearing her throat. "For as much as you . . . as it hurt me, you don't deserve to be enslaved again. I'd have messaged you but, well, I removed all digital traces of you a bit too well. So, when I got to your place and found it unlocked, I figured you took your freedom and ran. Which would've been the smart thing to do, you dick!" She tried to joke, but her grin was shaky and Casimir looked pained. Swallowing with difficulty, she said, "I thought maybe someone at your club would know how to contact you so I could at least warn you. I just overestimated my ability to find the place again."

"Oh, my precious Ollie," Casimir's voice was rough and husky, his eyes round and shimmering with emotion.

Olline tensed. "Don't call me Ollie," she growled. It hurt her heart too much to have him call her Ollie now.

She shook her head, but couldn't quite force herself to move out of his gentle grasp. "You have your freedom, Casimir," she said, trying to keep the quiver from her voice. "Why didn't you take it and run?"

"Because of you, *Olline*." He said it so matter-of-factly, like she should have known. She narrowed her eyes at him, and he smiled sadly at her in return.

"I spent all night wallowing in my home thinking of what I could do, what I could say to beg your forgiveness. Or if giving you space was the better option. It was driving me mad," he said with a heavy exhale. "I knew, even before you gave me my file, that I could never leave your side. I can explain better this time, I promise."

He took a deep breath and waited for her to meet his sincere gaze before continuing. "All I had to do was get you to like me. All I had to do was not fall for you in return. So blissfully simple, until I saw you at The Pit. My simple plan was undone the moment I saw you enjoying *life*. It was entrancing. But you," he cut himself off with a gruff noise Olline thought may be a growl. "You Olline," he began again, his voice softening on her name, "*you* are enchanting. You were the complication I could never have accounted for. Falling for you wasn't part of my plan. No matter how hard I tried to fight these feelings, I lost every single battle each time you smiled."

He sighed again, more wistfully this time, his breath tickling her face as he lowered his forehead to hers. Olline's heart was fluttering, hope rising like a wave. She was too afraid that if she blinked, if she moved, Casimir would evaporate and everything he said would be only a dream.

"It was you, Ollie," he murmured, his nose brushing the tip of hers in a gentle nuzzle. "It will always be *you* that undoes *me*. This freedom you've given me, it tastes like ashes without you here, with me."

Her breath caught in her chest as tears clouded her vision.

Every inch of her skin was tingling, too sensitive by half. She was too aware of him, of where their knees touched, where his hands held her, his nose brushed hers, how and when his brow crinkled as he waited for her to respond.

Words, for once, and at the worst time, failed her.

Casimir tightened his grip on her hand, his fingers trembling on her cheek as he whispered, "If I could take it all back, hiding the truth from you. Hurting you. I would. A million times over, I would take it back. I am sorry, Olline. I don't deserve your forgiveness, but I beg it all the same."

"Casimir," his name caught in her throat, and his hand moved from her jaw to cup the back of her neck as he breathed her in. She shouldn't forgive him, right? How could she believe him now, after everything he hid from her? But he also risked his freedom to stay, to find her, when he didn't have to.

She wasn't sure what to think, what to believe. Olline's heart thundered, clinging to the idea that this gorgeous man wanted *her*. She couldn't stop the comforting warmth that perfect dream brought with it from spreading through her, nor did she want to.

"For the first time in a century," he whispered against her cheek, "I was given a choice. And I choose *you,* Ollie. For the longest time, wanting anything was a death sentence because of what Etzel could make me do. But now . . . I want you to be mine. Selfishly, thoughtlessly, all *mine*."

Olline's chest constricted, her heart swelling, about to burst. This couldn't be real. Her only value to men like Achan and Casimir was what they could take from her and her work.

Yet Casimir hadn't taken her work, his file, and run. He had stayed. He had saved her life. The words were still lost to her and her disbelief. All that escaped her slightly parted lips was a tiny, sharp gasp of breath.

"I would face down every single one of Etzel's thralls for you, Olline, if that's what you wanted," Casimir said, his words an urgent plea. "Or you can say goodbye to me right now and I'll let you go. My heart will continue to beat, singing your name for the rest of my life if you walk away. I wouldn't blame you. I'm no better than Etzel for trying to manipulate you the way I did. But I'm hoping that I haven't fucked this up beyond repair. I swear, you aren't some mark. You never truly were. You're *everything,*" his voice caught on the word, his grip tightening a fraction before relaxing again.

"Say you choose me, Ollie," his voice was as rough as sandpaper, as deep as the night, her name a prayer on his tongue. "Choose me," he practically begged. "Or I will go and you never have to see me again. Your want, your desire, is *mine* to fulfill."

Olline could take no more. She removed her hands from his lap, and Casimir shuddered, his breath ragged as if his heart was cracking, believing she was going to push him away. The thought of him walking back out of her door, out of her life . . . the mere suggestion was soul crushing. Instead, she grasped the sides of his head and tilted his face up ever so slightly so he was looking into her eyes.

He looked scared, his brows furrowed in pain. *Afraid.* To hope, to love. Just like her. This was the Casimir she had fallen for. He was there still, deep inside, and he was *real.*

"I would like to kiss you now." Her own voice was a smoky whisper.

He blinked in confusion, before his expression changed, shifting to such a pure joy that it threatened to suffocate her. "I would like that."

His lips brushed hers, a feather-light touch that was hesitant.

Olline closed the distance, pressing her lips to his more firmly, marveling at how soft they were. A thrill went through her, finally claiming that coy smile all for herself. Casimir stilled for a heartbeat, his body tense, his hands gripping her like she was in danger of floating away, but his mouth remained kind and soft on hers.

Casimir pulled away. The kiss was so gentle and sweet, so at odds with him and his confession that Olline was light-headed. He rested his forehead against hers again, a slight chuckle rumbling through his hard chest. "You're the first person I've wanted to kiss in a century, my dear. I worry . . . I'm a bit out of practice."

Olline giggled, running her tongue along her top lip, savoring his taste. "We could practice together. If you want."

He watched her mouth, his eyes darkening with desire, his breaths coming in short bursts, but his gaze slid away, locking on the flecks of blood still on her, on his hands. He grinned, but pulled away a fraction. "I would love nothing more, but first," he said, pulling her to her feet. "We should clean this blood off."

CHAPTER 28

Olline was in a daze, her heart too full from Casimir's confession, her limbs still shaky from her near abduction. As soon as she stood, she swayed, and he frowned. He glanced around and, as Olline realized what he was going to do, he scooped her up into his arms and carried her through the apartment.

He held her so reverently, like she was the most precious thing he ever had in his arms. Olline snuggled closer, allowing herself to be held and taking the comfort he offered. That she deserved.

Stopping outside her closed bathroom door, his fingers dug into her body ever so slightly. "Are you all right to stand? Do you need help?" His words were so soft, so full of concern and want, that her core clenched in response.

She didn't *need* help, but she *wanted* it. And if Casimir was offering? Olline would take it. The way he looked at her, so open and like she was his beginning and end, sent her stomach fluttering into her throat. It made it easy to let him take care of her the way she was finally realizing she deserved all along.

"I'm fine, honestly, Cas. But we're both filthy. Seems silly to take turns." She slid from his arms, her body trailing down the length of him. Casimir stood rigid, his nostrils flaring, his eyes locked hungrily on every single one of her movements.

With a smile, she bumped open the bathroom door with her hip, then gently took his hand before she could overthink everything. "It's up to you, Casimir. If you'd rather take things slow after what you've gone through, I support that. I don't want you to feel rushed or forced ever again."

He stood motionless for a heartbeat.

Then his easy smile slowly bloomed on his face, making him glow. "The way you ask for my consent is perhaps the sexiest thing I've ever experienced. But what do *you* want, my dear?"

"You. This," she whispered back without hesitation.

A low chuckle rumbled in his chest. "Your wish is my absolute desire," he murmured, his words heated and breathy as he let her lead him into the bathroom.

Casimir kicked the door closed behind him. The crisp white light illuminated all the blood splatter in blinding detail. It hadn't fully hit Olline that Casimir would have killed Wolfe to protect her.

She should be terrified of that. A logical, sane person would be.

But all she could see was the man who would have gladly given up his freedom if it meant keeping her from harm. For someone who couldn't want or have anything of his own for a century, it was an incredibly selfless act.

Casimir's hands had rust-colored flakes caked on them, and streaks of dried blood marked his neck and face from where it had rubbed off on him—from her. She stole a look at herself in the mirror, and her eyes widened at the sight, suddenly bashful.

Bruises marked her wrists, and the shadows of welts in the shape of a giant hand marred her face, not to mention the blood. Olline hadn't seen what Casimir had done, where he cut or stabbed, but muddy red streaks painted the side of her face and neck. She was sure her hair was coated as well, but the dark moss and black of her hair hid it well. The bloodshot streaks from her tears and waning panic dulled the usually bright emerald green of her eyes. All of this was on top of the fact that, in her haste to find Casimir to begin with, she hadn't bathed or changed her clothes.

To put it nicely, Olline looked like shit.

Why would Casimir want her now? Perhaps this was a mistake. Maybe she should clean up on her own first . . .

Casimir followed her gaze to where she stared at herself in the mirror, her surprised look of horror plain to see. Slowly, tenderly, he released her hair from the hasty bun she had tossed it in earlier, and ran his fingers through the strands, detangling it. "You're a vision," he purred, pulling her closer, giving *her* the chance to pull away.

He was always putting her comfort first.

The realization broke the spell. She tore her eyes away

from her reflection, preferring to see herself as Casimir saw her, and hoping he, too, could see himself through her eyes. She gingerly reached up, cupping that sharp jawline in her hand, lightly pulling him toward her, their lips a breath apart. "I see you, Casimir. The real you. And you're wonderful."

His throat bobbed, his deep red eyes shimmering, and he lowered his lips to hers again. The kiss was soft, tentative, an entreaty against hers. She parted her lips, inviting him in. He moaned against her mouth, his tongue sliding against hers. His fingers, still tangled in her hair, tightened as he brought her closer, as he drank her in. She hummed in pleasure, and that little sound was his undoing.

Casimir devoured her like he had been starving all his life.

Holding her closer, his fingers wove through her hair, his mouth barely leaving hers for more than one shaky breath at a time. Her eyelids fluttered closed as contented bliss warmed her body, and she pushed his stained jacket off his shoulders. Her hands traveled down his stomach, dancing over every contour.

With a shudder, his lips left hers long enough to whisper, "Olline," as her fingers hooked around his belt loops. He moaned deep in his chest, making it sound like a growl, and he stepped from her embrace only to tear his bloodied shirt off and kick off his pants.

Olline didn't have time to admire him before his mouth was on her again. He peeled off her clothes, separating temporarily to pull her shirt over her head, as if any second where he was not touching her, where he was not kissing her deeply, was an eternity too long.

Cradling her head in his hands, his nose brushed hers again while she fumbled to turn on the shower. "You have haunted my dreams, Ollie. All of it was meant only to be a dream. You're too good for a scoundrel like me."

She smiled at him, gently nipping his bottom lip with her teeth like she had dreamed of doing. "You aren't. I like you, Cas. You and the softness you keep hidden under your sharp, hard edges," she admitted.

Casimir may have hidden the circumstances around how he came into her life, but he had never hidden his darker nature. Whether that was how he always was, or who he became to survive, it didn't matter.

His breath hitched, and then his arms snaked around her, gripping her tightly as he pushed her back, the hot water nowhere near as scorching as his touch on her bare, blood caked skin. Delicately, he trailed his fingers over her, washing away the stains from her neck, out of her hair. His eyes were wide as he drank her in, like he couldn't get enough. Suddenly, she felt shy under his adoration, the flush of her skin having nothing to do with the heat of the water.

As if reading her thoughts, he said, "You're glorious," and then did not allow her to respond as his lips brushed hers again, his tongue a gentle caress against her. Her body softened, and she gave into the desire she had felt for him almost instantly, magnified tenfold now because she *knew* Casimir.

His hands continued to roam, but she captured them in hers and carefully, deliberately, cleaned them. She had no words to express how little she minded what Casimir believed were marks against his soul, all those unspeakable things Etzel had forced him to do that he disassociated from. He was not stained, not to her. But if washing away the very real blood from him was the only way he could feel clean with her, then she would wipe every drop of gore from his body again and again, for as long as he would allow her to.

Casimir shuddered under her touch, as she wiped the stains from his neck, the flecks in his hair, and the few smears that had found their way to his shoulder and back. Her touches were soft but deliberate, and she could feel the effect her administrations had on him.

He had tortured her with his light, coaxing touches when they were working at Refractory. Now she would repay the favor. Olline's fingertips danced down his torso, lightly brushing the wet pelvic hair trail that started beneath his navel before her digits twisted to the side of his thigh. The ghost of a promise. His cock jolted, his body tensing as a ripple of pleasure coursed through him.

"Fuck," Casimir growled. He pushed her back until she was against the shower wall. His arms caged her in, hands pressed firmly on either side of her head as if he needed to be tied to the wall to keep from grabbing her. In that moment, Olline understood she was trapped, her emotions forming an unbreakable cage just like Casimir's arms around her body. Yet even if, one day, she freed herself from the affection locking her to Casimir, she would blissfully throw the key away with no regrets.

Olline smiled, tilting her chin up, an invitation he eagerly took. His teeth nipped along her throat, landing on the hollow where her shoulder dipped into her neck. Each little bite was an electric shock that shot straight to her sensitive clit. All the while, she softly caressed his taut skin with her hands, tracing every scar, showing him the care he had been denied for far too long.

Casimir's arms quivered around her as her touches brought her back to his shaft, lightly dancing around the base of his thick cock. His hips moved against her, his tongue flicking, his teeth tugging her skin, a promise of what he so clearly wanted to, and could, do inside of her. But he held back, letting her tease him, bring him to the edge, and *shit,* she was so wet from that knowledge alone.

She wanted—*needed* him to touch her, wasn't sure why he wasn't. When it hit her. Casimir would not take what hadn't been freely, and eagerly, offered to him ever again.

"You can touch me, Casimir. *Please.*"

No more needed to be said. His mouth was instantly on her breast, his teeth light as he nibbled the delicate skin until her nipple puckered. He drew it eagerly into his mouth, his teeth teasing on the right side of painful. One hand moved from the shower wall, tracing the outline of her other breast briefly before trailing down between her legs. That barren, cracked desert landscape that was her loneliness blossomed; a rainstorm that was Casimir's adoration watering the parched ground until Olline was positively blooming. She was vibrant and alive again in a way she hadn't been since Achan crushed her spirit.

All thoughts of her not-quite-ex fled as Casimir's long fingers moved between her folds to find her throbbing clit and rub it in slow, gentle circles, until she squirmed against him. Her lungs were on fire, unable to get enough air with how desperately she needed him to give her more, more, *more.* His thumb pressed down on the sensitive bud as one elegant finger slipped inside.

She opened like a flower under his touch. "Yes," she cried, tilting her head back and hooking her leg around his hip, needing him to go deeper, harder, faster. He gave a muffled curse around her breast, releasing her only to kiss her with an urgent hunger that stole all the fire from her lungs.

Even in the shower, she could feel the slickness of her desire as he worked her pussy. Rotating his finger, getting the feel of her, until . . . *there.* She moaned into his mouth as he found that sweet spot deep within her. She could feel him smile against her lips, before he pulled away slightly, admiring the flush of her cheeks, the bliss on her face as he brought her waves of pleasure.

Casimir made it impossible to think. Olline's blood was boiling, her legs shaking with the start of her pleasure beginning to crest. Her hands tangled in his wet hair, anchoring her. Her pussy clenched around his finger, and then that devil slipped another inside, opening her up. Her gasp did little to help inflate her lungs, her mounting orgasm taking up too much space as his fingers continued to twist and thrust and press down, harder, firmer on her clit.

"Cas," she moaned. "*Please.*"

He released her, and she nearly cried out with the loss of him, when his hands cupped her ass and hoisted her up. His strong fingers dug into the inside of her thighs, positioning her so that her legs were spread wide around his waist, making it impossible for her to wrap them around him. He positioned her in a way that spread her open around him, a position that should be obscene, but all it did was turn her on even more. Casimir met her gaze, his quick breaths matching her own, and she saw her own delight in the obscene mirrored in his eyes. The thick head of his cock sought entrance, and he held it there, teasing her. Olline whimpered. She wanted all of him in her until there was no more space between them, until his breaths were hers and their thundering hearts pounded in unison. She arched her hips forward until he was *finally* in her, where he belonged.

Olline gasped with the fullness of him as he pushed himself a little farther into her. He panted against her neck as he waited for her to get accustomed to the length of him, his girth stretching her out in the most pleasant ache she had ever experienced with any partner before.

He felt made for her. They were two broken pieces that became whole together and Olline didn't want to imagine a life without this—without *him* in it ever again.

With a deep growl that vibrated against her chest, he slammed the last inch home, burying himself in her until not even water could get between them. "*Olline,*" he cried, before rocking against her, finding the rhythm that carried her closer to the edge. He pushed her into the wall, releasing one hand from her ass to cup her head, protecting her from the shower tiles as he plowed into her.

She rocked her hips, angling down so she could rub against him as he drove himself into her, deeper, relentless. His breath was hot against her skin as he buried his face against her neck.

Pulling her leg up higher, he drove himself even deeper, and Olline cried out in ecstasy. "Fuck. *Yes,* Ollie. You're perfect. Perfect in every single way," he moaned against her skin, his tempo increasing.

Her orgasm was building within her with each desperate thrust. She threw her head back as much as she could, angling her body so he could hit that magnificent spot deep inside her again, and again, and *again*. "Cas", she cried, her breath hitching as a tingling, tickling warmth spread from where he was rocking into her.

"Say it," his words a demand, his tone a plea. "Say my name, my precious little caster. I want to hear you cry for me."

His thrusting turned frantic as he moved his hips harder, faster, her back thumping against the wall as he pushed as far into her as he could. And even then, it didn't seem like enough. Nothing was close enough. She wrapped her arms around his shoulders, felt the muscles bunching beneath her fingertips as her nails dug into his skin and she sank her teeth into him.

Casimir bucked against her. "I want to hear you," he rasped, his voice raw and husky with desire. "Scream for me,

Ollie."

It was how he said her name that threatened to push her over the edge. He made it sound like a precious, fragile bauble on his wicked tongue. Like she was the embodiment of magic, of *perfection.*

His pace was relentless, never slowing and then . . . *"Casimir!"*

Her orgasm was an eruption through her. She bucked against him, and he held her in place, drawing the wave out, rocking her through it as the currents of ecstasy tumbled over and through her, until her thighs were shaking and all she could do was hold on.

Olline wasn't usually a one orgasm kind of girl, but it had been so, so long since anyone had made her finish this hard. Her pussy tightened around Casimir, and he changed his pace, continuing to draw out her pleasure at the sake of his own. His strokes were long and slow before he plowed into her all the way again. The stone in her walls shuddered as she lost control of her powers, too wound up in the sheer pleasure that was Casimir.

Blissful contentment enveloped her, a warm completeness that had her seeing in ultraviolet as her magic and her heart became one under Casimir's reverence. It wasn't until her orgasm finally faded, the rivers of lava that were her pleasure cooling, and her arms slack and sliding off his slick back, that Casimir could hold back not a second longer.

His pace picked up, frantic and desperate. His fingers dug into her skin, urgent to keep her close, for her to take all of him. He grunted, and moaned, "Olline," drawing out her name until the sound was a sigh on his tongue.

With a final, violent thrust, he climaxed. His cock jerked in her as he slammed them against the shower wall. The vibration made her shudder against him, eliciting another moan from Casimir as he came deep within her.

They stayed that way for a moment, or perhaps an eternity. Olline didn't know and didn't care. The shower still steamed around them, but the water felt cool on her scorching skin. Casimir slowly, almost reluctantly, removed himself from her, and she could feel his cum roll down her legs as he gently lowered her feet back to the shower floor.

Olline was in a post orgasm glow, her mind hazy. How Casimir could think at all, she didn't know. His touch was worshipful while he cleaned her, making sure he had not added any new bruises to her back from his passion. He turned off the water, dried them off, and then bundled Olline up in the fluffiest towel she owned.

Casimir carried her again through her home, taking her to the bedroom. Her orchids arched contentedly as they passed, as caught up in bliss as she was. Checking her over one last time, Casimir placed Olline down in the bed.

She looked back at him sleepily and chuckled lightly. Grinning, she twitched back her covers and patted the bed next to her. Casimir licked his lips, staring at her like she was a goddess, too beautiful to behold.

Thankfully, he didn't need to be told twice because Olline was pretty sure talking was beyond her skillset at the moment.

Casimir slid into bed behind her, folding her naked body against the curve of his. He wrapped her in his strong, lean arms, and she melted against him. Olline burrowed against him until there was no space between them. His breath tickled her ear as he nestled his face into her hair, murmuring something she couldn't quite make out, before pressing a light kiss to the top of her head, and sighing contentedly.

Olline had never slept so well in all her life.

CHAPTER 29

Olline awoke naked and aching in the best way. At some point, in the delirium of the late night—or was it the early morning?—Casimir had woken her with a trail of wet kisses down the back of her neck, teasing her earlobe, until she had draped a leg over his hip, allowing him to slip inside her again. They had made love, slow and sleepy, their climax leisurely to arrive but still a torrent of warmth and shuddering ecstasy. They'd fallen asleep again, him buried deep within her, neither wanting to move and lose that connection.

Until now. When Olline woke up alone.

She groped in the tangled sheets, searching for Casimir's warm, firm body. Finding nothing, she opened her eyes a fraction, hoping beyond hope she would see him and be able to fall back asleep. Because that was the rule. If you didn't fully open your eyes, you didn't fully wake up. Seeing no familiar alabaster body, her eyes shot open and Olline's heart ticked up a beat. Sitting upright, she looked around, her chest heavy as her breaths came quicker. Did he leave? Perhaps he slipped away to get his things, or he was simply out of sight.

Olline tossed the sheets aside and practically jumped out of bed. She didn't bother putting on clothes as she raced through her apartment. Immediately, her thoughts went to Etzel, which is not who she wanted to think about ever again. How, in their immediate relief and passion, she had once again *not* used her power to disable Casimir's chip permanently. Panic stabbed at her chest, thinking that Etzel had found a way to turn the chip back on, to command Casimir away, to enslave him yet again.

She tore into the kitchen, eyes wide, breathing frantic, when she found an honest to goodness note on the counter:

"Only for you am I a morning person. Gone to get you that real coffee you love so much. I didn't want to risk breaking your ancient machine."

Olline read the note at least three times, breathing deeply throughout. She had to, to be certain it was real, that she wasn't still dreaming, that everything was fine. Trust Casimir to be so old-fashioned, and dare she say, romantic. Who took the time to actually put ink-based writing devices to archaic and fragile paper? Olline briefly clutched the note to her, then gently folded it and tucked it away somewhere safe. Maybe in years to come the sentiment would be meaningless, common even, but for now, she wanted to keep the note somewhere safe to revisit if she needed to. Tucking the note away, she suddenly remembered all the windows in her apartment, and that she was still very, very naked.

Olline took her time getting dressed, taming her hair

from the unruly aftermath of last night. Then cleaned up the apartment. The coffee kiosk Casimir was going to was deep in the city, which meant Olline had time.

After throwing their clothes into the laundry chute, she curled up on the floor and pulled out one of her holo-tablets. In theory, she knew how to disable Casimir's control chip. Based on the schematics she had from his file, it was the best she could do without surgery. In practice, though, Olline had no clue what to do.

She had never tinkered with a cybernetic biomagitech device before, let alone one still embedded within a person. This would not be like using her magic to rip out her own piercings for defense. Casimir *should* go to a hospital where a trained water caster physician could disable the device while also monitoring his vitals. But given who Casimir was, and what Etzel was capable of, even when Delora got the files and brought every lawsuit in Antal against Etzel, Olline didn't think it would be safe for Casimir to go to a specialist in a hospital or magitech facility. Etzel's claws were dug in deep anywhere biomagitech was concerned. Until they took him down, they couldn't trust that someone working at a cybernetic facility or a specialist in a hospital wouldn't tip him off, or worse, be a thrall activated to apprehend Casimir. Olline could always reach out to Lochan and see if someone within the Hayashi Corporation he worked for could handle a device like Casimir's, but securing safe travel out of Antal to Cyneburg with no one in the Government Plaza knowing would take too much time.

Olline hunched over the holo-tablet. The collar of her slouchy jacket finding its way into her mouth and she idly chewed, her eyes fixated on the schematics. She murmured to herself as she tried to work out the logistics of the device, and what she could finagle the pieces to do with her power based on several assumptions, when there was a knock at her door.

Rising to her feet, Olline was already smiling on her way to the entryway, the phantom smell of her coffee already teasing her even before she had the warm cup in her hands. Disengaging the locks, she made a mental note to get a key-fob made for Casimir so he could leave her poor doorman alone. As soon as she swung the door open, her smile faded.

"What—" was all she said before everything went blacker than the void.

WHEN IN HIS EYES

Watching Olline come undone around him had been the highlight of a very long and horrid century. She was an addiction he never wanted to come clean from. The heat of her skin as her pleasure mounted, the way she clenched around him as her climax hit, was exquisite. Even now, the memory had him growing hard as granite. He was a glutton for how she said his name. He wanted to drink her in until he burst with the taste of her. Yet, if Olline decided once he returned from his errand that they were, in fact, better as friends, he would gladly take that.

Well, not *gladly*.

Casimir would die inside if that happened. But he would take whatever little part of Olline she was willing to give, because even an infinitesimal amount of her was enough to banish the shadows shrouding his bloodied and battered soul.

Olline was saving him in more ways than one.

Casimir knew this was dangerous territory. That he

should temper these feelings. He had only been free of Etzel for a scorching hot minute and falling head over ass for the first person who showed him an ounce of care, of tenderness, of simple *decency,* was perhaps not the healthiest thing for him to do.

All of that was beside the point. Casimir needed to get his shit together. He had to make sure he was worthy of Olline, had to make sure she wanted him, the man who needed to rediscover who he was now that his chip was inert. He hadn't lied when he said no one—man, woman, or otherwise—was like her, and she deserved someone far less broken than he was. If Casimir had to spend the next century proving that to her? Well, he would relish the chance.

Casimir had seen enough shit, had dealt with it firsthand from people who didn't know he was screaming on the inside, to know that Olline was, well, special felt too simple of a term. She was simply Olline, and she meant the world and all its hidden stars to Casimir. It was a fact.

He wasn't "starting" to see what she could mean to him; it had already happened somewhere along the way. It defied logic and reason—on her part—but he wanted to get used to waking up in her bed every day, even if that meant his overwhelming joy had him getting up at the ass-crack of dawn to do something disgustingly mushy for her. Like get her real coffee.

It was such a simple pleasure, and so incredibly adorable, that Casimir would have traveled to the corners of Eerden to get her a cup of coffee just the way she liked it. Thankfully, he only had to go a bit deeper into Antal to procure his prize.

Casimir practically skipped back to her building, which was disgraceful, but he buried the urge. He tipped the coffee cup in salute to Olline's doorman and gave the man a wink that left the poor fellow looking more dazed and blearier eyed than usual.

By the time Casimir neared her door, he was already taking deep, savory breaths, as if he could breathe in her cucumber and mint scent from the hallway. He stopped at her door and gave his head a little shake. This, whatever *this* was he was starting with Olline, was too new and it would help no one to have Casimir so obviously mooning over this woman when they still had a job to do.

Even if that woman was his precious little caster.

He lightly kicked against the door; his hands too full with their expensive coffee to knock. He took a step back, adopted a flirtatious smile, a serene look of triumph ready for when Olline opened the door, and waited.

Nothing happened. Not even the whisper of sound from the other side of the door.

His grin turned mischievous, thinking of how he left her and trying not to pat himself on the back too hard for being such a consummate lover. He kicked against the door again, a little harder this time, in case she had slept through the previous knock.

Again, there was no response.

His heart began racing, on the cusp of exploding, and he became hyper-sensitive to all sounds, or lack thereof. He kicked against the door again, not caring if he scuffed it or the neighbors complained, and the door opened.

No one was on the other side. It shouldn't have opened on its own. He stepped inside and nearly tripped on a plant, its soil spilt and pot cracked, on the other side of the door. It was Olline's lovely little purple and green plant. It had a name he couldn't remember now, but in no universe would Olline ever have knocked the plant over, leaving it sad and trembling on the floor.

His hands shook as he put the cups down. On autopilot, he righted the little plant because, instinctively, he knew that's what Olline would want him to do. Its fuzzy leaves brushed against his fingers in gratitude, but he was too distracted by the pain in his chest to truly note the gesture. The world stilled around him at what he saw. Or, rather, what he *didn't* see.

Casimir turned on his heel and ran back the way he had come.

It wasn't cowardice that made him flee. Casimir would not waste a precious second tearing through Olline's apartment when he already knew what her unlocked door, her tipped over plant meant, and, more importantly, where she likely was. His lips pulled back, his teeth bared, as he raced away. The coffee stayed forgotten outside her door. His vision clouded as he tore from her building. His throat was dry from his rushed breathing, and an edgy, twitching feeling electrified his fingertips as they ached to curl around Etzel's throat.

For who else could have gotten to Olline in the brief hour

he had been gone but Etzel fucking Straub? Hadn't he known her moral heart was going to be the death of them?

Except . . . he liked Olline precisely for that good heart of hers.

Which meant this was all Casimir's fault; he had known better than to leave her alone. But he had wanted to do something nice for her, and now look where it got him. Funny though, through all the blame and rage and *guilt* he felt, never once did he question what he would do next, where he would go, or how far he would go, for that matter. Never once did he pause and consider this trap—for it absolutely was a trap of some kind—was one he could not disarm or walk away from. It didn't matter.

Olline was in trouble and he would rip apart anyone who stood in his way, and utterly annihilate anyone who so much as bruised that perfect skin of hers. So, without hesitation, Casimir marched back to the one place he swore he would never willingly return to after his chip stopped working.

Casimir didn't have to think about where he was going. His feet knew the way back to Etzel. They had returned him to Under Senator Straub countless times before. He stuck to the shadows, embracing the path he had slunk through too many times to count, but for the first time, he made the choice to go.

He lurked out of view of the nondescript warehouse district, his eyes fixed on one plain bunker in particular. One that he knew was a façade, one that stretched down farther than anyone but he and Etzel truly knew.

He counted the seconds, waiting for the flicker of light that meant someone was emerging out of the cloaked entrance on the far side. Minutes that felt like decades dribbled by. Each passing second tightened his chest and left him fidgeting with his mechanized stiletto, desperate to move, to do something, to get Olline out of there *right now*—

There!

He moved like lightning, zig-zagging across the concrete, slipping in and out of the hazy shadows too fast for the thrall to notice. With a swift strike to the back of the head, Casimir knocked the man out, and snatched his security credentials before he even hit the ground. Casimir made a point not to look too closely at who he struck.

Mercy was a luxury he couldn't afford.

Getting down to where Etzel conducted his *clandestine business* was so second nature to Casimir that it was easy—too easy, if he thought too long about it. It didn't matter, nothing would change his trajectory. It wasn't until he got to the labs that Casimir ran into any kind of resistance. Which was stranger still. Casimir could count on one hand the number of times this building wasn't crawling with personnel.

A small team of Etzel's private mercenary group lined the hallways. There were four of them, each equipped with *mostly* non-lethal rounds in their pulse-pistols and magitech tasers. He knew from experience. But enough punishment from even non-lethal rounds could be fatal. Casimir eyed them for a moment, his eyes darting from one to another, assessing the situation, before he rounded the corner.

"Hello, gentlemen," Casimir crooned, his hands in his pockets, expression nonchalant.

"Everhart?" One of the masked mercs said, their voice distorted through a filter for anonymity. "The boss's been looking for you. You ready to come quiet like? Mr. Straub's getting mighty tired of sending your friends after you, only for them to come back bloody. If they come back at all," he added with a mean chuckle. The merc shifted, perking up a fraction. "Say, what did you do to that thing exactly?" He tapped the base of his skull, indicating Casimir's chip. "Mr. Straub's damn near killed a few engineers trying to figure it out."

"Oh, I'm sure he has," Casimir said lazily. He took a few casual steps forward, angling his body just so. The forced nonchalance was making him sweat when all he wanted to do was race by and find his precious caster. But even Casimir's skills would be tested by the number of mercs facing him, and he would be no good to Olline if he had the audacity to get himself incapacitated so soon in the rescue attempt. "I'd be happy to explain, but it's all rather technical. Better yet, shall I show you?"

The mercs exchanged wary glances, before the one that spoke shrugged and lowered his weapon. Once the others followed suit, relief momentarily made Casimir light headed. He forced himself to move casually, the slowness of it stabbing his freshly healing heart, forcing him to imagine what Etzel was doing to Olline. If she was already implanted, he would never be able to forgive himself. He would . . .

He shook himself slightly, bottling the despair to fuel his

fury instead. Casimir turned his body ever so slightly and hoped the panic squeezing his chest didn't show on his face. "I'm surprised Etzel didn't want you to drag me to him dead after all the trouble I caused," he said with a theatrical sigh, pretending to be disappointed.

The first merc's eyes narrowed and Casimir was sure he was frowning, but it was impossible to see beneath his mask. "*Mr. Straub* thinks you're still too valuable to waste like that."

Casimir flexed his fingers, unable to remain still a second longer as the mercs finally got closer, weapons held loose at their sides, ready to see what Casimir had to show them. "Actually," he said, incapable of maintaining his bored drawl, his words nearly drowned out by the sound of his thrashing heartbeat. "Now that I think about it, an explanation or 'going quiet like' isn't something I'm all that interested in. You, however, will be silent as a grave."

The four mercenaries stiffened a fraction of a heartbeat too late, too lulled by Casimir's congenial manner, too secure in their biotech body armor to react as fast as they needed to. Casimir spun, flipped his stiletto open, and jabbed it into the space between the body armor and helmet of the closest merc before any of them even lifted their weapons. The merc gurgled and Casimir twisted him forward, using his body as a shield to take the first shot of a taser.

With a primal yell decades in the making, Casimir pushed forward, using the dying merc as a shield until he got to the next guard. With the hilt of his blade, he gave three quick jabs to the guard's face mask, denting it until it sparked. Casimir grabbed the merc's pistol and shot up under his chin in rapid fire until those concussive shots finally became fatal.

Two down, two to go.

One mercenary grabbed at Casimir from behind, trying to wrench his arm back. Casimir merely flipped the blade to the other hand, then he threw it with all his strength into the mercs boot, impaling him through the toe. Before the man could even scream, Casimir punched him in the throat hard enough to fracture the cartilage in the merc's larynx and trachea. He sputtered, air already escaping into his neck and chest. Which gave Casimir his next meat shield as the fourth and final mercenary finally got around his collapsed brethren in the narrow hallway and tried subduing Casimir with a club to the head.

Casimir jerked away almost too late. The club scraped against the side of his head as he pushed the choking guard into his "friend". Casimir dropped, yanked his dagger free of the dying man's boot, then slashed at the remaining guard's tendons.

The last guard cursed, Casimir's strikes only an irritant beneath his biotech armor. "Fuck taking you alive," the mercenary sputtered, changing his load out to lethal rounds. Which was, ironically, his fatal mistake.

Casimir had only ever needed milliseconds to strike. It was one of the first things he had learned to do in order to survive in Etzel's world. Casimir whipped his arm up. His blade curved in a graceful arc as he swung around. The guard leaned back, but not far enough. The sharp edge of Casimir's stiletto slashed across his neck, and no matter how firmly the merc pressed down against his own throat, there was no stopping his blood from spilling free.

The guard slumped to the floor, gurgling and twisting. Casimir carefully stepped around him to where the merc with the crushed larynx and trachea was, and gave him a swift kick to the head. Once he was unconscious, Casimir knelt down and disarmed the mercenaries. He pulled out their pulse-pistols, tried to flip them on to change their load outs, but each one had a biometric code that only responded to the mercenaries. The pistols were no better than pretty paperweights in Casimir's hands.

"We'll just do this the old-fashioned way," he grumbled, his words trembling with the worry he tried to bury. And yet, he not so secretly relished the idea of unloading his pain and fear on anyone who tried to get in his way. He sprinted deeper into the compound, where he prayed he would find Olline.

Before it was too late.

CHAPTER 30

Olline's head felt like someone was pounding an ice pick against her skull at irregular intervals. Her eyes fluttered open, and she wished she had stayed in the oblivion of unconsciousness. The light burned her eyes, intensifying the pounding in her head until she was nauseated.

When she could focus without threat of vomiting, Olline cautiously glanced around the room. She sucked in a ragged breath, her nausea returning on the heels of the horrifying realization of where she was. Casimir had briefly mentioned where he occasionally found himself after fulfilling orders from Etzel. She had never seen actual holo-footage of the place, but she instantly knew she was where Etzel took his marks to be implanted with control chips.

The warehouse was clinical, sparse and austere; a large room, mostly empty of furnishings beyond the steel tables of medical equipment. She thought the walls looked like stone, but she felt no call from the natural ores. The smell of disinfectant was so strong it made her eyes water, and Olline wondered if Etzel had recently implanted someone.

The more she took stock of the room, the more the walls seemed to creep in on her, choking her with a claustrophobia she had never experienced. Her breaths were raspy, scraping against ribs that felt too tight around her racing heart. Terror threatened to overtake her completely if she didn't *focus* and focus *right now*.

Because if she didn't, Olline Tavos would cease to exist.

She would be Olline the Thrall, her agency gone, her magic and brilliance used at the whims of a sick, twisted man's agenda. Her throat constricted, and she gulped frantically for the oxygen denied her in her blind terror. There wasn't time for her to panic, but she couldn't stop herself; being chipped, being *enslaved* by Etzel, where she wouldn't be able to stop herself should he command she hurt the people she cared about most . . . She wasn't as strong as Casimir in that regard, she would rather die than succumb to that fate. Yet that choice, of whether to live as a thrall, wouldn't even be hers to make if she didn't get out of this fucking room!

You're brilliant, Olline. You can get out of this!

The mantra was shaky at first, but the more she repeated it, the more it forced air into her lungs, the less her head pounded, and the clearer she thought. Still, she would give the mantra credit for pulling her back from the brink of losing her shit completely, not the increased airflow.

To calm herself, Olline compartmentalized the facts. Fact one: she was strapped to a gurney in a sitting position with medical devices pushed to the corner, waiting to be hooked into her. Her straps were a supple leather, not metal, which had its advantages and disadvantages. Fact two: there was a very good reason she couldn't feel if there was any natural material in the room—a pair of magitech cuffs glittered on her wrists.

Her magic was not completely dampened; it would answer her summons, it just couldn't escape her body. No matter how much she pulled on her power, how she grasped at the natural ores in the room, the power slammed against a barrier she couldn't break. The sense that her magic was still there helped keep her from panicking. That, and the mantra. She couldn't forget the mantra.

But now?

Dread welled in her, coating her stomach until bile inched up her throat. She felt a scream bubbling up, but the last thing Olline wanted to do was alert whatever doctor or magitech engineer was waiting outside. Or worse, notify Etzel himself.

Olline took a shaky breath and focused on the surrounding room. There were no windows, and she had to assume they were deep in a building Etzel owned, or at least had total control of. There was only one door, sealed shut with a complex security system that Olline would need full use of her hands to dismantle. Besides the medical devices, there didn't appear to be anything even remotely sharp in the room. Not that it would help with her chest, arms, and legs strapped to the gurney, and her hands cuffed in her lap.

I should have had Casimir teach me how he picks locks, she thought bitterly.

"Casimir," she gasped lightly, her voice like sandpaper in her throat.

Olline had underestimated Etzel Straub, and now she was paying the price. For as much as it tore her heart to shreds, she had to assume Etzel would use her capture as bait.

Forcing herself to take a deep breath, her lungs burned as they inflated to their full capacity. In this situation, her mind was her best asset, and she knew that if she let the panic win out, she would be in trouble.

Etzel wanted to add her to his collection of assets, had from the very start. Etzel lured her into his trap when she accepted the contract. If it hadn't been for her messing with the files, if her dummy update hadn't disconnected Casimir from Etzel's grasp, she would have been a pawn in Etzel's political machinations long ago.

Not knowing how much time she had before someone entered the room—she didn't see any security cameras, but that didn't mean someone didn't know she was conscious—Olline did the only thing she could think of. She flexed her arms and legs, moving her torso forward as much as she could, trying to get some slack in her restraints.

Someone removed her shirt and jacket, leaving her in a bra and her pants. As she wiggled her arms and strained against the restraint around her chest, sweat coated her back, making her skin stick to the plastic covering the gurney. A wet sucking sound echoed through the room each time she crunched her stomach, uncomfortably loud in the empty room.

With a *hiss* of air, the door at the far end of the room eased open, and Olline was alone no longer.

She froze, mid flex, slowly leaning back with the slim hope that no one had been spying on her and had witnessed her escape attempts. It might have been her imagination, but Olline swore the restraints were looser now. Perhaps she could use that to her advantage if she was clever and incredibly lucky.

Etzel Straub strode into the room, flanked by two medical personnel carrying trays of tools. Olline assumed that the two women had been chipped, but there was no real way of knowing, not with the magitech cuffs on.

"Ah," Etzel said, spreading his arms wide in greeting, his yellow diamond eyes gleaming. "Welcome, Ms. Tavos. It's a pleasure to meet you in the flesh." His voice was deep, a slight rasp belaying a youth of vices, but his tone was . . . *friendly*. Like this was some misunderstanding. There was nothing about how he spoke that would alert anyone to the monster he truly was. "Had Mr. Everhart done as instructed, this would have been much less dramatic, I assure you."

Olline sneered at him. "There's nothing pleasant about having a magitech device forcibly implanted in someone to make them your puppet, you rancid pimple."

Etzel blinked, the frown lines around his mouth pulling down and darkening his bright bronze skin. The tips of his long, pointed ears twitched, and his nostrils flared slightly. He cleared his throat and made a show of straightening the cuffs of his stone-grey tailored suit. It was the only sign that her words caught him off guard before his lips twitched in a smile that didn't reach his eyes. "What a vivid image. Your brilliance is clearly not limited to your technical acumen."

He tilted his head, giving her a sympathetic smile. Or the façade of one. "Well, you're *usually* brilliant. You did trust Mr. Everhart, and that was an objectively stupid thing to do." He sighed, shaking his head in disappointment. "But I can put that momentary lapse in judgment to good use."

He was every inch the slimy politician now, all fake charisma and sympathy. It made Olline's skin crawl like she was buried up to her neck in spiders.

Etzel's eyes remained on her face. He never once leered down at her half-naked body as he stepped closer. He was interested in one thing alone, and it wasn't her physical body. The two women perfectly mirrored him, step by step, their gazes vacant behind their protective coverings.

Definitely chipped then. Olline wasn't sure how intense of a command Etzel gave them, but neither woman seemed to be aware of their surroundings the way Wolfe had been when following a command.

Clasping his hands behind his back, the sterile light gleamed on his curved, soil-brown horns. "You know," Etzel said conversationally, "I've never implanted a caster before. Usually, I stick to useful lesser creatures. Humani mostly, the occasional seerani. Never casters or seersha. Far too noticeable. But then you showed up, so eager to prove yourself."

Olline glared at him. "There's that seersha arrogance I was waiting for." Not all seersha were arrogant, Olline knew, Goswin was a perfect example of that. Yet they had long, long lives, unique, stunning looks, and if they were also casters, that made them far more powerful than humani. And, well, it did things to a person. Her father's failed first marriage was a testament to that.

Etzel rolled his eyes. "It's not arrogance when it's fact. Seersha are better. You don't enslave a seersha," he said with a tight chuckle. "You can't! Our power is too strong to be contained by such primitive means, even with the most advanced biomagitech. And I'd know, I invest in it all. Not like you can with your kind."

Olline knew *for a fact* he was talking out of his ass. She hoped she had enough time to use that against him.

"Yeah, except seersha casters are stuck wherever they're born. If they leave, they lose that very power you say is so impressive. But I can go wherever I want and my magic remains just as strong. I'm not tied to any city like 'your kind' is," she spat back at him. It was the very reason Goswin and her brother could never leave Cyneburg.

"And yet, here you still are. Tied down all the same," Etzel responded, bored. He examined the women at his side for a moment and then shrugged. "Truthfully, I'd wanted you for your magitech expertise. You're truly brilliant, you know. For a humani. Having someone with your skillset at my disposal will make my work that much easier to control. I hadn't originally planned to make use of your caster abilities, but now I see how short-sighted that was of me." He tilted his head again, grinning to himself. "You're going to help me achieve great things, Ms. Tavos. Truly inspired things. All for the greater good of Antal."

Olline squirmed against her restraints. "I'm not here to impress you, you piece of shit. You don't care about this city at all, don't lie to yourself. Now let me go!"

Etzel shrugged, stepping back, though his thralls remained where they stood a few feet away from the table, holding the rest of the medical equipment. "You're smart enough to know I'm not going to do that. You know exactly why you're here. You were able to free Casimir, after all. I'm sure he told you everything if you hadn't figured it all out before. Which, given your clever little mind, I'm sure you did."

She was careful not to make the restraints groan as she continued to test their flexibility. There wasn't enough give for her to slip out.

Yet.

"I'll tell you everything I know, explain everything I did, if you let me go," Olline said, trying to make herself as pathetic as possible. Maybe there was an ounce of humanity left in him she could appeal to.

Etzel huffed in response. "No need for that, Ms. Tavos. I'll take the information once you're compliant. There'll be no risk of you lying then." He shrugged again, giving her a sympathetic frown as if he were actually sorry this was happening.

She flexed her arm and leg muscles again. *Nearly there.*

"Then why're you even here?" she spat. "Just looking to gloat? How cliché of you."

He chuckled good-naturedly. "I see how you'd get that impression from all this," he said, waving his hand in lazy circles to indicate the room around them. "It wasn't my intention. Honestly, I didn't even *need* to meet you, let alone like this. I could've waited until after the procedure. But I *wanted* to see you."

Olline narrowed her eyes, suspicious. Prickles of warning raced over her skin, but she couldn't stop herself from asking, "Why?"

Etzel had been looking at the door, but turned his gaze back to her when she spoke. He raised a brow at her like the answer should be obvious. Olline swallowed the lump in her throat, refusing to believe what her instincts were yelling at her.

When she remained silent, Etzel sighed through his nose. "I'm waiting for someone." Olline's body went cold at his words, the sweat on her back making her shiver as dread filled her. "There's no point in doing this procedure twice, Ms. Tavos. I'm a stickler for efficiency." Etzel glanced down at his wrist-communicator and grinned to himself. "Thankfully, we shouldn't need to wait much longer. Which is fortunate. I've more important matters to deal with." He glanced at her once more, his features darkening ever so slightly as he said, "Seems a political rival of mine has some aspiration of kicking me out of office. I need to nip that in the bud while it's merely an irritant."

It was all falling apart. Everything she and Casimir had tried to accomplish, all the careful steps they had taken to bring Etzel down with nothing coming back to them, had been for nothing.

Uninterested, Etzel turned back to face the door. The cold metal of the magitech cuffs bit into her still-tender wrists, and the pain brought Olline back to her senses.

If Etzel could be believed, Casimir hadn't arrived yet. Which meant she still had time, albeit very little time, to loosen her restraints.

She stole a glance at the two women who stood motionless, their eyes glassy and unseeing. Whatever their orders were from Etzel, it seemed like he didn't need them right now. No matter how she pleaded with her eyes for help, the women remained unmoved. She twisted on the bed, careful not to make any noise. Even with the two thralls facing her, they didn't move to stop her. Taking a deep breath, Olline redoubled her efforts.

To mask the sound of her straining against the leather straps, she asked, "Don't you have enough people in your *collection?* Why do you need Casimir back so badly?"

He chuckled, glancing down at his wrist-communicator again. "You mistake the situation. Casimir's a useful tool, an asset I can still utilize. I told you, I'm a stickler for efficiency. It'd be a waste to let that go when Antal still so desperately needs *me* to look after it." Etzel gave a long-suffering sigh, dropping his arms to his side. "This isn't personal, you know. You and Casimir play a part in the greater good I've envisioned for this city. You should be pleased I chose you at all."

Olline's stomach rolled, sour disgust flooding her system. Etzel played the compassionate politician so well that it was almost impossible to hear the note of greed undercutting each of his words. He *almost* believed in his own narrative. But someone couldn't willfully enslave others and claim that it's for benevolent reasons.

She twisted again on the table, pulling at her restraints. Olline's skin was so slick with sweat that she prayed she could slip through her bonds. It felt like all she needed was *one more* good pull.

"Right on time," Etzel said, swiping something on his wrist-communicator. The automatic door hissed open again, and Casimir stumbled inside.

Olline sucked in a quick breath as he entered.

His knuckles were bruised and bloody, the skin on the side of his head angry and raw. There were splashes of blood across his cheek and shirt, but he didn't appear to be wounded. Casimir was breathing heavily, murder flashing in his red eyes as he glared at the seersha politician. He had fought through whatever personnel Etzel had to get to her, even though they were a smokescreen to hide the fact that Casimir was barging right into a trap. Her heart swelled with hope, with happiness that he came. *He came for her!* She was so relieved she could weep. Until the reality of what that meant crashed into her, flattening her and squeezing all her organs like a roller construction truck was driving over her.

"Get out, Cas!" Olline gasped before she could stop herself. "He's going to activate your chip!"

"I know," Casimir said, voice hoarse, as the door slid shut behind him. "Trap or not, there was no way I'd leave you to this monster, Ollie."

Olline's chest warmed at his words for a fraction of a moment, before she went back to urgently straining against her restraints. All those times he hid the truth from her, it was to protect her from his horrid reality. It might have been misguided, but he did it because he cared. Truly and deeply *cared for her* like he claimed. Could this mess have been avoided if she had believed him sooner?

Casimir's eyes snapped to her briefly, taking her in. The tremble in his hands steadied when he saw she was relatively unharmed. His eyes narrowed back on Etzel, and a silver blade appeared in his hands. The mechanized stiletto Kullen had gifted him before selling him to Etzel.

"Touching," Etzel murmured. Looking down at his wrist-comm, he turned his back on Casimir and walked toward Olline, as if Casimir was no threat to him whatsoever. She only had a second before Etzel would look up and notice that she was finally, *finally,* wiggling off the gurney. "This should make everything easier for you then, won't it? You two can be *companions* as I complete my life's work."

Olline's blood turned to icy sludge in her veins. Anything good that she could have had, could have built with Casimir, would be gone. They would be trauma bound. A life forever stained with knowing they were the conductors of each other's pain, had been an active part in their complete loss of freedom.

They would be together forever, with no choice. It was the last thing she wanted, for either of them.

Etzel looked at her then, drawn by the movement of her sliding beneath the restraints. He scowled, but Casimir was already racing forward. Olline made the mistake of looking at him and not focusing on Etzel.

Without even glancing behind him, Etzel swiped through something on his wrist-comm and Casimir stopped mid-stride as if frozen. "It took an embarrassing number of people to figure out what you did to his chip, Ms. Tavos. It's impressive and made me want you for myself all the more. Thankfully, the assets I do possess could give me something to bring Mr. Everhart back into the fold."

Seeing Casimir freeze, his deep garnet red eyes glaze over, broke something in Olline's chest. A strangled cry tore through her and, with no other options, Olline did the only stupid thing she could think of.

She rushed at Etzel, side-stepping the doctors flanking him. She lowered her shoulder, hoping to tackle him to the ground, but the old seersha was spryer than she gave him credit for.

He pushed her aside and, with another of his long-suffering sighs, said, "Subdue her."

She wheeled around toward the doctors, ready to dart past them and rush at Etzel again.

But he hadn't given either of the women the command.

Casimir's strong arms wrapped around her, pinning her arms to her side. His once so comforting scent of lavender and eucalyptus had her tensing in terror now. That firm body she had delighted in having pressed against her the night before held no tenderness for her now. Tears stung her eyes with the utter betrayal that her lover could not *see her* cleaved her heart in two. A distant part of Olline knew Casimir wasn't responsible for his actions, but it was still his nimble, strong fingers digging into her, causing her pain, now.

Olline gasped. Casimir easily lifted her and slowly walked back toward what would be the operating table. "Cas, no!" she pleaded, twisting, making him stop to get a better grip on her. "This isn't you!" But she knew there was no way for Casimir to fight the command either, not with the chip functional again.

She didn't want to hurt him, but Etzel wasn't giving her any other options. As Casimir shoved her past the table, she slammed her head back into his face.

With a grunt, Casimir stumbled, releasing her. Olline's head throbbed, but it didn't matter, she knew where the tool she wanted was. Even with her hands cuffed and her vision blurry, she was able to grab the laser scalpel. Etzel had fallen to the same mistake she had: underestimating the person they were up against.

Too late did Etzel give the doctors the command to help get her under control. Her hands closed on the device and with a recklessness that would have given her father a heart attack, she turned it on and cut through the chain on her handcuffs before slicing through the magitech on her wrists. She was too focused on the cuffs to feel the pain as the laser sliced into her wrists, causing blood to coat her hands and pool on the ground.

Casimir had recovered by then and resumed his chase,

following his orders, but Olline's magic was free now. All she needed was a moment to identify what in the room she could use. Her piercings had been removed, but there had to be something else she could use. Maybe Casimir's knife—but looking at Casimir was a mistake. Looking into his eyes, she saw nothing of the charming seerani who fought his way to free her, who had gotten up early to get her coffee after loving her all night long. Her skin burned where he had gripped her, replacing the sweet memories of his gentle caresses. The horror of realizing the man she was starting to—no, that she did *love* was aiding Etzel in turning her into a thrall nearly incapacitated her with hysteria. Her heart hurt so much Olline wanted to scream until her throat caught fire. Only clinging to the fact that Casimir had no choice kept her mobile.

There were only trace amounts of iron in the door, in the walls, in the stainless-steel medical devices. If Olline's heart hadn't been breaking, her vision not going fuzzy at the edges, she might have been able to concentrate and take the iron right out of Etzel's blood. But the bigger trace amounts in the room would do nicely.

Or they would if Olline had *one fucking second* to grab the iron and manipulate it.

It was getting harder and harder to avoid the two women and Casimir as they tried to grab her and hold her without seriously hurting her. In an ironic twist of fate, the bloody wounds she had given herself from cutting off the cuffs made her a slick target to pin down.

Etzel, for his part, merely leaned against the door, looking both bored and exasperated by the whole situation. Like it was taking too long to enslave her, and he had better things to do.

What an absolute *asshole*.

"Enough. Take her, by any means necessary," Etzel said in a dispassionate drawl. Olline chanced a look at Casimir at the same instant her ethereal fingers clasped the metals in the room and connected them to her earth magic.

Casimir's movements were jerky, his red eyes unfocused, teeth bared as he clenched his jaw. It took her mind too long to recognize that there was a part of Casimir still aware of what Etzel was commanding him to do through the chip. And he was fighting. His fingers would flex at the last second, ensuring he never got a good grip on her, his knees locked at every still moment, slowing him down and tangling him with the doctors, who moved clumsily around him. It was pure misery to realize that she was wrong, that he was still there when she thought no trace remained after Etzel issued his command, that she nearly doubled over with agony.

Yet the control chip, with the new code that Etzel's team had uploaded on the local network, was too strong. A cold stoicism fell over his face, one not so dissimilar from the marble mask he wore when he was trying to protect his thoughts.

He lunged at Olline.

No longer commanded not to harm her, Casimir's movements were faster, more violent than Olline was prepared for.

He tackled her to the ground. Her head bounced on the hard floor. She groaned, her vision swimming, her magic slipping, while Casimir cut off her airways. She had less than thirty seconds to do something, *anything,* before it was too late.

There was no trace of her Casimir left in that vicious sneer now. There was no mischievous light dancing in the deep ruby-red irises. Still, she didn't want to hurt him. But Olline was running out of time. They both were.

Drawing on the fantasy of what they could have, might have had if Etzel hadn't gotten to them both, Olline *pulled* at the magic one last time.

She clenched her fist and forced the iron free of every device she could in the room. There was no gentle coaxing, no finesse to her pull that wouldn't damage the room or the people in her way. With a slight twist of her finger, she shaped the iron into a messy ball, all while gasping for breath, her throat on fire, praying for a bit more time before her brain shut down from lack of oxygen. She blinked rapidly, trying to focus, when at excruciatingly long last, all the magic snapped into place.

Olline swung her arm as hard as she could. The ball of pure iron flew through the air guided by her magic, and her hazy memory of the operating room, where the magitech devices were located, and where Etzel had been loitering. Her aim was true, that much she knew, before everything went mercifully black.

CHAPTER 31

Olline slowly came back to her senses for the second time in less than a day. It was not a record she thought she would break, ever, but here she was.

Her eyelids were heavy, her head fuzzy like there was cotton shoved in her ears. The iron tang of blood coated her tongue, and everything *hurt*. You weren't supposed to feel pain anymore when you were dead, right? Because that's what Olline had sworn had happened. And yet, her throat was a raw, scorched mess where even the cool air ripped through it like a rusty saw. Her hands throbbed, heat pulsating from where they were bandaged—

Bandaged?

With a violent gasp, she forced her eyes wide open. Scrambling for leverage, for some kind of weapon . . .

Olline was back on the gurney. The medical devices she had seen earlier were closer, with pale blue tubes attached to her arms.

Oh no. No, no, no!

Her painful, labored breathing picked up as panic demanded she call on her power again, hoping against hope that she still had access to it. The table vibrated, relief flooded her, when:

"Easy now, love, you're okay," a raspy female voice said from behind her.

Olline whipped her head around, her vision spinning, and it took her a second to focus on the doctor she had seen earlier. She raised her aching hands, eyes wide with terror, ready to impale this woman to the wall and run, dragging Casimir with her if she had to—her breath caught in her throat, making her sputter. Where was Casimir? Did Etzel send him away?

"We're free, for the moment," the woman explained hastily, raising her wrinkled, soft brown hands in placation. Olline still eyed her warily. Slowly, she released *most* of the magic she had summoned to her, as the doctor didn't move closer and she wasn't strapped to the table. "You were in awful shape, we couldn't leave when you . . ." the doctor trailed off, waving her hand toward the figure slumped behind her.

Etzel was unconscious on the floor. *That* wasn't Olline's doing. Did Casimir do that? If so, where was he now? Why had he left her alone with a stranger?

She blinked, trying to focus her attention through her mounting panic. Her eyes snapped to the destroyed wrist-communicator. The coil in her chest eased slightly seeing the demolished device. It had been a gamble, sending her ball of iron careening into the tech. She hadn't been positive that destroying it would disrupt the signal and free Casimir. Olline was seventy-seven percent sure it would, since Etzel sent the update from his wrist-communicator, and had waited until Casimir was near. She was glad her assumption paid off, but it didn't account for why, or how, Etzel came to be in the sorry state he was in now. Nor where Casimir was, though she had to assume he wasn't following anyone's command but his own. She *had to* believe that or drown under the force of her anxiety.

Following her gaze, the doctor sighed and hesitantly went back to checking Olline's hands. Olline lurched back, licking her chapped lips, not letting the doctor closer until she had a moment to study the surrounding serums. Once positive they wouldn't be used to sedate her, Olline allowed the doctor to tend to her injuries.

"Where is he?" Olline demanded, voice little more than a strangled croak. "Where's Casimir?"

"The moment Casimir returned to his senses," the physician explained softly, "he tackled Etzel before he could summon his security detail. He couldn't give us new commands, and you were technically subdued, so our minds became ours again. Etzel was the only threat in the room." The doctor rubbed more serum into Olline's tender neck, letting the healing nanites repair the damaged tissue at an accelerated rate. "Once Etzel was unconscious, Casimir and my wife went to make sure we wouldn't get any nasty surprises while I tended your injuries. Nasty bit of work you did on your hands, love. You're lucky you didn't cut them off with that laser scalpel."

Olline gave her head a little shake and turned her attention back to the doctor. "Your wife?" she asked, her voice cracking.

She swallowed anything else she wanted to ask about Casimir, about what he had done to her. Olline wanted to believe that he would never consciously hurt her. But she had never seen him like that before, had never known him when he was a true thrall. While her heart yearned to reassure herself that he was safe, that their actions—Casimir's and the doctor's—didn't define them, especially in this case, Olline would be lying if she said she wasn't a bit glad she didn't have to face him immediately.

The woman's grin was tender, though her hazel eyes remained sad. "She's a specialist, my Isobel. She is, *was,* a cybernetic surgeon before Etzel got his claws in her. We were already married, but I'd wager that if I hadn't been a doctor, and a damn decent one at that, Etzel would've had me *discarded.* He likes to toss rubbish before it gets rank if you follow me."

She spoke with such a detached nonchalance that Olline's heart broke. "Did—" her voice caught, and she couldn't blame it on the magitech serum. She cleared her throat and began again, "Did Casimir bring you . . . I mean, was he ordered to, you know . . ." Olline bit off her words, floundering for the right way to ask how she came to be here.

The doctor faltered slightly; the sadness deepening in her eyes. She brushed back a wisp of silky, cool brown hair and shook her head. "No, love. Casimir wasn't the one who lured my wife here. Even if it'd been him, we wouldn't hold it against him. Isobel and I, we've been part of Etzel's menagerie long enough to know that none of us are here by choice, and none of us would do a fraction of the things he forces us to do."

Breathing, Olline found, was marginally easier at hearing the doctor's words. It was the comfort Olline needed, whether or not the doctor knew it.

The older humani checked the fluid bags attached to Olline's arm once more and then gave her shoulder a gentle squeeze. "I'm Sofia, by the by. And, in case I don't get another opportunity to say it, *thank you* for breaking the control Etzel had on us. You're a proper saint, you are."

"Is it over then?" Olline asked, her eyes darting to Etzel again, hoping Casimir and Isobel were all right, and wondering when they would return. Mostly Olline wanted to know if she still needed to fix Casimir's chip, if they still needed Under Senator Delora and her mountain of lawsuits against Etzel at all.

Olline's nerves were fried, and if she could be done with this entire business, she would jump at the chance. In theory, doing the right thing was perfect. It was, well, the *right* thing to do. But the trauma of nearly being implanted with a control chip . . . Olline wasn't designed for that. As she watched Sofia fuss over her, she had a new appreciation for what this woman had gone through, and the gentle care she was still able to provide.

Sofia lifted a shoulder in a slight shrug. "Couldn't tell you, love. Etzel had contingency plans, yes? But it went further than that. His entire organization's a machine like none

I've ever seen. Quite literally. His being incapacitated doesn't shut the machine down. If it did, the prick wouldn't be able to sleep. Far as I can tell, everything's still very much operational and this is just a momentary reprieve."

"Then what do we do?" Olline asked in a quiet voice.

Sofia gave Olline a sad smile. "I know why Etzel wanted you. Your magic, for certain. But your expertise, love. He wanted to take advantage of that mind of yours." There was a pause. Sofia gave her a pleading look before quietly adding. "If anyone can dismantle this whole operation, it's you. If you feel up to it. Or want to."

"Of course, I want to. I will," Olline answered immediately. No matter that in her weakened state, it wasn't a guarantee she would succeed.

No pressure.

"There," Sofia said, adding a bit more biomagitech serum to her wrists where the bandages ended. "That'll fix you up nice and proper now. You'll not lose any mobility in your hands, but I can't speak to the sensitivity going forward. You sliced big chunks out of your palms, love. You'll need to take it easy for a while."

Panic had her heart fluttering again. "I'll need my hands to work," she said, her throat constricting on the words.

Sofia bit her lip, then her shoulders slumped in a sigh. "Nothing to be done for it, I'm afraid. You have some mobility, but the magitech nanites in that serum can only do so much, work so fast. It shouldn't affect your ability to cast. So that's good news, yes?"

Olline wasn't sure. It was *something*. But was it enough?

She had enough time to flex her stiff fingers before the door hissed open again. Olline's heart stopped, her breath escaping in a *whoosh* of air, eyes wide with dread. The other doctor, Isobel, entered the room. Her lungs squeezed, suddenly unable to breathe when she didn't immediately see Casimir. She sat up straight on the gurney, swinging her legs off, ready to run to save him if she needed to. Olline swayed, trying to see around Isobel, hoping, praying that Casimir was behind the woman.

Despite her worry, Olline noted how petite Isobel was, how almost frail the older humani looked, but she had a severe beauty to her free of her protective gear. Her blue eyes held a fierceness that made them burn with icy flames, her pale blonde hair was pulled in a tight bun atop her head, not a single strand out of place. Despite how small she was, how delicate she looked, there was a strength to her that had Olline swallowing the lump in her throat as Isobel strode toward her wife.

But where was her Casimir?

Then, the door opened once more and a familiar seerani entered the room. Tears welled behind her eyes to see him, back and himself again. She couldn't speak around her joy, instead making an intelligible sound deep in her chest.

Casimir didn't approach Olline when he reentered the room.

Her heart plummeted. He hadn't even noticed she was awake after what he had done to her. Had Sofia been wrong to think that Etzel's thralls wouldn't do the things he commanded them to if given a choice? Had part of Casimir wanted to hurt her, and now he couldn't look at her because of the guilt?

No, she told herself fiercely. She knew better. She knew Cas better than that. He would never want to hurt her, but that wouldn't remove the guilt he may feel over being forced to do so.

He stood over Etzel, his shoulders rising and falling in time with his heavy, trembling breaths. Casimir clenched his hands so tightly at his sides that Olline could see the white of his knuckles from where she was on the bed. He had eyes only for Etzel, whose face was twitching with faint grimaces, slowly coming back to consciousness.

Sofia and Isobel were murmuring to each other, checking in with one another. If either of them noticed Olline carefully pulling herself off the gurney and using the IV pole for support as she got to her feet, they didn't stop her.

"Cas?" she whispered, but he didn't respond.

Olline took a shaky step closer, unsure of what was happening, what Casimir was thinking, as she carefully drew nearer. "Cas? Are you okay?" she asked again, her voice a little louder this time. Was he ignoring her? Too guilt ridden to look at her? Her heart twisted, wanting to hold him, but the memory of his hands crushing her throat made it almost impossible for her to get closer, to touch him.

"I found it," he said. His voice was so raspy and low that it came out as a growl.

She was almost too afraid to ask what he found. But that

had never stopped her before. "What're you talking about?" Olline said, carefully inching forward, her hands throbbing around the pole they held for support. But the pain in her hands was a sweet balm compared to the anguished ache of her heart.

"The control room," he answered, like it should have been obvious. He still didn't look at her, didn't react like he truly knew she was there. He locked his red eyes on the man who enslaved him, his body coiled tight like a steel cable about to snap. "Where Etzel makes us all dance, where he keeps the keys to the kingdom. I found it, and I . . ." he trailed off, before taking a deep ragged breath, his body tensing even more—something Olline didn't think was possible. "I could take it, with your help. Transfer all that power, that data, to me. I could run this operation. Make Etzel one of *my* assets instead." His voice became fevered, laced with manic desperation. "I'd be free. Safe forever. I could keep you safe. *Us* safe. If that power was mine."

Olline sucked in a breath, tentatively reaching out to him. She could understand the longing Casimir had, empathize with it, even. This shouldn't have been a surprise to her, his words and desire. Casimir had openly told her this was an option he was considering. But she had thought he was joking. Had hoped he was joking. And after what Etzel had made him do, to her of all people, she had believed he would have let this desire go completely.

"You're still mixing up freedom with power, Cas," she reminded him, her voice barely above a whisper. She didn't know if any of the arguments she had given before would work now, but she would try. Even if it took all the air in her lungs, and all the strength in her aching heart, she would say anything to keep Casimir from going down that path. What was the point of saving him from the control chip if she couldn't save his soul along with him? She would rather die than see that happen.

"You don't have to turn into Etzel to be free of him. We're already doing that. We're nearly there! No one should have the kind of twisted power Etzel claims, built off the backs of enslavement, kidnapping, blackmail, and so many other terrible crimes." She took another shaky step closer, as if afraid to spook him, afraid he'd lash out at her if she did. It was a fear she never would have had if Etzel hadn't forced Casimir to lay hands on her. "If you want to be free of Etzel permanently, and truly heal and grow, then you need to *destroy* his empire, his political career, not step into his shoes."

Casimir whipped his head toward her, his red eyes blazing with furious fire. "I've dealt with a century of pure *torture*. I deserve better! I'm owed better."

The room stilled further, and Olline risked a glance at the two doctors. Their eyes were hard, hands slowly inching toward scalpels and laser cutters. *They'll kill him,* she realized, taking a sharp breath. She couldn't let that happen.

Holding up a placating hand, Olline tried to put as much tenderness—not pity—as she could in her face. She tried to hide the fearful tremble of her hand as she stood before him, this man she wanted to save so badly her lungs constricted with the need.

"You *are* owed better," Olline agreed. "But so is everyone else Etzel implanted. What about them, Cas? What about Sofia and Isobel? Would you really continue to do to them what Etzel did to you? What Kullen sold you into?"

He flinched, his whole body curling in on itself at the mention of his older brother. The fury blazing in his eyes died down, the feral rage dissipating to where Olline saw the man she had fallen for reemerge.

Until Etzel groaned, rolled over, and tried to get to his feet, anyway. The bastard had *the worst* timing.

Casimir's face hardened, lips pressed into a firm line, and the fury reignited in his eyes. He grabbed Etzel by his hair, twisting it in his fist to get a tight grip. The Under Senator gave a sharp, ragged breath, and sputtered, "Let go of me, you rat!"

Casimir sneered, kicking his tormentor over so he was on his back, forced to look Casimir in the face. Olline watched, wide-eyed, too stunned and paralyzed to move.

"We're going to dismantle the political empire you built, Etzel," Casimir seethed, crouching on Etzel's chest. "Everything you've built for the past century, poof! Up and gone with no fanfare. No one to laud your accomplishments, no one to care when you're gone." He glanced quickly over his shoulder at Olline, and that's when her stomach sank. A chill ran through her, raising the hairs on her arms in warning.

"She's right, you know," Casimir said, his voice a deadly, heated whisper. "I don't need any of the tainted power you hold to be safe. But to be free? Well, as long as you draw breath, there'll be no freedom for any of us."

That flash of silver again fell from Casimir's sleeve into his waiting palm. Olline registered it as the knife Kullen had given Casimir, the one token he kept from his brother all these years. In an instant, she remembered what Casimir said about why he used this blade—so the blood would be on his brother's hands and not his. Too late, she shouted, "Wait!"

Casimir thrust the blade into Etzel's chest. Etzel gave a wet gasp, yellow eyes large and unbelieving, the blade buried to the hilt. He clawed at the weapon when Casimir yanked it free and plunged it in again.

And again, and again, and again.

Etzel stopped gurgling long before Casimir dropped the gore-covered dagger. Olline couldn't tear her eyes from the dead body of Etzel Straub. Coldness pumped through her veins, too shocked perhaps to register the brutality of what she witnessed. She should feel horrified; but if Olline was being truthful, she didn't care. She didn't care that Casimir had killed his abuser.

Etzel had deserved it.

Casimir rocked back on his heels, spent. Blood covered Casimir, with arterial sprays all over his chest and face, and his hands dripping with gore. He looked down at them, marveling, before a ragged sob cracked him in half. He threw his head back and yelled, his cries so full of pain. His hands rested in his lap, dripping, but Olline didn't care. She stumbled, her knees slamming to the ground as she fell next to Casimir and pulled him to her.

She cradled him as he cried, and yelled, and raged. She didn't say anything as the tidal wave of emotions rolled through him.

Olline let him know through her embrace that he wasn't alone.

Soon the tsunami of grief pulled back, or it could have been hours later. She didn't know, and she didn't care. Olline would have stayed like that forever if that's what Casimir needed. But, eventually, his screams of pain turned to hiccupping sobs of relief.

His arms tightened around her briefly as the last of his anguish bled from him. With a strangled sigh, Casimir rasped, "He's finally gone."

CHAPTER 32

Olline disassociated a bit after that, and really, who could blame her?

The simple fact remained: they had killed an Under Senator of Antal, and if they weren't careful, authorities would arrest all of them for it—control chips or not. Casimir, Sofia, Isobel, Bode, and everyone else had suffered too much at that monster's hands to be burdened by his death now.

With silent communion, the women got to work.

Sofia checked Casimir for injuries and removed every drop of Etzel's blood from his clothes, skin, hair, under his nails, and probably even his pores. She used another of Etzel's illegal biomagitech devices to destroy the blood stains as if they had never existed.

Isobel, meanwhile, worked on Etzel.

Her gloved hands worked with a scary fast efficiency, masking the stab wounds so they appeared to be crushing blows instead. How she managed it without magic at her disposal, Olline didn't want to know. Watching the doctors work,

Olline knew with a chilly certainty they had often cleaned up scenes like this under Etzel's command.

For her part, Olline rested her bandaged and throbbing hands against the icy wall and closed her eyes. She called her magic, let the magma in her core leech out through her arms, down her wrists, and through her numb fingers. The power snaked from her, crawling through the walls, the mortar, the stone, and steel, on a quest. Like calling to like.

There wasn't a lot of natural material to pull from. She wasn't even sure if there was enough to collapse the room. That was the plan. She would make it look like a localized explosion, an accident that would match the fresh injuries Isobel was making. Olline needed to do something Under Senator Delora Peralta could sell to the press in order to keep her case, and the lawsuits, clean. Etzel Straub could not for a single second look like a victim.

What the room lacked in natural material, it made up for in wires and cables. A network of copper wires ran through the walls, keeping the room shielded and off the grid from the rest of the building, and probably all of Antal. It wasn't ideal, given Olline had limited use of her fingers, but she could work with this.

With less delicacy and finesse than she would have liked, a running theme for her as of late, Olline *pulled*.

With each wire, Olline tugged out the elements that sang to her power, hauling them through the walls and weakening them. Hopefully. Olline hadn't exactly done this before. But in her head, this plan was going to work beautifully.

The alloys and elements lay buried deep within the wall. They had to be twisted and coerced into something new, so they didn't kill them all instantly—which would not only be bad, but embarrassing—so it took more concentration than Olline expected. Even if blood loss had not weakened her, the work would still have left her spent. Olline thanked the nanites coursing through the healing serum for keeping her as coherent as she was.

Once everything was in place, the proverbial clock began ticking. They had maybe twenty minutes before the weakened walls and support struts finally gave way, and when that happened, they definitely needed to be out of the room, preferably on a different floor. That left Olline with just enough time.

With sluggish steps, she made her way over to Casimir and Sofia as the doctor placed the materials she used into a mobile incinerator. Casimir still seemed to be in a state of shock, and Olline wasn't sure if she should try to bring him out of it yet. Luckily, she didn't need him to do anything for this to work, either.

She bit her lip, inhaling deeply through her nose, hoping the quiver in her stomach from the stress would lessen. It didn't. She licked her lips and hoped she looked more confident than she felt. "Turn around," she said, her voice a nervous squeak. "I need to fix your chip. Or, no, sorry. Not *fix it,* fix it, I mean break it."

Smooth, Olline.

Casimir blinked slowly at her once, twice, before his

brows furrowed in confusion. Olline stifled a sigh and offered a sympathetic smile. "Isobel, Sofia, and all the others, they've the newer chips. With the killware I gave Delora, once that program runs, their chips will forever be inert. Yours is different. Old. Even with Etzel dead, some other evil bastard hoping to step into his shoes could, theoretically, reboot your chip. I want—I *need* to make sure that never happens again." She didn't say she needed to do it for herself as much as him. As long as his chip had the potential to be reactivated, Olline didn't think she could fully feel safe in his presence.

"Have we the time for that?" Isobel asked softly.

Olline nodded, straightening her shoulders and looking slightly more confident than she felt, never taking her gaze away from Casimir's face. "It won't take long, I promise. It's better I do this now before anyone comes snooping."

Sofia nodded, patted Casimir on the shoulder, and went to join her wife by the door. Both were ready to bolt as soon as she was done.

In a daze, Casimir turned around and Olline gently lifted his shirt so she could better feel where the chip was in his spine. She recalled all the schematics she had been studying before she was kidnapped, pulled her exhausted magic to the surface once more, and placed her hand on Casimir's clammy skin.

Could Olline have waited until they were in a medical cybernetic facility to do this? Yes. *Probably*. But with how sideways everything had gone, she didn't want to risk it. Until the killware went through the system, and Delora brought the legal hammer down, who was to say the hospital she took Casimir to wasn't one in Etzel's pocket somehow?

Taking a deep, fortifying breath, Olline shut her eyes and pressed her palm more firmly on Casimir's back. She pulled up a mental image of the materials list she guessed would be in the chip, the biomagitech nanites that were still alive and left dormant buried deep in Casimir's spinal column.

Warmth bloomed from her palm like feathery vines, moving through her and into Casimir, slithering into his bloodstream, and searching for the components she knew were buried beneath skin, muscle, and entwined in his nervous system. Casimir shivered under her touch, a breathy sigh puffing from his lips; the only sign he felt her power at all. With her eyes closed, she let her magic paint the picture for her. It was like a holo-projection beneath her eyelids that flashed whenever her earth abilities found a biomagitech nanite, or a minuscule part of the centuries-old control chip. With each brief pulse of light, the picture in her mind became clearer and clearer, until the outline of the control chip so firmly implanted in Casimir became visible.

Sound ceased then; she couldn't even feel Casimir's skin beneath her hand. She was so absorbed in identifying the microscopic hardware and software that she lost all track of her surroundings, including the time. Sweat began collecting on her brow as she concentrated, using her magic to command this part of the chip to shut down, while that nanite needed to move and block that pathway—*no, not that way!*

Olline took another breath; she couldn't afford any mistakes. Even a minor error could lead to paralysis, or alter Casimir in some other way. The ultraviolet vision of her magic in her mind's eye flickered as anxiety stabbed at her chest. Casimir was already acting oddly. Would she even know she had fucked something up before it was too late? Her magic pulsed again, warming her body, flooding her senses with flashes of the life she wanted, and may not get, if this didn't work. A life free of working in the Government Plaza, tied down by some sneaky fine print, a life with Casimir lounging on her couch, playing with her hair as she showed him the latest orchid she'd crafted. The fear of losing that gave her weakening magic the boost it needed to finish the job, but mentally, could Olline withstand the pressure?

She risked an infinitesimal moment to calm her racing heart and steady the ethereal fingers of her magic. It brought her out of her magic enough to notice the vibration in Casimir's back beneath her palm. Olline assumed someone was talking to him, but she was too focused to make out what anyone was saying. Pushing her hand more firmly against his back, Olline braced herself by gripping his shoulder and resting her forehead against the back of his head, taking gulping breaths of his calming scent. Olline needed a bit more time to carefully complete the delicate work and guarantee Casimir's freedom for the rest of his life.

Which Olline hoped was long, and included her in some way, in *any* way.

Everything about Casimir was complicated, yet it didn't scare Olline anymore. She didn't feel the need to bury herself in her work and pretend she didn't need, or didn't want, someone in her life. No, not *someone*. She wanted Casimir, no matter how heavy his baggage was. She would have to remember to thank her father for that bit of wisdom, assuming Casimir could still look at her after what he had been forced to do.

Worry about that later.

She commanded the copper in the connecting wires to disconnect in their sheaths one by one by one. Olline bit her lip, searching for the last wire. She was certain there was another tangled in his spinal column somewhere, having grown with the near sentient biomagitech in his system. There was more rumbling beneath her hand, harsher, sharp little bursts this time as Casimir spoke. She screwed her eyes tighter together, focusing on her waning power and tuning out even that sensation. Iron filled her mouth as she bit her lip too hard in her concentration.

Olline's heart was racing again, beating erratically and with hammer-blow force. Her chest was on fire, breathing painful as her ribcage constricted. The sweat on her brow was suddenly cold, the ultraviolet vision of what her magic saw as it twisted through Casimir's body flickered.

Her power was almost completely exhausted and had pulled on her weakened body instead. Olline's muscles trembled, her hands shaking so hard she could barely keep a hold on Casimir. She knew she was close to running on fumes, but she had thought, she had hoped . . .

She ground her teeth. Her magic wasn't depleted yet,

and she wasn't done. There was still one active biomagitech nanite that might undo everything. And where Casimir was concerned? Olline would not take any chances.

The vibration was back again. This time, however, it wasn't coming from her or Casimir.

The room around them was shaking. Olline's previous work was about to come to its inevitable conclusion. Standing was becoming more and more difficult between her weakening muscles and shuddering floor. She couldn't tune out the frantic, sharp voices of Isobel and Sofia this time, nor the soft pleas from Casimir.

Her mental image flickered again. When it snapped back on, she had the last nanite cornered. *Got you, you slippery shit,* she thought before crushing the biomagitech device, allowing Casimir's body to filter it out harmlessly, with the very last ounce of her power.

With a heavy, ragged sigh that hurt more than she was willing to admit, Olline pulled herself out of the control chip.

Olline was nearly back in her own body, her own mind, when her hand slipped off Casimir. The room was shuddering, and Olline toppled over.

She would never know if she hit the ground or not. A black nothingness so complete enveloped Olline that she was aware of nothing but the sad fact that she had, once again, beaten her own record for number of blackouts in a day.

Awesome.

CHAPTER 33

Olline was floating. Heat cocooned her body, electrifying her nerves as *something* pulled into them. Like a mental sigh that slowly eased all the tension out of her, her once brittle bones, the muscles so tight they were about to snap, relaxed one by one by one by one.

Until Olline was alive again.

With a shuddering, sharp intake of breath, Olline sat upright and opened her eyes. She couldn't see anything; her vision was out of focus even though she knew she was no longer in the dark. Her heart rabbited with worry; had they succeeded? Did they get away in time?

In truth, Olline hadn't *died,* but damn if it didn't feel like it.

She had never used her magic to depletion—or near depletion—before and she was not eager to ever, *ever* do it again. With a start, the reason she had nearly imploded came back, hitting her like a fist to the temple. Her reckless overexertion of her power trying to dismantle Casimir's—she cut herself off with a gasp.

"Casimir!" she croaked, her throat dry and scratchy like she had been guzzling gravel.

No one answered, and slowly her vision returned. That's when she saw where she was: back in her apartment, but it was all *wrong*. Every single one of the dozens of plants she had so carefully cultivated was dead, nothing more than brown, withered husks. Her pothos and philodendron were black, withered vines. Her succulents were so shriveled they held no shape in their fat leaves. The purple passion plant was nothing but dust, and her ferns and massive monstera lay on the floor, a breath away from disintegrating.

Now the sensation made sense: the little magic she had remaining called back the pieces of her from the only source it had available. Her precious plants. Olline's posture crumbled under the weight of her grief. These were her creations, *her friends,* and they all had returned the life she given them so she could live. It didn't seem fair that she should remain hurt and depleted, while the very things that had buoyed her through loneliness, heartbreak, had seen her grow and make life altering changes were now . . . gone. Tears burned her eyes and her heart thudded dully in her chest. Olline was glad she couldn't see what had become of her precious orchids. That would have been one blow too many to her cracked and battered soul.

"Cas," she said again, her voice cracking with defeat. But this time, she got an answer.

"Ollie," her name was a hymnal on his lips. "You found your way back to me." The bed dipped next to her, and even with her vision blurry with endless tears, Olline would recognize that lavender and eucalyptus scent anywhere.

She reached out blindly, and Casimir caught her fingers in his strong, elegant hand, careful not to crush her still-healing hand. "I'm right here, my precious caster, and I'm not going anywhere."

Olline closed her eyes, slumping into Casimir's warm embrace. Her strength was coming back to her faster now, even though she hated knowing the source of that strength. Even so, she could only manage a whisper to ask, "What happened?"

"Collapsing the room worked, maybe too well," Casimir said, his voice nonchalant, though she suspected that was for her benefit. "But we couldn't reach you. You were wasting time on me, of all the silly things. Isobel knew we couldn't move you safely until you finished what you were doing, but Sofia was starting to panic." Casimir's body shifted, tensing as he moved closer, but held himself back. She could feel Casimir's shoulders drawing up, and him tucking his elbows into his sides, his guilt over his actions a physical barrier between them. "I felt your power withdraw as the first chunks of the ceiling came down." Olline stiffened and Casimir took a deep, pained breath. "No one was hurt. We got out all right, thanks to you, my dear. Though, did you really need to worry about my chip right then and there? I didn't—I don't deserve such consideration after . . ." Casimir trailed off, his voice thick as his throat constricted and he averted his gaze, unable to look her in the face.

Realization over how much his treatment had scared him, had hurt her, squeezed Olline's gut. The horror and guilt of his actions kept Casimir close, but unable to offer the comfort of his powerful arms like he had when Wolfe attacked her. Olline was torn. Logically, she understood Casimir wasn't responsible for his actions under Etzel's influence. Emotionally . . . her wounds were still bleeding, and she suspected Casimir's were just as raw. Healing would take time, but perhaps that was a journey they could make together.

Olline pressed her lips together, burying the fear that made her chin tremble. Reminding herself that the man currently on her bed was the *real* Casimir, and the version of him that had attacked her was only a nightmare now. She snuggled closer and put her head on his chest. They remained that way, silent for the moment, while Olline listened as his erratic heartbeat slowly became steady again.

"Yes," she said simply. She cleared her throat. "I couldn't risk you again. I didn't . . . I couldn't risk someone else flipping your switch on. Not again."

"I'm so, *so* sorry, Ollie." Casimir's voice was tight, as if regret were strangling him. He rubbed his face with his hand. The other was poised, hovering around her, afraid to touch her, like he was no longer worthy of touching her. "Etzel succeeded in turning me into a monster. At least in your lovely eyes. Hasn't he? There's no recovering from this blow." His shoulders quaked with repressed sobs of remorse.

A strange sense of relief tugged at her, a tiny ember of warmth chasing away the numbness in her chest. It would have been easy, even natural, for Casimir to merely wave off what he had done as having nothing to do with him. In a way, he would have been correct. But him owning up to the wrongdoing, the pain and fear he had caused, even if it was not his choice to do so, gave her hope. That this, while a terrible blow to the fledgling relationship growing between them, was indeed something they could recover from.

She shook her head lightly. "*You* didn't hurt me. Etzel did. He made you . . . *subdue* me. I know what that chip does to you, Cas. I know you'd never hurt me. My body may just take more time to remember that fact. If I flinch or cower, it's not because," Olline couldn't finish, the muscle memory of his hands around her throat made that impossible, even if it proved her point. She clasped her hands in her lap to stop them shaking and waited for the pain in her throat to subside as she slowly relaxed against Casimir's chest again. "I'm not afraid of you, but I am—was afraid of what others could force you to do. Taking the time to make sure that couldn't happen again? Well, it was a risk I had to take. You were—*are* worth the risk. But if you need to hear me say it anyway, I forgive you."

Casimir sucked in a ragged breath, blinking rapidly at her in disbelief. Before a slow smile of relief tugged at his lips, bringing a touch of color back to his pale cheeks. His arms tightened around her, anchoring them together, as he buried his nose in her hair and his warm breath washed over her. "You are a wonder that never ceases. If I have to spend the next century atoning for bruising your delicate skin, I'll gladly do so. If you wish, or allow me to," he whispered back, his voice husky with emotion. "Thank you."

The tension ebbed a little, but Olline kept her eyes closed until she was certain tears wouldn't blur her vision anymore. "How long was I out for?" Thankfully, her voice was a little stronger this time, the raspy tremor nearly gone. Her plants, her creations, and the power she gifted to sustain them, their sacrifice was doing wonders to bring her back to her old self. Which hurt her heart almost as much as her still aching, fragile body.

"Close to twelve hours."

To be so close to death, so completely depleted of life energy . . . She shouldn't have woken up, at least not here. Maybe if they had taken her to a hospital that specialized in seersha and caster patients, maybe, *maybe* she would have recovered. But this? This didn't make sense.

Sensing her turmoil, Casimir said, his tone soothing, "You were so unresponsive that Isobel suggested we come here. I agreed, explaining your apartment was filled to bursting with your plants. I thought they'd bring you comfort, being somewhere safe and familiar. But Isobel's worked on enough casters in her day job to know that if I brought you here, the magic you used to make your darling little plants would come right back to the source. She tried explaining it, something about natural preservation instincts. Admittedly, it was hard to pay attention when you were so faded in my arms. She was still worried, though. We all were. Sofia did her best, but," a chuckle that might have been a sob of relief cut Casimir's words off, but he continued before Olline could make sense of it. "But your plants, your power, Ollie, it's all so incredible. *You're* incredible."

Casimir took a deep breath, gently brushing the hair off her forehead and tucking it behind her ears. "There was so much *life* in your plants that you, well, you're here. Back, and safe."

That knowledge was too big, too much for Olline to handle. All those times Olline swore her plants were reacting, were listening to her as she bustled about. She had brushed it off. It had been safer to believe she was personifying her plants rather than acknowledge she had created living batteries through her love and magic.

Olline had always known such a thing was a possibility. Many casters created such batteries to carry with them in case they needed their power to defend themselves against a more powerful entity. But Olline had never intended that, had never consciously chosen to make batteries. All she had wanted to do was create beautiful plants, to fill her space with greenery and give herself something to focus on during those moments when she wasn't in the office.

Her breath rattled in her chest, she hadn't wanted this to happen, had always been so careful so it would never happen. She knew how deadly it could be to overexert herself. And yet, here she was now, alive because her passion had her putting more magic in her houseplants than most earth casters would bother with. She would mourn her plants, but she would also honor what they had given back to her, too.

However, Olline wasn't the only miracle in the room, the only person who was back and safe, forever. Her eyelids stuttered open, making her lashes flutter as she looked up into Casimir's face.

Her vision cleared, and she traced the sharp line of his chin with a finger that no longer shook. She traced the contour of his mouth, the plump lower lip that arrested the breath in her lungs with his sleepy smiles, his *genuine* smiles. Olline's fingertips danced away and his mouth parted, his gaze locked on her. Those deep garnet eyes that had seen too much pain without recollection looked at her now like she was the answer to every question he could ever have. Her hand cupped the side of his face before moving to his forehead, brushing back those silky silver-white curls, tucking the strands behind his tall, pointed ears. Her fingers trailed to the back of his head, where she gently brought his face to hers until their foreheads rested against one another.

Olline inhaled deeply, filling her lungs with this incredible man, this survivor. He could have taken all of Etzel's files, all his power, and used it like Etzel had. Casimir could have lied to himself, trying to convince himself he was doing it for a greater purpose. Only to succumb to the same trap of power Etzel had. Instead, he had given it all up. She didn't think he would appreciate it now, but she was so, so damn proud of him. One day she would tell him, maybe when he wasn't so raw, maybe when she finally processed that her dormant power in her plants brought her back. Casimir had been so scared of Etzel and what he could do and take from him for centuries, that simply killing him had, ironically, been an act of restraint.

"You are too, you know," she murmured, her lips a hair away from his. "Back and safe, I mean."

"Because of you," Casimir cut in quickly. "You saved me, believed in me when no one else would have. I'm only here because of you."

She smiled, her lips barely brushing his in the action. "We saved each other, Cas. And we can heal from this. We *will* heal. Together. We make a good team."

He shifted, holding her more comfortably but never moving his forehead from hers, his lips still a breath away. "You're far too modest. We make a *perfect* team," he said, and she could hear the smile in his voice when all she could see was the sparkle in his eyes. "I'd like to kiss you now," he murmured after a moment, his voice husky and breathy all at once.

"I hope you'll do more than kiss me." Casimir stilled, his arms tensing around her. He pulled away enough for her to see the worry in his eyes as they trailed over her injuries. She rubbed the tip of her nose against his, grinning. "It's fine. *I'm* fine. After everything, it'd just be nice to feel . . . alive again."

He made a humming sound deep in his chest, his arms relaxing, but his hands still held her possessively. "You are my life," Casimir said so faintly she almost couldn't believe she had heard him correctly. But then his lips were on hers, so achingly soft and sweet that Olline couldn't think of anything. She didn't want to think of anything but the press of Casimir's body against hers. The tenderness of him now was what she wanted to remember, to replace her muscle memory of him from a mere twelve hours prior.

Casimir shifted them both, so careful, so gentle not to hurt her damaged hands, handling her like she was fragile, precious glass. She wanted to tell him he didn't have to be so careful with her, but that would require her moving her mouth away from his, where his tongue was softly seeking entrance. She arched against him, giving him permission and full access to her body.

He kept one arm around her waist, moving her hips so they perfectly lined up with his. His other he used to ease off the stretchy pants and the oversized shirt he had put her in. A shiver raced down her as the cool air hit her bare skin. But it soon disappeared, replaced by the heat of his body as his mouth was on her once more, trailing down from her lips, brushing her neck, nipping at her tattoo like he seemed to love, before his tongue flicked over the hollow of her throat.

The aching terror from before melted from her mind and muscles under his touch. One day, she wanted to enjoy all of Casimir without near abductions being their cruel foreplay. But for now, they both needed to be reminded that life was good. It could be sweet. And what could be better than reminding each other of that fact, together?

With a delightful pang beneath her sternum, Olline realized that, despite everything, she had no desire to be anywhere else but right here in bed with Casimir. That frozen, grief-stricken part of her thawed, and a familiar warm, peaceful connection to life the flora in her home had once given her, enveloped Olline once more.

He trailed one of his long, graceful fingers around the swell of her breast, her nipples pebbling instantly. His body rumbled against her, a moan of satisfaction deep in his chest. He trailed more kisses down the center of her chest until he was pulling her nipple into his mouth, running his teeth along the sensitive skin until her breath was coming in fast bursts, a moan of pleasure building in her chest that was echoed by the spreading heat between her legs.

All too soon, Casimir was moving down her body again, trailing kiss after kiss down her stomach. He pulled her with him so he could kneel off the bed, his hands positioning her closer to the edge of the mattress, draping her legs over his shoulders. He looked at her then, a hungry desire plain in his gaze, but so was a question. If she didn't want this, if she was too tired or achy, he would stop. But she didn't want that.

Their existence over the past day had been fraught with so many near misses. They had come far too close to losing each other. That Olline's heart ached for Casimir. She *craved* him. All of him; mentally, physically, whatever he was willing to give. Like a transplanted flower, her roots needed to anchor her home once more. Emotionally, that would take time, but physically? They could at least begin forgiving each other with their bodies right now.

She bucked her hips up, arching her body in an invitation. "Take me," she said, her voice low and smoky.

"With pleasure." And he was lifting her to him, his mouth on her in an instant. His tongue was almost cold with how hot and wet she already was. He hummed against her as if she were the most delicious thing he had ever eaten. His teeth grazed her sensitive clit, his tongue licking her deep inside. Olline swore she could see bursts of color, hundreds of tiny blooms, as he speared her with his tongue again and again, devouring her.

His tongue moved in dizzying patterns, and Olline could not get enough. Reaching down, she tangled her fingers in his cloud-like hair and pressed his face firmly against her. Casimir moaned with such intense pleasure at having his face buried deep within her that, beyond the blinding pleasure, Olline thought she would burst with the sheer bliss of having this man at all. He sucked on her bud greedily, teeth grazing it enough to make her gasp before he was drinking her in again, letting the wave of pleasure recede before bringing her back to shore a second later with that wicked tongue. Her hips bucked, fingers gripping his hair ever tighter, her pleasure so intense it nearly tickled. But she continued to hold him firmly against her pussy, grinding against him as he moaned into her.

Olline gasped, her pleasure coming quick and hard, building faster, mounting higher. She whimpered, trying to bury her moan of pleasure, but it was a losing battle. His tongue twisted in her, coaxing her to the edge, and then—"Casimir!"

Her orgasm swept over her like a landslide. She twitched against him, and still, he held her firm against his wicked mouth as he savored her pleasure, bringing her carefully not quite to the shore, but within sight of it. Only then did he lift his face from her. His mouth glistened as he smiled teasingly at her, but all Olline could think was how glorious he looked kneeling between her legs.

Without delay, he shoved his pants down, his erection already at her entrance, as he lifted her hips with him as he stood. His hands cupped her ass, spreading her wide before him so he could marvel at the entirety of her.

She looked up at him, at how devastatingly beautiful he was with her wetness all over that perfect mouth. He looked down at her, his gaze greedy on her bare breasts, her face, and yet, he hesitated. "I want you, Olline," he said, his voice gravelly with desire. "I want you so badly all the time."

Olline knew he wasn't just talking about the obvious, but fuck if she didn't want him filling her up again *right now*. Regardless, she didn't need to think of her answer.

"I want *you,* Casimir. I forgive you." Like a healing balm spread over her, merely speaking the words aloud had a radiant glow of adoration heating her bruised and battered heart. "And I'll happily take *all* of you."

He smiled, he wasn't oblivious to the innuendo and in one swift movement; he thrust himself into her. At this angle, he was able to hit deeper than he had before, and even before he found that perfect rolling rhythm of his, she was already moaning in ecstasy.

He held her hips up as he thrust deeply into her, all the way to the base of his long cock each time. Always so careful and gentle with her, like he was apologizing with every roll of his hips. Soon his careful, torturously slow, steady thrusts, where she felt every single glorious inch of him before slamming back in, picked up in speed and tempo.

Casimir was about to lose himself completely.

"No," she said, her words mixed with a moan. He slowed but didn't stop, and she propped herself up. "Together," she panted, pulling him down onto the bed and flipping herself onto him so she was straddling his hips. "I want to watch you cum with me this time," she said, repositioning herself to take him again.

She rode him mercilessly. Her hips rocked in hard, quick motions. Casimir's fingers dug into her hips and thighs as his own orgasm quickly approached. He threw his head back, biting his lip, trying to make it last, but Olline was too close again to stop. The friction from grinding on him was too much and soon she was calling his name again, and he was lifting his hips to meet her, thrusting deeper until there was nothing but him and her and them together, connected.

"Olline," he cried her name, a gasp, a prayer of ecstasy as they climaxed together.

He twitched beneath her and Olline lowered herself, covering him with her body, careful with her bandaged hands. Casimir wrapped his arms around her, holding her in place, neither moving until sleep claimed them.

Olline woke with Casimir lightly sliding her black and deep jade hair through his fingers, twirling the strands idly before running through her hair again. Olline sighed contentedly and draped her arm over his chest, snuggling into his warm, firm side. He nuzzled the top of her head with his chin, inhaling deeply, as if he couldn't believe this was all real.

Same, Cas.

For as much as she wanted to have this moment be the only one that mattered for the rest of all time, the creeping vine that was her anxiety twisted through her. She had been deep in a healing sleep for so long before, well, *before*. She couldn't avoid reality any longer, nor did she really want to. Too much was at stake still to ignore what had happened to Etzel Straub, and their part in his downfall and murder—there was no prettying that up, even if the bastard deserved what Casimir did to him.

As Olline searched for the right words to break this beautiful moment of serenity, she slipped a leg between Casimir's, letting their feet touch and rub together. It was such an innocent gesture that Olline was surprised by how Casimir reciprocated the movement. It made it easier to ask, "Did Delora do it then? Did she enact the killware? Is it . . . over?"

Casimir didn't answer for about three seconds, which felt like thirty years to Olline, who couldn't help but hold her breath through the silence. He stretched an arm out of the bed, careful not to move Olline away from him, as if any loss of her skin against his would be an unspeakable crime. He placed one of her holo-tablets on the bed next to them, its screen still dark.

"Find a news feed," was all Casimir said.

She didn't even need Casimir to specify which news feed. Delora Peralta's face was everywhere Olline looked.

She wore a pristine red and white pantsuit during the press conference, which complimented her ebony skin and the black halo of her curls, making her look like some avenging angel—Olline was certain that she did it on purpose. The news ticker under her listed lawsuit after lawsuit, violation after violation, and all the names of the corporations and biomagitech developers tangled up in Etzel's web of corruption, blackmail, and even murder. Delora didn't mention how she got the evidence, she didn't need to. With Etzel dead, it allowed the Under Senator to expedite her proceedings, no longer needing to tread carefully lest Straub catch wind of what she was up to. Standing around her were some of the victims Etzel had used his control chips on; she only knew because she spotted Sofia, Isobel, and even Bode lurking in the back.

Olline opened several tabs containing different feeds, some showed Delora detailing all the crimes, others had anchors commentating on Delora's findings, and some showed live footage of investigators pouring through one of Etzel's sky-towers, and clearing debris from the bunker basement Olline had collapsed on Etzel's body. She got snippets here and there, but all the sources said the same thing: Etzel was being charged, posthumously, of severe corruption crimes against the city-state of Antal, and capital offense crimes against the ninety-three people he had implanted with illegal biomagitech control chips. Those people had been used to blackmail, coerce, and murder a nearly unimaginable number of people and corporations alike over the years.

One of the news feeds she maximized was a loop of Delora making a big show of running Olline's killware. Olline nearly cried with relief, and she hugged Casimir all the tighter, knowing that, while she had sabotaged his chip personally, everyone like him was free now, too.

She searched, but there was no mention of Etzel being murdered. Olline breathed easier at that. Delora seemed to go with the cover story they had left her, and whether she knew the truth, or chose not to look into the circumstances around the room collapse and his death, it didn't matter. The result was the same: Casimir was free. They all were.

Olline sighed, letting the feeds run as she turned to look up at Casimir. "You didn't want to be there for the press conference? None of this would have happened without you. Antal should know you exist and thank you for ending Etzel's corruption."

Casimir gave her an unreadable look for a moment, then shook his head, a faint smile on his face. "And miss being here when you woke up? Perish the thought, darling." She rolled her eyes at him, despite the heat of her blush.

"I'm serious!" she said, tracing the lines of his muscles around his chest and shoulder. "You deserve to be standing there beside Delora."

Casimir didn't answer. Instead, he flicked to another news feed, one Olline had minimized earlier to look at the investigators pouring through Etzel's building. On this news feed, people complicit with Etzel's plans were being arrested. Some names and faces were familiar, sending a coldness through her that shouldn't have shocked her: her supervisor, Karter Wayser, was named, as was the IT personnel he had brought to her office, Camirin. However, what shocked her the most was that the security guard, Brayden, hadn't been listed. Seemed like he was just "following orders". Thankfully, Briallea Jensen's name didn't come up anywhere, and Olline made a mental note to reach out to the friendly woman when she was well enough to see her. She was about to ask what she was looking for when she saw *him*.

Kullen Everhart.

She barely recognized him; he bore so little resemblance to Casimir. Kullen was like sour milk compared to Casimir's marble physique. It was clear Kullen had lived a rough life; he looked ancient even though he wasn't terribly older than Casimir. Still, Olline couldn't even pretend to feel sympathy for that walking hemorrhoid.

The holo-tickertape at the bottom listed him, as well as a dozen others, as accomplices that had sold people to Etzel in order to get out of their own debts. Olline's stomach twisted, and she searched Casimir's face, looking for . . . she didn't know. Regardless of her condition, it made sense why he wouldn't want to be around when his brother was arrested. Casimir still had thorny feelings around his big brother, to put it mildly. Feelings he would need to address one day, feelings he could finally heal from now that his brother would face justice.

Olline propped herself up on her elbow, resting a hand on

Casimir's chest, wishing the bandage wasn't separating her from the full force of his heartbeat—which was beating calm and steady beneath her palm. "Are you all right?"

He covered her hand with his and gave her one of his slow, sleepy smiles that melted her insides every single time. "I am. And I've you to thank for that. For the first time in over a century, I'm *me* again."

CHAPTER 34

Even with some of the prep work Delora had done ahead of bringing Etzel's atrocities to the public eye, it still took another month to sift through the century-long list of accomplices, teasing out those who were there by choice or coercion. In terms of politics, that was lightning fast, but for Olline and Casimir, it felt glacial.

Olline was in a type of limbo while her contract was modified. The Police and Securities Department had decided to keep and honor the contract, so she wouldn't be homeless and need to move back to Cyneburg. Which was nice of them, she guessed. But ratifying the contract was taking time. Which was great news for Olline's rapidly healing hands.

In a few weeks, she would be back in the sub-basements of the building assessing security threats, using her magic to change the evidence storage hardware so that exploitations like Etzel's couldn't happen again. Or that's what they told her. Olline wasn't so naïve anymore. Etzel Straub wasn't the beginning and end of Antal's corruption racket. But this felt like a genuine step in the right direction.

She was actually looking forward to going back to work in a few weeks, of starting, hopefully, a real friendship this time with Briallea without interruptions from shady supervisors. Being idle, glued to the news feeds to avoid watching Casimir carefully collect her plant debris while her hands finished healing, was driving her crazy.

Casimir hadn't wanted her to go back to work in the Government Plaza, but contracts were dangerously funny little things. He had encouraged her to do something with her magic that would bring life and light to Antal instead. Maybe she could open a virtual-simulator café where she not only sold her plants and brewed real coffee but also offered hardware or software work on a contract basis. It would combine her two loves and protect her from ever getting mixed up with slimy politicians again. She was partial to the idea, but it wasn't feasible.

Yet.

Casimir lost his little apartment. Though he wasn't sad to see it go. The apartment had been owned by Etzel, another way to keep those he controlled under his thumb. Through some unspoken magic, Olline didn't even have to ask Casimir to move in with her. Instinctively, he knew he belonged there.

Though he often said he would, "get out of her hair, and give her some space". Olline wasn't sure if he meant that, as the days turned to weeks and he made no moves to leave. Not that she wanted him to, ever. But her anxiety kept whispering to her, telling her that today would be the day he left.

During that month, Casimir had sold off all his brother's clubs, including Refractory, and cashed in whatever stock options Kullen had in his name. He didn't speak to his brother during that time and didn't bother seeing him as he was processed. Casimir had Delora talk to Kullen whenever necessary. Olline had asked if he wanted to be a part of Kullen's eventual trial, but he shook his head, claiming he would not lift a finger to help nor hurt his brother, unlike how Kullen had treated him. The only businesses he kept were the little artist's havens that were tucked into the forgotten spaces of Antal. Casimir was working on a business plan to make those more viable long-term.

Despite his claims of giving her space, not once did he look for a new place to live. Not that she was aware of.

She didn't want him to move. She had gotten so used to the shape and feel of him in her bed, in her *life,* that she was too afraid to bring up the topic lest he remembered that leaving was something he said he would do. But the limbo of what they were was making her teeth itch. Olline was already dealing with too much uncertainty out of her control with her contract. But knowing what she and Casimir were? That at least was in her control, and she hoped simply knowing would, at last, remove the gnawing anxiety from her gut.

Casimir was fussing with the night orchid she had given him. He was trying to find the right spot for it still—this was the third time he had moved it in four days—when Olline approached him. She watched him for a moment, gnawing on her lower lip and twisting her now fully healed fingers.

He gave her a side-long glance, hands on his hips, as his slow smile tilted the corner of his lip up. “You’re still so adorable when you’re trying to think of what to say, Ollie.”

She narrowed her eyes at him, but there was no heat in the smoldering glare she gave him. Olline hadn’t prepared what to say. She was no good at speeches or romantic declarations, not the way others were. Gestures, like the black orchid, she could do. Finding the words now felt so wholly inadequate, but so desperately vital she couldn’t breathe properly until she said what was in her heart.

“After Achan, I didn’t know what real looked like,” Olline began hesitantly, dropping her gaze to her fidgeting fingers. “I thought I knew and then, well, you know what happened.” She saw Casimir’s feet shift, so he was facing her, but she didn’t dare turn her gaze up to meet his yet. “But before there was Achan, there was my mom. What she had with my dad was so special and achingly beautiful, and it ended far too soon when she got sick. She was here one day, gone the next, and none of us got a chance to—” she swallowed, her throat tightening and tears stinging her eyes like they always did when she thought of her mom. “Well, a lot was left unsaid. My dad, he, well, he never really recovered despite the smile he shows the world. I promised I wouldn’t let that happen to me. If I found someone, had something like that, I’d make sure they knew every single day, every second I could.”

Olline took another deep breath, slowly exhaling until her voice steadied again. “I don’t want you to ‘get out of my hair’. I want you to stay. Here, with me. If you . . . want this too. If you want *me*."

This was the worst déjà vu she ever had, but it *had* to happen. Hopefully, this time, no one would try to kidnap them before they figured it out.

She could hear Casimir breathe deeply, but still, she didn't look up, she couldn't, not until she got this all out. "You're special to me, Cas. You always were. And I know everything's still kind of fucked up but I have to know." Taking a final deep, fortifying breath, she said, "I have to know what we are. What I am to you. Because I think—no, I *know,* I've fallen for you. Hard. I-I adore you, Casimir. And you don't have to say anything," she added quickly, "that's not what this is about. I just need to know what we're doing here, if this is *something* or . . . something else."

She couldn't quite bring herself to suggest what they had was a temporary fantasy. She wouldn't pressure Casimir. He had only just gotten his autonomy back. If he wasn't ready for this and needed someone kind to help him get his life sorted again, well, she would learn how to cherish the little time they had together.

Olline had forgotten how to breathe properly as she waited, not meeting Casimir's gaze. He was silent for a millisecond before he gently tilted her chin up so she had to look at him. His deep red eyes were soft, sweet almost, as he looked at her, giving Olline every ounce of his attention as he closed the gap between them. He wrapped an arm around her waist, his hand splayed over her lower back and the top of her ass, pulling her closer in a gesture that was so possessive Olline almost swooned.

"I'm sorry, Olline," he said, lowering his face a fraction closer to hers. "Sorry it wasn't obvious that you're the air and without you, I can't breathe. Those three little words aren't enough, but they're yours: I love you. I have for an embarrassingly long time and I should've said it sooner, so you didn't have a moment of doubt. You're all I want, Ollie. Now. Forever. Until forever falls apart. You're *mine*. I'm yours, and I'm not going anywhere."

Relief like sunshine flooded her veins, and her whole body softened in his arms. She clung to him more fiercely, a hiccupping laugh bubbling out before she could stop it as she cried, "I love you too! Oh, thank goodness, that felt so good to finally say."

Her laughter overpowered her, and she shyly glanced at him, only to see amusement and joy warring for purchase in his smile. "That's what I really wanted to say, well, say a while ago, but it seemed too fast and I didn't want to scare you." She realized she was babbling and abruptly cut herself off when she felt his chest thump against her with his chuckle. "I love you too, Casimir," she said again, calmer this time now that the relief had run its course.

Casimir pulled her closer and kissed her so thoroughly that she did actually swoon this time. He tilted his head back enough to take a deep breath, their lips so close that she could still feel the warmth of them. He lowered his forehead to hers and said, "Let's make something real. Together."

EPILOGUE

THREE YEARS LATER

Casimir didn't like dealing with Darrin and Lochan. He supposed Lochan had his moments of being congenial toward Casimir, given what her brother believed Casimir had put Olline through. But Darrin never let him forget he was due a throttling for lying to Olline, even years later. Casimir admitted he deserved it, but he would be damned if he ever told a meathead like Darrin that. Still, Casimir had no choice but to speak with her brothers occasionally, especially now.

The boys liked proof in Casimir's devotion to Olline to be tangible. That, despite him being a seerani like them (sort of), there would never be an imbalance of power in the form of longevity between them. So, today, Casimir obliged both Lochan and Darrin and reminded them he was already close to two-centuries old, and with Olline being a caster, there would be no imbalance of power in terms of years, anyway. In terms of actual power? Well, Olline had that in spades. Lochan was moved by his speech, Darrin . . . not so much. But Casimir had gotten what he needed from them in the end, and that was the important part.

Zachery, Olline's father, was a delight, however.

Casimir had only met him face-to-face once over the past three years, but that was more than enough to know that Olline took after him in the most charming ways possible. After Olline had told him of their relationship, and how it came to be, including the bag of shit that was Kullen, Zachery had practically adopted Casimir.

He couldn't remember what it was like to have a father figure, but Zachery couldn't have been a better model. Not that he would say that to Zachery Tavos, or, if he did, he would need to do it somewhere where his sons couldn't hear. They would only become more insufferable.

Casimir shook his head. None of that should be what he was thinking about. Not when it was such an important day for his marvelous little caster.

He focused on the path beneath his feet and dodged all the people who had the audacity of slowing down and stopping to gawk at something right in front of him. Today, of all days, he could *not* be late.

This wasn't like his brother's trial, or even the prison visitation hours. Those he didn't mind being late to. Routinely. Olline had convinced him to go, to talk with Kullen, that it would be good for his healing journey with Etzel being dead or some other overly pleasant tripe. He hated she was right . . . But loved her for it, too.

He didn't think he would ever forgive Kullen, even if his brother apologized. And yet, Kullen had been a whole person before the drugs and alcohol and Etzel. If *that* man still existed, well, Casimir wanted to find that version of his big brother again, someday.

But not today. No, today was all about Olline.

He clenched his hand in his pocket, pushing through the crowd to get into the shop. A line was already forming, the inside far too crowded to squeeze into, but Casimir was a VIP and these people would move for him. He would make them if need be. He wouldn't miss Olline's grand opening.

Delora had tried to tempt Olline into a permanent position on her staff, but Olline had turned the offer down, even without Casimir having to say anything. She, like him, had her fill of politicians. Once she was free of that bloody contract, Olline had taken Casimir's advice and opened her own place. A multimedia café and greenhouse.

Olline had even tempted her friend, Briallea Jensen, away from the Government Plaza to work with them. Despite the pay cut, the woman had been eager to join. Briallea wanted to work with tech and breathing people again instead of having only droids for company in the sub-basement with Olline gone.

Nothing like the multimedia café and greenhouse had ever existed in Antal before, and it was a risk, but one that Casimir's instincts told him would pay off. It combined Olline's amazing talent with plants and her joy of manipulating technology, and married it with the artist havens that Casimir had a penchant for. The result was a café where people could dive into their virtual blogs, simulators, or murmur over real coffee while a solo guitarist crooned on the small, elevated stage. All while browsing for spectacular plants they could purchase. At a *premium*. Casimir had made sure Olline would agree to that or none of this would work.

And if someone needed their magitech hardware or software amplified with a bit of magic? If they needed a digital past wiped clean so they could be free of a past they had long outgrown? Olline and Briallea were available for hire.

Admittedly, Casimir hadn't anticipated the grand opening of Night Orchid going this well. Olline had a way of attracting people to her that he hadn't foreseen, though he should have. He had been no exception to that allure. It didn't hurt that all the people who had once had control chips in them had been the shop's biggest advocates—especially for special software like the killware Olline had made.

He stayed out of the way as much as possible. This was Olline's moment, and he wanted her to savor every second. She had earned this, and no one else deserved to be marveled at like she did. Watching her, flushed with excitement, her black and dark jade hair slowly unraveling from the neat bun she had put it in rather than her normal Mohawk, her impossibly bright emerald eyes flashing with joy, Casimir had never been prouder of her.

Or more in love.

He kept his hand in his pocket the whole time, waiting for a lull in the grand opening, but one never came. By the time Night Orchid quieted down, it was time to close. Olline had nearly sold out of all her plants and been hired for three hardware projects. Their barista was dragging their feet, having worked far too hard on too many custom orders despite their opening-day menu. The musician had finished, and Briallea was helping them pack their amp and clearing out before Casimir finally had a chance to wrap Olline in his arms.

"You're a vision, my love," he murmured, kissing her on the forehead. "I'm so proud of you."

She smiled at him, her cheeks rosy, making her smattering of freckles darken. "Thanks," she murmured, tucking her hair behind her ears. "But I couldn't have done this without you. Night Orchid is *our* triumph, not just mine."

He lifted her chin with a finger so she was looking him straight in the eye when he said. "I simply gave you a nudge. This is all you. I'm honored to merely share the space with you."

She rolled her eyes, but her blush intensified in that way that made Casimir want to pin her to a wall and devour her whole.

Later.

Olline was pulling away, going to help Briallea, no doubt. Casimir let her go so he could finally take his hand out of his pocket. By the time she turned around, ready to close Night Orchid and go home, he was down on one knee, the black box open on his palm.

"Cas," she gasped, her eyes wide as they fell from his face to the ring in his hand.

There was no way he could make a ring as spectacular as she could with her earth magic. But he did his best.

He had gathered the debris from the plants that had brought her back from the brink of death and kept them safe. In truth, he had known right then and there what he wanted, but he was such a mess he absolutely could not thrust himself at Olline in that capacity. The sweet woman may have acted merely to make him feel better, which simply would not do. So, he kept the remnants of her plants safe until he was positive he was finally worthy of her.

And until he found the right earth caster. One who could take the material and transmute it into a perfect, black-gold band that twisted like the vines that were creeping back over her windows.

In the center of each curl of metal was a small pink sapphire, a tiny bloom that framed the large teardrop diamond in its center. The diamond had been her mother's, and Zachery had been all too happy to give it to Casimir for this occasion—once he had gotten her brother's blessings.

"Over the years," he began before his voice could crack with emotion, "I've called you my precious little caster, my darling, my love, Tav, Ollie, and a million other little endearments. But what I really want to call you is my wife." He took a deep breath, and asked, "Olline Tavos, will you—"

But she jumped on him before he could finish, drowning him in kisses as she cried, "Yes!"

ACKNOWLEDGEMENTS

This book nearly didn't happen.

Coming out of a traumatic delivery of my first child, the NICU, the sleepless nights, and then the colic, I kind of assumed I'd be "done" writing for, well, if not forever, then at least for several years. Then, my first video game love finally added another installation into the franchise I've adored for over twenty years. Baldur's Gate III. Spending my late nights up with those characters when I was on little sleep and had no brain space left sparked that creativity I thought, frankly, was gone after so much time away. And so, the first draft of Encryption of the Heart was born.

And still, this book nearly didn't happen.

Close to the finish line of getting EotH published, my father passed away. He had been feeling uncomfortable for a week, went to the ER, and spent a week there as they tried to determine what was happening. He was diagnosed with cholangiocarcinoma, a rare and aggressive form of cancer. With no good options, he came home and spent his last days with us. From diagnosis to his passing, only five days had passed.

I'm sharing this with you as a way of acknowledging the emotional hardship that I encountered during writing and publishing a book. Although I genuinely love this story and these characters, that love wasn't enough. Thankfully, I was not alone during this process at any step.

This book would not have happened without my support system of fellow mom authors, my friends that are like family, and my blood family who supported me in every sense; from holding my hand during my first time mom struggles and scares, to beta reading the early versions of this book, and then holding me together through grief.

They know who they are. I carry their names with me, engraved on my heart forever. Thank you for helping me cross the finish line and getting Olline and Casimir's story out there despite, well, everything. I would have dedicated this book to them and my dad, but given the nature of this story, that felt a little weird.

And thank you, dearest reader, for letting me take the time I needed to publish, and reading EotH. I hope Ollie and Cas live forever rent free in your head like they do mine.

ABOUT THE AUTHOR

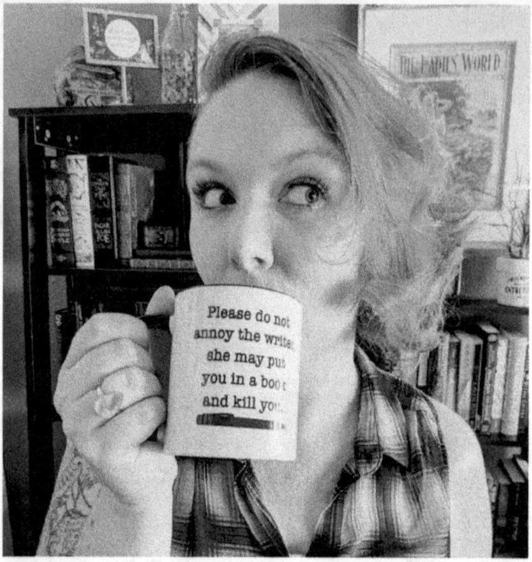

C. E. Clayton is the author of the young adult fantasy series "The Monster of Selkirk", the creator of the award winning cyberpunk Eerden Novels, and her horror short stories have appeared in anthologies across the country. By signing up for her newsletter, you'll immediately get a novella set in the Eerden universe!

www.ceclayton.com/newsletter

When she's not writing you can find her treating her fur-babies like humans, constantly drinking tea, and wrangling her tiny tyrant child. And reading. She does read quite a bit. More about C.E. Clayton, including her blog, book reviews, social media presence, and newsletter can be found on her website.

FOLLOW C.E. CLAYTON

- BookBub: bookbub.com/profile/c-e-clayton
- Instagram: instagram.com/chelscey
- TikTok: tiktok.com/@chelscey
- Facebook: facebook.com/CEClayton
- Goodreads: goodreads.com/chelscey

www.ingramcontent.com/pod-product-compliance
Lightning Source LLC
Chambersburg PA
CBHW072016020726
47501CB00006B/1828
* 9 7 8 1 9 5 2 7 9 7 1 2 5 *